OLENA N

FANGS & FAMILY

AMBER LEGENDS

CONTENT WARNING

Dear Reader, we appreciate that everyone has a different level of sensitivity and may be triggered by different topics. It is up to your discretion whether you can handle the content in our books.

The book is intended for a mature audience of particular interests and contains a certain amount of coarse language, graphic sex scenes as well as sexual innuendo. You can also find scenes of death and physical and emotional violence, as well as scenes of nonconsensual mind control.

Contents

CHAPTER 1

I'd hoped it was just indigestion, but my gut feeling told me I should have called in sick today.

It must be something I ate. I tried to convince myself, but this heaviness inside, the one every seasoned nurse gets when she knows the night will be difficult, refused to subside, souring my mood. Who knows, perhaps my friend Sara, the *"Oracle of Gdansk,"* as I'd started calling her, had exposed me to her mojo. I could do with her special insight, but it was probably just because I knew working nights during an election campaign meant raised passions and more raised fists.

The fights that broke out over prime poster placement or open spaces for the soapbox orators never failed to send their victims through the doors of not only all emergency departments in the city but also our special hospital.

'Nina, we need you; there's another batch.' The triage nurse had poked her head out of her bay. Her slightly wild-eyed, frazzled look sent me an instant warning. I looked past her, taking in the half-drunk but fully enraged group of men fighting over whose politician was best, each of them sporting bruises, cut faces or bleeding noses.

'Quiet!' I shouted, marching through the door.

My expression was one of thunder and outrage as I faced down the imbeciles when they stumbled to a confused halt.

Our hospital, beautiful as it was, had been an engagement gift for my best friend from her Forest God-turned-mob boss and now slightly reformed, doting husband. As with any gift, expensive and shiny, it soon stopped being fit for purpose.

At first, it was intended to be a small hospital where both humans and the Elder Races could be treated, no questions asked, but soon, humans, ever eager to bypass a waiting list, became our main clientele. We were such opportunistic creatures that it didn't surprise me the Elder Races preferred the Nether to this world. There, they were able to heal any injury without the indignity of prying human eyes.

'How may I help you, gentlemen? Before we start, if you're thinking of continuing your brawl, I want to make you aware of our security. Those two kind souls will ensure you will leave much faster than you entered.' I informed them, pointing toward the massive shifters that had entered the room, waiting for my signal to intervene.

'No, no ... we're good, Sister,' one of the drunkards mumbled. He briefly glanced towards the imposing duo, who acknowledged my introduction with two very wolfish grins before all the patients promptly sat on the chairs. *Sister*, how I hated that outdated term; its origins from the time when nurses were mainly nuns. I heard it so often that sometimes I wanted to roll up my nursing diploma and shove it where the sun didn't shine.

I nodded at the twins working the security shift today. I liked them. They were men of few words but very effective in calming the crowd. It still baffled me how so many creatures of the Nether could hide in plain sight, Shifters especially. They looked like ordinary humans, perhaps with overly built bodies and grumpy manners, until they transformed. However, since Sara's husband had purchased half of the Kashubian Forest from the government and gifted it to the Tricity pack, there was never any danger they would be seen when they ran and hunted.

The Nether itself was a marvel only a few chosen humans were aware of. A world, or rather a sphere of existence, between the physical realm and the afterlife. The land of gods and monsters, as Sara used to call it.

Most of Earth's magic went into maintaining the Nether, with only a tiny amount left behind for the survival of the fantastical creations of the gods and their descendants. There were entrances to the Nether sprinkled all over the material world, which were commonly known as "Gates." They were guarded by powerful entities who sacrificed their power to sustain their existence. Tricity was lucky to host three Gates, one of which was in the Dockland district.

I looked at the waiting room. None of its current residents had any idea they were sitting in a place run and financed by literal monsters, and I bit my lip to hold in the chuckle.

'So, who's first?' I asked, and the man with a bleeding nose stepped forward.

'Can you sort this out, Sister? Or should I go to the proper place and see a doctor?' He asked, and I rolled my eyes. My newest patient had barely opened his mouth and had already annoyed me twice.

'My name is Nina Zalewska, and I'm not your "*Sister*". You may call me Nurse, Matron, or by my surname. Also, this is a "*proper*" hospital, and the doctor will be with you shortly. In the meantime, our triage nurse will assess you,' I said, pointing to the doors of the open bay.

Maybe I shouldn't have taken my frustration out on him, but Sara was late for her shift, and lately, any minor inconvenience was setting me on edge.

Well, not lately, but exactly two weeks to the day, which was the first time I'd seen Adam since throwing him out of my life two years ago. Physically, he hadn't changed. He was the same sinfully handsome man with a prideful look on his face, but there was something different about him. The arrogance that so pissed me off was... well, not gone, but dimmer, and the question of why was stuck in my mind like an intrusive thought playing on repeat.

When he'd approached, there had been an intensity in his gaze, a focus I hadn't seen before. I was petrified. Did he want to confront me about what I said two years ago? Now? In the middle of Sara's party? The last thing I wanted was to cause a scene, so I turned away, focusing on entertaining the patrons of the hospital. What confused me the most was Adam's gaze, which darkened with each passing hour until he stormed away. I'd avoided a catastrophic scene, but I hadn't been able to stop thinking of him ever since.

Now, I was frustrated because it felt like the last two years of working to forget about him were for nothing, and I was stuck in a perpetual Stockholm Syndrome.

My conflicting emotions must have been painted all over my face because the gathered crowd quietened, eying me warily. The first patient meekly followed the nurse to her bay while I headed back to my office, with its supply reports and recent attendance documents piled up on my desk.

Half an hour later, Sara ran in, her honey-gold locks in glorious disarray. 'I'm sorry, Leszek came home late, and I had to...' she started, but I waved her off.

'You had to wait until he gave you a lift to work because your "Horned and Horny" has to give you a goodbye kiss.' I said with a soft chuckle.

Sara blushed cherry red at my nickname for her husband, but since she'd told me about him suddenly sprouting antlers during their first intimate encounter, I couldn't help myself. Of course, I never said it to his face.

'He has a name, you know,' she grumbled, but I could see the smile teasing her lips. 'Anyway, enough of my man's special extras. What's on the menu today?'

'Another pre-election night. You already have a probable broken nose accompanied by a rowdy bunch of idiots with bruising and lacerations. Thankfully, our wolf duo nicely subdued them with their unyielding glare.'

'Ugh, I hate this time of year,' Sara complained with a sigh. 'Yesterday, Leszek went to meet with his preferred candidate to tell him about the Nether and put him under a geas[1] . Normally, it goes flawlessly. They might fret or panic a little, but when their predecessor reassures them it's all true, they accept it. Then you can tell them about the agreement and offer your help with the election, but not this time. This guy was a moron. He tried to push Leszek out of the door, claiming that *"This shit isn't real"* even

---

1. *Geas: an obligation or prohibition magically imposed on someone.*

when Leszek transformed into his stag avatar.' She said, dressing in scrubs, and I shook my head.

Sara had been seeing shadows since childhood, so accepting the Nether came as easily as breathing. For myself and the rest of our little found family, a pack of misfits Sara had gathered around her. Well... we just followed her lead. It was easier to accept something so monumental when the sister of your heart was an integral part of it.

'Sara, be fair. The poor man probably crapped his pants seeing the Forest God in all his horned glory,' I said, passing her the patient's records.

'I am fair. You accepted it all with no issues, even sleeping with a vampire and letting him bite you. Which was, by the way, the most stupid thing you've ever done. So why can't the new councillor candidate accept the obvious, especially when *the obvious* is standing in front of him, surrounded by fireflies and magic? It's ridiculous that Leszek has to repeat this circus every four years.' She said, taking the files.

I didn't comment. Sara was right, but she was also very wrong. I didn't want to dwell on my strange relationship with Adam, Leszek's second, and the vampire who, for several weeks, became my bodyguard, taking it far too seriously.

'Just go fix some people and call when you need me.' I said as she closed the door, and Sara sent me one of her blinding smiles in reply.

I loved her. She was my best friend and the best doctor I knew. Sara was now the Soul Shepherd, a woman with the rare ability to anchor a soul to a physical body so it could be healed or killed. Her power had no limits. Any spirit, even the gods themselves, submitted to her touch. Gods were especially attracted to her, like moths to a flame. That's how she ended up bound to what the university books described as Leshy, an ancient and atavistic Forest Deity worshipped by prehistoric Slavic tribes.

We knew him as Leszek.

Since learning about the Nether, I'd always hoped there was something in me, a grain of magic, some unknown lineage, that would allow me to see Gedania and the legends of old, but I was all human with no magic of my own, so the mirror city of Gdansk, and that part of Sara's life, was forever closed to me. I had to stand in the corner and watch, envious and excluded. All because I was 'normal,' or as 'normal' as a thirty-two-year-old divorcée from a broken home could be. Just an ordinary woman who was heading straight toward a midlife crisis, who'd just happened to befriend a Seer, when all I'd known about Sara was that her 'hunches' were always correct.

'Nina, there's a man here insisting on seeing you.' One of the wolf twins said as he shoved his head inside the office.

'Tell him to go to triage. I'll be there shortly,' I answered, putting the stack of papers together.

'He's not a patient. He looks like a junkie but says he's your brother.' He said it so casually, but I felt my heart drop. I hadn't seen Pawel in ages, and before that, he'd dipped in and out of my life, mainly to ask for money or hide from whoever wanted to beat him bloody.

'Fine, let him in.' I said, preparing myself for another one of those conversations. One where he'd beg, and I'd refuse before he angrily stormed off. I loved my brother, but sometimes love isn't enough to save a lost soul.

It was less than a minute before he rushed into the room, looking exactly how the wolf had described him, twitchy and nervous. His raven black hair, whilst the same colour as mine, was lank and greasy. His washed-out blue eyes were in stark contrast to my almost black irises, but the deep, dark circles under his eyes made them stand out more than usual. *Is he here to ask for methadone*[2]*?* I wondered, trying to hold back another sigh. My estranged younger brother, whom I loved and hated, nervously paced around my office, and the space suddenly felt too small.

'Hey, how's life?' he asked, dropping onto the chair across from me.

'What do you want?' I asked curtly.

---

2. *Methadone is a medication which has been used for decades in Medication-Assisted-Treatment (MAT) to help treat people overcome their addiction to heroin, other opiates or narcotic pain medications.*

I didn't have time for his games or excuses. He'd already extorted enough money over the years to pay off the mortgage for a small house, even in a city as expensive as Gdansk.

'Aren't you happy to see me? How long has it been, Sis? Feels like ages. And look, I find out you're in charge of such a posh place. That friendship with the blonde doc must have finally paid off,' he rambled, fumbling in his jacket pocket before pulling out a silver locket. 'Look what I have for you today.'

The necklace looked old, with a dark patina obscuring the engraved silver, but there was something vaguely repulsive about it that forced me to avert my eyes. *Why the fuck did he have to bring silver?* I thought, gritting my teeth.

The hospital policy was that all silver, jewellery or otherwise, should be removed before entering the premises. Just in case our shifter staff needed to examine you. Not that such a little thing could truly harm them; if something didn't kill a shifter instantly, they would likely recover, but my recent experiences told me you could never be too careful. Besides, why expose them or any of the Elder Races to a potentially lethal metal?

'Put that back in your pocket. Who did you steal it from, and why did you bring it to me?' I snapped, feeling as if something was screaming from inside, trying to crawl out of its silver prison. 'I don't want it. You should trash it or pawn it. Just get rid of it.' I added, gesturing to him to take the thing away. 'Now tell me what you want and leave. I have work to do.'

The hurt expression on his face played on my conscience, but I couldn't give in. It was always the same with Pawel. Some small talk, a gift that left me feeling guilty, and finally, the request for money, a prescription, or sometimes both.

'Twenty-thousand zlotych, or the equivalent in dollars or euros. I remember you saying you had around five thousand dollars in a foreign bank account that you'd squirrelled away after the repossession agent sold your flat. I know it's a lot, sis, but I really need it. I'll pay you back, I promise. I've got a big gig coming, but right now, I have to let the heat cool off,' he said, looking at me with those sad puppy eyes that always tugged at my heartstrings.

How the hell did he remember I had that account? I'd kept it secret for years. An old habit I picked up after my gambling, cheating, now ex-husband left me broke. That was my untouchable money, my insurance policy to never feel helpless and at someone's mercy again.

Mom, why did you make me promise to look after Pawel? Just why? I thought, and the only explanation was that she never knew her little angel would grow up like our father; always in trouble, always running with the wrong crowd.

'No. I don't know who told you that, but I don't have that kind of money, and even if I did, I wouldn't give it to you. Enough is enough, Pawel.'

'Can't you ask Sara? I know who she's married to. I'm sure her husband wouldn't even notice if she borrowed a bit of his fortune.

I really am in trouble, Sis. I need you. Please, Nina, I really need you this time. They're going to hurt me really, really bad if I don't hide. You know I love you, and I wouldn't come if I wasn't in dire need. I know you are getting better, and I'm trying not to be a burden, but I really need your help,' he begged, standing up and walking toward me until he crouched beside my chair. 'Please, you don't want to see me here as a patient, do you?'

Emotional blackmail? It was much better than his previous begging, but I was adamant I wouldn't listen. Not this time. No matter how much this useless brother of mine hurt me.

'Get out.' I rasped, closing my eyes, trying to ward off tears. 'Just get out. I never want to see you again.' I felt something fracture inside. Maybe it was the last vestiges of trust or hope that we'd ever be a family again, but I felt the last fibres of our familial bond snap, and now the twenty-five-year-old man next to me felt like a stranger.

'Nina, c'mon, don't be like this,' he pleaded, placing his head on my knees like he used to do when we were children. 'I don't have anyone else. We have only each other, same as always. Don't do this to me, sis.' Pawel was so very, very wrong about that. He'd always had me, but I'd had no one, not until Sara found me crying in the storeroom and helped me piece my shattered life back together.

'Get out, Pawel. Don't come to me or call me, and don't even think about asking my friends for money. You're an adult now, and I've had enough of being responsible for your bad choices.' I stood up and pushed him away. I saw the understanding dawn in his eyes, and genuine emotion leaked out for the first time. Not anger this time, more like understanding and... fear.

'I'm sorry, Nina. For everything, I... I wish things were different. You are right. I'm sorry, sis, I love you. You deserve better than a brother like me,' he said and turned away, walking out of the office.

I'd never seen him like that, so sincere and apologetic. I stood there, stunned by his words, with my hand on my chest, trying to calm the rapid beating of my heart. I don't know how long I lingered, but when I rushed to call him back, he was already gone, and security didn't know which direction he'd taken.

'Thank you,' I said to the shifter and returned to my office, closing the door as gently as possible. What was done was done, and I had work to do. I pulled out the first large folder with a list of supplies that need restocking and those close to their expiry date. Medical equipment and drugs had to be checked regularly, and it had always calmed me down.

After staring at the numbers and dates without seeing them for a while, I noticed how they distorted and smudged in front of me, and when the first wet drop landed on the paper, I realised I was crying. *What if I'm wrong? What if he really is in trouble?* Whispered the tiny voice in my head. The pressure in my chest built up, threatening to split me in half.

'FUCK! Fuck! Fuck!'

The folder's plastic cover cracked when I smashed it onto the edge of the desk. I hit it again and again until the door to my office slammed open, and Sara rushed in together with half of the shop floor personnel. One look at me, and she took control.

'Everybody out. Now!'

I was making a fool of myself, but I just couldn't stop. Especially when she wrapped her arms around me and pulled the folder out of my hands.

'It's alright, Nina, whatever it is, we will fix it. The twins told me Pawel was here. Did he ask for money again?' She asked, gently stroking my pixie-cut hair. I could only nod, and she sighed slightly.

'If you need money, I have some saved, or I can ask Leszek,' she soothed, but I shook my head.

We'd had the same conversation years ago when she found me crying and scared, with no place to sleep after I lost everything, abandoned by my husband, penniless and broken. She offered me the use of her apartment while she went to Kosovo. Instead, I signed up and went with her and the boys. What I saw there changed me forever, toughening me up, but now, here I was, breaking again, with Sara once more holding the pieces together.

'No, I don't need money. It's just... I told Pawel I never wanted to see him again, and he looked so scared. He told me he had some trouble, but I thought it was just his usual bullshit. Now I'm not sure,' I explained, pulling away and wiping my tears. 'I'm sorry. So, did everyone see me make a fool of myself, or are there still some poor souls unaware of my meltdown?' I asked with all the bravado I could muster.

'Nina, everybody cries sometimes, even a hardened biker bitch like yourself,' Sara teased to distract me, a nod to my weekend rides with the local bikers. 'Don't be too hard on yourself. Your family always had its issues, but it isn't your job to fix them. If you're still worried tomorrow, we can ask Adam to dig—' she said, but I instantly stopped her.

'No, not Adam. He and I... we're done. I don't want any favours from him.'

I saw Sara ready herself to argue, but after a slight shake of her head, she sighed.

'Fine, I will find the second-best bloodhound in Tricity to locate your troublesome brother.' She smiled, winking, and wiped away my smudged makeup with a tissue from the box on the desk. 'If Adam hurt you, just tell me, and I will rip his fangs out myself. I know you split up when Leszek and I had our... difficulties, but if this was because of me...' Her voice trailed into silence, and I saw the uncertainty in her eyes.

'We didn't split up because, technically, we were never a couple. Adam lived in my apartment because Leszek thought protecting me was protecting you. I let him feed off me once out of curiosity and because I knew he'd get his head ripped off by the Forest Lord if my death made you sad. It was a pleasurable experience, but that was it. Other than that, he was an annoying womanising prick, and you know that's not my type.' I said.

Sara didn't look convinced. Hell, I wasn't convinced either because, deep down, there was more to it than that. We'd promised nothing to each other, but I'd grown fond of the roguish vampire during the very short time we'd had together and decided to give it a shot. That's why the pinnacle of our non-committed relationship was marked by my total melt-down, so complete that I was still ashamed of it.

'He's not well, you know,' Sara mumbled. 'I know you had your reasons, but I think it was a mistake,' she added, and I looked at her sharply.

My friend was not one to meddle in other people's affairs, so why, all of a sudden, did she mention Adam? I hadn't told her what had happened between Adam and me. It was so embarrassing that I wished I could forget it.

Two years ago, I'd snapped over something petty, packed his things and told him I didn't want him in my life. There was no reason for him to stay any longer. The danger hanging over my head was long gone, but he still hung around like a bad penny. It was the right thing to do, but the way I did it still made me groan in shame.

His assignment that day was the last straw and triggered me in a way I didn't think was possible.

He told me to be ready by six because he wanted to take me to dinner. So I dressed and waited, then called, calling again when he didn't answer, all for nothing.

He turned up in the middle of the night when I was about to phone Sara, worried sick that whatever he was doing for the Syndicate had left him wounded or dead. He didn't even look apologetic, just smiled as if nothing happened when I opened the door dressed in my pyjamas.

'Why didn't you call me if you knew you would be late?' I'd asked calmly, even though I felt tension coiling in my body, ready to explode.

Confusion marred his beautiful blue eyes, 'I was busy, Nina. I had a few things to do. I had to visit the brothel before I could see you and needed to use my vampire charm on the ladies working there, which took longer than expected,' he said with a flippancy that made me see red, and I lost it.

I really fucking lost it.

I didn't let him explain. One by one, I threw his belongings in his face, calling him every offensive name under the sun. All I could see was the face of my ex-husband lying to me, telling me he was on a business trip when I knew he was with another woman.

I should have known better. Why did I think the arrogant vampire would be any different? As soon as I let my guard down and thought of taking the next step in our relationship, I ended up with another man who didn't have the decency to talk to me. Instead, he went elsewhere to scratch his itch.

Adam must have forgotten he'd invited me out for dinner. I'd dressed up in my finest because I wanted it to be a date, our first date, and I was hoping it would be the first of many. Instead, I'd felt humiliated and hurt. My life was a vicious circle that had brought me another womaniser who didn't give a flying two cents about my feelings, but this time, it wasn't too late to say no.

I couldn't face being discarded again. I couldn't face being coerced into taking him back, to cave in under an avalanche of lies and apologies. I'd been there, and it had cost me everything.

So I decided to protect myself and never see him again.

Adam Lisowczyk was who he was, and it was just my bad luck that I'd fallen for a damn vampire.

CHAPTER 2

ADAM

'I'm going to stake him. First, I'll find the oldest, most potent aspen tree, take the gnarliest branch, then ram it through his heart the hard way.' The angry voice somewhere deep in the building was eclipsed by heavy stomping and the trashing of furniture, but I couldn't care less. My mind was floating on a cloud of pleasurable oblivion thanks to the fresh whiskey-infused blood I'd been drinking for the last hour or two. While I usually stayed away from mind-altering substances, I had kissed my last fuck goodbye and headed to the nearest blood brothel to drink myself blind.

I looked at my donor, her eyes struggling to focus even as her expression gave away her distaste for my favourite tipple. Her hand brushed idly at the needle mark left from the discarded transfusion kit that lay beside her.

Her disdain at my choice of this method had annoyed me. 'That's not how things are done,' she'd said, and I'd ended up paying double to shut her up.

Most of the staff here worked for more than just money, desperate for the pleasure a vampire's bite could induce. Despite my present circumstances, I couldn't face biting another woman, and I wasn't interested in catering to another annoying female's demands. This was a blood brothel, so I didn't care if she felt slighted. Even if it was the only place that catered to my kind, and it would have to be with a name like "Suck and Fuck", I wouldn't yield to her demands.

Unfortunately, the idle thought didn't distract me from the desire to bite someone, and I felt my anger rising as, in my befuddled state, the redhead's hair darkened, reminding me who it was I really wanted to sink my fangs into.

'Fuck!' I cursed, throwing my empty tumbler across the room, the illusion of that woman filling my vision, her heart-shaped face and dark expressive eyes that burned so bright I felt my heart wanting to beat again just to make her smile.

Nina. I wanted to bite her, to rip into the flesh of that sensual neck for what she did to me. I still remembered our endless conversations, the times we sparred, letting her win to have her jump into my arms, laughing so freely, like she wasn't embracing a monster.

She wasn't afraid of me, challenging me at every step. She also gave me a home, warm and welcoming despite my presence being forced on her, and it felt good, so I tried hard to be good enough for her. I was ready to offer her the world. I didn't even ask for her blood, only taking what she offered on that one incredible night, holding back despite the burning craving her taste left in my body. Stupid vampire, falling for the first woman who wasn't trying to use me for sex or money, only to fall apart when she tossed me aside like week-old trash.

My thoughts began spiralling as I grabbed another glass for another drink, my mouth twisting in disgust at the now foul-tasting blood. The curse I uttered as I looked down at the lukewarm liquid was full of spite, but I downed the drink, refusing to let that woman spoil my last pleasure.

I was cocking back my hand to throw another glass at the wall when the door burst open, startling awake my donor. The woman didn't hesitate to flee the room unsteadily without a backward glance.

'Adam, that's enough. Shift your worthless arse out of that seat. You're coming with me.'

The distaste in the newcomer's voice had me raising my middle finger even as I flinched in self-recrimination. I tried to ignore the imposing figure that stood in the doorway, radiating power like some avenging spirit.

'Make me!' I replied, laughing at Leszek's darkening expression before I waved him away. 'Go back to your woman and just leave me alone.'

As the Forest God's body blurred, I squinted, trying to focus despite the bright glow that came from fuck knew where. I was sure it wasn't daylight yet, and whilst the sun couldn't kill a vampire, we definitely knew when its glare touched our skin, the pain it caused, which thankfully lessened the older one became. Still, as with any night predators, vampires liked it dark, and my eyes needed a moment to adjust.

'Make you? Oh, with pleasure. Get up, you poor excuse for a Vampire Master. You have a job to do, and you will do it even if I have to break your bones. Where the fuck have you been? You were supposed to supervise the shipment on Monday and check the bank account of that Austrian merchant. Care to tell me why I have to come to a brothel to drag your half-naked and wasted body back to work?' He asked, not bothering to hide his displeasure.

'Then just break my bones. I'll heal anyway. I always do.' I replied quietly. I wanted to feel pain. I wanted to feel something, anything, that would mute this longing that had torn at my soul since I'd seen Nina at the charity event. We had a history; it may have been short, but that brief period was the most alive I'd felt in decades, until one petty argument that left me confused and on the street. Now, she ignored me and acted as if we were strangers while I felt every emotion I'd bottled up break loose and smack me in the face.

'Why do you care, anyway? Am I disrupting your perfect marital happiness with my problems?' I sounded pathetic even to my own ears now. *Maybe it's time to stop drinking,* I thought, especially when the enraged Forest God grabbed me by the collar and lifted me off the sofa.

'It's been two years since you broke up with Nina. Two years. For fuck's sake, pull your head out of your arse and talk to her. Didn't you learn anything from my fuck up with Sara?'

'And tell her what, exactly? Don't you think I didn't try? She doesn't want me. If she did, she would have looked at me at least once during your party. Why didn't you tell me she was going to be there? I saw her, smelled her... I can't... you don't know how it feels to be ignored by the woman whose blood still sings in your body as she flirts with a horde of men. For her, I'm nothing. Do you hear me? Nothing! So spare me your divine wisdom. Nina is not like Sara. She will never accept me. I know because I fucking bent over backwards to be good enough for her!' I shouted in his face, drunk and uncaring. It was the first time I'd told Leszek about my longing for Nina.

'What the fuck is going on in that thick skull of yours, Adam? Stop being a fucking jerk and fight for her if there's even the slightest chance she could be important to you,' Leszek snapped out, dragging me toward the light.

'Our situation is different,' I said, but he only shook his head.

'Oh, for fuck's sake, grow a pair,' I heard my boss mutter before he dragged me out of the room.

I hissed, covering my eyes, wondering when I'd last stepped outside. A day? Maybe two? Leszek said I'd missed a shipment, so it may have been a week, but it could have been longer, as I couldn't remember anything after storming out of the charity event. I wouldn't have gone if I had known she had been invited. Still, when I saw her, I'd stayed until... fuck, why did I stay?

I'd watched her like some creepy stalker while remembering the time we spent together, me as her bodyguard, her my pain-in-the-arse client, testing my patience and goodwill at every turn. I moved closer in an attempt to bury the hatchet, justifying my actions to ease the tension when we inevitably crossed paths, as we were both in Sara and Leszek's social circle.

It was a mistake. I knew it the moment Nina tilted her head to the side, watching me, her brow lifted in annoyance, but I was one step too late. Nina's scent hit my nostrils, and my body reacted, canines elongating, my saliva filling with pleasure-inducing venom.

I still could recall the taste of her blood, so full and sweet, like the best Hungarian Tokaji[3] , Nina's surprise at the erotic sensation of my bite, followed by the throaty purr as she leant into the feeling, whispering my name while her hands found their way under my shirt....

---

3. *Tokaji Aszú - Hungary's most famous dessert wine. The legendary elixir. sweet, sophisticated, and historically sought. The wine is part of the compelling story of Hungary's role in the modern history of wine.*

Vampire venom, excreted at will, was an adaptation my kind had developed for survival. Whilst a victim in pain was more fulfilling, the times of killing with impunity were long gone, so we changed our hunting practices to avoid the pitchforks and fire of the enraged victims' families. Now, instead of screaming and thrashing humans, our bite made our food into a pliable puddle of lust, easy to drink from and craving more. Unless we wanted them to suffer, which we sometimes still did.

Nina was no exception. I could have made her give me everything, taking her body and anything else I chose to possess, but I stopped before the venom-induced lust could overwhelm her free choice.

I was a fool. A softhearted fool who hadn't wanted her to hate me later. Not that it helped, and Nina made a point of completely ignoring me at the charity event. I would not make the same mistake again, and I wouldn't beg for her attention.

'Adam! Adam, look at me!' I heard Leszek shouting, and I opened my eyes, his anger burning through my alcohol-induced stupor.

'Fine, fine. Give it a rest, I'll go with you.' I said, standing. 'I can go to the dockyard tomorrow and check the next shipment. Just... give me an hour or two, and I need a shower.'

'You're fine as you are,' he said, smirking as we walked to his car. 'We're going to the island. Sara wants to talk to you.'

The change in the tone of his voice amused me. Leszek might be the prodigious God of Forests and Wilderness, the powerful Leshy who guarded the gates to the Nether in Pomerania and the man who controlled the Amber Syndicate in the Baltic, but both man and god quailed before Sara, the human doctor and Soul Shepherd, the one being loved and worshipped by this terrifying entity beside me.

I could barely understand that kind of attachment.

Leszek was different. He was the original shifter and shared their need to form a permanent bond with their mate. Vampires were not made to be monogamous. Since we'd stopped killing our prey to enhance the chance of survival, we began taking from multiple donors, and with the pleasure our bite induced, it was nearly impossible to be faithful to one person. None of the vampires I knew had a bonded mate, their At'kar[4] . The vampire ritual of mating for life was gone, replaced by a lifestyle no one wanted to talk about.

Now, the only thing that could make us crave one person and no other was the Blood Fever. Or the Vampire Bane, as some called it. It was an aberration, an addiction that turned a vampire into an obsessed fool attached to his donor beyond any reasonable justification. Sometimes, it came with affection, but most cases were tied to violent mood swings and bursts of insanity. Eventually, when

---

4. *At'kar – "Beloved" is both the term of endearment and a mark of commitment between the vampires.*

the donor died, and they always did, the vampire would follow, unable to find any joy in their existence. It was far too similar to how I was acting now for me to feel comfortable.

As Leszek drove us through the city, I analysed my predicament. I didn't exhibit the typical symptoms of Blood Fever. I didn't stalk Nina or force-feed off her. In fact, I had left her alone since I'd been thrown out.

I was functioning reasonably well, doing my job, caring for the Syndicate and my own small nest. The last incident wasn't typical, so I could forgive myself for that brief episode, but no matter how hard I tried, I couldn't forget the woman with the obsidian eyes. *Maybe it's because the time you spent in Nina's company was the happiest you'd felt in years?* Whispered the voice in my head that I didn't want to acknowledge.

The curse that slipped out in answer to my inner dialogue caught Leszek's attention, and he looked over, concern flashing in his eyes, but as with any alpha male, he knew when to leave talking about emotions well enough alone.

'Drink this,' he said, pulling a flask from the glove compartment, and I scrunched my face in suspicion, expecting one of his healing tonics. 'I will not talk to a drunk. Drink it, Adam.' He ordered, and with a heavy sigh, I put the flask to my mouth, following his curt command.

Magic punched me in the guts, and I welcomed the distraction.

'I have a job for you. It's well suited to your particular skill set and might even help you get back to your usual self.' Leszek said after the moment of silence.

'Which skill set do you mean? The one that finds people or the one that makes them disappear?' I asked, hoping for the second option. I might not be allowed to show my anger, but the opportunity to unleash some of it? That I would welcome.

'Your tracking abilities. I was contacted by a wealthy client, an ancient vampire currently living in France, who's had a family heirloom stolen and wants it returned as soon as possible.'

With a raised eyebrow and a knowing smile, my annoying boss pulled over and, without another word, climbed out of the car. I followed him like a lost puppy staring at a bone until he snorted and stopped.

'I thought you might enjoy letting off some steam in a treasure hunt, so I already accepted the offer.'

'Why? I don't know what Sara sees in you. You're more annoying than that windbag Stribog[5] . Didn't you ever consider asking me first?'

I put my heart into acting affronted, but we both knew I loved nothing more than ferreting out secrets, so Leszek's laughter wasn't unexpected, and neither was the gesture I gave him in reply.

---

5. *Stribog – in Slavic mythology, he is the deity and spirit of the winds, sky, and air.*

I caught up with my friend, and we walked to the entrance of his home. I should say mansion, really, because Leszek's home was old and beautiful. Its white walls and wooden beams were covered with wisteria, giving it an otherworldly feel that made it feel natural and not man-made. The imposing structure was surrounded by oak, elder and walnut trees that remembered a time before humans set foot on the island, when the Elder Races lived free of persecution. That, of course, was long before the creation of the Nether, the magical refuge for those hunted to near extinction by humans.

Only three of the Elder Races could live in the purely physical sphere now, and all of us shared some human traits: shifters, mages, and vampires. Anyone else, mainly spirits and gods, could only visit this realm from the Nether, and all with significantly reduced powers. All except Leszek, of course. The god-like power of the Leshy was forever tied to the Gates, anchoring them in the physical realm.

'You know where the guest room is. Take a shower and maybe have a nap. We'll talk later,' Leszek said, opening his arms as Sara rushed into his embrace.

'Hi darling, I see you returned our lost sheep to the fold,' she said, grinning at me before stretching out and grabbing Leszek's beard, pulling him down for a kiss.

'Get a room,' I said, their display of affection rubbing me the wrong way, and I felt my mood darken again.

'We need to talk, Adam. Come with me,' Sara ordered, moving toward the living room. I followed before Leszek's words stopped me.

'Let the man rest, my Firefly. He needs a shower and sleep to clear his head. You can talk in the evening, and I can assure you his brain will be working much better by then.'

'Fine, but...'

'No buts, love, give him a moment, and I will keep you busy in the meantime.' Leszek scooped up his wife and headed toward the bedroom. 'There, Adam. You are safe for now. Go sleep. Honour the sacrifice I'm making to give you a few hours free from the inquisition,' he said, laughing when Sara punched his shoulder.

'Oh, really? If it's that much of a sacrifice, then get on your knees, Bambi, and worship your Goddess.'

I shook my head at their exchange. I knew she referred to Leszek's stag avatar, but... Bambi?

'I didn't need that image in my head.' I muttered, moving toward the guest room. The muffled sounds of vigorous lovemaking interspersed with bouts of giggling and squealing made me smile even as I cringed at overhearing something so private. Leszek deserved his happiness, especially after he fought so hard to be with Sara. *Maybe I should bind Nina to me like he did with his woman?* I thought, undressing in the bathroom.

I turned on the water to drown out the sounds of the vigorous pair and looked in the mirror. A pale, masculine face, full of sharp angles, looked back at me. There was always a hint of crimson in my dark blue irises, at least as far back as I could remember. My hair was so black it seemed iridescent in a particular light and was longer than I usually kept it, giving me a messy, *bad-boy* look. I wasn't as well built as Leszek, but he was a shifter, and they were just built differently. Still, I was tall with defined muscles, and each time I went to the club, I garnered enough female attention to say I was attractive... except for the one woman who didn't want to look at me.

I wiped the steam off the mirror and smiled at my reflection.

'Is Leszek right? Should I fight for you, Nina? Or maybe I should punish you for showing me how good life could be before taking it away without explanation? Oh, my Obsidian[6], two years is enough. Enough of this torment, enough of your tantrum. I will find out what happened. I will ensure you will never want to be free of me, but this time, we will do it on my terms.' I said to my reflection in the mirror. I craved her, but she didn't want me when I tried to be a better person, so I would be the worst and make her love it.

---

6. *Obsidian is a volcanic glass that forms naturally. It is naturally black and has a glassy texture with a vitreous lustre. It is also sharper than any steel blade and, in magic, is used as a crystal that wards off negative energy and channels magical energy in rituals.*

I didn't have a plan, but I'd made the decision, and somehow, those words calmed me, so after taking a shower, I went to bed to sleep off my recent overindulgence like a good vampire.

Sara was waiting for me in the living room, relaxing on the sofa with the ugly beast she said was a cat. Her familiar, or companion, as she preferred to call him, looked up when I approached, and I swear it sent me a warning with his eyes before jumping down and sauntering out of the room.

'Feeling better?' She asked, turning in my direction. I nodded, running my hand through my hair, which had dried into unruly waves.

'Yes. You said you wanted to talk?' I queried, curious as to what she might want.

'Adam... I know we haven't seen eye to eye in the past, but I need your help. This is about Nina,' she started, and I froze, shocked at the timing of her statement. I needed a plan, and it looked like Sara was gifting me with not only the perfect opportunity but also a reasonable excuse. The worry about Nina, mixed with the excitement of the hunt, was burning in my veins, but I forced myself to keep still, feigning disinterest.

'What about her?'

'Her brother visited the hospital yesterday, claiming he was in trouble and needed money. I want you to check on him. It is likely another one of his scams, but just in case it isn't, I want to find the truth. She is anxious this might be serious this time. Pawel's not a good person, but to Nina, he's still her little brother who needs to be looked after. So if you can find his whereabouts, please do it, but make sure you're discrete. She wouldn't be happy knowing I asked you.'

Sara's last sentence wasn't surprising, but it still stung. Nina wouldn't ask for my help, even knowing I was the best tracker and hacker in the Tricity area and had the Syndicate resources at my disposal. I knew I was going to do whatever Sara asked me to do, but I couldn't keep the sneer from my voice.

'Why should I help her if she's so adamant she doesn't want me involved?'

'Because she needs you, even if she can't admit it,' Sara replied simply, and something inside of me snapped.

'Needs me?' I asked incredulously. 'Are we talking about the same woman? The one who packed my things, throwing me out like I was trash? The woman who called me a clingy blood-sucker and a manwhore when I tried to talk to her, accusing me of every possible sin when all I did was follow your husband's orders? She doesn't need me, Sara. I can help, of course, if you ask me nicely, but let's not pretend Nina needs me for anything.'

'That bad, hmm...? I didn't know any of that. Nina only told me she didn't want you to live in her apartment any longer.'

'Yes, that's what's happened. Leszek asked me to check one of Nadolny's brothels. A short, undercover surveillance to see who uploaded some VIP's videos to the internet. All I had to do was to search for hidden cameras and interrogate the girls under compulsion. It's my fucking job. I'm head of security for a reason.' The anger that bottled in me for the last two years exploded, and Sara bore the brunt of it. 'Nina wouldn't even let me explain, and now she needs the same services. What a fucking irony.' I snarled and, as if on command, Leszek walked out of his office, lips curling into a warning growl.

'It's alright, my love. We were just talking. Adam was simply shedding some light on a certain issue, but we both know he can control himself.' Sara said, and after a brief staring contest, my boss shrugged and turned to leave.

I looked at Sara, who was biting her lip, clearly weighing her next words carefully. Just as I was about to stand up and leave, she looked me straight in the eye.

'How much do you know about Nina's past?' She asked, and for the first time, I shuffled uncomfortably.

I know her parents died, her father when she was a teenager and her mother soon after graduation. I know she was married and then divorced, but nothing more than what you could find in the government's databases.

'I run a basic check for everybody that enters Leszek's social circle.' I answered, noticing Sara's shoulders sag, but her determined look told me whatever she was going to say would be worth hearing.

'So you only know the bare bones. Well, buckle up, boyo, and I'll tell you why she reacted so badly after finding out you visited a brothel.'

By the tone of Sara's voice, I knew it wouldn't be a pleasant story, but I needed to know. Nina's reaction had plagued me ever since I'd found myself on the street with my belongings strewn at my feet, staring at a silent and very sturdy door. Why, despite my earnest explanation, the door remained closed, and the sound of some operatic heavy metal drowned out my voice. Maybe knowing would ease the burning anger I felt each time the memory of that day resurfaced.

'Go on,'

'Well, be ready for a "it's not you, it's me" story, or rather how to waltz from one trauma to another, giving yourself PTSD and trust issues. Certain things in Nina's past left scars, deep scars that can trigger reactions beyond any reasonable measures.' Sara sighed, and I saw sadness clouding her eyes. She looked at me, her lips tightened in a pained grimace.

'Nina doesn't trust men, but you should already know that. She was hurt so much by them that I was shocked when she allowed you to stay in her home. Her father... I didn't know him, but from what she told me, he was an alcoholic who resented his family, and the only memories Nina had about him were the constant shouting and violence whenever he drank, which was often.'

I nodded, keeping quiet, afraid any comment from me would silence Sara and leave me in the dark.

'She needed to escape that toxicity, and unfortunately, she grabbed hold of the first man to show her affection. It was fine... at first. When I first met Nina... she was different. A bright soul with a heart as big as the ocean, an excellent nurse who'd be a better fit for paediatrics or convalescent care than the emergency department, but no, she wanted to help. Needed to, I suppose, taking every shift, every holiday, every night no one else wanted. She was practically living in the hospital, eating from the cafeteria and working, constantly working. I only knew she had a husband because she talked about him constantly, how loving and wonderful he was, how he fulfilled her every dream, and how they were building a future together. She seemed so happy... until the day I found her collapsed on the floor crying as if the world had ended.'

'So, he cheated on her?' I asked, my voice distorted by fangs that elongated, responding to my anger. It was a guess, me connecting the dots, and I held myself back, knowing where this story would end.

'Are you sure you can handle it?' She asked, the understanding and sorrow in her voice instantly cooling my anger.

'Yes, I need to know.'

'I didn't know what to do when I found her. Her grief was so raw I thought someone had died. Nina didn't want to talk at first, but between sobs, she told me a man had turned up at her home and repossessed every valuable she had, told her their bank account was frozen, and she was issued an eviction notice. All that time, whilst she worked all the hours of the day to give them a good life, the husband she loved so much was throwing everything away faster than she could make it on gambling and his "special" friends. I think every brothel in Tricity knew him by his first name, but that wasn't the worst of it. She thought it was all a terrible mistake. She still believed him, but as she was working, she got a phone call from one of his *fiancées*. Her husband had two other lovers, and when the repo man came to her house, that bastard simply switched his home address, telling the other woman it was Nina's fault, and the stupid bitch called to berate her. The day I found her on the floor, she was essentially penniless, homeless and with a broken heart.'

I held my breath, rage filling my blood. 'And you are telling me just now? If I knew... What's the name of the arsehole?' I asked calmly, without trying to hide the menace in my voice.

'No, Adam. It wasn't my story to tell, and I didn't tell you all this for you to seek vengeance. So no, don't look at me like that. I know what you're thinking because I know what Leszek would do if it happened to me. Nina doesn't need that kind of trouble.'

'Not your story? Then why are you telling me this now, Sara? You must have known... know what I feel for her. Aren't you afraid of what I'll do to get her back?' I couldn't help myself.

'No, Adam, I'm not afraid. Oh, and the reason I didn't tell you till now? You'll find that out soon enough,' she said with such chilling certainty that, for the first time, I felt afraid of the seer's power.

CHAPTER 3

NINA

I'd been questioning my response toward Pawel for nearly a
week now, the anxiety growing as I analysed every moment
of the encounter. The truth was, I loved my brother, troubled
as he was. I was harsh because I thought cutting him off would
force him to mature, but he was family, and I might have left
him without a sliver of hope for help.

*What if he really was in trouble this time? What if his life was
in danger because I'd turned him away, worried he'd spend the
money on maintaining his extravagant lifestyle?*

I look around my tiny apartment. One bedroom, one bathroom
and living room with a small kitchenette area. That's all I'd been
able to afford once I crawled back to my feet. My ex-husband left

me with nothing, well, except maybe a broken heart and trust issues after I'd been blindsided by all of his affairs.

In the beginning, this place felt like failure, with the dreary, mildewed walls and thrift store furniture gifted to me by my friends and the hundreds of stairs that turned each journey into a chore. However, I grew to love it, and after several painting parties, along with the colourful, mismatched throws I'd collected, it perfectly encapsulated my healing journey. Nothing expressed this more than the World War Two bayonet I'd embedded in the front door during one drunken pity party with Sara. She'd laughed so hard when, with much pomp and circumstance and an unsteady flourish, I'd punctuated the end of my wallowing, scaring my neighbours half to death with my enthusiasm.

I admit I had anger issues when I returned from Kosovo, and my distrust of men deepened after witnessing those horrors, but working beside Sara and the boys gave me a sense of family I'd never experienced before. Still, reality snapped back into place as soon as we returned, leaving me angry, betrayed, and fighting a messy divorce. Not that there was anything left to fight over, but my lawyer found enough evidence to save me from paying alimony to my freeloading, cheating ex.

Fuck! Why am I thinking of that again? I wondered, losing grip on my anger. My chest heaved, and my hands shook, almost as if I'd regressed to the time right after my divorce when I was a skittish, shaking mess of pain and betrayal. It had taken Sara's help and a life-changing mission in Kosovo for me to decide no man would rule my life ever again. The teasing I'd received from my friend when I cut my hair and bought a motorcycle still made me blush.

It took me a moment to calm my breath before I stripped down to a sports bra and sweatpants, picking up the boxing gloves. The male training torso looked at me with empty eyes when I dealt the first blow, then the next one, and on till I was covered with sweat and panting, but the negative emotions refused to die down.

The last time I felt like this was when the god of woe and darkness, Czernobog, had nearly killed Sara. I'd seen the concern in Adam's eyes when he saw me pounding my fists into the dummy's body until tears blurred my vision.

I felt like he'd saved me when he grasped my hands, pulling me away from the mannequin. He pressed me to his chest, and for some reason, in those powerful arms, I could breathe again.

'It's alright, Nina. She will be fine. Leszek will take care of her. It's alright, sweetheart, you can cry with me,' he'd murmured, and my knees buckled, unable to keep my weight before he lowered us both to the floor. It had been the only time since my divorce that I'd allowed a man to console me. To melt into his arms while he rocked me gently, wiping my tears away.

I missed him. Despite being an annoying, egotistical arsehole who thought he had a divine right to tell me what to do because the mighty Forest God made him my guardian, Adam had his moments.

I still remember when he saw me playing Fortnite, then rolled his eyes and took me to the middle of the room to show me some *actual* fighting moves.

I'd been so happy when I'd finally landed a punch that I threw myself into his arms, laughing like a madwoman. At that moment, Adam looked at me like I'd knocked away his blindfold, and he finally saw me, the real me, and he liked it.

'What did you do to me? How do you make me feel so alive again? You are my Obsidian, so brittle I could crush you by mistake and so sharp that your smile can cut me open. You make me feel vulnerable, Nina, and I don't know what to do with that,' He'd said, leaving me speechless.

Fuck, I did it again. I thought, replaying that scene like a bad commercial that I couldn't get out of my head. However, those moments weren't enough to make me forget he was a vampire who enjoyed the pleasures of the flesh a little too much while I was a mundane human.

Adam had proposed turning me, but I refused. Submitting myself to anyone's dominance and control was not on the menu, not even to Adam's. He was a Master of Tricity Seethe. All the vampires bowed to him, showing almost unquestionable obedience, and if I were to be a vampire, he would be my master, and I would bow to him.

Romancing your boss would be a helluva conflict of interest, but without the transformation, all I would ever be was another fling in his long, immortal life. I can't go through that shit again. I just can't. Even the comfort he brought was not worth it. I thought, pulling my gloves off.

A sharp knock on my door startled me, and without a second thought, I went to open it. Two sombre-looking men stood in front of me. Their eyes assessed me from top to toe before their gaze finally fixed itself on my face.

'Mrs Zalewska? Nina Zalewska?' Asked the taller of them, and I nodded in confirmation.

'Could we have a moment of your time?' He asked, flashing his badge and pushing forward to enter my apartment.

'Until you tell me what this is about, there's no way I'm letting you in, and I want to see your badge properly before you start if you please.' I said, putting as much displeasure in my voice as it was possible. It wasn't difficult, as I was still on edge.

'Of course, Mrs Zalewska, my apologies. Here is my badge. We would like to talk to you about your brother,' answered the shorter male, placing a hand on his counterpart's forearm.

Perfect. Now, I knew who'd be playing good cop. I thought, examining the warrant card that proved their identity and rank in the police force after he pushed it under my nose. One way or another, I had to let them in. I needed to know. Whatever trouble my idiot brother got himself into, I needed to know, and maybe, with a bit of luck, I would be able to help him.

I gestured to the policemen, pointing to the sofa and bracing myself before I asked the question.

'What did he do this time?'

'We were hoping you could tell us, Mrs Zalewska. Our colleagues from South Poland sent an alert that he might be in danger. We would like to find him and ask him a few questions regarding his recent whereabouts.' Mr Good Cop said, looking around the room while the others' gaze stayed glued to my breasts. I looked down, only now realising that my sports bra left little to the imagination, and with as much dignity as I could muster, I went to grab my discarded shirt.

'First, it's Ms Zalewska. Second, why ask me? I'm sure whoever Pawel's been mooching off would know more about his whereabouts than I would. I haven't seen him in ages, two years at least.'

'The men Mr Zalewski was seen with are dead, I'm afraid. Dead and gutted like sacrificial pigs, so I suggest recalling when you saw your brother last because it might just save his life.' Mr Bad Cop stopped staring at my tits long enough to threaten me. I think I preferred it when he was preoccupied with the puppies to this.

'Gutted?' I asked because Pawel, even unhinged as he was, didn't hang around with killers. He was more hedonist than fighter, always seeking pleasure in life; even his loan shark never threatened violence.

'Yes, gutted. Drained of blood, hung upside down with an open abdomen and strangled by their own intestines like they wore a bloody necklace, and the only connection between all five was your brother,' said Bad Cop, grimacing. 'I saw the pictures, Miss Zalewska. Gutted is the only way to describe what was done to those poor souls.'

'Oh, fuck!'

I must have looked like I was going to black out because the shorter man rushed over, grasping my arms before lowering me to the armchair.

'Can I get you some water, some tea?' He asked as I struggled to contain the sudden panic attack.

'No, It's fine. Do you know who did it?' I asked, but both men shook their heads.

'No, that's why we want to find your brother. This looks like a mafia vendetta. It was meant to send a message, especially considering those men were no saints. Burglary, larceny, and even the desecration of graves.' The shorter man said, finally releasing my arms.

'I don't know where Pawel is or how to find him, but if he contacts me in the future, I promise to let you know.' I answer curtly, now in control of my breathing and eager to get them out of my apartment.

'Are you sure you don't have any information we could use?' The nice one asked again, but I had already stood up.

'No, as I said, I haven't seen my brother in ages,' I reminded them, walking toward the door and opening it. 'I will contact you if I learn anything. For now, please leave; this has all been very upsetting.'

They weren't happy being forced to leave, Mr Bad Cop sending me hostile glares as he left, but unless they arrested me, they had little choice. It wasn't my first rodeo of law enforcement looking for Pawel. This and years of working in emergency had taught me exactly what powers the police held.

As soon as they left, I went to the kitchen and pulled out a half-empty bottle of vodka kept there for special occasions. *Or the world ending*, I thought, my heart hammering so hard I could hear the blood rushing through my arteries. I didn't bother to reach for a glass, simply opening the bottle and taking a swing.

The harsh, burning sensation of alcohol cascading down my throat made me cough and splutter, but after a moment, my heart slowed down, muffled by a sudden wave of dizziness. Then, still holding the open bottle, I went back to the living room and sat on the sofa. Grabbing my phone with my free hand, I scrolled through my contacts with shaking fingers until I finally found the correct number and called.

'Sara, I need your help.' I said as soon as the call connected.

'I'm on my way.' That was Sara, never asking why, just dropping everything for family. I put the phone on the table and took another swig, feeling a glimmer of hope in my despair.

The bottle was at my lips again before I realised. *Gutted*, fucking *gutted* by the mob. *Pawel, what did you get yourself into now? And why the fuck do I have to solve your problems again?* I felt like crying, but would my tears help anything? They never did, not when my mother died and not when my husband cheated on me. The only time crying didn't feel like failure was when Adam held me and made me feel I wasn't so utterly alone.

Fuck, I wanted that. I would give anything to feel the vampire's embrace chasing my fear away, but it's not like I could call him. Instead, I walked to the wardrobe and opened the bottom drawer. His old T-shirt, the same one he wore as we sparred after the Fortnite game, was still there. I found it in the washing basket days after we split, and I just couldn't bring myself to throw away the last reminder of the little spark of happiness he'd brought into my life. It still smelled like him.

Before I realised what I was doing, I tipped the bottle back, draining it dry before I pressed my face into the fabric and screamed.

I tried to keep focusing on one thing instead of letting my eyes float to the sides like some weird chameleon when the door opened and Sara marched in with a massive pizza box.

'I see you started without me.' She said, pointing to the empty bottle before placing the pizza on the table. 'C'mon, spill the beans. What happened?'

The compassion in her voice broke the last string that held me together, and I felt the tears pour down my cheeks again.

'The police came asking for Pawel. They said he was involved with some southern gang or something, and the men he was with were killed. I can't believe it, Sara. They said those men were gutted, torn open and....' I couldn't complete the sentence, too horrified at what that might mean. 'And I sent him away when he came asking for my help. What if he... if he....' I couldn't talk. My throat tightened at the thought my brother could be out there, hanging upside down with his stomach torn open and dying.

Sara didn't say a word, sitting beside me, gathering my unresisting body into her arms, and then stroking my hair until the tears stopped flowing.

'He's fine, Nina. You know what Pawel's like. He has more lives than a farmer's cat.' Her voice sounded different, but it didn't register as she handed me some tissues. 'Eat. I don't want you passing out drunk on an empty stomach. While you gorge on cheesy goodness, I'll make a few phone calls.'

I ate what tasted like ashes to my anxious brain, my eyes following Sara as she talked to Leszek, the mobster Nadolny, and then her ex, the former undercover cop, Kamil, before returning to sit with me.

'None of them knows anything about Pawel, and there are no new bodies in the morgue, gutted or otherwise. Both Leszek and Nadolny will keep an eye out for strangers asking questions, and

Kamil promised he would find out more about what happened in the south.' With that, Sara grabbed a slice of what I realised was a tuna and mushroom pizza and proceeded to stuff her face, groaning obscenely as she ate.

'So we still have nothing. Can you maybe do your thing? Please?' I asked, knowing my friend could summon visions of the future, especially when it involved death or violence. A talent that had saved many of her patients in the past.

'I can try, and well, I've been getting a lot better, but when it comes to people I don't know well or can't touch? It's patchy at best. Are you sure you don't want me to call Adam? If anyone can find Pawel, it's him.'

'Fuck no,' I exclaimed in a drunken panic, then blushed as I caught sight of his tear-stained T-shirt hanging off the chair. I took a moment to calm down and answer properly. 'At least, not yet. We didn't part on the best terms, and I'm sure he'd take great pleasure in seeing me beg for his help, but I'm not yet ready for that.' The suspicious smile that blossomed on Sara's lips set off all my alarms, and I knew something was up.

'I'm sure he deserved whatever you did to him, but I'm not here to judge, so get yourself dressed because we're going to Sopot.' She said, pointing at the door to my bedroom.

'To Sopot, wait, you want us to go to the Coven?'

I had been to both Sopot and the Coven's villa before. The city was in the middle of the three cities, a beautiful part of the Tricity area that was geared almost entirely toward tourism. Somewhere in the undeveloped area that separated Sopot from Gdynia was a sprawling compound the Coven called their villa. It was an administrative hub for witchcraft, their *university,* and the seat of their current leader, Veronica Sandoval. I knew very little about Veronica, but the few times I'd seen her with Sara or Leszek were enough to realise she had a commanding presence with a temper as changeable as the element of air she controlled, and her anger could be as cutting as a winter storm or as gentle as a summer's breeze.

'I told you evoking a vision of Pawel might be difficult. So we need to go to ask Veronica for the Coven's help. If they allow, I can call on their power to make it happen, and as he's your brother, we might need your blood to focus on his presence in Dola's[7] tapestry,' Sara explained as I hurriedly dressed.

'Whatever, the sooner we find him, the better, so I can kill him myself. What the hell did he get himself into this time?' I said, feeling so much better now we had a plan. My friend got the job done, and if there was any solution to my current problems, Sara was going to find it.

We soon arrived at the Sopot villa despite the afternoon traffic, the white walls appearing like magic from the surrounding trees. I

---

7. *Dola - the Polish goddess of fate and fortune that weaves the tapestry of fate for every living being*

know it was just an effect of good landscaping, but the sight never failed to impress. It was a beautiful property, and despite its size, it reminded me of Sara and Leszek's home with its calm, welcoming atmosphere. Humans with magic, it seemed, liked to be in touch with nature as much as any of the elder races, and this Coven was no different.

When Sara discovered she was a Soul Shepherd, a Seer with powers over spirits, she brought me here, and the feeling of family and acceptance made me wish, just for a moment, that I had that spark of magic that would allow me to join these incredible women. Unfortunately, I was only a human. The only supernatural thing I had in me was the remnants of Adam's venom from our first and only encounter, but even that must have faded away after so long.

'Sara? How may I help you? I don't recall any scheduled meetings.' Veronica welcomed us into her office, and I could see we'd surprised her while she was drawing what looked like alchemical diagrams and... a man's portrait. I noticed Sara recognise the subject as her eyebrows shot up, and she quickly glanced at Veronica, who scrambled to hide the sketch under her other notes.

'Hi Veronica, we didn't schedule anything, but I need your help. We're trying to locate Nina's brother,' she said, and I felt uncomfortable when Veronica's gaze slid over me.

'Are you willing to pay the price?' She asked, and I quickly glanced at Sara, who nodded, so I trusted her judgment and looked back at the witch.

'Yes, I am,' I said a moment later.

'You know what to do, Sara,' Veronica remarked. The office was a dark, cosy room with a lounger and a few comfy armchairs, and my friend pulled out her blouse before positioning herself on the lounger. I knew Sara had been training hard here for the last two years, barely finding time for any other activities, but I still felt uneasy seeing her like this, especially when Veronica approached me with a small black-handled knife in her hand.

'What are you going to do?' I asked, backing up a little, making her frown.

'Didn't you tell her?' She asked Sara, and my friend gestured me closer.

'The knife is an athame[8], Nina, and whilst very sharp, will not be used to bring harm to you. Remember how I said we'd need a little blood? Well, the athame is made from a material that won't interfere with magic. We only need a few drops to help locate Pawel through your sibling bond and my special mojo.' Sara was using her calming doctor's voice to reassure me, and I couldn't help giving her a little evil side-eye before I held out my arm to Veronica.

The cut was shallow but surprisingly painful. It was almost like the knife was made of acid that now burned my skin. *Clearly, Sara had a different idea to me of what harm was*, I thought.

---

8. *An athame or athamé is a ceremonial blade, generally with a black handle. It is the main ritual implement or magical tool used in ceremonial magic traditions.*

Veronica gathered the blood and moved toward Sara. My friend paled slightly but nodded her forward.

'I'm ready,' she said, but the strain in her voice pushed me forward, and I grasped Veronica's shoulder to hold her back.

'Is it dangerous? For Sara?' I asked. It was one thing for me to do something stupid to find Pawel, but I wouldn't endanger the woman who was like a sister to me.

'I'll be fine, but it'll be a little messy, so look the other way if you want.' Sara said, and before I could stop her, Veronica smeared my blood onto my friend's chest, drawing a sigil with the tip of the knife.

Sara's body arched, and she gasped when a painful spasm twisted her spine. For a split second before she closed her eyes, I saw a milky, otherworldly film obscure her pupils.

Veronica positioned herself behind Sara, supporting her weight and placing her fingers on my friend's temples whilst muttering an invocation.

Silver strands flowed into the room from various directions and slid beneath Victoria's fingers.

'What the fuck...?' I muttered, and the coven mistress answered.

'Our sisters are sharing their strength.' She said, continuing to channel the strands, and I watched as if hypnotised. I wished... *Why can't I be one of you?* I thought, feeling the prickle of envy.

Ever since Sara introduced me to the Elder races, I found myself connecting with the people in this new reality, but I still had the feeling I didn't truly belong. I would love to join the Coven. The way witches and warlocks supported each other spoke to my very soul. The pack was like a family of growling bastards held together by the stern discipline of the Alpha, a stern version of a father figure, ready to sacrifice himself for his people.

Adam's Seethe was ruled with similar authority, but maybe more like an iron fist in a velvet glove. Even with its ostentation and politics, the vampires presented a united front to any external danger. Leszek, out of all those I knew, had led a solitary existence until Sara entered his life.

But the Coven... the Coven was like a family. It wasn't necessarily the magic that attracted me to it but the bonds they created. Unfortunately, without magic, I was, and always would be, an outsider.

The minutes dragged by. I gnawed my fingernails to the quick as I decided I needed to have a good talk with Sara about what she considered fine, and I'd probably throw in a sentence or two about harm as well; my arm was still smarting from the cut.

Suddenly, Sara jerked, falling onto her knees and heaving as she knelt on what looked like an expensive Persian rug, which had Veronica cursing up a storm as she grabbed a box of tissues to stop her from making a mess. After a few moments of coughing and spluttering, Sara looked up, her eyes now clear but filled with guilt.

'I couldn't see him, Nina. I'm so sorry. All I caught were glimpses of the past and a vague sense that he was alive. It felt like banging my head against a brick wall, and nothing I tried could break through. Whether it was a spell or someone's will, it protected him from being found. I'll have a chat with Leszek and ask for his help. I'm so sorry. I know you were hoping for some answers,' she said, staggering to her feet as I looked on, feeling defeated.

'It's alright, we'll try something else. At least we know Pawel's alive, and that's all that matters,' I said, jumping when the phone in Sara's pocket blasted out, "Cry Wolf," and my friend gave me an apologetic smile.

'I'm sorry. Leszek must have felt my distress through that bloody soul fragment he shoved in my chest,' she grumbled, answering the phone. It wasn't the first time she'd complained about how the way he saved her life came with the price of being hard-wired to his spirit. I heard her launch into a terse explanation before angrily ending the call.

'Damned overprotective men, antlers or not. Let's go. Some-one will come to pick me up from your apartment because, guess what? I'm not supposed to drive after scrying in case I have a dizzy spell.'

The outrage in her voice dragged a smile from my lips despite the situation. Leszek's orders were utterly ignored as she apol-ogised to Veronica and formally thanked her, then bundled me into her car, driving to my place like a maniac.

'Why don't you tell him to stop acting like you're made of glass?' I asked, holding onto the door handle during one of Sara's wilder manoeuvres.

'Because it wouldn't change anything. After I almost died, Leszek sees danger in everything. Besides, if pampering and protecting me makes him happy, I'm willing to put up with the minor inconvenience.' She grinned, taking another turn. 'He feels better that way, and I still do what I want, but the difference is now I can always call my forest-scented cavalry for help.'

Despite the dread of my situation, I couldn't help but laugh. My friend had her divine-powered husband wrapped around her pinky, and they both were thrilled with this arrangement.

'Come on, you. Hand over your feminist membership card,' I joked.

We were still laughing when we pulled into my parking spot, but when I saw who was there to take Sara home, the laughter died in my throat. The person leaning against his car so nonchalantly was the one I wasn't ready to face.

Adam looked dangerously handsome. His dark hair curled behind his ears, giving his face a roughish charm. He looked good in his modern cut three-piece suit, but somehow, despite his pose, he looked tense. When we exited the car and Sara hugged me goodbye, he approached with a sarcastic smile lingering on his lips.

'I thought Leszek said no driving for you today?' He commented, nodding toward Sara, but his gaze never dropped from my face.

'I thought you knew I never listen to orders.' She answered, giving me a quick peck on the cheek. 'I'll see you later, Nina.'

Adam opened the door for her, and when she was seated on the passenger side, he turned toward me. After a prolonged silence, his intense gaze slid over my face, and I swallowed hard, doing my best to act cold and distant as if this were a random encounter with a chauffeur.

C'mon, Nina, you'd at least greet the chauffeur. I thought, pulling the tight smile on my face while my heart hammered in my chest.

'Hi, Adam.' I must have been tired or just too stressed to think clearly, but even after all this time, I swear his beautiful dark blue eyes lit up when I spoke.

Adam came closer, so close I had to tilt my head back to look at him. I was startled when he lifted his hand to touch my face. Unsure of what he wanted to do, I flinched, stepping back. Something dark crossed his expression before the corner of his mouth twitched, showing the arrogant smirk I knew too well.

'Call me, Nina. Don't overthink it, just call me... please,' He asked, and my breath caught as hope suddenly blossomed together with a warmth spreading through my chest right before the arsehole added. 'Don't drag Sara into your mess. Leszek won't be happy if she's hurt again.'

CHAPTER 4

ADAM

I drove carefully, desperately trying to concentrate on the road, conscious of the precious cargo beside me. Sara sat slumped in the passenger seat, struggling to stay awake. Her silence made me wish for her sarcastic observations to distract me from my thoughts.

Nina's expression dominated my thoughts, the sight of her dark eyes warming when I asked her to call me, then instantly icing over when I warned her about Sara's involvement. Still, I needed her to phone me, and after she flinched away from my touch, proving she still wanted nothing to do with me, I used her concern for Sara to force the issue.

I wasn't proud of myself, but I didn't regret it either. The analyst, the level-headed security chief in me, knew there was no wrong way to achieve a favourable result and the thought that I'd made a mistake. I decided to ignore it, even if I hated how it made me feel.

I knew Nina would call me. Maybe not today, but soon. She could be stubborn. We had sparred verbally enough times for me to understand that the impossible woman never gave an inch, always needing to be in control, but I couldn't blame her for that as I wasn't any different.

Even when we'd first met, and the truth of the magical world was new to Nina, she'd insisted on examining my fangs. When I'd refused to show her, she'd tripped me up and shoved her fingers into the side of my mouth, positive I was trying to scam her best friend.

The memory of her body pressed against mine, her small breasts awakening urges I'd been stupid enough to act upon. *Fuck!* My mind drifted again, and the car swerved, waking Sara.

'Are we home?' She muttered, turning toward me. 'Adam, are you alright?'

'Not yet, sorry, and yes, I'm perfectly fine.'

'Yes, you're bloody wonderful, with the emphasis on bloody. Your lip is bleeding.' Sara rolled her eyes, pointing to my face, and instinctively, I licked my lips, my tongue scraping against my elongated fangs.

'Just a minor accident, nothing to concern the mighty Oracle. Go back to sleep.' I snarked, trying to discourage her from enquiring further.

'Gods, you are such an arsehole sometimes. Just tell me. I saw your face when you got in the car. What's gnawing at you?'

'I don't want to talk about it,' I said, hoping she would let it be, but Sara was Sara, and she simply sat up straight and focused all her attention on me.

'It's Nina, isn't it? She'd set you on fire, and you don't know what to do with those feelings, do you?' She said it as if she hadn't just condensed two years' worth of anguish with one sentence, and my answering groan drew a sympathetic smile from her lips. 'Adam, I don't need my seer abilities to notice how you look at her. The hunger in your eyes turns them into seething pools of crimson fire, but of course, if you don't want to talk about it.'

'No, I don't. So drop it.' I snapped, much harsher than I intended, making her frown before she turned toward the window.

'Fine, suit yourself. I was only trying to help because I know how much Nina likes you.' With those words, she closed her eyes, curling up in the chair, and I felt like a complete bastard or, even worse—a fool because all I wanted to do now was to ask why she thought Nina liked me.

Leszek was waiting to greet us, pacing outside his mansion, and as soon as I pulled over, he helped Sara from the vehicle. I saw indulgent amusement in Sara's eyes as he fussed over her, the love they shared as clear as day. I could only shake my head. They'd been together two years now, but my boss was still stuck in the honeymoon phase.

I parked Sara's car in the underground garage, blending into its shadows to transport myself to my apartment. It was a valuable skill to have. The ability to manipulate the magical borders of the Nether called the Shadow Realm, folding them to move from place to place, had saved my life enough times that I paid particular attention to perfecting the technique. I didn't know how most vampire magic worked, my sire having abandoned me before I awoke, so everything I knew was learned in the school of hard knocks. Every skill discovered was practised until I could perform it without thinking.

I didn't like to remember the moment I awoke from death's embrace all those years ago, my body contorted by the agony of blood deprivation. If not for the accidental meeting with Leszek in the foggy banks of the Motlawa, I would have died in the first blush of dawn.

Now, I can walk in the sunlight with little discomfort, only sensitive to direct exposure, and not even that when well-fed. However, newborn vampires, before their first feed, cannot face the dawn without being immolated, *which explains all the vampire myths*, I thought. All our terrible fame probably came from the newly turned, crazed, starving, and caught unawares by daylight as they searched for sustenance.

I was an unclaimed vampire, and that bothered me. Someone created me without care or by accident. I clearly wasn't a choice; I was more likely a victim of an accidental draining and the potent magic of Gdansk's old town instead of a traditional blood exchange. At least that gave me the freedom few vampires, especially those as young as myself, could enjoy.

I shrugged off the random thought, just happy to have survived. Leszek went even further, though. When we couldn't find another vampire willing to take in a stray, he took on the role of Seethe Master until I gained enough self-control not to kill indiscriminately.

I emerged from the shadows in my penthouse, the nearest sensor catching my movement, and a light flared to life, the modern system programmed to give the impression of welcoming candlelight. At the beep from a small console, I reached over, entering the code to disarm the security alarm, and the apartment came fully to life.

Leszek liked his mansion to be as close to nature as possible, each unused space full of plants. I was the complete opposite, enjoying the amenities that science offered and revelling in its precise geometry and symmetry, the shiny metallic surfaces and polished concrete floor giving my penthouse a sophisticated industrial look. Electronic devices were everywhere, and the only soft, plush textures were those I used for sleep and sex, not that I have had much of either the last two years.

'Lorelai, dim the lights and run the bath,' I called out, and she dutifully answered, 'Yes, Master,' in a soft female voice. Lorelai was the best thing I'd ever received in payment for my services, and I was glad I gave in to the client's begging.

That client had been a fellow tech head and warlock whose family grimoire had been stolen. I accepted his offer because even though his morals were on the darker shade of grey, he'd never crossed the line into human sacrifice. Upon completion, the warlock handed me an iron box with strange engravings and a USB cable attached. At my raised eyebrow, he had explained that it was the magical version of artificial intelligence, so I accepted, the techie in me gleeful at acquiring a new toy.

Weeks later, after a fruitless search for whoever was leaving wet footprints on my concrete floors, I discovered the sneaky shit had bound a kikimora[9] to a computer and that the glitches in my Home AI were her trying to escape. Thankfully, after pulling in a few favours from the local witches and a long discussion with the grateful spirit, we came to a mutually beneficial arrangement, and I now had an assistant who could run everything in my home without the usual repetitions and frustrating mistakes.

I undressed in the bedroom and headed toward the bath, knowing I had to relieve the tension in my body or I'd never be able to think clearly. In the past, I would simply call a discrete agency for

---

9. *Kikimora - (pronounced Kih-kee-mora) is a female house spirit from Slavic lore who can be helpful or malevolent depending on the behaviour of the homeowner. In differing versions of her stories, there are two kinds of spirit, one generally helpful and the other harmful; both depicted as a woman sometimes with a bird's beak and legs.*

someone willing to make a donation and, depending on how they felt, possibly do something a little more pleasurable. Now, though, I had to rely on bagged blood and the microwave. My head was too messed up for anything else.

'What have you done to me, Nina?' I said, sliding into the bath and letting the water cradle my tired body until sweet oblivion gathered me in its arms, leaving only the image of her beautiful Romani eyes[10] in my mind.

It had been two days since I'd talked to Nina, and it took all of my willpower not to drive to her apartment. I wanted to see her, but that would only repeat the mistake I'd made in the past. My assumption that she felt the same as I did ended with the door being slammed in my face, convincing me I'd assumed wrong. This time, Nina had to come to me; it had to be her choice. The other, less noble reason I hadn't gone, was to prove to myself I was stronger than my need for her. Two years of stewing in doubts and anger, unsure of what I'd done wrong to deserve her outburst, still hurt like a festering wound, and I would not beg for her attention.

10.*In Polish culture, Romani eyes is a term of endearment as Gypsy/Romani ethnicity is famous for their beautifully expressive dark eyes.*

Two days! How long will you make me wait? I thought, buttoning my shirt, this time carefully, as the previous attempt left me looking like a child who didn't know how to dress. The tension was wearing me out, and I felt physically tired while waiting for Nina's call. I spent my time investigating her past. Even with Sara's revelations, I couldn't find much, and it only angered me when I found out how much her brother and her husband had taken from her.

The telephone rang, reminding me of a meeting with a client. There was no number on the screen, only the word private flashing repeatedly until I picked it up.

'Yes?'

'Adam ... it's Nina...erm... can we talk?' Her voice sounded hesitant, but the sound of it left me smiling like a fool. *Finally, my darling. You finally called, and now we can play.* My thoughts raced, overjoyed by the end of this waiting game.

'Adam? Are you there? Gods, I thought this was the right number. I'm sorry, my bad.' She blurted out, and before I could answer, Nina ended the call.

'Fuck!' I looked at the grey cellphone as if the lump of electronics was to blame for my blunder. Calming my breath, I tapped in Nina's number.

'Hi, Nina. Sorry about that, I was with a client,' I lied, the words flowing from my lips smoothly to explain my lack of response.

'Ah, I'm sorry. I can try again later.' She said, but this time, I didn't let her finish.

'No, you wanted to talk, and it took you two days to decide on calling me. So we'll talk.' I answered harshly and heard her sucking in her outrage.

'Well, if you wanted to talk to me sooner, you should have called me. It's not like you don't have my number. Oh, and there's no need to worry; I won't be asking Sara to scry for me again.' The anger in her voice drove out the hesitancy, as she sounded more like the Nina I knew.

'Oh, should I call you? After calling me a man-whore and, if I remember correctly, an obsessive leech, then telling me if I ever called you again, you'd stab my withered heart with a splintered stake?' The silence from Nina made me curse my lack of control, which made the two years of suppressed anger spill out.

As soon as the words left my mouth, I realised they still hurt. Nina had wounded me more than I'd ever admitted, and a small part of me wanted justice for how she made me feel. Still, I shouldn't have brought it up now, no matter how good it felt.

After a long pause, Nina spoke, her voice quiet but determined, almost emotionless.

'I'm sorry, alright? I was wrong. You're not an obsessive leech. Can't we just forget about it, have a normal conversation and try to get on? Leszek and Sara won't be splitting up anytime soon, and it'll break their hearts to see us continually fighting.' The reasonable request grated, especially following the incomplete apology, but I held my temper and turned on the false charm.

'Of course, Nina. We can even be casual acquaintances if that'll make you happy. So what can I do for you?' I said, grinding my teeth while fighting with conflicting emotions.

'I need help finding my brother. I tried every other option, but when they failed, everyone pointed me in your direction. I will pay for your time, of course,' she said, and I barked out in surprised amusement, annoyed she didn't ask me as a friend, clearly putting money as a barrier between us.

'Did the nurses suddenly get a pay raise? I don't think you can afford my services.' I couldn't help myself.

I worked for Leszek's Amber Syndicate, but he didn't mind if I took a side job every now and again. However, my services didn't come cheap, and my clientele were either wealthy or talented individuals with something unique to offer in payment. Even if Nina sold all of her possessions, she wouldn't be able to afford me. Not that she needed to. I was going to help her anyway, but she didn't need to know it. I wanted her desperate to agree to anything I proposed because I knew what I would ask of her would be a difficult pill to swallow.

'You're an arsehole, you know that, don't you?' she said with a sigh before adding. 'Fine, what do you want?'

I want you. I want to see you, touch you, taste you...I want time to convince you that you never want me to leave, whispered the voice in my head. Unfortunately, I couldn't say that because if Nina suspected that was my intention, I would have the proverbial door slammed in my face again.

'This isn't a conversation to hold over the phone. Let's meet. I know a place in town, a steak house.' I said, hoping the smell of raw blood and roasted meat would distract me from the intoxicating scent of Nina's skin, which I remembered all too well.

'You in a steak house? No irony there, then. Fine, when?' she asked, and I quickly sent her the name and address.

'This evening, Nina. I'll meet you there at seven and make sure you have an appetite. I don't want to attract attention talking over an empty plate.'

'Oh, what else? Will you tell me what to wear too?' She said, and for some reason, her snappy tone made me happy. That was my Nina, the woman who pushed her fingers into my mouth to examine my fangs.

'Wear the red one, sweetheart. Your skin looks ravishing in red.' The image of her in the short red dress with her pixie-cut hair enhancing the curve of that delicious neck sent a shiver of anticipation straight into my groin.

Well, thank you, Pawel, I whispered after she ended the call. I didn't care about that bastard's life. He was my chance to get closer to Nina, and I was going to take it because simply talking to her made me happier than any moment over the last two years.

I arrived early at the restaurant in order to use the time to have a brief conversation with the manager, using a little compulsion and no small amount of money to persuade them to keep the tables surrounding our booth free from customers. The aroma of sizzling meat and blood washed over my heightened senses, distracting me, and I congratulated myself on the choice of venue.

Then I waited.

The tumbler, with its aromatic whisky, was heavy in my hand as I rolled it between my fingers to control my rising anxiety. Nina's slightly raspy voice had managed to overcome my defences over the phone, and the thought of meeting face-to-face now gave rise to a whirlwind of emotion that I didn't fully understand.

'Welcome, madam; your partner is already waiting at your table. If you'd follow me?' I heard the waiter's greeting, recognising the scent of his companion easily in spite of the distance.

Fuck! The stirring in my trousers grew bolder as I caught sight of my guest. Nina almost flowed as she walked toward me in a skin-tight crimson dress. It wasn't the garment I expected. This smooth, sleek dress was a modern version of a Chinese cheongsam[11] that clung to every curve of her svelte body, leaving me breathless

---

11. *Cheongsam - a straight, tight silk dress with a high neck and a slit (= cut) in the side of the skirt, in a style that became popular in China, especially Shanghai.*

and forgetful of my manners as the waiter pulled back Nina's chair.

'Thank you,' she murmured to the young man, and as soon as he left to bring the menu, Nina turned toward me. 'Well?'

That woke me up from my dazed stupor, so to cover for it, I gifted her with my most dazzling smile. 'Nina, as always, you subvert my expectations in order to shine brighter. I must say you look splendid.'

With rolling eyes, my beautiful guest sighed.

'I'm glad my look pleases you, but can we get down to business? I need you to...' Her sentence cut off as our waiter returned with menus and the wine I'd ordered earlier.

'Our business can wait the short time it will take to enjoy a meal, can it not? If it makes you uncomfortable, consider it part of the payment for my services,' I said and saw her hand clench on the linen tablecloth until the knuckles went white.

'I can return later if you wish?' the waiter interrupted, clearly sensing the tension.

'No, we're ready,' Nina said without even looking at the menu. 'Steak. Medium rare for me and rare for my partner with boiled potatoes and a salad, any kind of salad. Oh, and bring me a beer.'

'Yes, ma'am. Of course, ma'am,' the poor man stuttered at Nina's authoritative matron's tone as she ordered without once taking her eyes off me.

'I hope you'll enjoy my choices for you,' she said, then mumbled 'before you choke,' making me smile. 'Can we talk about my problem now?' The question sounded almost civil through her clenched teeth, and I felt pleasure spread like molasses through my chest. I loved to spar with my sharp-witted woman.

'How have you been, Nina? Anything interesting happened since we parted ways?' I asked casually, ignoring her glare.

'You want to play like this? Fine!' she snapped, placing her hand on the chin before a soft smile curved her lips.

'I am fine, Adam. Thank you for asking. The hospital is great, and since Leszek increased its financing, I could say it is the best place for healthcare workers in Tricity. And yourself? How have you been?'

Her hand slid to her neck, and casually, she popped the button that secured the high Mandarin collar. I traced each movement, watching her dainty fingers, the nails painted crimson, sliding along the jugular vein as she slowly lowered her hand to the table.

'I'm doing well, Nina, business as usual,' I said, trying to shake the mental image of my lips following her path.

'Oh yes, of course you are. What was the usual, hmm...? That's right. Seedy nightclub surveillance. I'm sure you are outstanding at that job. Maybe I should try it one day. Do they have something for my tastes, or is Tricity still so outdated that those places only focus on male clientele?'

I knew she was trying to get under my skin, but the thought of Nina with another man almost stripped away the polished, gentlemanly veneer I worked so hard to maintain.

'Unfortunately, you'll find out that none of the establishments in Tricity will cater to your preferences, even if they have the appropriate personnel.' I said quietly, fighting the instinct to grab her and tell her that no club in Pomerania would provide her with a male escort because as soon as I got hold of my computer, I would blacklist her from every single one of them.

'Oh, never mind, then, I'll find another way to scratch this itch.' She said with a dazzling smile that almost ripped my heart out. Thankfully, the food arrived, and Nina attacked her meal with gusto, leaving me with no option but to follow her lead.

She'd won this round fair and square, and I had to admit, just by being herself, Nina could elicit emotions I'd forgotten existed. This woman was my weakness, my addiction. I thought I'd learned to live without her, but all it took was one look, and I was more lost than when I'd tasted her blood. It took me a moment to ease the tension in my body before I could speak.

'Tell me about your brother,' I asked quietly whilst cutting a small piece of bloody meat. I saw her small sigh of relief, and then the story started. I ate slowly, trying to not reveal my thoughts, but despite Nina's attempt to hide how the situation affected her, I could hear the anxiety and guilt in her voice, her rich, sweet scent corrupted by the sourness of her fear. I already knew how Pawel's friends had died, each one tied up and gutted like prime hogs, but I waited until Nina told me herself, knowing that unless she could open up about this, she wouldn't open up about her feelings.

'That's all I know. Please tell me you can find him. Whatever hornet's nest he's kicked, Pawel is still my brother and the only family I have left,' she said, and I nodded slowly.

'I can... for a price, of course.'

'Name it. I have some savings, and I can... I can sell the apartment if needed.' I could hear her desperation and restrained my predatory nature by sheer willpower. Desperate people would always reach for any lifeline and make the impossible choice.

'I don't want your money, Nina.' I said slowly, reaching for her hand.

She didn't protest, but her pupils widened when I stroked her wrist. I noticed when she shivered gently under my touch, uncertainty flashing in her eyes.

'Then what do you want?' she asked suspiciously.

I didn't plan it. I wanted to make Nina spend time with me. Grasp the feeling of vitality we'd had and take petty revenge for how she made me feel before I considered the next step. Instead, seeing her so defiant and yet vulnerable, I couldn't help myself.

'I want you, Nina. I want your blood and your time. I want you to move into my apartment and let me feed off you until I find your brother,' I said, gripping her hand when she tried to pull it away, pausing a moment until I released her, my smirk letting her know it was my choice to let her go.

She stood up so rapidly the chair fell to the floor, the hollow thud followed by a loud bang when she slammed her hands on the table.

'Are you fucking insane? There is no way in hell I'll let you sink those fangs into me again, and I definitely won't live with you. Adam, why can't you just help me? For fuck's sake, please. Anything but that, please?'

I saw Nina's eyes turn watery as she fought back her tears, and guilt burned in the cavernous pit of my heart, but I wanted her too much to give in now. I'd made a mistake pretending to be human the last time. It was time for honesty. It was time for the Vampire Master to stake his claim because Nina was mine. She just didn't know it yet.

'I can't. Those are my terms. You will have my help. I swear if you accept it, I will do everything in my power to find your brother and keep him safe, but you will live with me, Nina Zalewska. That is non-negotiable,' I said.

Nina shook her head, but I could see she was considering it as her face grew paler with each passing moment. Finally, she exhaled, rubbing her palms on the silky fabric of her dress.

'I hoped you had changed, but you are, and always will be, an arsehole. I was right to kick you out. I will find another way. Thank you for dinner, but I refuse to be your victim.' She said, and when I nodded, she picked up her clutch and left the restaurant.

Maybe I was making a mistake, but we lived by her rules the last time, and it didn't work for us. Now, even if it hurt us both, it was time she accepted me for who I was, and I wasn't a nice man.

CHAPTER 5

NINA

A dam walked into my office carrying a stack of folders. It appeared he was making it his personal mission to discuss every single issue I had with running the hospital. He showed up the day after our argument in the restaurant, announcing that as part owner of the business, he would keep a close eye on the finances and administration, especially since he discovered a few issues with our suppliers.

It was bloody annoying, as the man who hadn't shown his face inside this building since we'd opened, disinterested in how it functioned, suddenly wanted to know the smallest detail.

I checked with Sara, but unfortunately, Adam was telling the truth. He owned thirty percent of the clinic's shares, and I couldn't just kick him out.

'Nina, focus please. The single-use masks and aprons. I see we already paid the invoice, but they didn't deliver the shipment,' he commented, placing the folders on my desk while I ground my teeth and huffed an irritated sigh.

'Yes, but they phoned and apologised, giving a reasonable explanation and time frame for delivery. The supplies will be here within the week as soon as they replenish their stores. That's not an issue. We still have plenty of boxes in the basement.'

'Replenish their stores? They wouldn't have to do that if they hadn't sent their merchandise to a private clinic in the capital. I will talk to them, Nina. Let's see if they can find a way to fulfil our order,' he said with a predatory grin before pulling out his phone. I threw my head backwards, wondering why he was hellbent on giving me a headache. Adam sorted out the issues but in old-fashioned mafia style, and I wondered if once he'd finished proving me incompetent, I would have any contractors left to work with.

The first time the vampire made a call, it had taken me by surprise. It was a warehouse that provided cleaning products. I wanted to renegotiate the contract with them, but they'd been putting it off for several months. It took Adam one quiet conversation, and we were free from being overcharged.

This time was no different. As expected, half an hour later, a truck filled with boxes of masks and aprons was parked in front of our loading bay. Another issue solved by the vampire. I was grateful, but he also made me feel inadequate.

'Why are you doing this?' I asked quietly, closing the blinds when I noticed him squinting, blinded by the morning sun.

'Because I want to. I can't let anyone mess with my hospital and my... my personnel. Don't read too much into it, Nina,' he said, but I knew he was a lying toerag and calling me personnel made me want to punch him.

'Right, because I'm naïve enough to believe you.' I mumbled, 'If you want to help, find my brother.'

Adam flashed his fangs in a smile that grew wider when he bent, whispering into my ear. 'I will, Nina. All you have to do is to accept my conditions.'

'No,' I answered. 'That will never happen, but I want you to know I appreciate your help here. Despite all the bullshit reasons you might have, you've really made a difference. Even if you made me feel incompetent, what you did was good for the hospital, so thank you.'

Before I knew it, he was leaning so close I could smell the sandalwood in his cologne, and when I gasped, Adam stroked his thumb over my cheek.

'It was not my intention to make you feel bad. On the contrary, I am impressed with how you manage this place. Some tasks simply require a different touch, and I can assist with that. I can help you any time you want, my Obsidian.'

He played this cat-and-mouse game for several days until all of our files were backed up to external servers and any problems were solved, leaving me with barely anything to do.

He was a predator hunting his prey, and I swear I could see his annoying smirk whenever he looked at me. *If he thinks he can wear me out, he's sorely mistaken,* I thought, even if I couldn't deny that seeing him around helped ease my anxiety in the same way as his help in the hospital eased the burden on my already overstretched nerves. My job was stressful at the best of times, and with my own search for Pawel failing, my mind was close to breaking.

Another week passed. After several days ended in another failed lead, I fell into a funk that even Sara couldn't alleviate. I'd even talked to Kamil, who, as an undercover policeman, had connections I'd never have access to alone, but even he couldn't find anything and when he'd tried flirting to cheer me up? I'd kicked him out of my apartment with a stinging cheek and a few choice swear words.

I hired a private detective, but the days flew by, and he couldn't find anything, so he gave up, increasing my frustration.

It felt like fate was stripping me of options, but I wasn't yet ready to sell my blood to the vampire.

Today, I was at my wit's end, struggling to even dress before heading to work. I drove slowly, not trusting my own abilities, with my mind constantly analysing my dwindling options. My resources were limited, my wallet was emptying fast, and I was no closer to finding Pawel. I couldn't ask Sara to scry for him again, not after she told me about the block and I'd seen the toll it took on her. If she said someone or something was hiding my brother, they were, and there was no point asking her to do it again.

I remembered how we searched for Czernobog's disciple when the God of Darkness threatened Leszek's domain, but this time, it wasn't a powerful organisation that was difficult to hide. It was one human who was good at disappearing.

'Can't you just phone me? You've never listened before when I wanted you to go away; why this time?' I questioned, wishing Pawel could hear me.

My question left me sighing, tightening my grip on the steering wheel. If only the sibling link so popular in movies actually existed, but no, even Hollywood failed to help me.

'Why does my life have to be so fucked up? Just *once*, I wish I could have some happiness,' I grumbled, allowing myself a moment of self-pity before heading to work.

I parked the car and looked at the front of the beautiful clinic that, despite being near the dockland area, seemed to blend into the surrounding natural features. I loved working here despite doing more paperwork than I would have preferred nowadays. Being a nurse, facing the challenges of treating not-so-human patients, and the thrill of working with a team who were more family than colleagues was a dream come true that I wouldn't give up for the world. Yet today, I wish I could just skip a day or more because I didn't know if I could face everyone and keep a professional demeanour.

'Come on now, Nina, leave your troubles at the door. The people inside need to see you as capable and professional.' My pep talk was awful, but it still worked as I walked through the door, and reality came to smack me in the face.

'Nina, thank god, we're short-staffed today. The triage nurse called in sick.' The day shift lead said as soon as she saw me. I wasn't even properly at work, still wearing my civilian clothes, and I already had a problem to solve.

'Fine, I'll do it.' I said.

That's one way to keep my mind occupied, I thought, and part of me revelled in the thought of being on the front line. Triage was always busy, with little time to think or dwell on your problems and emotions. It didn't take me long to change clothes and sit in the triage room. There were already a few patients waiting to be seen, none of them in need of emergency treatment. I checked them over, measured their vital signs, and gave them advice and any prescriptions before sending them on their way.

'Nina, do you want some coffee?' Asked a junior nurse when she came to check up on me, and I nodded to her.

'Sure, it's been a little busy here, and I could use five minutes to stretch my legs. My backside is getting flat from sitting in this chair.' I said, stretching to ease my tense muscles.

'Then maybe you should send some patients our way. The duty doctor keeps gushing about having the calmest night in ages. Be careful, or you'll end up our permanent triage nurse,' she laughed, and I smiled back, taking a moment to feel proud of my hard-earned competence.

'What can I say? Most people didn't even need to be here, but we had the lights on and the door open, so…' I let my voice trail off, sharing the unspoken joke, and my colleague burst into laughter.

'Whatever you say, oh mistress of boo-boos. Your coffee will be in the break room whenever you're ready, and maybe you'll even get some cake if you don't dawdle,' she joked. I took a quick look at the chart. There was only one more patient to go, presenting with an "open wound to the forearm." So once I was done with him, I could go for a well-deserved break.

'Leon Sapieha,' I called out to the waiting room. I didn't know what I expected, but the man who walked in wasn't exactly someone I often saw in our clinic with any illness, let alone an open wound, but accidents can happen to anyone, so I shrugged it off.

First of all, he didn't look distressed. He didn't cradle his wounded arm or display any signs of pain. Instead, he inclined his head, looking around as if he wasn't sure what to do before I pointed to the chair next to my desk.

'Please have a seat and tell me what brought you here, Mr Sapieha,' I said, taking a good look at him. He was forty, maybe fifty years old, with short tawny hair dusted with silver on the temples and a timeless, handsome face. He was attractive, but the way his eyes bore into mine with an unsettling intensity instantly put me on my guard.

'Nina Zalewska?' He asked with a hint of a foreign accent, pointedly looking at my name badge as if daring me to deny it. 'I'm glad I was given the opportunity to meet with you this evening. I was wondering if you could help me with my… issue.' He took off his jacket and rolled up his shirt sleeve, revealing a large cut on his arm.

It wasn't bleeding. The skin looked pale around the edges, almost as if the patient tried to cauterise the wound. Still, it was too clean and looked self-inflicted from the angle and location, making me wonder just what was going on.

'Did you cut yourself on purpose?' I asked, watching his expression closely for signs of distress, so it came as a surprise to see him smirk slightly before answering.

'Yes. It was a requirement for some personal business. However, that is unimportant, so can we ignore the why and focus on repairing the damage?' He answered perfectly politely, and I felt my hackles rise in response. I took another look at him, assessing who he might be under his immaculately tailored clothes, trimmed hair, and handsome features. He felt old, and sure as hell, he wasn't human. After two years of working here, I could easily identify the elder races.

'Of course, Sir. If you don't mind, may I ask what kind of... person you are? I wouldn't wish to apply a treatment that might potentially bring harm to someone of a certain sensibility.' I didn't like being subtle, but with so many needing to hide their background, you learned to come at the critical questions from the side.

'A vampire,' Mr Sapieha replied, smiling widely to reveal his sharp canines for the first time.

I blinked rapidly. Vampires don't come to the clinic. You killed them, or they healed themselves by doing some otherworldly juju that came with black smoke and temporary disappearance. Yet, here was one, and he was sitting calmly in a relaxed pose, observing my every move. The entire scene felt off, and if life had taught me anything about vampires, it was that they could move incredibly fast.

This one didn't display any aggression, but under his polished sophistication and elegance, I could feel the coiled violence, and my body instinctively reacted to the threat. However, it wasn't the first time I stared death in the face. *Fake it till you make it,* I thought, approaching him with confidence.

'I'm glad you came to us. This clinic is under the protection of the Leshy, so feel free to relax. I'm happy to help you with your injury, so I'll just grab a suture kit,' I said, trying to keep my expression calm after hinting that Leszek would protect the staff and not just the patients.

I used Leszek's divine name on purpose, knowing not everyone would know his modern version, but part of me wondered if I was acting irrationally in a perfectly innocent situation. After all, this man had done nothing threatening and came here for help like many of the elder races did, but his presence set me on edge.

'Thank you.' He said when I returned with the suturing kit and cleaned his skin. 'What is a human such as yourself doing in a hospital that caters to the Unseen?' There was no command in his voice, but I felt compelled to answer, my confusion at his term for the elder races pushed aside as I spoke.

'Working? Everyone working here is fully aware of the Gates and the Elder Races, and we all swore to protect that knowledge as well as do our utmost to encourage a better understanding of each other,' I said, reciting the corporate spiel we used to reassure our patients before reaching for Mr Sapieha's injured arm. 'Now, let me put in a few sutures to close your wound. I may need to cut the cauterised edges of the skin to help close it.'

'Do what needs to be done, Nina. How does your family feel about your circumstances? Are you sure they'd approve? After all, most people you encounter here are less civilised and more dangerous than humans. Not everyone can restrain themselves like us vampires,' he said, observing me without flinching when I cut away a thin strip of damaged skin and sank the needle into his flesh.

'My family has no say in where I work.' I answered with a frown.

Why was he asking about my family? Was this just a polite way of talking from olden times, or was there something amiss? Whatever it was, I didn't want to give him any details.

'Oh? Well, of course, you're an adult, but no matter how old we are, we occasionally still listen to our parents.' Mr Sapieha's comment was a little annoying, but I shrugged, ignoring his remarks to focus on my work. I felt much calmer now and wondered what had prompted my initial suspicions. After all, this man was trying to be friendly, even if his polite conversation touched on a sore subject.

'Both of my parents are deceased. It's only me and my brother.' I answered.

'With only the two of you, you must be close. Does he work here too?' He asked, and I frowned again. Something didn't feel right, but I felt like something was numbing my senses, and each time my worry spiked, I felt instantly calm, as if my cares had been washed away.

'No, Pawel isn't suited to helping people. Our paths diverged when we were young, and it wasn't amicable, to say the least. My brother has... well, he follows trouble like a lost puppy, and I grew tired of it years ago.' I didn't like to talk about Pawel, but with this man, I felt like I could share my troubles. His gaze was so patient and understanding.

'Oh, Nina, is he alright? If you are worried about him, maybe I could help? It could be my way of thanking you for the excellent care you are showing me. I must admit, over the years, I have made many connections with powerful people, so I'm sure my assistance would be useful.' I found myself smiling at Mr Sapieha's offer, tears threatening to flow in relief, and only my professional pride stopped me from embracing the generous vampire.

'Thank you so much. I wasn't expecting a stranger to care...' My voice broke, and I exhaled slowly to centre myself.

'Of course I care. Do you know where your brother is? As soon as I speak with him, I will ensure his troubles will never bother you again.'

'But I don't know where he is. That's the problem. Can you help me find him?' I asked, and the vampire narrowed his eyes. I felt so attuned to his emotion that I knew I'd disappointed him. Still, after a moment, a gentle smile ghosted over his lips again, and I relaxed. I barely registered when his hand landed on my cheek.

'Nina, you will tell me when your brother contacts you.' He ordered, and I felt the strength of the command in his voice. The warm fuzzy sensation was gone, replaced by fear. I jerked backwards, trying to get away from his reach, but he was faster, grabbing the back of my head and pulling me close to him.

'You will tell me where your brother is as soon as he contacts you. Make no mistake, little human, I won't ask twice. I will get what I came for,' he snarled before his fangs sank into the soft flesh of my neck, and a wave of overwhelming pleasure swept away all thought.

'Nina, wake up, come on, please wake up.' A stubborn voice repeated those words, refusing to let me ignore them until finally, I opened my eyes, only to close them, hissing in pain at the uncomfortable intensity of the cubicle lights.

'What the... What happened?' I asked, wondering why my head was pounding and I was lying on a trolley.

'You blacked out in triage. Your patient shouted for help, and we found you on the floor. I took some blood samples. Your sugar levels are low, and you're anaemic. Seriously Nina? Did you forget to eat before you came on shift?'

Now I knew who was talking. Only Sara could make me feel like a ten-year-old with their hand in the cookie jar. I tried to recall what happened, but all I remembered was suturing a charming man with a minor cut.

'Oh fuck! Is he alright? I didn't face-plant in his wound, did I?' The speed at which I sat up left me dizzy, and I took a moment to stop the world from spinning.

'No, he's fine. You'd finished before pulling your dying swan routine. Luckily, he caught you before you injured yourself and lay you down, and then the team called me. You're going home, and I'm covering your shift.' Sara looked at me sternly as she handed me a large muffin. Strangely embarrassed, I wished the ground would swallow me up, but there was something that bothered me about this story. I'd been this hungry many times without passing out, so why now?

'You can't do it. You're a doctor. This place needs a triage nurse,' I argued, trying to preserve the last shred of dignity. I was a Matron[12], and she was sending me home like an unruly pupil.

'And my majestic doctor's crown won't fall off if I do some triage duties. So stop arguing the toss. You are going home tonight, and I will come by in the morning to check up on you,' Sara ordered. She was rarely in her bossy "don't argue, or you die" mood, but today was the day, and I didn't have the strength to disagree.

'Nina!' the roar from the doorway made me scramble to the back of the stretcher, and Sara instinctively took a defensive stance. It was Adam, but like I had never seen him before. The bad boy nonchalance was gone, replaced by a condensed fury that eased only a little when his gaze fell on me.

'What the fuck happened? Why did they call Sara, saying you were unconscious?'

'What are you doing here?' I asked, shocked by his appearance.

'Are you monitoring my calls, Adam?' Sara's voice was filled with menace, but he didn't flinch when she approached him.

'I listen to everything. What else do you think the security chief for the Syndicate is fucking doing? Talk to Leszek if you want to

---

12. *Matron – European phrase for Nurse in Charge. The highest rank, the nurse in charge of other nurses.*

be off the list,' he said, and I wondered when Sara would punch him, but then he added.

'Is she alright? What can I do?'

At the earnest concern in his voice, some of the tension in my friend's shoulders melted, and she sighed deeply, shaking her head.

'You are such an arse, and I'll definitely talk to Leszek about you screening my calls. Now take Nina home, please, and make sure she eats something before going to bed, even if you have to use compulsion to make her do it.'

My head snapped around at her instructions, the sense of betrayal making me lose control of my temper, especially since Adam already had his arms beneath me to lift me up.

'You're taking this too far. I'm perfectly capable of looking after myself, so stop treating me like a bloody toddler. Also, out of everybody here, you chose Adam to be the responsible adult? Seriously?'

'I'm worried about you. I wish I could stop Pawel from dipping into your life and messing you up like this. I know you, Nina. I know you're worried sick about him, but please, this time, let me look after you. I will come by tomorrow, I promise, and I'll let you berate me to your heart's content, but for now, let Adam take you home, please?'

'Fine,' I said, pushing the vampire away while climbing down off the trolley, instantly feeling giddy. I put my hand back to support myself on the railing when, in a blur of a movement, Adam scooped me up.

'Put me down.' I snapped, but he shook his head, and his stubborn expression told me he wouldn't listen no matter what I said. Instead, he turned toward Sara.

'Leave it to me. I will make sure she rests. Thank you for your help.'

'Put me down!' I punched his chest, but he didn't even flinch. When I stopped, his dark blue eyes focused on my face.

'It's not up for discussion. Besides, do you want to cause a scene in the waiting room, Nina? You can barely stand, and if you fall again, I will have to pick you off the floor. So let's do it in a civilised manner, one where I drive you home and then you can kick me out... again. One way or another, you are under my care tonight, and you can enjoy my temporary help or fight it kicking and screaming.'

'Sara's right, you are such an arsehole.'

'Yes darling, but we established that a long time ago. I'm simply ensuring you will be able to keep your side of the bargain once you decide to take it. Personal care comes with the package, so calm down and enjoy the ride,' he said.

I wanted to scream, but what choice did I have? Adam did what he always did, and that was whatever the fuck he wanted, but this time he was right. I didn't want to cause a scene. Also, despite him speaking like a total jerk, his touch was always so gentle, and

I would be lying to myself if I claimed I didn't like it. If I couldn't fight, I might as well enjoy it, so as soon as he carried me from the room, I embraced his neck and lay my head on his shoulder, giving the appearance of a lovers' embrace much to the enjoyment of all the patients waiting to be seen.

'You will regret this,' I whispered into his ear, and I felt him tense again.

'I already am. The stench of another vampire is all over you. Did you find a replacement for me? Someone whose bite you can tolerate? Do you really think he will help you find your brother?'

His questions took me by surprise, but more the tone of his voice. Adam sounded angry, jealous even, but underneath the anger was genuine distress. It would be easy to let him think I'd chosen someone else to bite me. It would ensure Adam had no delusions that I'd agree to be his blood donor, but I couldn't bring myself to do it. I didn't want to see him hurt, I just didn't want to be hurt by him either, and the closer he got, the more likely it was that would happen. Not to mention, I might still need to ask for his help.

'My last patient was a vampire. It appears he caught me before I hit the floor and carried me to the nursing station,' I said.

Adam's steps faltered. His hands tightened on my body as he pressed me to his chest. He didn't look at me, his gaze fixed on something in the parking lot.

'Thank you.' The words were so quiet I barely heard them, but they allowed me to relax while he carried me to the car.

We drove in silence until he parked next to my apartment complex.

'I can manage from here.' I said, opening the door, and I heard him cursing quietly.

'Come on, don't make my life difficult, please,' he said, offering me his arm. I took it. It was easier than trying to argue with him, especially since I suspected Adam was determined to fulfil Sara's order to the letter.

As soon as we entered my apartment. Adam led me to the bathroom.

'Take a quick shower while I make something to eat,' my determined babysitter said, like it was the most normal thing to do. When the door closed behind him, I undressed and turned toward the mirror. Since I'd fainted, this was the first moment I'd been alone with any time to think. I felt unsettled with a vague sense of violation. It was as if nowhere was safe anymore, and something had been taken from me without my permission. Not knowing what it was made the situation worse, and the only sense of security was Adam in my kitchen, making food like we had never parted ways.

I turned on the shower and walked into the stall, letting the water wash away unsettling thoughts. I stood there for a long time before I was ready to exit, and when I did, I found my oversized flannel pyjamas warming for me on the radiator.

'You didn't have much in your fridge, but I managed some cheese toasties from what you had,' Adam said, walking toward me with a plate. He put it on my nightstand before turning toward me.

'You should eat in bed,' he said, his roughish smile brightening his face, and I had a flashback of the night I met him. He'd taken me home and made me a sandwich before making himself a bed on the sofa. It felt good to have him here. I know it was wrong, that I was using him for comfort, but I needed Adam and this awkward sense of normality he brought into my chaotic life. I wrapped my hands around him, placing my head on his chest.

'Please, just for a moment, could you hold me?' I asked.

Adam looked down, and I felt his hands embrace me, gently stroking my back. He reached up and tucked a wet strand of hair behind my ear before bending until his nose touched my temple and inhaled deeply.

'I missed this, Nina. I missed you.' He said, pulling me closer. I didn't expect this. The old Adam would say something snarky, sexy, or patronising, but those words sounded sincere.

'Will you help me find my brother? Please? I need you. I really need you,' I begged, leaning toward him, craving more of his tender touch.

'Will you agree to my terms? We could be happy, Nina. If you only consider....'

I put my hand on his mouth to stop him. That was not the decision I could make today or ever. How could I risk agreeing to live with him, to be bitten when he decided? To lose my independence and trade the life I'd built for one where I'd depend on my vampire master's whims and needs until he found my brother or got bored with me?

I couldn't do it.

I knew my weakness, and Adam... even with his ridiculous demands and the way he bossed me around, made me feel safe, and safe was just a step away from love.

How long would it take till I opened up and gave him it all?

It was always all or nothing with me. When I loved, I didn't hold back. It was a devastating force, and it nearly destroyed me once. Adam, the new Adam, was pulling at my heartstrings harder each day. I wanted more of him, but I didn't want to be broken again.

'No, that would never work. If you can't do it for me as a friend, then please just go.' I said, pulling away only to see his eyes darken, crimson overtaking his irises.

'As you wish, Nina. If you come to ask for my help again, remember the price you will have to pay,' he growled, coldness seeping into his voice, and I could only stand there quietly watching as he walked away.

CHAPTER 6

NINA

Adam's hand trailed over my lips as he pinned me to the wall.

'Do you know how beautiful you are? I could spend eternity looking at your face and hearing your laugh, my brave Nina, always ready to fight for those she loves. I hope one day I will see the fire in your eyes when you fight for me,' He murmured, his lips trailing lazily over my neck, pausing for a moment on the collarbone.

I felt his body pressed against mine, but I didn't object. I wanted this, wanted it so much that my breath quickened as I trembled in anticipation. Two sharp points grazed over my skin, and I gasped as fear and desire warred within me. I stared into Adam's eyes, pushing aside the apprehension and almost daring him into action, when I tilted my head to the side, exposing the length of my neck to his teeth.

'I would never hurt you, Nina. Not now, not ever. If you want me to stop, say it because, for you, I would wait an eternity. I would never take your blood without your consent. No matter how much I crave it. Don't be afraid of pain because what I offer is only a pleasure.'

'Stop talking.' I almost growled as I spoke, still gazing deep into Adam's captivating eyes, and his throaty laugh vibrated on my skin.

'As you wish, my Obsidian.'

He bit me, but even as the sharp teeth cut into my flesh, the pain disappeared, replaced by the most sensual pleasure I'd ever felt in my life. My body was on fire. I wanted him on me, inside me. I wanted to give him everything and let these flames consume me. I would do anything he asked me just to prolong the transcendent euphoria that engulfed my senses, bringing me to orgasm quicker than I thought humanly possible.

I was floating in bliss, but something had changed. Adam's touch was no longer gentle. Instead, he grabbed my hair, pulling until the painful moan escaped my lips. The torment tainted the intimacy of the bite, telling me something wasn't right. I knew Adam. I knew my vampire, and he would never make me suffer, so I hissed, looking up to tell him to stop.

The words died on my lip as Adam's face faded away, only to be replaced by the vampire from the hospital, his bloody fangs tearing into my flesh. It has to be a dream. It has to be a fucking dream. I'd never let another vampire touch me.

Why does it feel so real? Wake up, Nina, wake the fuck up!

My helpless body thrashed and fought to escape, the pleasure overwhelming me now a sickening parody of the feelings I'd experienced.

'Adam!' I screamed as if his name could save me, and the vision tore as I flung myself onto the floor, panting like a hunted animal, unsure where I was and what had happened. 'Fuck, no... just no,' I cried, wishing the words could erase the image of that bastard violating my body and mind.

The four walls of my bedroom slowly came into focus, and I shook, suddenly cold and drenched in sweat. 'It was just a dream, nothing else.' I croaked, then repeated, my voice strong and determined, as if saying that would make the situation better.

My dreams had always been wild and incredibly vivid, full of fantastical creatures that were a blessed relief from my ordinary life. I could explain the first part of the dream easily enough. My unfulfilled desires and seeing Adam again had clearly triggered the memory of the moment he had fed from me. It was so intense and rich in detail that it felt like we were doing it again as I melted in his arms, the feeling of those powerful muscles holding me tight, calling me his Obsidian. The second part, where the dream became a nightmare, I didn't know how to explain or why I'd even conjured such a scenario.

'Maybe fate is trying to tell me that Adam is dangerous and to stay away from him?' I asked the universe, half-hoping for an answer as I climbed back into bed.

'It's not like my fucking patient bit me with no one noticing, is it?'

That thought made me frown, something niggling at the back of my mind, and a stray memory surfaced. Adam once told me that as vampires aged, they gained certain perks, but I'd been distracted at the time, and he hadn't elaborated. I'd thought Mr Sapieha seemed older, but could he drink my blood without me remembering? It sounded ridiculous, but I had fainted, and I couldn't rid myself of that feeling of violation; that something was stolen, and I was forced to enjoy it. It felt so wrong that I wanted to scream again.

The safety of sleep no longer held any appeal, so I stood up and headed to the bathroom. Sharp white illumination flooded the small space when I flipped the light switch, my eyes fighting to adjust to its intensity. I pulled at the collar of my pyjamas to examine my neck.

The reflection of unblemished skin mocked my fears, not even a bruise or soreness anywhere to be seen. I remembered the day after Adam had bitten me, his smile of sultry possession. '*I like to see my mark on you,*' he'd said, and even as I bristled in anger, something within me had melted at those words. Now, looking at my neck,

I could see no evidence to support last night's nightmare or the feeling of disgust.

'So it was just a dream,' I said to my reflection, but the pale woman with dark shadows marring her eyes and tense, worn-out expression didn't look convinced. *Perfect, I'm talking to a fucking mirror,* I thought before turning away and dragging myself back to bed.

The following days passed quickly. I'd taken every long shift, so when I came home, I ate ready meals, fell into bed exhausted and slept, thankfully, without nightmares.

I didn't give up on trying to find Pawel, but my worry for him eased a little after meeting with Kamil, who commented that if my brother was so good at hiding, maybe it was better if he stayed hidden and that I'd probably cause more problems if I found him.

It didn't sit well with me at first, but the more time that passed, the more tired I felt, and the only option left for finding Pawel was to accept Adam's proposal in order to access his network.

'Not happening,' I said to myself because, since the nightmare, the thought of a vampire biting me and commanding my body became unbearable. I trusted Adam, but even with him, I could not allow myself to be helpless. I'd fought so hard to have total control over my life, to not feel like a trashed, used toy when my heart ached for a few kind words. The idea that a simple bite could reduce me to feeling like one terrified me.

Today was Sunday, the first day off I'd taken since this nightmare had started, though not by choice. Sara had taken it upon herself to remove my name from the roster and told me not to argue. I still did, but not too strongly and accepted my fate with only a short grumble. In fact, today, I would typically ride with my local biker club.

I loved the time spent with the wind in my hair and a coarse joke on my lips unburdened by the day-to-day troubles, letting the open road ease my worries, but today, I dreaded it. My mind was torturing me with guilt at being unwilling to sacrifice my time and a small amount of my blood for my brother's safety. I could just stay home, but being locked behind four concrete walls was no better, leaving me with too much time to dwell on those negative thoughts.

I went to the kitchen to make myself a meal and stared at the inside of the empty fridge with an idea slowly forming in my head. My house was a mess, but I hadn't had the time or energy to clean it. My dirty clothes and dishes rose high in separate piles, and my fridge contained only two bottles of beer. If I was going to put my life back on track, I had to start with shopping and cleaning, and that should keep me sufficiently busy to not brood over things that were, for the moment, out of my control.

I squeezed my butt into a pair of skinny jeans and threw on a fluffy, oversized turtleneck sweater. This, together with a windproof coat and high boots, would be enough to protect me from the unpredictable weather of early spring. The Baltic Sea was capricious this time of the year, and you never knew what mood it would be in. It might bring beautiful sunshine, rolling fog or sudden hail that produced patches of black ice that gave me so many patients.

This time, however, it looked like the gods favoured me because the sun was shining, and I took my time going to the local farmers' market, determined to start with buying fresh produce for a healthy diet. I'd lost so much weight lately that my pale face could easily pass as a skeleton cosplay at a costume party.

I was halfway through picking the best celeriac[13] from the stall when my phone rang. I must have given an entertaining performance juggling overgrown vegetables in one hand whilst trying to dig my phone from the tiny back pocket of my jeans before dropping them both in a muddy puddle full of slime and dirt.

'Oh, for fuck's sake.' I cursed, provoking a few snickers, but as I bent to pick up my electronic device before it succumbed to its watery grave, a man's hand appeared in my view.

'Let me help you, ma'am.' He said, picking up my phone and, after checking the screen, wiping it on his cashmere coat before

---

13. *Celeriac - versatile, turnip-like root in a range of seasonal recipes, from hearty soups and gratins to wintry salads*

handing it back. 'You'll have to be more careful if you don't want to lose it.' He said as I stared, aghast, at the muddy stain my phone left on his clothes. *Why would anyone do that to such an expensive garment?* If I could afford a cashmere overcoat, no one would be allowed to approach me without washing and disinfecting their hands at least three times.

'You're not the sharpest tool in the shed, are you?' I heard myself saying, and the man's polite expression turned into a grimace. 'I mean, thank you very much, but it was unnecessary, and I'm afraid your coat now needs to go straight to the dry cleaners.' I said, only slightly embarrassed by my previous comment.

'That won't be a problem,' he answered, giving me an unfriendly glare, then, after nodding his head, disappearing into the crowd. I rubbed my neck under the woolly collar, wondering how he could withstand the heat of the spring sun that seemed to take pleasure in pretending to be high summer. I already regretted my own fashion choices, and the fact he also wore a fedora and a scarf meant he must be overheating in this weather.

I glanced at my phone. The notification from the call still flashed on the screen but was coded as private, so I put it back in my pocket. It was likely another scam telling me I was involved in a car crash or trying to sell me solar panels. I picked up the rest of the vegetables and was on my way to the homemade liquor stall when my phone rang again, and another withheld number alert flashed on the screen.

'Look, I'm not buying anything, so this is me politely asking you to bugger off,' I said, but before I hit disconnect, the voice on the other side made my heart stutter.

'No, sis, wait! We need to talk. Nina, please!' When I heard Pawel's voice, I almost dropped the phone for a second time. He was alive, and I stood in the middle of the market, trying not to burst into tears.

'Pawel? Where the hell are you? Come to my house, we can talk. I know shit happened, but I'll help you,' I said when I could control myself enough to talk.

'I can't, sis. I'm risking enough phoning you, but if something happens to me... I'm sorry for everything. I just want you to know I love you and that I'm so sorry. Be careful. He'll send his men to watch you... fuck... I'm sorry. He knows you're my sister. Don't trust strangers. Go to Sara, her man. He won't mess with that bastard. I don't have much time, but I wanted to tell you that before I have to go.'

'No, wait! I have someone who can protect you. Pawel, meet me in our old playground. Do you remember where? Please, I'll meet you there, and my friend, he can take on anyone, I promise. Just trust me.'

'I – I don't know, I'm so tired, Nina, so very tired. I love you, sis,' he said, sounding just like the boy I knew before the life he led turned him into a crook. My heart was breaking for him, but before I could reply, I realised I was listening to the silence of a disconnected call.

Dazed, I stood in the middle of the path, gasping for breath as my mind raced, even as I struggled to not fall to my knees. *He's alive.* I felt a tremendous sense of relief and worry that tightened around my heart like an iron band. Nothing mattered now except for keeping him that way. His past actions be damned, he was my brother. I couldn't live with myself if I left him to face this problem alone. I knew the fate his future held if his enemies caught him, so taking a deep breath to calm my racing heart, I looked at the phone and found Adam's number.

'Nina?' The smug pleasure in his voice didn't bother me this time.

I would suffer either way. Whether it was losing my brother, butchered by thugs, or losing my heart when Adam eventually broke it, I couldn't win this, so I cut my losses. The vampire would get what he wanted, even if it cost me all I had.

'I agree to your conditions. Every single one of them. Meet me at the Green Market and bring weapons. We are going to meet my brother.'

'Where? Are you safe where you are?' His voice lost its polished timbre, hardening into something truly frightening.

'I'll tell you when you pick me up. I'm not sure, but there might be someone watching me. Just say you'll help me, please, and I'll be your blood whore for as long as you want,' I said. The painful resolve hardened inside my mind with each passing minute.

'I would never treat you like a whore, Nina. Find the most crowded area in the market and wait for me there. Don't move, and don't let anyone lure you away. If anyone arrives claiming I sent them, they will be lying. Everything will be alright, sweetheart, just wait for me.'

He disconnected, and I walked to the middle of the square, sitting on one of the benches provided for those eating from the food trucks. I felt numb inside. I'd just sold myself for my brother's life, but everything felt so surreal. My mind collapsed as if I had stepped out of the flow of time.

I wasn't afraid of Adam. The cold-hearted bastard would never harm me, but it felt like I wasn't in control of my life anymore. Whatever I did, fate pushed me into Adam's arms, and I didn't trust how long I would be able to resist the temptation, losing myself in his love.

I sat there waiting, absentmindedly toying with my phone. My thoughts were a tangled mess that isolated me from the world as I tried to straighten them out, and it was several seconds before I noticed the shadow blocking the sun. When I finally looked up, I flinched at the look of concern in Adam's eyes.

'Nina, what's happened?' He asked, forgoing the usual platitudes in favour of meeting the problem head-on.

He wore what I could only describe as casual combat gear. Dark cargo pants with pockets filled with God knows what, steel-toe boots and a leather jacket that made him look deadly, beautifully deadly. *That's what I bought with my blood, a lethal weapon*, I thought, sending him a tight smile.

'Thank you for coming, but we need to go. Pawel may already be waiting for me, and it sounds like he's in danger,' I said, avoiding his outstretched hand, afraid that if I touched him again, it wouldn't stop there, and I'd end up crying in his arms because that's exactly what I wanted to do.

'Fine,' he replied, tightening his hand into a fist and dropping it to his side. 'My car's in the parking lot.' He continued, and we walked toward it in silence.

'Where to?' he asked once we were settled in the car, and I gave him the description of the overgrown, unused playground in the New Port district. The place had been derelict when I was younger, just like the entire district. Even though the area had been gentrified recently, the old playground, close to the abandoned shipyard, was still there, covered in so much wild vegetation that the rusted equipment and evidence of casual drug use were well hidden. Despite that, it was still the happiest place of my childhood.

After I repeated the conversation with my brother, we again lapsed into silence. Adam's attention was entirely on the road, manoeuvring his car skilfully through the dense traffic. My mind was reeling in fear and anxiety, thinking about all the worst-case scenarios, but I kept my lips sealed. I could no longer pretend I could sort it out myself, hating every minute I knew I was not capable of dealing with my family troubles.

I studied the man next to me. I bought his service, and I intended to fulfil our contract, but why was he willing to help, especially after setting such ridiculous conditions? I don't think I'd ever treated someone so poorly, yet here he was. Adam had an agenda, but he was very open about it. I knew he wanted me, though I didn't know exactly what he wanted. Revenge for how I'd treated him? My blood? My body? If he was going to punish me for how I ended things between us, I would accept it. Maybe that's why he insisted on reversing our situation, forcing me to live in his home. Still, right now, he was here, and that was all that mattered.

I reached out and touched his thigh with my fingertips. I didn't want to look at him, but I wanted to feel he was real and I wasn't alone.

'Thank you,' I whispered, and Adam's hand slid from the gear stick, covering mine. It was a small, silent gesture; he didn't even take his eyes off the road, but it meant the world to me, and finally, I could breathe easier.

'This dump is where we're meeting your brother?' Adam asked when we parked next to the barbed wire fence.

'Yes, a veritable childhood paradise, but only Pawel and I know we used to play here, so....' I answered, getting out of the car. 'I'll go first. That way, he'll know it is safe.' I couldn't help noticing the questions forming in Adam's eyes, but he chose not to voice them for the moment.

I slipped through a hole in the fence and headed into the former playground toward a concrete structure that resembled an old steam train. It was the perfect place to hide, and of the places we spent as kids, I knew I would find Pawel there, except I didn't even get halfway there before three men emerged from the overgrown bushes.

In a blur of movement, Adam pushed me behind him, positioning himself like a shield.

'Identify yourself,' he barked, expecting an answer.

'We are not here to cause trouble, Spymaster, but this woman has answers my Lord seeks. Step aside, and no one needs to get hurt,' said the likely leader of the group, his two cohorts falling into formation behind him.

'You come to my land and dare to demand I surrender my human?' Adam was outraged. I saw his muscles tense when he looked the leader of the group in the eye. 'Get the fuck out of my way and tell your boss the next time he wants to visit Tricity; he should introduce himself as per custom instead of sending his spawn to do his dirty work.'

'He did, to the Leshy, the true master of this land. You didn't break your tethers, and you are not recognised as the Master of the Seethe. Therefore, you won't be treated as such. All we want is the woman behind you, and I can even promise that as long as she cooperates, we will return her to you unharmed.'

'We both know the only reason I didn't break the tether is that I don't know my maker. But I'm not here to explain myself. Tell me what will happen if I choose to refuse your generosity?' Adam slid one of his hands behind his back, and a short hunting knife appeared in it, which he passed to me.

'That... would be unfortunate. We simply need the female to lure her brother into the open; that's all my master wants. He knows you are meeting with him here, so all we need is for her to encourage the boy to surrender, then you can have her back,' the leader said as he held his hands up in a non-threatening gesture, taking a step in our direction.

'Touch her, and I rip your heart out of your chest. Tell your master that I will meet with him and compensate him for what her brother stole, but he must cease the hunt.' Adam's insistence and cold fury shocked me, and I couldn't help but stare at him. He knew something I didn't, but as long as this worked, I would not undermine him by asking questions.

'I'm afraid that will not be happening. I will warn you one last time; step aside or be made to.'

I knew that tone of voice from the time I'd spent on the humanitarian mission in Kosovo with Sara. The men in front of me were fanatically dedicated to their leader, and unless Adam yielded, there would be violence. Fuck, there's three of them to his one.

I didn't hold any illusions that I could help, these bastards had supernatural written all over them, but if I surrendered myself... Adam's hand pressed against my chest as if he knew what I'd been thinking. I saw a menacing grin spread over his features, almost as if he welcomed the challenge.

'No, I think I'd like to see you try,' he smirked, enunciating every word, and then all hell broke loose.

CHAPTER 7

ADAM

I sneered, confronted by three foreign vampires who acted far too comfortably in my territory. The sheer audacity of coming to another nest's domain without asking permission violated one of our most fundamental laws. They were set in place to prevent overpopulation, overfeeding, and exposure to human authorities. However, these bastards not only pretended I wasn't the master of the territory but insulted and belittled me in front of Nina. Worse, they were partially correct. I couldn't gain independence because I didn't know my sire. Somewhere walks the bastard who made me who I am, binding my life with his, and I couldn't do anything about it.

I might have let it slide under different circumstances. Leszek didn't need another war in the region, but there was no way I'd allow someone under my care to be taken, especially not a woman I cared for. No, I only had one answer for such impertinence: pure, unbridled violence.

This was my domain, my woman, and no one would take either from me without killing me.

I smirked and wiggled two fingers, daring them to come closer, mocking their greater numbers, and the two underlings charged forward in a blur of movement.

I was already moving, knives appearing from their hidden sheaves as if by magic, but I hadn't expected the leader to stay back, especially when he flicked his wrist and a rusty metal pole launched itself toward my chest. That little fucker was an elder and had significant power. Curses slipped from my lips as I twisted to the side, narrowly avoiding the pipe as it sailed past, my knives flashing out to parry an attack from the charging enemies and riposte, gouging a deep cut into one of the idiot's faces.

Frustration burned in my chest as I knew I could easily kill these fools if not for their elder's power and the need to keep Nina safe. I exhaled, reining my temper and slammed my fist out, punching my dagger into the side of one attacker, twisting and forcing him to stumble into his compatriot.

I suppose I should be grateful that only the leader was an elder, but in my fury, I didn't care. Anyone threatening my Nina would die, and die regretting their life choices. They fought with tooth and claw, disdaining the use of weapons, and I was carving them to pieces with ease, almost enjoying their foolish arrogance.

I would later thank Nina for bringing us to such a desolate place. It allowed me to forget about potential witnesses and let myself go, using my full strength to rip them to pieces. Unfortunately, I realised my mistake too late as Nina gasped in fear, and I noticed I'd exposed her to an attack by the leader of the group. As I turned to rush to her side, a clawed hand tore across my forearm, leaving it numb, and my dagger fell harmlessly to the floor. Instinctively, I dropped my other weapon, willing my hand to transform and, with a wordless scream of rage, lashed out, hammering my clawed hand through his chest until my fingers closed around his withered heart.

I saw his eyes widen as the realisation of true death flashed across my enemy's features, but my hand was already exiting his body as I rushed toward Nina.

The second vampire knocked me to the side, but this time, I was quicker, rolling with the impact and lashing out. My claws tore out the idiot's jugular, leaving him incapacitated, as I leapt to my feet again. I was about to finish the job when a piercing scream forced me to turn away.

'Adam!' Nina's body was pinned to the tree by the power of the last vampire. He stood there, not even glancing at his captive as he looked me dead in the eye while her hands desperately clawing at her throat.

'You are good, but you are no elder,' he gloated, his contours blurring, and I knew he was going to enter the shadows, taking Nina with him.

'Don't you fucking dare touch her!' I shouted, pushing the bleeding vampire's body to the side.

The elder vampire was wrong. I had faced my challenge and survived. It'd started one night two years ago when a woman with eyes of obsidian fire had offered herself to me. Despite knowing there was something different about how I felt around her, I accepted. It took one drop of her blood to know she was the sweet darkness that whispered in my soul. She filled me up like no one ever could.

I could enthral her, feeding off her until she died, or I could accept a life filled with burning agony because of the thirst she awakened, but I wanted more than just blood. I wanted Nina. That night, I made the choice that started my blood rite. The choice of not draining the woman with fire in her blood.

The blood rite was always about choice. Every vampire could undergo it once in their lifetime. Some failed, while others proved themselves as masters, gaining unique skills that allowed them to break the tether if they so chose.

For most of the vampires, it happened at a time agreed on by their sire, the master deciding when the spawn was mature enough to resist the bloodlust. The ritual was simple. The vampire was starved to the point of madness before being offered a human. They could bleed the victim dry or hold back the hunger, triggering vampire magic that allowed them, in time, to inherit some of their sire's magical abilities.

Unclaimed mutts like me had little chance to complete their blood rite, as no vampire alone was able to bring themselves to near-death starvation. If they were lucky, it happened by chance when they fed on blood that tasted like no other and awakened the blood rite craving.

Nina didn't know she was part of my blood rite, and I chose to keep her in the dark, allowing her to be free in a moment of unexpected selflessness. As soon as I withdrew my fangs, I felt something change. The sliver of humanity left inside me grew, pulsing with unknown magic, and when Nina's life was threatened by Czernobog's madness, I felt a connection with Leszek that manifested my power. I hadn't used it since, but it had been etched into my soul, waiting to be called.

My eyes never once left my opponent's smug visage, and I felt the smile grow on my lips as I drew upon it, wings bursting from my back, tearing apart the fabric of my clothing as if it were tissue paper.

With feathers as dark as my black heart, their silken sheen disguising vicious, razor-sharp edges, my wings were a weapon sharper than any knife. I saw Nina's eyes widen in horror as darkness surrounded me like smoke, her struggles ceasing as she stared, but I didn't have time to worry about her reaction. I pulled the darkness closer, using it to propel me forward at an incredible speed, closing in on my opponent before he could blink in surprise.

My grin grew wider and more savage at the vampire's shock, his confusion at someone so young gaining such power fuelling my strength. Unfortunately, he was not surprised enough. I almost missed it, barely able to twist away, when the knife Nina had dropped embedded itself in the base of my wing.

I faltered, almost falling to the ground, but I was already beside my opponent, my clawed hands reaching out.

'It can't be possible,' he muttered. Dirt and debris peppered my body, raised by his mind, but nothing could stop me now. He'd hurt Nina, and for that, he would die.

He didn't see it coming, my body formless within the shadow, but as my hands tore into his flesh, my wings swept forward, shrieking worse than any banshee's scream, the razor-sharp feathers ripping through his neck, severing his head in a bloody explosion of fury.

With the vampire's death, the storm of debris ceased when the power fuelling it was gone. Nina's choking gasp and the thud of her helpless body falling to the ground were loud in the sudden silence, and I rushed to her side, barely stopping her head from hitting the concrete debris.

'Dracula can kiss my arse,' she whispered as I pulled her into my arms, unable to hold back my chuckle at her brazen words.

My merriment died when I noticed her shocked expression and the wild, bewildered look in those black eyes, and I worried what Nina's reaction would be. Still, I held myself back, knowing I needed to check if she was injured. Loosening my tight grip on her body, I moved to examine her but stopped as she whispered a quiet question.

'How... wh... what just happened?'

'It's my ability, Nina, something vampires gain after...erm... living for a certain amount of time.' I finished with a white lie, unwilling to admit she was the one who had enabled my gift.

'I know it's a little different, unusual even, but I believe it's due to Leszek's influence, as he's the closest thing to a sire I have.'

At least that part was true, but I saw the lack of understanding in her eyes. I shrugged it off, taking advantage of her confusion to examine her, explaining the origin of my gift to distract her.

'As we age, vampires face a challenge. Think of it as us growing up, and when it happens, magic forces a transformation. It is called Ascension, and one needs to face fear, cravings, and obsessions to survive. One's master usually guides the vampire through the blood rite because it comes with great suffering, but sometimes it happens spontaneously during intense emotional stress. Tomasz, the werewolf alpha, insists on calling it "vampire puberty," but that's because he's an immature arsehole. The creature that attacked you developed telekinesis, whereas I developed a form of shapeshifting, hence the wings.' I tried to keep the discussion light-hearted, but the smile I gave Nina was tense and more of a grimace.

I hadn't intended on sharing that aspect of my life with the woman in my arms. I knew the shadows and wings looked like something dragged from the depths of hell or some twisted horror movie, but it was done now, and I would have to deal with the consequences.

'Can we talk about this later? We need to find your brother,' I said when I couldn't find any injuries, and Nina muttered a curse. My distraction had worked well if she'd forgotten the main reason we were here in the first place. I tried to fold back my wings, but the knife deeply embedded in the bone made it impossible. I transformed my hands effortlessly, but each time I tried to banish the stubborn appendages on my back, the blade prevented it. Nina observed me for a moment before losing her patience.

'Stay still. This is too painful to watch,' she said, approaching me.

'Not as painful as trying to take it out would be,' I snapped but allowed her to continue, closing my eyes when she laid her hands on my feathers.

'Be careful, those are damn sharp,' I warned, knowing one cut and the smell of her blood could set me on edge again. Nina traced the edges of my wings, and I enjoyed it way too much; having those dainty hands caressing my body made my anguish from the last two years melt away.

'Motherfucker, why?' I cursed, jerking away when, with the sickening sound of scraping bone, she yanked the knife out.

'Calm down, Archangel, it's out now. Try flexing your wings, then see if you can fold them back. We can't have you walking around like a Halloween party reject; people will start asking you to bless their tattoos.'

I snorted with laughter, feeling more blood gush out of my wounds. 'Please have mercy. I will bleed to death if you keep making me laugh.'

'You are not allowed to die without my permission, and I won't let it happen on my watch.' she answered, rolling her eyes.

Nina and her no-nonsense attitude always left me gaping, never knowing whether to be impressed or insulted as she ploughed through every problem and worried about feelings once the dust had settled. Right now, I was trying not to laugh at her joke as she thrust her hands into her pockets, a strange look on her face.

'Your feathers are... they felt...' Nina fell silent and turned away suddenly, but not before I noticed the blush blossoming across her cheeks. I bit back a curse as I startled, twisting my wound painfully as I realised my Obsidian liked my wings.

Nina caught my wince and began unwinding her scarf, clearly intending on wrapping the still bleeding wound, but I held up my hand to stop her.

'No need for that,' I said, concentrating and forcing my body to change, banishing the wings. 'I heal quickly. I just need a moment to focus and step into the shadows. That's why you've never seen an injured vampire in the hospital. Shall we go now? I want to ensure the area is clear before we head out.'

My shoulder blade was aching, pain radiating down my arm and blood trickling down my back, but I didn't want to leave her alone. Not even for a moment, and that would happen if I shifted. I could heal quickly but not as fast as a shifter, their transformations healing damage almost instantly, so for now, all that was needed was to ignore the excruciating reminder that telekinetic arseholes with knives were dangerous.

It only took a few moments to search the playground, and it was a small mercy that Nina was so focused on finding her brother that she didn't notice me stumbling every now and again when the pain darkened my vision.

'Do you think he ran away?' She asked when we ran out of options and hiding places.

'I don't think he came at all, but I will find him for you. Just give me a few days to work on it. I have a couple of questions, though. How did those goons know you asked your brother to come here? Did you contact anyone else after we talked?' I asked.

The leader of the group, whose earthly remains were now fertilising the weeds, gave me the impression they knew precisely when Nina would be here. I knew we weren't followed, as I was meticulous as we drove here, and yet they'd been here before us.

'No, I only talked to you. Then I waited where you found me, but the man who spoke was at the Green Market. There was an accident, and I dropped my phone. That man, vampire, I guess, took my phone and cleaned it. Could he have done some of your weird mojo then?' She talked like we were partners, with only friendly curiosity flashing in her eyes, and I could barely look away, captivated by their radiant beauty. I'd set the conditions for my help to force her to spend time with me. To let her know I was a vampire who wasn't afraid to be ruthless, but now I was second-guessing myself, enjoying the warmth this casual conversation brought.

'I will check later if your phone was tampered with.' I said, gesturing her closer. 'But first, we need to go to the island so that I can talk to Leszek. This fight shouldn't have happened, and I want to know who thought they had permission to hunt on my grounds without talking to me.'

Nina walked closer but paused at the last moment, looking around at the impromptu battlefield. 'The third one, he's escaped!' she exclaimed, and I calmly nodded.

'Yes, but he's injured, and we had more pressing matters to deal with than dealing with an incapacitated vampire. Besides, I needed someone to send a message to their Master.'

'A message? What kind of message?'

'That I am the Master Vampire of Tricity, and if anyone lays a finger on you, they will die. You know, the usual.' I casually answered, giving Nina a rakish grin, hoping it would offset the darker meaning of my words. It didn't, and I knew it when Nina gasped.

'You don't own me, Adam.' She answered quietly, but I moved in closer, brushing a stray lock of hair behind her ear.

'No one owns you, Nina, and as long as I live, no one ever will. I want you safe, and if the entire world believes that you are mine, then they won't dare to touch you. For them, you are my woman, and today, I proved to them that whoever touches something of mine will die. Now, it's time to go. The sooner I talk to Leszek, the quicker I can discover where your brother is hiding.'

Nina bit her lip, and I knew she wanted to say something, but in the end, she shrugged, letting me lead her back to the car.

This time, the silence was more comfortable, even if my reason for not speaking was the need to concentrate on the road, as the pain from my wound made the traffic swim out of focus with alarming regularity. Maybe that's why I almost crashed the car when Nina spoke.

'The fight was... you'll probably think I'm horrible for not caring about the deaths of those men, but... you were amazing. I couldn't see everything, but what I did see was you tearing apart an enemy without breaking a sweat, and if I hadn't been in the way, I doubt they'd have even touched you. It wasn't much fun standing around like some damsel in distress. Maybe that's why the fucker caught me; I was staring at you like you were some sexy, avenging angel.' she said, and I laid a hand on her thigh to reassure her, biting back my reply to the sexy comment, just as she continued. 'I want you to know that I'm very grateful, and I will fulfil my part of the bargain. I will do whatever you ask, I... except Sara, no one ever fought for me. I just want you to know I'm grateful.'

I winced as a twinge of guilt pricked my conscience. Was this any better than Nina telling me she didn't want me in her life? Probably not, but I wanted her, and my selfish desire beat any remorse I might feel for how I managed it. At least now she knew she wasn't selling herself cheaply to some schmuck who couldn't look after her. As for the future, hopefully, after she spent some time with me, there might be a chance for feelings to grow.

'I'm glad you're willing to stick to your side of the bargain because right after I finish my business on Leszek's island, I'm taking you to my apartment,' I said, wincing, the pain and guilt making me sound harsher than I intended.

'Fine! Can't you just... be a little nicer about it? I know I have to go, but can I at least pack some clothes and a toothbrush? Or do you want me barefoot and chained to the fridge like an easy snack,' she retorted, and I barked out a laugh at the image, immediately regretting it as a sharp pain shot down my arm, numbing it.

'There's nothing easy about you, Nina, and yes, I'll take you home to pack.' I said, but something inside me wanted to distance myself from the men from her past and offer an explanation for some of my motives.

'I know the bargain we struck sounds one-sided, but the situation has become dangerous, and yes, I was a dick about it, and I'm sorry for that. My need for your blood isn't some twisted kink to make you suffer; I will need to be stronger, and for that... well, you know.'

The image of Nina chained in my kitchen, with not only her feet bared to me, flashed before my eyes, and I smiled in wicked delight. 'Of course, I remember how adventurous you could be, so if you want to be chained up in my home, I'm sure we could arrange it.' The words slipped out before I realised, so the punch to the shoulder wasn't entirely unexpected.

'Can't you be serious for more than five seconds? Do you think they'll try again?' She asked, the second question more subdued than I liked.

'They'll likely try again, yes, but you're with me, and I won't let anything happen to my favourite snack.' I teased to ease Nina's tension. It earned me a thunderous glare that made my grin wider, especially when I noticed her lip twitch in a hesitant smile.

'You care a lot about your diet, it seems,' Nina said as she turned away, looking through the side window, but I could see in the reflection she was trying to hide her smile.

'You have no idea,' I answered, feeling happy for the first time in two years.

CHAPTER 8

ADAM

I called Leszek as the traffic slowed to a crawl, letting Michal, his assistant, know we were coming. I could hear Sara's excited voice in the background, asking if there were snacks in the pantry or if she should order pizza. It was good she was there as it helped relieve some of the tension in Nina's shoulders. My woman needed her friend, and I intended to give them as much space as they desired before I told Nina what I'd already learned about her brother's past.

We were barely through the door when Michal and Sara appeared in the hallway.

'Oh fuck! What happened? Michal, we need the first aid kit and towels, lots of them. Oh, and grab Leszek's sweats for Adam!' Sara shouted, waiting until Michal left before embracing Nina and guiding us into the living room. Leszek must have heard the commotion because he emerged from his office, his eyebrows lowered as soon as he saw me, then grabbed my shoulder, pushing me toward the wet room. I cursed when his fingers dug into the still-bleeding knife wound, sending me to my knees, trying to catch my breath and fighting against the excruciating pain.

'Adam!' Nina was instantly by my side, wrapping her arm around my waist and pulling me upright.

'You are still injured? How?' Leszek looked positively bewildered, and I would have laughed at the Forest Lord's confusion if not for the pouring blood from the wound his friendly grasp had reopened.

'You told me you would heal! You moron! I can't believe I let you drive in this state. Why do I keep trusting you?' Nina was frantically shouting at me while I tried to support my own weight.

My woman baffled me. Nina had kept her cool when her brother called and seemed calm after I fought with the other vampires, but now she completely lost it. She grabbed one of the knives strapped to my belt and used it to rip off the remains of my jacket and the shirt beneath it. I should have stopped her and simply shifted to the shadow, but... I didn't want to, enjoying the dramatic expression of her worry for me, so I sank back to my knees, letting her do as she pleased with my clothes.

'Sara, do you have a suture kit?' She called over her shoulder, and the doctor gave a mocking salute and trotted to the bathroom.

'On it, Matron,' she replied, rushing at Nina's impatient glare.

'I thought you'd heal like shifters do when you banished your wings. Why did you have to pull this macho, silent bullshit in front of me? You know, we could've gone to the clinic and had it fixed, but, no, you had to come back and talk to your boss about the fight. Gods, I could strangle you right now.' Nina kept talking while cleaning the wound.

I occasionally hissed as the pain grew too much, but I loved every second. I could deal with much more just to know she cared. Nina was worried because I was injured, and that felt good. I had to admit, despite berating me like a stray dog that had stolen a sausage, her ministrations were gentle, efficient and much less painful than I expected.

'Wings? Did I hear something about wings?' Sara asked, returning with gloves and unpacking a suture kit.

Nina grinned, and for some reason, I began to worry.

'Oh, tall, dark, and sparkly here, has two massive fluffy angel wings, though I think his halo might have fallen off a while ago, as he thought lying to me about his injury was perfectly acceptable. He assured me that this would heal, but it's still bleeding.' She said, stepping away to show my back to Sara.

'Sparkly?' I asked, my lips twitching in barely restrained laughter, especially when Nina nodded eagerly.

My gaze met Leszek's, and my boss, the all-powerful god of wild places, raised his hand in a gesture of surrender and, with an all-knowing smirk, he quietly withdrew to the office. 'When they are done with you... Sparkles, I will come back with some medicinal whisky and a clean set of clothes. Your mess, you deal with it.'

'Coward.' I mouthed silently, feeling the sting of a needle piercing my skin, having second thoughts. I should have locked myself in the bathroom and shifted to the void instead of allowing the ladies to practise embroidery on my skin with their human healing techniques while my friend abandoned me to my fate.

Half an hour later, my back no longer felt like one massive gaping hole, and I finally started relaxing. Nina and Sara went to the bathroom to, in their words, deal with the gory aftermath and discard my shredded clothes while I sat there half-naked in my briefs with a skilfully bandaged shoulder. Leszek emerged from his office holding two tumblers of light amber whiskey and a pair of sweatpants thrown over his forearm.

'Here, put these on before I go blind and tell me how big a problem we're facing,' he commanded, and I shrugged.

'Enormous and not helped by the fact you ran away and hid, leaving me alone with those two witches. You should've told them I would heal if they'd leave me to focus for five minutes.' I said, saturating my voice with sarcasm.

'I've learned to pick my battles. Nina freaked out, seeing you hurt, and Sara would do anything to make her feel better. So be careful because one day Nina will ask her to sew your mouth shut, and I will have to hold you down while Sara does it,' he said.

I felt my muscles loosen as I sampled the fiery liquid in my glass. It almost felt like home, the relaxed atmosphere of sipping on my drink while the ladies discussed our latest complication in the privacy of the bathroom. Tiredness from my fight forced my eyes to close, and it was a shock to hear a quiet sob. I jumped to my feet, ready to rush to Nina.

'What the...?'

After tapping his chest, Leszek waved me back. 'Leave them be. Sara is calm, so it's not an emergency. Better tell me what happened and stop fretting. Nina will feel more comfortable talking to someone she trusts. It must have been a helluva lot to deal with, judging by the state you both arrived in.' He said.

'She can trust me,' I snapped, but Leszek rolled his eyes, and for a moment, I saw gold specks dancing in his verdant green irises.

'Does she? You two have nowhere near the level of trust Nina needs in order to be vulnerable in front of you, but I have to admit you're making some progress. At least now I don't have to schedule events around you two to ensure you won't meet.' He said.

'You did what?' I asked, deeply affronted.

'Well, Michal did. You know my assistant's the only one talented enough to organise my life into some sort of order. Will you tell me what happened, or would you prefer to avoid talking about it for another hour or two?' Leszek was just finishing when the ladies returned from the bathroom. Nina looked calm and composed again, wrapped in Sara's dressing gown, her eyes only a little puffy, and I was glad to see the shy smile teasing her lips as she sat on the sofa.

The shy smile disappeared when Nina turned to Leszek. 'We were attacked by three vampires, and Adam did wonders protecting my sorry arse. I barely survived there, so give him a break.' She stated, her eyes flashing with passion, ready to defend me, and I groaned in embarrassment when she added more calmly.

'And give him a raise. I've never seen anyone fight like that before, and I hope I never will again, but he was incredible and saved me from being kidnapped,' Nina asserted before turning to me and smiling again. 'Thank you, Adam. Truly, thank you, and I'm sorry you got injured because of me.'

Her smile and the sincerity in her words undid me. I wanted to cross this small space and embrace her. The need to ensure she was alright and not blaming herself for what happened dominated my thoughts. The pain I had accumulated during those two years was melting away faster than I would have thought possible. I hesitated, remembering how trying to deny my nature had led to the acrimonious ending of our relationship. That she didn't want to witness a repeat of this evening's fight left me worried she wouldn't accept that I was a killer and the Master of the Tricity Seethe, a vampire more than comfortable slaughtering his enemies.

I inclined my head, masking my feelings with a self-deprecating smile.

'You are welcome. After all, you hired me to find and, I assume, protect you, and I always deliver the best service. Besides, I would have to deal with those mutts and their Master sooner rather than later, despite them claiming Leszek allowed them to enter Tricity without announcing their presence to me.'

My friend looked at me, and I saw the question in his eyes. 'Why do you say I allowed it? I would never disrespect your authority in front of your Seethe, same as I wouldn't undermine the role of Alpha in Tomasz's pack.'

'I know. That's why I came here to discuss the matter calmly and not shouting like a self-righteous arse. It doesn't explain their assurance that they had your approval.' Once finished, I raised an eyebrow in polite inquiry, to which Leszek frowned and pulled out his phone to look through his correspondence.

'I've only had one meeting with a vampire in the last few weeks. The one looking for his family heirloom, if you recall? I allowed him to travel to Tricity to visit me. I'm sorry, my friend. I never thought he would try to bypass you. Let me check if there were any other requests that Michal or I received, just in case I'm wrong.'

With a shake of my head, I replied. 'There's been no other electronic requests. I check everything that comes from outside of your domain, and I would have remembered seeing them. I know some of the old ones dislike technology, so thought it best to talk to you just in case.' As I watched Leszek still checking his phone, my smile grew. I realised he'd missed my teasing about old ones and technology, though it was a slight disservice to the Forest Lord as he did at least try to stay up to date. However, the mention of technology reminded me of the not-so-accidental meeting with the three vampires.

'Nina, would you pass me your phone, please?'

My request startled her, and I realised her thoughts were far away as she was lounging with her head on Sara's shoulder.

'Yes, sorry, it's in my bag in the bathroom. Give me a moment, please,' she said. As soon as Nina left, Sara looked at me. I swear I shrank a few centimetres under her glare.

'She's barely sleeping or eating lately. You will find her brother, Adam. This is no longer a polite request but an order. I know you leveraged her living with you as payment, as well as donating her blood, so now I'm telling you. I'm not happy. No, screw that; I am fucking furious, so if you're going to continue with this farce, then I will only allow it under one condition. You will ensure she sleeps, eats and rests, and... for fuck's sake, spoil her a little; she deserves it. Also, you won't feed from her unless she gives you consent. Leszek will rip your head off if you force her.'

'Will I?' Leszek looked at his raging wife with barely hidden amusement.

'Yes, you will, or you and I will have a problem.' Sara answered, not once taking her gaze off me.

'You heard what my Firefly said, Adam, so be good. I like to think we've become friends, but unlike you, I don't enjoy walking around covered with someone else's blood.'

Nina chose that moment to return from the bathroom, so I couldn't reply to Sara's threat, but it didn't matter. I was more than pleased that Nina had such a fierce defender. Even if it was my boss's wife, the most annoying woman on this side of the Motlawa River. Nina looked at us, confused by the lingering tension, before she passed me her phone, trying to hide a yawn.

'Feel free to snoop,' she muttered, sitting next to Sara and curling up on the sofa.

The phone was unlocked, and I quickly checked to see what number Pawel had used to call his sister. Instead, I found something strange. A few moments after their conversation, she'd called me, the ID of *'Arsehole V'*, a dead giveaway, but that wasn't the strange part. No, after our call, Nina had phoned someone else, and the number had a foreign prefix, but when I'd asked her earlier, she'd been adamant there were no more calls.

'Nina, are you sure you didn't make any other calls?' I asked, and she shifted to look at me.

'No, I followed your instructions and waited,' she said, and I felt uneasiness building inside me.

'Someone abroad, maybe?' I asked again, and she looked at me in complete confusion.

'What are you talking about? Why would I call someone abroad? Why would I even take the chance of missing a call from you or Pawel?' She asked, now fully alert, a panicked look in her eyes, so I handed her the phone to show her.

After glancing at the phone, she frowned before handing it back. 'What are you talking about? There's nothing there.' Nina was clearly exasperated, but even from this distance, I could still see the number displayed on her screen.

'Fuck!' The curse slipped out as I rushed forward, and Nina jerked away, frightened. I grasped her head, tilting it to the side and thrusting my face close to her skin, searching for any signs of damage, but frustration left me snarling at the lack of evidence.

With a whispered apology, I pressed my lips to Nina's carotid, lightly grazing my tongue along its length, tasting her sweet skin. There was a low gasp of surprise from her, but instead of tensing and pushing me away, Nina relaxed, tilting her head to the side in complete trust. I nearly came undone at her reaction, but just as my body began to respond, I tasted the barest hint of the sourness of vampire venom and cursed again, pulling away suddenly. Retreating to my chair, my phone already in my hand, I hit speed dial three, calling Veronica Sandoval.

'What do you want?' she asked curtly, and I wondered what insulting tag she had my number saved under.

'I need your help. Send a Psychic Witch to Leszek's mansion. Find one who can remove a geas placed by an elder vampire.'

'Sara?' she asked, and I quickly answered.

'No, Nina, her friend.'

'You're asking a lot for a human, but fine. Twenty thousand zlotych, and I will send you my best witch first thing in the—' She hadn't finished before Leszek ripped the phone from my hand.

'You will send one now, and I will double your price. Now, Veronica. It's important.'

Ignoring Nina was a mistake, and when her panicked voice overrode Leszek's, I turned back, ready to apologise.

'What's going on? Can someone tell me what the fuck is going on?!'

If looks could kill, I would have been dust at that moment, but before I could speak, Sara answered Nina's question.

'I'd say Adam discovered you were bitten by a vampire and that the bastard has you under a compulsion to do whatever he tells you,' she said, and I watched the colour drain from Nina's face.

'That can't be true. It was only a nightmare,' she whispered before her eyes rolled back and she fainted.

I had Nina in my arms before I even thought of moving, gently laying her helpless body on the sofa. When Sara came to our side to examine her friend, I nearly attacked the Seer, but expecting my actions, she merely knelt down and smacked my nose, then ignored me as she worked.

Moments later, her sigh of relief eased the knot in my chest, and I sat back, Nina's hand in my own, my fingers running across the veins for reassurance.

'Foolish man, she was just overwrought, exhausted and anaemic from the bite.' Sara's words, meant to be comforting, had the opposite effect on me, and her next question angered me beyond sense. 'I'm assuming you haven't bitten her as well?'

'No, and I will stake the motherfucker who touched her! He must have compelled her to call him when she had any contact with her brother. Fuck, where is that damn witch?'

I could barely contain my fury. The mark of another vampire on Nina's neck was evidence of my complete failure. Maybe if I'd contacted Nina as soon as Sara asked me to investigate, this wouldn't have happened. My spiralling thoughts broke off when Nina slowly opened her eyes, her gaze meeting mine with eyes that were hard and unyielding, filled with a hurt I wished I could erase.

'You will fix this, Adam. Do whatever it takes, and I will give you whatever you want in payment,' she said quietly but implacably. I simply nodded, unable to console her while my head was filled with rage. I sat next to her on the sofa.

'As soon as we're done here, you are moving to my apartment. It isn't just about your brother, Nina. I can't allow anyone to hunt on my territory.' I said, and her eyes widened at the vehemence in my voice.

That wasn't the whole truth, but still, it was a better explanation than mentioning the thought of her alone and unprotected drove me mad. Now came the challenging part, the one I knew she would oppose. 'You will also take a leave of absence from the hospital. You will be by my side or with Sara, but never alone.'

'You can't be serious! I can accept living with you for now, but how can you expect me to pay my bills if I'm not working? Rent won't pay itself just because I temporarily changed addresses. I know what you're saying, but I can't let this fucker stop me from living my life. He already did... I can't let him rule over my life, Adam,' she argued.

The last sentence was a pleading whisper, and I wanted to give in, tell her she could live as free as before, but what would stop that bastard from coming for her then? What if he lost control, draining her dry without bothering to turn her?

It was this fear that hardened my resolve.

'I am serious, Nina, and you will accept it, or I will let your brother die in whatever shithole he's crawled into.' I said, and Nina turned her head toward her ally.

'Sara?'

'I'm sorry, I know it's not ideal. Trust me, been there, seen it, and nearly strangled Leszek with the tee shirt, but this time, Adam is right. Although he could be less of an arsehole in how he goes about asking,' Sara said with a glare in my direction, and Nina instantly deflated.

'Fine, but when you've dealt with him, we're done,' she all but snarled.

'After I finish with him, you can choose how you want our interactions to continue, and I will abide by your decision. Until then, you will do what I say because not only is your brother's life at risk, but your own is too,' I replied, driving the point home as her expression darkened. 'I know you hate what I do, but I do it to protect you. Deep down, you must know this,' I added. My beautiful brittle Obsidian looked so broken that I reached out and placed my hand on her cheek, tilting her face up.

My breath hitched when she nodded, her lips brushing the inner side of my palm as she spoke.

'I know, but it's still a bitter pill to swallow.'

'Then I will sweeten it for you. This isn't our first rodeo, after all. This time, we'll get to sleep in comfortable settings.' My little tease didn't chase away all the clouds from her expression, but I saw the corner of her lips twitching as she pulled away from me.

'You will regret this, bloodsucker,' she teased without a hint of malice in her tone.

Michal's entrance interrupted our discussion, an elderly lady following him inside.

'Adam, this lady is here to administer the assistance you requested,' he said, politely indicating the woman beside him before bowing to Leszek and giving the rest of us a very reserved, respectful nod.

'I understand this issue is urgent. Where is the victim?' She asked, and Nina stood up from the sofa with a wry answer on her lips.

'That would be me, although I wouldn't describe myself as a victim.' I moved to follow her before the witch stopped me.

'Not you, Seethe Master. Only my sister's presence is allowed,' she said, with a pointed look towards Sara, who immediately stood to attention.

'Of course. Let's go to the office,' the Soul Shepherd said. Both Nina and the witch followed Sara as she led them to Leszek's private sanctuary.

Leszek observed the women disappearing behind the heavy oak door before he sat in the armchair. 'What are you going to do because I hope holding Nina under a protective umbrella isn't your only solution?'

'Give me all you have on this treasure hunt you signed me up for. The timing is too coincidental for it not to be connected, especially since I found Nina's useless brother teamed up with those Lost Ark idiots.'

'The ones that named themselves after the movie?' The eye roll that accompanied Leszek's question was of epic proportions, but I couldn't blame him. The Lost Ark group were a group of feckless dilettantes that, thanks to their various vices, were now more grave robbers than amateur archaeologists. Unfortunately, somewhere along their descent into criminality, they learned about the Nether, and in the last few years, the group began targeting the elder race's sacred grounds, graveyards, and temples, searching for magical artefacts to sell on the black market.

'Yes, those. However, whatever those cretins' latest little caper was, it got them killed. Nina's brother is the only one not wearing his entrails as an overcoat.' My brutal answer didn't phase the Forest Lord in the slightest, his slight shrug indicative of his feelings.

'Small loss. I take it you think the killer is here to finish the job?' He asked, sipping his whisky. I noticed a frown appear on Leszek's face as he reached up to massage his chest.

'We have Pawel's sudden appearance, then disappearance, rogue vampires and some old Master seeking a family heirloom. There are too many coincidences, and that leads me to only one conclusion. That idiot stole something from the Vampire Master, who is more than happy to trample over the laws of hospitality in order to retrieve it. So I need the contact details of the man who wanted to hire me, and if I confirm his involvement, he will die.' I said, looking at him, expecting Leszek to stop me.

'Protect your woman as you see fit, just... don't involve Sara. Use whatever Syndicate resources you need to do it. I don't like strangers disturbing the peace, so send him on his way or to Veles' pit, whichever is easiest,' he answered, deeming the matter finished.

'I doubt your father would accept a vampire into his realm. After all, Veles's pit is for the souls of the living, not the dried-out husks of the monstrous dead,' I said, the smile on my face one of bitter amusement. 'Maybe you could ask him to make an exception.'

Since his union with Sara, the Forest Lord had regained most of his divine power, so much so that his home was reborn as a sacred grove, allowing the elder gods to roam freely over his island whenever they wanted. Which meant he really could ask Veles to accept a soul if he didn't mind dealing with his father.

Suddenly, Leszek jerked forward, grabbing his chest, the sound of retching from the office making us both turn in that direction. In the blink of an eye, I was at the door, ripping it from its hinges.

All three women turned sallow, nauseous faces toward me, and I noticed Sara holding Leszek's favourite Yuka plant on her lap, the ceramic container full of vomit.

'You owe me big for this one, vampire, and don't you forget it,' said the witch as she attempted to leave, but before she passed, I grabbed her arm, only to feel the trembling muscles beneath my hand.

'Who was it?' I asked.

'An elder, a powerful one with psychic skills that almost broke me. If not for the Seer, your little human would never have escaped his control,' she answered, shaking her head. 'Let me go. I need a scalding hot shower and a bottle of vodka after that, and so does your human.' She pointed toward Nina, who sat on Leszek's chair, dazed and exhausted.

When I went to scoop her up, she didn't try to fight me, her head dropping against my shoulder, so I held her a little tighter, feeling Nina's erratic heartbeat thundering against my chest. 'It's alright, sweetheart, let me take you home,' I murmured, feeling the rightness of those words.

Leszek was already crouching next to Sara, taking the violated plant from her hands. 'Are you alright, my love?' He asked, and she grunted something in response that caused my boss to sigh heavily.

'That's fine, but why my favourite Yuka? Out of all the plants...' He hadn't finished before I heard Sara's voice.

'Oh, for fuck's sake, you don't get to berate me because of a plant. You can sleep on the couch tonight,' she snapped.

'Fine, but remember, each time you kick me to the couch, you end up complaining there's not enough room there for both of us.'

The rest of their conversation was cut off by the front door as it closed behind me. I looked at Nina, still pale, as she rested in my arms. This was not how I envisioned taking her to my apartment for the first time, but as long as I got her there, nothing else mattered.

CHAPTER 9

A dam held me like his life depended on it, and I gave in, basking in his embrace. I should object and assert my strength, but exhaustion had leeched away my ability to find any reason to reject him.

Do I even want to anymore?

My thoughts were filled with so many conflicting emotions that I simply switched off and let him bundle me into the car, then drive through Gdansk to Granary Island. I had a lot to process after the latest revelation, but for now, it was all going to be locked into the deepest, darkest pit in my mind till I had the energy to deal with it.

There was one memory I especially shied away from. Sapieha's biting me. When we'd broken through the mind control, my memories from the moment flooded back, but that bastard's attack and the way I reacted to his venom? I flinched as shame burned through my body.

The rational part of me knew it wasn't my fault. I'd fought with every fibre of my being until I couldn't fight anymore, but the shame was still there. Whether it was his mind-control magic or that weird vampire venom, I surrendered to the pleasure until something broke inside me. I gave him whatever he wanted, and my body enjoyed it.

I felt dirty, so utterly broken. Adam must have realised something was wrong because I could see the concern in his glances reflected in the window I was pretending to look out of. Part of me craved his compassion, wishing he would just hold me. I knew he would never judge me for what had happened and that he was willing to look after me, which made the entire experience feel less... tainted.

Another part of me hated that he knew. I could no longer be the haughty Nina, looking at the world with a strong, unbroken spirit, claiming I would never yield to a vampire. All it took was one man, one bite, to break me.

I'd insisted on knowing, but now I almost wished we hadn't broken the geas. Tension rose in my chest again. *So much for cramming my emotions into the back of my mind,* I thought, realising I was hyperventilating. My breath was so fast and deep that my fingers started tingling, and my muscles spasmed.

I exhaled slowly, focusing on the changing panorama outside of the car as if I were seeing it for the first time. Granary Island was the most exclusive area in Gdansk. It was an island in the middle of the Motlawa River, connected with the old town by countless bridges and walkways. For years, it stood empty, the ruins of medieval granaries enticing adventurous artists who created a community of misfits and rebels, until a mysterious corporation bought it from the city and built ridiculously expensive apartment buildings with exclusive shops and businesses.

Even though the island had been thoroughly gentrified, the corporation left the majority of the vegetation alone, creating an almost wild, untamed haven for the rich and famous that incorporated the medieval buildings almost seamlessly into the modern, sleek architecture. It was a place of beauty and harmony, and as I studied the exquisite surroundings, I came to a sudden realisation.

'Leszek did this, didn't he?' I asked, finally distracted from my panic. Adam's reflection nodded before he spoke.

'Yes, we knew it would happen. The city council wanted to revitalise the economy, and several companies were competing to ruin the island with concrete and glass. We simply changed their minds and invested our own money, ensuring that any so-called *improvements* were palatable to the Elder Races.' He answered.

'We?'

'I designed the outline and provided security for the island. Because of our reputation, it was difficult to get the city council to approve the purchase unless I promised them it would incorporate the old medieval granaries. The island looks so much better from above. I will show you when we get to my apartment,' he said proudly, but I couldn't contain my sigh.

'So it's happening, then? My jail time in your custody?' I meant it as a jest, but Adam's shoulders instantly stiffened. He didn't say anything, but I knew I'd hurt him. We drove the rest of the way in silence, and I opened my mouth a few times to apologise, but something always stopped me. The bitter old part of me, so afraid to be hurt again, prevented me from saying those precious words to let him know I never meant to hurt his feelings.

He parked the car in the underground garage. 'Wait,' he commanded when I reached for the door handle.

The authority in his voice stayed my hand. I frowned, but it was his place, so I waited. Much to my surprise, Adam walked around the car, opened my door and reached inside to help me out like a gentleman from an old-fashioned movie.

It was sweet, and not entirely out of character for an almost two-hundred-year-old vampire, so I took his hand, enjoying the gentle warmth that spread inside me. My muscles trembled when I stood up, and I used his strength to avoid falling.

'Thank you...' I hadn't finished speaking when he scooped me up, closed the door with the kick, and marched toward the elevator. 'Adam, put me down. I can walk.'

'Oh yes, that's why you held my hand so hard that I felt my bones creaking. It is time for your incarceration, remember? So I advise you to follow my rules, and don't forget that I will do as I please in my house.'

'Oh yes, Master, your captive is at your command, oh Dark One! What kind of medieval bullshit is this?' I quipped, rolling my eyes.

'If you insist on calling me Master, do it in the bedroom, chained to the bedpost, like a blushing virgin in good, old medieval times,' he answered with a smirk, nuzzling my temple with his nose, and it instantly piqued my interest.

'You have a bed with bedposts? Like a real vampire?'

'Oh gods, give me strength... I am a real vampire!' He muttered, but I saw a corner of his mouth twitching before he turned toward the elevator control panel and barking out the command. 'Penthouse.'

'Voice recognition confirmed, access to penthouse granted. Welcome home, Mister Lisowczyk,' the elevator announced at its arrival.

We entered the plush interior, gliding towards the top of the building before the door opened onto the enormous hallway.

'Lorelai, soft mood lighting and run the bath for Nina. Use my herbal blend.' He said impatiently, kicking his shoes off, only slightly tightening his hold on me as he did.

I expected the housekeeper to appear and greet her boss. Instead, an overexcited voice shrieked from the speaker on the ceiling.

'Of course, Master. You finally brought her home. How exciting! Will you be taking her to bed? Your mate should sleep with you, of course.' The female voice said, and suddenly the lights dimmed, and the soft, alluring voice of Sade[14] filled the apartment, singing *Smooth Operator.*

My chin hit the floor, especially when a blush blossomed on Adam's pale complexion, and he roared.

'Stop the music, and do as you are told!'

'Of course, Master. Your humble servant follows your every command.' The voice from the ceiling answered. I could clearly hear the sarcasm and offence in her voice. One thing was good in all this, I was so focused on this bizarre situation that thoughts of the assault and worry about my brother dimmed a little in my mind.

'*Smooth Operator*?' I asked, pressing a hand to my lips to prevent the mad laughter from escaping when I saw the blush darken on his cheeks. He was still walking, and I was wondering where Adam was taking me when he crossed his 'steel and concrete' decorated living room.

'She likes this song. Lorelai can be wilful sometimes, but she is an excellent housekeeper,' he answered curtly, and I was wondering how often his wilful servant played this and for how many women.

'Oh well, I'm sure it will be a novelty to not have your conquest sleep in your bed. Lorelai will be shocked, poor thing,' I said.

---

14. *Sade – Nigerian-born British singer known for her sophisticated blend of soul, funk, jazz, and Afro.*

Unfortunately, sarcasm was unable to hide the undertone of hurt in my voice. Two years ago, despite becoming close, Adam didn't once offer to bring me here, yet his servant immediately assumed his female visitor would be sleeping with him. *Smooth Operator, indeed.*

'Nina, you're the first woman I've brought here to stay the night, so don't read too much into Lorelai's assumption.' He said, lowering my feet when we entered a large, modern bathroom.

Could I believe him? Everybody knew vampires weren't big fans of chastity. On the contrary, if you wanted sex in any configuration with any partner or partners, their kind was happy to oblige.

I wanted to believe him, but all I could see in my mind was the image of a stream of women entering this beautiful room, Adam biting on their necks, feeding and pleasuring them. At the same time, soft music played in the background. I didn't like it one bit. It shouldn't matter, but it did. We weren't a couple, but I felt strangely possessive of my vampire. Whoever warmed his bed was none of my business, but the thought of Adam with another woman pissed me off so much that I pushed him away.

'Well, I'm safe now, so you can call one of your charitable donations because you're not feeding from me tonight. You don't have to be so nice, you know. I preferred it when you were being an arsehole. At least then I knew what to feel.'

The unfiltered thoughts poured out of me until I took a deep breath, angry that I let my feelings escape my control. I was still reeling from the magic and subsequent memories. It wasn't the best moment to talk to Adam about anything, not when I felt like this. He did nothing wrong, yet I was lashing out because I needed him, and I didn't know how to ask for his help. I was better than this. He deserved better than this.

'I'm sorry. I shouldn't have said that. Can you...? We have a deal, but I'm exhausted. Can we not do it tonight? You will feed from me just... leave me alone for a moment, please?' I said, standing up.

The water was already running in the large sunken tub, the decadent marble reminding me of ancient Roman baths. A combination of steam and the tart scent of male grooming products was intoxicating and made my legs buckle. If not for Adam catching me at the last moment, I would have crashed helplessly to the floor.

Until now, I hadn't realised the huge toll the last few weeks had taken on me. How utterly depleted my body had been because of the constant worry, blood loss and fighting the geas. This latest outburst had burned through the remains of my energy, and Adam must have sensed it. Another embarrassment to add to the growing list. I tried to show Adam I didn't need him, but the only thing that stood between me and face-planting his marble tiles was this damn vampire.

'Thank you. I'm good now,' I said, hating my own weakness as he wordlessly helped me to a chair near the vanity stand.

I knew I needed a bath, and not just to clean away the dirt of the day. The session with the witch had been exhausting. She returned my memories, making me relive the events for my conscious mind to acknowledge the reality while Sara held my hand, grounding my spirit and witnessing what happened. It was like a nightmare I couldn't wake up from and left me covered with the stench of fear, a layer of sweat, and aching muscles. In the end, the witch ripped away the vampire's compulsion, and my heart almost stopped when the spell rushed through me.

I couldn't blame Sara for retching. She was in my head when the witch connected us and felt how I reacted...

The memories of the pleasure forced upon me by the stranger's bite left me feeling tainted, unclean in a way I wasn't sure soap could ever erase. *No, I needed to wash it off.* I didn't care how irrational it sounded or that I would most likely drown in the deep bathtub.

I didn't want Adam to see my weakness. Not him. I could deal with the bite, but not with the pity in Adam's eyes, and I wasn't sure if I could stop myself from crying.

He crouched next to me, placing his hands on my knees. My breath hitched, and all I could feel was the heat of Adam's touch because he didn't hesitate. Something had triggered this reaction, and I saw his eyes change from deep blue to black, and I drowned in the boundless depths of his irises. His touch was still gentle, but his expression was not, and I flinched seeing pure, unbridled fury before he bent his head downward, hiding it away.

'Nina, do us both a favour; shut up and let me look after you. I don't need your blood, and I'm not being nice to get it. Whatever you think of me, we both know you need my help. You're in no shape to bathe by yourself, so be a good girl because I'm not leaving you alone like this,' He stated, his voice quiet but unyielding.

Adam emphasised his words with a gentle squeeze of my knees, and I felt like he was reading my mind. I knew this was stupid, but I didn't want his touch when he was so angry, not when he thought he had to do it.

'I'm no one's good girl!' I said, standing up rapidly, only for a wave of dizziness to leave me falling back down onto the chair.

'Well then, could you be a smart one before you crack that thick skull of yours and get blood on my tiled floor? I'm sure a nice bath will help us both relax and be a little calmer. So unless you want to earn yourself another bite from an out-of-control vampire, I suggest you just suck it up and accept my offer. What is so fucking offensive in my trying to help you, anyway?'

It was the last sentence that stopped me in my tracks.

Did he think I was repulsed by his touch? I wondered, looking at the bath and imagining myself naked with him there. *I don't have a problem with nudity, so what's stopping me?* I weighed my options. I felt Adam's hand tense, and he looked at me with an uncertainty that suggested he needed it as much as I did. I could work with this, and for as long as we help each other, I could accept his offer.

'Fine, but no funny business. I've had enough bloodsuckers hanging off my neck to last a lifetime,' I said, and my reluctant au pair sighed heavily, grabbing the rim of my jumper.

'Lift your arms,' he ordered, and I followed his instructions, letting him strip me of the clothes I'd borrowed from Sara.

Still, I pulled back when he reached for my bra, and Adam smirked.

'Oh please, after the things we did together, you're suddenly shy?' It felt like my acceptance of his aid removed some anger and brought back the more appealing traits of his personality. Now, with a mischievous salute, Adam continued. 'Scout's honour, your virtue is safe with me. I will simply help you bathe. Treat me as an upgraded version of a male nurse. Just with better pecs,' he teased, and I couldn't help smiling. He didn't push or try to overpower me, simply waiting for my decision, and that was good enough for me.

'Fine, do what you want... nurse,' I said, letting him reach behind me to unhook my bra. *Thank fuck we don't have nurses like this in the Emergency department; everyone would be tripping over themselves to get injured.* My mind stuttered over the thought as Adam slid the bra gently from my shoulders.

'I cannot do what I want. You are not ready for that, but I will help with whatever you need. I'm not him. I won't hurt you, Nina. I'm sorry for what he did to you. He will pay for that, I promise,' Adam whispered, suddenly serious, so close to my ear that it made me shiver. The raw need in his words was more potent as I sat there in nothing but a pair of panties.

Adam quickly stripped away his borrowed clothes, leaving only boxer briefs, before he scooped me up and carried me into the steaming bath. I gasped when he sat me between his legs, his chest touching my back as I pulled my knees to my chest, feeling vulnerable as the memories repeated in my head.

I shivered as they started again, but Adam's hands began stroking over my arms, driving away the goosebumps. It was a small gesture, but with his body surrounding me, I felt safe for the first time since remembering my assault. I wanted to turn to thank him for his silent support, but I wasn't entirely free of the fear.

Adam didn't say a word. All he did was apply soap to my shoulders, continuing to stroke me. The fluid round motion and firm touch were so soothing I melted against his body, laying my head against the soft hair of his chest.

When he finally broke his silence, Adam's words washed over me as smoothly as water. 'You've had a tough day, Nina, so just relax. Nothing and no one can hurt you here. I won't fail you again, please trust me,' he murmured as he tenderly kissed the top of my head, his fingers moving over my tense muscles, easing the knots one by one, intuitively lessening the pressure when he encountered a painful area.

With my thoughts turning sluggish, I wondered why he hadn't tried to make this sexual. I'd expected him to show his true colours, grabbing me and trying to have sex, especially since I felt a rising erection pressing against my back, but not once did his hands do more than massage me. Adam was entirely focused on me, kneading my muscles, letting his touch and hot herbal bath relieve my stress.

Then it hit me. This was all about me. Adam wasn't trying to trick me into being intimate or to submit to him. In his own rakish way, he was helping me the best way he knew. I was sitting between his legs, naked and vulnerable, and Adam didn't take advantage of it. He could toy with my body, possess my mind, and make me do things like the other vampire… instead, here he was, playing nurse and asking for nothing in return.

He cares for me. This realisation broke me. All the feelings I'd suppressed since breaking Sapieha's compulsion surged up into loud, ugly sobbing, and I turned around and buried my face in Adam's chest to hide myself from the world. Adam's hand stilled before he embraced me, his mouth pressed to my temple in the lightest of kisses.

'I'm so sorry, Nina. If I wasn't such a prideful arsehole, you would have come to me earlier. This was not your fault, sweetheart. Nothing that happened was ever your fault. Whatever you felt, it was all on him. Fuck, I will kill him for you. I will rip his heart out for you to crush under your heel. You're safe now. I won't let anything happen to you. I know you are in pain now, and if I could take it away, I would, but you are strong, and I promise this memory will fade away,' he whispered, his powerful body wrapped tight around me, hands once more stroking over my back.

Adam held me like that without another word until my desperate sobs subsided, my emotions more settled than they had been in days. In the end, his words helped me to smile again. Typical Adam, offering me the still-beating heart of my enemy.

'Thank you... but no rotten hearts, please.' I said, pulling away, and he instantly opened his arms, letting me go.

'Whatever you wish, Nina. It's your call, but I can't promise I won't rip his head off for his other transgressions,' he stated firmly as I shook my head and slowly stood up.

Adam was instantly on his feet, reaching for the towel to wrap it around my body, but instead, I took it out of his hand, my fingers lingering against his to express my gratitude.

'I'm better now. You were right. I needed it, and... thank you. You would make an excellent nurse.' I saw the lines around his blue eyes harden again, and I wondered if he thought I was pushing him away. Instinctively, I put my hand on his cheek.

'You helped a lot. Somehow, you found the right way to ease my mind, but I'm not good at crying. I've always had to be the strong one. It's...' I trailed off before continuing. 'I just need a moment for myself, but I'm good now... and starving.' I added the last bit, not really feeling hungry, intending it as an excuse Adam could use to avoid feeling awkward.

'Fine, I'll be in the kitchen when you're ready,' he said, taking the hint. As soon as he closed the door, I fell heavily on the chair, stunned by the realisation that Adam had given me precisely what I needed, and I wasn't sure if I was ready to admit how that made me feel.

'Your clothes, Mistress.' Lorelai's voice startled me, and I promptly turned around to see a humanoid shadow, strange and disproportional, disappearing around the corner. With the servant's name on my lips, I noticed the clothing she'd left behind: a bathrobe with a simple cotton t-shirt and a pair of shorts left in a pile next to my chair.

The bathroom had only one door, and I'd been facing it the whole time. That meant Lorelai must be one of the Elder Races that was able to survive in the mortal realm.

'Thank you, Lorelai, whatever you are,' I called out, slightly embarrassed, before dressing. Cheerful laughter followed my words, and I tried to ignore the shiver that slid down my spine.

The t-shirt was a plain grey, covering me to mid-thigh, almost hiding the cute little boy shorts, and when I slipped on the fluffy black dressing gown, I was surrounded by warmth and the uniquely masculine scent of Adam. I didn't know where the rest of the outfit came from, but with the dressing gown on, I suddenly didn't care.

I walked toward the kitchen, the polished concrete floor surprisingly warm under my bare feet, almost as if a sleeping dragon warmed it from beneath. Just as my imagination began taking flight, I stumbled to a halt, the mouthwatering smell of pancakes overwhelming my thoughts.

Adam stood shirtless by the cooker, flipping the heavenly perfection with practised ease. I vaguely remember telling him that pancakes were my favourite comfort food from my childhood. The only moments in my chaotic life that weren't filled with arguing parents were those times our mother had sent Pawel and me to our grandmother's, and she'd made us pancakes. The only moment that I'd truly felt loved and looked after was when I didn't have to protect my brother.

Now, Adam was doing that for me, and I couldn't find the words to thank him. My chest burned because I suddenly felt so vulnerable. He was peeling away the layers of my defences with his kindness, and it felt almost as bad as being mind fucked by a vampire. I wanted this, wanted him, but it felt wrong. Me, a bitter divorcee, pining after an immortal vampire? Fairytales like this never lasted, and sooner or later, someone's heart, most likely mine, would be broken.

'Your food's ready,' Adam said without turning around. His enhanced senses must have alerted him to my presence, and I wondered if that was the reason for the tension in his muscles because he looked like he was ready to kill.

'Thank you,' I answered, sitting in front of an empty plate, which he then filled with fluffy goodness. 'Also, thank you for the bath and for defending me.' Pointing to the now full plate, I continued. 'You didn't have to do all this. You could have just pointed me to a bed. I can look after myself.'

'Or you could eat your pancake so we can talk. I feel things are changing between us, and I thought maybe you could tell me the real reason you kicked me out on the street like a stray dog,' Adam said, placing a pot of jam and a pot of cream next to my plate.

'I had my reasons. Not very good ones, but they were still reasons.' I said quietly, picking up the fluffy pancakes, but not before I saw Adam grimace.

'I know. Sara told me about your ex-husband. Who, by the way, recently had all his assets as well as his current lover's money seized by the Tax Office after some good citizen anonymously tipped off the authorities.' He said, and I choked.

'What did you do?'

'What he deserved. Sara asked me not to kill him, and I honoured her wishes, but my little prank will cost him dearly.' He said it so casually, as if destroying someone's life was part of his day-to-day routine.

'And before you ask, I put aside a little protected nest egg for his latest victim, as long as she isn't up to her neck in his dirty deeds.'

'Why?' I asked

'Because he deserves it. He hurt you, and I couldn't let it slide. What that bastard did to you took two years of my life. I was wrong to set the terms, but you were wrong for not trusting me. Even after today, you barely accepted my help. I want to be more than just a man you hired to find your brother. So, please, what is so wrong with me that you keep pushing me away?'

I looked at him, and I barely recognised the man who lived with me in the past. He was perfect. What he did for me, not just today, but in the days leading up to the attack itself. The little things that helped me manage the hospital's affairs when I could barely hold my life together. Fuck, I was falling for him, and it scared me no less than the first time because I knew unless I took his offer and let him transform me, time would eventually break us apart and my heart with it. Still, being his spawn was not an option, and I had to find a way of explaining why.

If only I could protect my heart, to keep it safe till our time together was over, maybe we could try to be happy, even if only for a moment.

'I will tell you, I promise, but not today, not after everything that's happened, I'm sorry. I just can't face that.'

Chapter 10

Adam

Tonight had been a catastrophe. I should have known better than to ask that question, but knowing I hadn't protected my woman made my anger burn brighter than ever. I wanted to find the cause of my failure to ensure she would come to me if she needed help again. Instead, I sat there, looking at her pained expression and knowing this time I was the cause.

She opened up to me, let me hold her, care for her. I thought she was ready to talk about the past, about us, because I was. Feeling her cling to me in the bathtub as she cried in anger and sorrow had changed something for me. I wanted to be the man she trusted to hold her when she was at her most vulnerable. I was ready to deny my very nature to be the hero in her story, and suddenly, I felt nothing except blinding rage.

Since learning what happened to Nina, I'd tried to hold myself together, to think of her, to help her, and suddenly I couldn't. It was my failure. In pride and impatience, I had demanded a set of conditions that left Nina unable to trust me and vulnerable to attack.

I felt bloodlust and rage clouding my judgment, threatening my sanity. I wanted to go back to that damn playground, hoping more of her enemies turned up because I wanted to rip something apart so very, very much.

An incoherent growl formed in the back of my throat, and I saw Nina's pupils widen, the scent of uneasiness permeating the room. She didn't run away, but I saw her body tense, hands trembling even after she put them flat on the counter. She was worried I'd attack her. I couldn't even blame her. I was a vampire, the same kind as the bastard who assaulted her, and now I was on the edge of bloodlust.

'Calm the fuck down, or she'll think you're a fucking monster.'

The words formed in my head, but I was beyond my ability to control the urge. I needed to feed and not from a bag this time. I had starved myself for too long. The blood loss from the fight and intense emotion triggered the beast in me. I ground my teeth and steadied my breath, the irony of the situation hitting me hard.

At a time when I should be at my best for her, I was at my worst, reminding her of the bastard who attacked her.

'What is going on? Your eyes… we can talk. What can I do to help…' she said, attempting to calm me down, but I cut her off.

'Make yourself at home. My apartment is large enough for you to avoid me if that is your wish. Our arrangement is now null and void. I won't bleed you, Nina. Not when you are afraid of me, but you will stay here for your safety. I will find your brother and protect you because I can't allow some piece of shit Vampire Master to run around my city like he owns the place. When I'm done with him, you will be safe to leave,' I said, rubbing my neck.

My home felt so suffocating. I needed to get out, and I needed to go now before I broke my word and fed off her. My inner beast was raging inside, and the longer I smelled Nina, the more unpredictable I felt.

'You're leaving me alone? What should I do?'

'Do whatever you like here while I'm out. I'll be back first thing in the morning,' I said, and Nina looked at me sharply.

'Where are you going? What's going on?'

'I'm going to feed,' I said, watching as her eyes widened and face drained of colour. 'Make yourself at home and wait. The rest is none of your fucking business.' I said sharply, choosing my words on purpose because the longer she stopped me, the less control I had over my hunger. I needed to end this conversation, even if it meant she was hurt and angry, before I ended up on her neck, turning into the beast she hated.

Without waiting for a reply, I moved toward the shadows, my form melting as I slipped along the edges of the Nether.

'Adam, wait!' I heard Nina's voice, but I didn't listen. My Obsidian had never seen me like that. Her fear, her scent, and her heartbeat were pushing me over the edge, but she did nothing to deserve the monster I was becoming.

Everything was grey in the shadows, but even knowing that fact, I couldn't resist looking back. The icy touch of the void calmed me enough to manage that much.

Nina held her chest, breathing rapidly while her tears slowly dropped on the countertop. A look of devastation overtook her features before she straightened and scowled at the corner I'd disappeared into.

She was regal in her anger, and despite everything, I was proud of her strength. She turned away to sit in front of the now-cold pancakes and began eating. *There you are, my Obsidian. I will make it up to you, I promise,* I thought, feeling the pain of hunger twisting my insides.

I quickly shifted to my bedroom and changed clothes. A glance in the mirror reminded me of the saying, *'dressed to kill'*, and my smile turned predatory. Nina's blood was sacred, everyone else was fair game.

I headed for The Anchor, the notorious nightclub and head-quarters of the Syndicate's human partner in crime, Zbigniew Nadolny. I would not be using a blood brothel this evening. No, tonight I would hunt. I needed the thrill, even if the method I employed was more sex appeal than devouring violence. Nadolny's club was always full of young women who would shed their inhibitions to take a perilous walk on the wild side.

My form coalesced in the alley next to the club's main entrance, preventing passers-by from realising I had appeared from nowhere. The bouncer recognised me immediately, opening the symbolic rope to let me in, much to the displeasure of the waiting patrons.

Loud music assaulted my ears as soon as I entered, my eyesight obscured by the chemical smoke popular in these places, highlighting the occasional flashes of strobe lighting, distorting the gyrating bodies on the dancefloor below. Of course, I knew the real reason for the smokescreen was more to hide nefarious deeds than to add an atmosphere of mystery, but tonight, that was precisely why I was there. As I stalked toward the bar, my eyes scanned the area, constantly aware, always searching, both for threats and potential victims, my anger clearing the way without the need to touch any disgustingly sweaty bodies.

'Welcome, sir,' the bartender was as quick as the bouncer to acknowledge my presence. 'The usual Bloody Mary, or would you prefer one of our specials?' He asked with a smile, and I nodded toward the alcohol.

'The usual, please,' I answered. It never ceased to amaze me how easily the personnel of this club adapted to change, accepting the presence of the Elder Races without a single misstep. That open-minded approach turned the Anchor into a safe space for those with unusual needs and dietary requirements. This barman was no exception, his laconic gaze unblinking as he casually offered me a willing donor to drink from.

The cocktail appeared almost immediately, and looking around, I noticed the inviting glances from a couple of young women as they drifted to the dance floor, their stares growing bolder as they performed in front of me. I smiled at them but shook my head. They were looking for entertainment, and I was not in the mood to indulge them.

A lazy stroll through the club didn't reveal anyone who caught my interest. Those who managed to pique it all seemed to repulse me whenever I came close enough to catch their scent. After I dismissed the fourth, it hit me. They weren't Nina. That was the only thing that was wrong with them. A slender, boyish figure and pixie-cropped hair were not enough. I needed Nina, the woman whose essence made me salivate at the mere thought of her. She was so strong, resisting me, yet so vulnerable. My Obsidian. So sharp yet so brittle, the mere thought of her and I felt the uncomfortable pressure of my hard cock pushing against the inadequate restraint of my clothing.

'Fuck!' I snapped out, my exclamation loud enough to catch the attention of a boisterous group of young men.

'What's your problem, pretty boy?' asked a belligerent, stocky male, and I smiled. *The Gods reward those who take what they want,* I thought, stepping forward.

'Oh, my problem? I'm looking for a new plaything to beg me to take his arse, so if you play your cards right, I might reward you with more pleasure than you thought possible.' The tone of my voice made the provocative words sound more like a threat than an offer, but I began to enjoy myself as the group bristled.

'Who the fuck do you think you are, arsehole?' he snapped, and I sauntered toward him, standing closer than my antagonist liked before speaking.

'I'm the man whose cock you'll be begging to suck in a second. So, why don't you get down to business? I can see you are the type who would like it.'

As if listening to my plea, fate granted me a guilt-free hunt when the rest of his friends stood up, their intentions written all over their drunken faces. I had no qualms about using those bullies for my snack. They deserved it all. My anger, my pain. I would thoroughly enjoy unleashing myself on them. I barely noticed my fists clenched as my hunger for violence grew, my goading having the desired effect as the three bigots in front of me pushed forward.

Unfortunately, just as the fun was about to start, the music escalated to roaring cacophony, and the Chief-Spoilsport arrived.

'Adam, get the fuck out of my club if you're going to be like this.' Nadolny stood at a respectful distance, his demeanour one of unyielding command, but I wasn't in the mood to play good little soldier. I turned toward him with a look of pure innocence pasted onto my face.

'Whatever could you mean, old friend?' I asked, and he rolled his eyes in response.

'You will kill no one in front of hundreds of people with smart-phones ready to record everything. You know the rules: you can persuade a donor or pay for your drink, but no one dies in my club. Take your anger elsewhere, or I'm calling Leszek.'

'I'm not angry,' I said, feeling my muscles tensing as my blood-lust tested the limits of my control, but Nadolny simply laughed.

'Of course you aren't. Still, it is time you left. If you do still feel murderously not angry when you're outside, I hear a group of foolish men are causing trouble down in the docklands.' Nadolny's smirk told me this wasn't just an idle comment. He wanted me to despatch those men so that he didn't get his own hands dirty.

Normally, I would have laughed in his face, but the timing for this request couldn't have been more perfect.

'I'll see what I can do, but you'd better be prepared to dispose of the bodies.'

Nadolny's nod was all I needed to remove the self-imposed leash I held on my instincts. Leszek would crush my balls in a vice for this, but for tonight, I couldn't find the energy to care.

'Happy hunting,' the club boss offered, but I was already pushing through the crowd toward the exit.

I released my hold on the shadows as I neared the dockland area owned by Nadolny, listening to the eerie silence for any sign of my soon-to-be victims. With heavy fog rolling in from the sea, the environment was perfect for the misdeeds of the wicked, splendidly fitting my mood. I'd never taken the lead in the enforcer side of the Syndicate business, leaving that to Tomasz and his werewolves. Any killing done in the past had been in a purely kill-or-be-killed situation, but tonight, I needed the freedom of unfettered violence. Maybe then I could process the storm of emotion that were my feelings for Nina.

My feet barely made a sound on the cool tarmac as I began my hunt. The last time I'd hunted humans was two years ago when Sara was taken by Chernobog, and Leszek gave my Seethe free rein to pursue those that hurt his soulmate. Today, I had no such permission, and that just added to the thrill.

A pained moan caught my attention, and within moments, I was kneeling next to a human, the man lying in a pool of his own blood. His face was a mangled mess of broken bone and flesh, but he was alive. The victim was wearing a security guard's uniform, the poor idiot too brave to have backed down from a more numerous enemy. Still, in order to help him, I turned him onto his side, rearranging his limbs into the recovery position, which seemed to help with his breathing. Unfortunately, I recognised the signs of impending death. I doubted he was innocent, working for Nadolny didn't go well for ordinary people, but in death, he felt like one. I was forced to watch as he breathed his last, cursing the bastards that did this.

Sounds of a struggle started further along the street, dragging my attention from the dying man, and I noticed a truck next to the open doors of an unlit warehouse. It looked like whoever was stupid enough to rob Nadolny came well-prepared, but they weren't prepared for me. A scream of pain followed the sharp snap of breaking bone. Someone was still fighting inside, praying for a hero. Instead, they would get me. A vengeful vampire.

'Just shut him up already. We have the passcode. We don't need him making noise and bringing more fucking witnesses.'

I rushed inside at the finality in the voice's tone, but for all my speed, I was confronted by the sight of a lifeless body crashing to the floor as the baseball bat used to crush his skull swung around his killer's laughing face.

The rage I'd bottled up erupted in an explosion of bone and feathers as my wings tore my shirt apart.

I don't remember moving, but as my claws tore through the killer's surprised face, the sour taste of chemically enhanced blood hit my tongue. The cocktail of drugs he took, likely to suppress any doubts or inhibitions, splashed across my mouth, and I licked my lips.

With disgust twisting my features, I tore my hapless victim's throat apart before turning to his terrified companions.

My enemies' initial shock quickly changed to fury, goading them into action, and they attacked, screaming and cursing, wielding whatever they had to hand.

I laughed in derision at the knives held by the first two. I almost felt sorry for the idiot with the crowbar, but he at least seemed in complete control as he barrelled into his compatriots, stopping them in their tracks. The little moue of disappointment I offered the men increased their anger, but I stepped back and concentrated, banishing my wings and straightening the tie on my ruined shirt.

'I must be going soft.' I held my hands up to prove I had transformed fully. 'I'll give you a chance. Well, it's not much of one. Even so, I want a little entertainment before I kill you.'

My provocative words didn't have the effect I intended. The three men stood there, frozen in fear. I had surprised myself when I'd stopped my attack, my conscience pricking me for slaying an unprepared opponent, but now, despite their lack of ability, they at least had a choice at what happened next.

When they still didn't move, my anger grew, and I shouted out in frustration.

'Fight, you cowards!'

My command broke through their daze, and they looked at each other and their weapons, communicating silently. A wordless bellow echoed through the warehouse as they charged, the knife-wielding fighters circling to the sides as the furious male with the crowbar advanced, his weapon held above his head.

The rapture of battle made my lips stretch wide, my smile making my attackers stumble, but it was too late; my fist was already hurtling forward, and I felt the resistance of the man's muscles tearing apart. I focused my attention on my opponent's face as the pain registered. Each moment passed in slow motion, his eyes dilating till the iris disappeared, his features twisting, contorting into a rictus of agony. Finally, as my hand thrust up into his chest and tore away his heart, blood burst from his mouth, covering my face with his life's essence.

The blood tasted of fear and cocaine, its velvet smoothness enriched by the intensity of his emotion. It was nothing like Nina's. Her blood, sweet with the lingering spice of her beautiful soul, tasted like home. She was my fate, my kismet, and I left her all alone because I could not contain my inner monster.

The one I drank from now was screaming in utter terror. This taste, this feeling, matched my desperation. In my darkest hour, I took his life to sustain mine. I snapped my head forward, plunging my teeth into his artery, drawing as much pungent liquid as possible.

I laughed, the sound tinged with madness as the sharp stabbing pain of a knife plunging into my kidney reminded me of the presence of my other attackers. The pain felt good, and for the first time in so long, thoughts of Nina weren't dominating my mind. I allowed myself to be impressed at the skill used for the strike, the blow a killing one if I were human. Unfortunately for this man, I wasn't human, and I proved it as I crushed his fingers to a pulp and ripped the knife from my body.

The poor bastard didn't have more than a moment to regret his choices, as with a twist, I broke his arm and buried the knife in his skull, not even looking as his body fell limp and dead to the floor, my attention already on the final opponent and his pathetic weapon.

I studied the man before me, the shaking knife, the wild, panic-stricken eyes and sweat leaking from every pore.

'Not so brave now, hmm, little mouse?' I couldn't resist licking the blood coating my lips, all the while looking into this pathetic bastard's eyes, feeling like the proverbial cat playing with his prey.

A large gulp preceded the loosening of my opponent's grip on his knife, but before the weapon hit the ground, I held my victim by the throat, his feet dangling helplessly in the air.

'You weren't thinking of leaving so soon? Things were just about to get interesting,' I said, flashing my fangs. The sour stench of fear intensified, and he tried to escape.

The darkness I tamed my entire existence rose to the surface. The scent of his terror was delicious. The hunger, unquenched for the last two years, exploded inside me as I pulled the man closer.

I licked my victim's throat, enjoying his flinching reaction and the speeding pulse, adrenaline pumping so hard I could almost taste it. I shouldn't play with my food, but I couldn't resist.

'There is a woman, you know. One drop of her blood would satisfy me in a way that all of yours never could, but I cannot touch her. Nina. She's the reason for your death. I want you to know her name, and I want you to take it with you to the underworld. Find the soul of the bastard who attacked her, and tell him his undead husk will be next because you will die, my delicious morsel, and I won't be calling you back.'

'Please... please, I have a family.' He begged, hands beating helplessly against my body, trying to push me away.

'You want mercy? What mercy did you show to those guards? What about their families? Did you stop to ask if I had a family when you attacked?' My voice held derision, but that couldn't hide the bitterness. 'If the world knew mercy, I would be holding my woman, kissing away her tears. There is no mercy, not for me, and certainly not for you.'

With a growl, I sank my fangs into the man's carotid. The artery pulsed faster under my mouth as I drank. It only took moments before his pulse became erratic. I would usually finish my feed at this point as anything more could hurt the human, but not today. This man deserved to die, and I was so very, very hungry.

I didn't inject the pleasure venom to ease him into the after-life. His fear satiated my hunger. Cheap alcohol and a cocktail of illicit drugs added to the vintage. The adrenaline in his blood boosted my strength, increasing the speed of my healing. I felt like a god reborn, enjoying the moment his pulse slowed down and struggles became weaker, the moment of death approach-ing. I felt the instant his spirit fled, leaving behind a lump of dead flesh in my hands.

As I lifted my mouth from my victim's neck, I couldn't help looking into his dead eyes. He was the first person I'd killed whilst feeding, potentially my first spawn.

If I left his body untouched, so close to the Gates of the Neter, the magic of this place would rise him at sundown tomorrow, confused and frightened, just as I was all those centuries ago.

The hunger... I shouldn't forget that urge, the insatiable thirst for blood that would drive a fledgling vampire into the sun, desperate for sustenance. However, if I were there when he awoke, I could guide him, and he would do anything I asked in unquestioning obedience. That's how the Seethe worked. No youngling could resist an order from their Maker, but I'd never wanted that, never wanted a slave.

I grabbed the corpse's hair in my other hand and twisted his neck, casually tearing him apart. I promised not to call him back from death, and I was the man of my word. I picked up my phone and called Nadolny's assistant.

'Tell your boss the warehouse is free of rats, but he needs a cleaning crew... and the funeral wagon for the guards. I arrived too late to save them.'

A twinge of guilt made me feel uncomfortable, and I rubbed my neck, but there was nothing I could do for them. Instead, I had avenged their deaths, enjoying myself a little too much in the process. I looked down at my clothes. They were covered in blood and gore, but I was calm, maybe slightly high, an unexpected bonus of my cleaning services. Since I'd been sired, I'd tried so hard to protect the part of me that was human, but tonight, it felt like that bridge had been burned, and I had to accept what I'd become.

I walked back to my car, putting a waxed sheet over the upholstery, not wanting to get congealing blood over the pristine interior.

I was satiated, my presence no longer putting Nina in danger, and it was time to go home, preferably before any of the Elder Races discovered what I'd done.

CHAPTER 11

I couldn't open my eyes; no, I didn't want to open them. If I could convince the world I was asleep, then I could pretend yesterday's events were a dream and not my life falling apart in my hands. I was no closer to finding Pawel, and I'd learned that some Uber-powerful vampire had snacked on my blood, then fucked my mind up with a wave of his hand. To make matters worse, I was in Adam's house, and after yesterday's metaphorical open heart surgery in the bathtub, there was little hope he still saw me in the same light.

Especially after he stormed off like a madman when I refused to discuss the past.

My mind kept trying to dissect what exactly happened. One moment, Adam was caring and patient, calming me down when

I needed it the most. The next, he was a raging ball of fury, and I didn't know what had triggered the transition. I just hoped that wasn't me because I didn't like being afraid of him. It felt... unnatural.

I dragged my feet off the bed. I needed to go to the bathroom before I went to see Adam and find out what had happened. Whatever it was, I had to find a way of fixing it.

If it meant putting on my big girl pants and answering his question? Well, that wouldn't be easy, but he deserved an explanation. I had to do it. For Adam, for myself, and for Pawel. Especially for my brother. There was nothing more important, and our feelings could wait until Pawel was safe.

The apartment was silent as I made my way across the warm floor, my footsteps failing to banish the eerie feeling of emptiness. I hugged the oversized t-shirt to my body, shivering despite the warmth of the blinding dawn sun. If Adam was asleep, there was a slight chance I could make myself look human before I pissed him off again.

My cavernous yawn reminded me of a particularly bad dream, which was my excuse for the squeak I made at seeing the bloody bathroom and crimson-stained clothing. I was so surprised that even as I recognised Adam's clothes from the night before, I failed to notice the man himself step from the shower in all his naked glory.

I blinked twice before reality reconnected, and I realised that much blood meant he must be injured again. As worry overcame me, I rushed forward, grabbing Adam by the shoulders as I searched his body for injuries, my confusion returning after finding nothing wrong.

'What the fuck? What happened? Did you get hurt? Did anyone else? Is it Pawel, Sara?'

I couldn't stop looking, my fingers prodding and poking with professional expertise while I had a mini breakdown.

At a hitch in Adam's breathing, I looked up, biting my lip as his strong fingers captured my hands and pressed them to his chest. My gaze fell into his eyes, with pupils so dilated they overtook the blue of his irises staring down at me, and my tongue slipped out to lick my suddenly dry lips.

'Good morning, Nina. If I'd known all it took to have you lay your hands on me was copious amounts of blood, I'd have opened a vein months ago.' Adam stepped closer, his chest squashing my arms between us. 'Of course, if you'd like to feel the effect you have on me....' his gaze dropped, and my own followed, widening at the sight it beheld.

'What the... can you stop thinking with your dick and tell me what happened? I was just worried you were injured. Just... Let me go, you big oaf.'

'Why would I do that? You started it, coming onto me, touching and prodding my body without invitation. Knowing how much you care for my well-being, well, I'm truly flattered, but is that the only reason? Touch me more, sweetheart, or should I make a new deal? One where I never let you go.' Adam said it so casually, even as his eyes smouldered with a passion that made me squirm.

My intuition told me something was very wrong with him. Not that Adam was ever a prude, but this unbridled lust was new and, combined with the carnage surrounding us, set my mind on high alert. I had a naked, unhinged vampire in the bathroom, and I didn't know how to deal with him. I would really like to touch him more, but now wasn't the time or the place, especially since I didn't know the reason for this sudden outburst of passion.

I stopped struggling and finally met his gaze head-on. My best option was to stop playing his game. I needed to regain control of the situation before I let him bend me over the sink and fuck me senseless.

I bit my lip as that image dominated my thoughts, surprising me with its intensity. I hadn't taken things that far when we were together, but Adam seemed hell-bent on fucking me, and I wasn't sure I wanted to object. I needed a distraction, preferably before I waved goodbye to my common sense.

'Focus, Adam. Whose blood is this if it isn't yours?' I asked, struggling not to look down, and when he didn't answer, I freed one hand and pinched his nose, pulling him down to my level.

'What happened last night?' I questioned, enunciating each word slowly until, finally, something more than pure lust appeared in his gaze. I focused on Adam's mouth as he began speaking, and the sight of his fangs sliding over his bottom lip caught my attention.

'Nothing happened. I'm a vampire. I hunted down my prey and fed from them. What did you expect it to look like? It's a messy business.' The strange note in Adam's tone made me frown, perplexed.

My friendly neighbourhood vampire had never mentioned hunting before, often referring to his feeding as charitable donations.

'The person you fed from, are they still alive?' I asked quietly, pretty sure I knew the answer.

Adam released me, and I backed away as his eyes were overtaken by a crimson hue that reminded me I stood before an apex predator.

'Shit,' I muttered, falling back further, but all for nothing. The next moment, Adam's arms embraced me, his hands gripping my buttocks as he lifted me onto the vanity unit. I yelped in surprise, fighting to free myself, but his throaty laugh told me he enjoyed my struggles. He released my rear to grab my hands, placing them back on his bare chest as he pushed between my legs.

Was he going to force himself on me like the other vampire had? My thoughts were racing, my heart beating so loud I could hear it drumming in my ears. Adam must have heard it, too, because his lips slowly moved, kissing down the column of my throat, his breath teasing it as he whispered.

'Yes, my prey is dead. I couldn't find the one who hurt you, so when my hunger grew too strong to control, I found someone else who deserved to die. My beautiful, cruel Nina, you broke me. I no longer desire to give my donors the pleasure of my venom. That will always be yours alone, but I can't touch you, not after what this bastard did to you, so I fed on their pain.' Adam's breath trailed over my skin as he inhaled my scent while his tongue traced the artery that pulsed rapidly to the drum of my racing heart.

'You are my weakness, my obsession. I want you so much I could rip that shirt away and fuck you, filling your body with bliss while I feed on you... but you don't want that, don't want me. Gods, your fear is like an obsidian dagger buried deep in my heart,' he murmured, shaking his head as if he woke up from a fevered dream.

'Can you please... Calm... the fuck... down. What can I do to help you? Adam, this isn't normal. Yesterday, you were so angry I thought you were going to break my neck when I refused to answer your questions, and today I find you like a horny dog ready to hump everything that moves. Please talk to me. How can I fix this?' I said, placing a hand on his forehead to check for a fever. 'Are you ill?'

I hadn't finished talking when he vanished. One moment, he stood there pressing his body to mine; the next, he was gone, only to reappear again a few moments later. I yelped, unsure of what had just happened. Still, he appeared much calmer, and his eyes had lost their glassy sheen.

'Yesterday, I was struggling, but how could you believe I'd hurt you? You are the only one who should never be afraid of me. No matter what you say or don't say or how deep your insults cut, I would never hurt you. I wish you could see past my nature and see the man who would lay the world at your feet, but you only see the monster, don't you? A bloodsucker, no different from the one who attacked you.' The self-loathing in his voice broke through the fearful thoughts burning through my mind as I realised he thought I'd detested him.

I pushed Adam away. He winced, tilting his head and avoiding my gaze, so I grabbed his chin, forcing him to look at me.

'You said I shouldn't be afraid of you. Well, I'm not. You left me here all alone, with no explanation, and the last thing I saw was an enraged vampire, but I didn't run away, did I? I didn't call Sara for help. I just waited. I waited for you without knowing what would happen when you returned. So stop this bullshit because I'm at my wit's end right now. If you don't tell me what happened and why you're acting as high as a kite, so help me, god, I will shove your naked arse under an ice-cold shower until you can think again.'

He snarled. He actually snarled at me, but I already knew I'd won the argument when the tension left his body.

'I haven't fed in a while, and the fight in the playground, together with the blood loss, left me starving. I could barely control myself. I had to go, Nina, or I would have hurt you. I crave you, and what a man could easily control, a starving beast couldn't. Yesterday, I was more of a beast than a man. Do you understand now? There were some raiders at Nadolny's warehouse,' he ground out, angrily pushing forward and placing his hands on either side of my body, caging me in. 'They murdered two security guards before I arrived. Five men. Stupid bastards with blood full of drugs and with simple brutish weapons. I killed them all, and I enjoyed every last moment,' he snarled, as if challenging me to condemn him.

My sigh of relief was loud, even to my ears. I don't know why, but Adam's revelation eased something in my chest.

'You are an idiot, Adam,' I said, noticing the question in his eyes. 'I'm sorry? Should I react differently? Did I not meet your expectations? Oh, forgive me, Master. So you wanted to paint yourself as a monster because you killed thugs who murdered two guards? Maybe you should find yourself some oversensitive damsel in distress because the only thing I care about right now is you and... feeding...? You should have asked. You fought for me. If you'd explained about the hunger, I would have accepted it.' I said, but he shook his head in denial.

'You didn't want that. Nina, you were afraid of me. I may be a bastard, but I would never demand that from you,' he insisted, and I wanted to punch him.

'And? I was scared because I didn't know what was going on. We are partners, for fuck's sake. I may not enjoy it, and I would certainly ask you to not do the pleasure thing, but I would do it for you. We are in this together, and since you're working for me, you should at least ask me. To give me a chance to be there for you. As for the killing, I know you would never take the life of someone who didn't deserve to die. Oh, and next time? Choose someone who's only drunk. You are an obnoxious arsehole when you're high.'

I kept pushing, watching as he relaxed a little more with each sentence. Whatever was in his head, Adam craved redemption and understanding. I lifted one hand to his throat, sliding my fingertips over his soft skin before lightly pressing as I studied his expression, and when Adam didn't react, I tightened my grip, pulling him closer.

This man, no, this vampire, had just killed five men and now stood there as my nails dug into his flesh without flinching. It shouldn't have aroused me, but it did, and I pressed even harder.

'If you knew what I've seen... what I'd done to survive in Kosovo. Those men were the real monsters. No, I don't condone your actions, but you didn't murder some poor innocent on the street, so stop acting like an idiot, and next time, give me a fucking choice.' I punctuated my speech by pushing him back, his response another wordless snarl as he reached for my arms.

'Oh no, none of that. I'm so angry at you right now I'd sooner kick your bollocks than let you touch me,' I said, batting his questing hands away. 'Also, unless you want a puddle on your pristine floor, you'll give me some privacy. If you're that desperate to please me, you can make those scrumptious pancakes from before. Maybe then I'll forgive you for all this mess.'

I dismissed Adam with a casual flick of the wrist and moved toward the toilet facilities, a little intrigued by all the buttons.

'When I'm finished, we can have a civilised conversation. You promised to find my brother and the vampire that bit me. If you feel such a strong need to kill, I will find you a better target than some random idiots.' I couldn't resist a look over my shoulder, glancing down at the impressive hard-on he was sporting, almost like our argument was foreplay for him. 'Oh, and don't forget to leash the beast. We wouldn't want it drooling during our discussion.'

His jaw dropped, then he took a deep breath, and I braced myself for the screaming threats and arguments, but in the end, he just shook his head.

'What are you doing to me, Nina?' he muttered, but left me alone.

As soon as the doors closed behind him, I fell to the floor. The ugly truth was that he killed someone because I'd disrupted his life so much that he'd lost control. The darkness he kept hidden away had emerged so unexpectedly, it left my head spinning. Still, even when drugged and suffering, my monster didn't turn on me.

I felt like I was betraying my profession by excusing his actions, and God knows why I felt so damn thrilled to have so much power over him, but I couldn't deny the darkness I held in my heart any more than I could deny my attraction to him.

My noble monster. Adam could unleash himself on the world, but all he did was kill the murderers.

I need to call Sara, I thought, picking myself off the floor. My feelings were a mess, and I needed to talk them through with my friend, but first, I had to talk to Adam and judging by the aroma, he'd taken the pancake business seriously.

I quickly showered, brushed my hair and walked to the kitchen table just as Adam dropped the fluffiest pancake I'd ever seen on a plate in front of my chair. He looked like a sinful god with black silk trousers and nothing else, and I quietly moaned, suspecting it was his 'home casual' style.

'I'm sorry for earlier and for yesterday. It is difficult to control the hunger when I'm in that state. I should have explained it, but I wasn't sure if I could restrain myself,' Adam said, avoiding my gaze but clearly in control of himself despite his pupils still flashing with hints of crimson.

The bastard knew precisely how good he looked dressed like this, and I had a feeling after our bathroom encounter, he was testing me now.

'I told you to dress,' I said, changing the subject, and he pointed to his trousers.

'I did, putting the *"drooling monster on a leash,"* just as you requested,' he said, and I rolled my eyes.

'Tell me about this hunger. What is it? Does it happen often? Should I do something when it happens again?'

'No, last night was the exception. I neglected my meals, and your call took me by surprise,' he said before the corner of his lip up-turned in a mischievous smile. 'The Hunger is like the deep-seated craving that pushes you to cook for a woman when all you want is to taste her lips.'

'Later...' I coughed when a piece of the pancake stuck in my throat at his words. It was definitely time to change the subject. 'I mean, we will *talk* about it later. I need you to tell me what you know about Pawel. And stop acting like an arsehole. You know how important this is to me,' I said, annoyed by his comparison and the way it sent heat sliding down my spine, but my Freudian slip didn't escape his attention.

'I can accept *later*.' He said, flashing me a sinful smile. 'Alright, let's talk about Pawel. Your brother got caught up with a loath-some group. They are, or I should say they were, grave robbers. They called themselves the Lost Ark,' he said.

I snorted with laughter, and Adam nodded, amusement evident in his tone as he continued. 'I know, right? They were not the smartest tools in the shed, but they were efficient. They've been operating in Southern Poland on the Ukraine and Belarus borders. Their modus operandi was simple. They'd find a burial ground of prominent noble families or those of the Elder Races that lay forgotten, and under the guise of the government's historical renovation, they'd dig up the graves and steal whatever they found, selling to unscrupulous antique collectors.'

'C'mon, that's disgusting, but grave robbing is hardly worthy of being gutted and hung up to die. If those graves are forgotten, then the only people involved are the dealers they sell to. That's hardly the sort of person to commit such atrocities,' I argued.

Adam smirked and shook his head. 'Even beneath the most polished veneer is the ugliest truth. Just because someone sips champagne from a delicate crystal flute doesn't mean they aren't capable of the worst humanity has to offer.'

I knew he was right, but that didn't make the situation better.

'Do you know who it was?' I asked, but he shook his head.

'Not yet, but I have a lead and one solid suspect.' He said, and I continued stuffing myself with pancakes. 'When your brother came to see you, did he leave anything behind or talk about needing to sell something?'

'A necklace. Pawel was trying to give me an old silver necklace. I didn't accept it.' I answered, and Adam stood up, gesturing for me to follow him. I was confused by the request but didn't want to spoil his cooperative mood. We walked through the living room towards a solid, steel-reinforced wooden door.

'Lorelai, open my office.' He said, and I had to bite my lip to avoid laughing as his command sounded suspiciously like *open sesame* from *Aladdin*.

I heard the clunk of the lock and the quiet whoosh of steel bolts sliding into the wall. The door opened, revealing a creature so strange I yelped and jumped on Adam, climbing him like a tree.

'Shit, I'm sorry, you startled me, appearing like that.' As an embarrassed aside, I turned to Adam, releasing my hold on his neck. 'I'm sorry for grabbing you again.'

I couldn't help frowning at Adam's laughing face or his refusal to allow me to escape my embarrassment, his arm holding me close.

'Nina, this is Lorelai. She is... she makes sure everything runs smoothly in the apartment.'

With that, my annoying captor nodded respectfully to the strange creature before us, who returned his nod with a bobbing curtsey. I might have worked in a hospital for the Elder Races for two years, but I'd never seen someone so unusual.

With the beak of a bird for a mouth and cute swept-back horns peeking out from a mass of curly moss-green hair, the female was still quite beautiful. Her traditional Polish peasant garb high-lighted her feminine curves and mostly hid the unusual bird's feet that poked out from beneath the hem of her skirt. I had never met someone of her kind in my time at work, and I wondered how such a magical creature could live outside of the Nether.

'Lorelai is bound to the electronic heart of my home and lives in her own sphere of reality.' Adam said, answering my unspoken question.

'Pleasure to meet you, Lorelai. I'm sorry for the trouble.' I said politely, and she nodded her head.

A soft female voice spoke from the discreet speakers behind me.

'My pleasure too, Mistress. I've been waiting for your arrival for so long. Master dreams of you so often and so intimately that I was surprised he didn't bring you home earlier. Was the room to your liking?' I whipped my head around, staring at the speakers. I could see the person in front of me, but her beak hadn't moved, and the phenomenon confused me for longer than I was proud of.

Adam came to my rescue, covering for my faux pas.

'Lorelai is a kikimora. She can manifest her body, but her spirit is trapped in the electronic unit that controls the house. She can also see your dreams and will offer her opinion on them whenever she wants to cause mischief. Before you ask, she is happy here. I offered to find a way to free her, but she refused.' He said before pulling me gently into the dark room. Lights were blinking everywhere, and several computer screens flashed with streams of data that boggled the mind, especially when you remembered Adam was hundreds of years old.

Unbidden, the remark, 'I guess you can teach an old dog new tricks,' slipped from my lips, and an electronic snort issued from a speaker on the desk.

Adam ignored the exchange as he led me to the nearest desk.

'I want you to describe the necklace in as much detail as possible,' he requested in a snippy tone before sitting on an oversized, comfortable computer chair.

'It was silver, old, with some engravings on both sides. I think it was a locket, or at least it looked like one. The pendant itself was quite hefty and round. The chain looked plain... that's all I remember.' I said. I couldn't recall more. Even closing my eyes didn't help.

Adam sat staring intently at his screens as his left hand moved a stylus over his desk whilst his right typed furiously. I was quietly impressed at his skills and about to comment when he gestured for me to join him.

When I stood behind him, peering at the computer screen, I saw a picture that bore a remarkable resemblance to the locket we'd discussed.

'Put the engraving around the edges, and that will be pretty much what it looked like, though, I think the chain was thicker? Oh, and there was this weird double arrow in the middle.' I said, leaning over and pointing at the middle of the locket.

Adam didn't look at the screen. Instead, he turned his head, his lips millimetres from my cheek when he inhaled deeply. I should have pulled away, but I froze, still talking about engravings, pretending his warm breath didn't give me goosebumps. The tension in the air was palpable, and I waited for the bubble to burst or for

Adam to pull me onto his lap, trying to manhandle me like he did in the bathroom. This time, I was more than ready to submit and give him whatever he demanded. It looked like I had a soft spot for bad boys, especially when they were good to me.

'I have a meeting with a client looking for a stolen heirloom. He is a wealthy and powerful man, so if this locket is what he is looking for, we will know who's trying to kill your brother.' He whispered as we both pretended there was no tension between us.

'And if not?' I asked, stunned when he pulled away from me. I saw the hunger and lust in his eyes, but there was something more. A tenderness he was trying to hide, and darkness, an all-consuming darkness that threatened to turn him into the monster he believed himself to be.

'If not, I will search deeper. I've barely started, Nina, but I won't fail this job...'

'I know you won't,' I cut him off. I wished I could prove to him I knew he was doing his best, but I felt words were not enough. Adam wasn't a fool. I knew he expected trouble, yet he helped me, and I wanted to let him know I appreciated it. All of it, his help, the way he looked after me, his protection, and if all he wished for was a kiss, I was more than ready to grant it.

I drew a shallow breath and bent over, placing my lips on his. I kissed him gently, unsure if I was doing the right thing. Love was too complicated, but why should I deny us a few moments of happiness? There might not be forever, but I was happy with *"for now"* because whatever started when I saw him at the party felt real.

Or as real as five dead bodies and a drugged vampire could be.

As soon as our lips connected, Adam gasped, hands grasping the chair handles as if he was afraid that once he touched me, he wouldn't be able to stop.

'Open your mouth,' I whispered, nipping his bottom lip, and he instantly complied.

I slid my tongue into Adam's mouth, teasing the edges of his fangs with the tip. It was reckless, stupid even, but it felt so good, so liberating, to finally touch him. He'd shown me he wanted me, and now it was my turn to take the next step. I pushed the fear away, curious how far I could go with him while still staying safe and unhurt.

'Fuuuck…' As soon as a droplet of my blood formed on the tip of my tongue, Adam groaned, sucking at it desperately. His hands reached for me, but I was already pulling away, and after a moment of hesitation, he sat back, breath heaving in and out of his chest.

I moved away, my own breath ragged and urgent, but I couldn't tear my eyes from the pink tinge of Adam's fangs. When his features twisted into a grimace, I looked up into the crimson eyes of a vampire fighting to hold himself back from taking everything I'd just offered on a silver platter.

Gods, that was so stupid of me. How could I goad him like that and expect him to take it? I scolded myself, moving away, my hands in front of me in a defensive position.

Adam moved. I don't know how, but he erupted from the shadows right in front of me and captured my hands, preventing my escape.

'Are you playing me, Nina? You know I want you, and your blood... is this another of your little tests?' The groan that escaped his clenched lips was filled with pain and confusion. Not the reaction I'd been aiming for with my reckless behaviour.

'No, you said you wanted a kiss, and I wanted to...' I said, swallowing hard, unable to avert my eyes from the swirling crimson pupils.

'A few weeks ago, you didn't think it was possible to be near me, but now you are kissing me? Please, Nina, no lies, just tell me why?'

Adam's desperate plea tore at my heart, his grip tightening when I tried to pull free until, reluctantly, he released one of my hands. I raised it to his cheek, tentatively stroking it like I would a dangerous beast on the verge of tearing me asunder.

'Because I wanted to. You made me want you. I like you and... I don't want to fight you. Please understand, I don't want a relationship. I may never want one, but each time I touch you, it feels so right. I want to try something with you... to see what is possible. This is embarrassing enough as it is, but I want you. Can we... I don't know, can we maybe try to have a good time? We've been forced together again, but we don't have to make the same mistakes. We could be friends and just enjoy things as they are, no expectations, no strings attached, and I could help you with this hunger if it gets too much.'

'So you want me to fuck you, feed on you but not love you?' He asked. His face turned so grim that I swallowed hard.

'If you put it that way, maybe it is not the best idea. I just thought..., but no, you're right, it was stupid. I'm sorry.' I answered, unable to keep the embarrassment out of my voice.

'Oh no, Nina. I accept. After all, I'm a man-whore, remember? How could I waste such an opportunity? Take what you want, my Obsidian. I'm all yours, and as you wish, no strings attached.'

His choice of words made me realise how utterly screwed I was, and this time, I couldn't even blame Adam.

It felt like I'd made one mistake after another, and I needed to talk to my friend, because this clusterfuck with Adam messed with my head so badly I didn't recognise myself.

Chapter 12

Adam remained silent after my reckless proposal, and I grasped hold of the reprieve with both hands, desperate to take a moment to think while avoiding looking at his sinfully beautiful body.

He noticed my gaze sliding over his bare torso. A mischievous smile ghosted over his lips, and before I knew it, he had tensed his muscles.

'Show off,' I muttered, feeling the warmth of a blush crawling over my cheeks, and his eyes crinkled in amusement.

Since I'd seen him in the parking lot when he picked up Sara, our worlds gravitated toward each other, and despite his attitude occasionally irritating me, I liked the man I saw under the vampire's cold veneer. The man with an inner darkness who, like myself, struggled with his demons, but no matter what I did or how I acted, he had never purposely hurt me.

I'd teased him to the brink of madness, testing his self-control. I'd let him taste my blood, but he didn't cross the line. Only looked at me with those bright blue eyes that burned as if he wanted to devour me, making me want to surrender completely.

Fuck, I'm falling for him. The thought didn't surprise me, well, not exactly, but it certainly reinforced my need to talk to Sara.

'Could you please take me to the island today? I want to see Sara,' I asked, flinching when his mobile phone suddenly rang.

Adam looked at the screen and sighed. I saw his lips tighten for a moment when he answered the call, listening in silence.

'Yes, I'll be there. Is Sara home today? Nina would like to see her,' he asked, and I heard an angry voice snap a few words from the tiny speaker.

'Yes, I understand. No, you won't need to send the wolves. I'll bring Nina and come straight over,' he said, ending the call. The quiet hum of computer fans filled the temporary silence. Adam looked so tense. Whatever was said during this bizarre exchange had left a foul taste in my companion's mouth.

'It looks like your wishes and those of the Forest Lord are aligned. We need to go to the island. Please be ready in twenty minutes. In the meantime, I need to code a facial recognition search before I finish here.'

'What happened? Are you in trouble?' I asked.

I hope no one found the bodies. I thought, instantly wincing, that my first thought was of protecting Adam and not those who'd died.

'Yes, I'm in trouble. My actions last night weren't sanctioned, and I didn't report it to Leszek straight away, but whatever the Leshy wants to do to me, it won't stop my search,' he insisted, pointing to his workstation where the shots from a multitude of cameras started flickering. 'I will find Pawel if only for the pleasure of watching you rip someone else a new arsehole,' he said, waving me out of the computer room.

A few minutes later, we were on the road, and I couldn't stop thinking about what Adam had said.

'Is this about the men you killed? What will Leszek do?'

'Yes, and I don't know. I don't think he cares too much about them. Leszek is more concerned about the discovery of the Elder Races. That's why we're not supposed to kill whilst feeding, and the werewolves aren't allowed to kill human prey. Still, you don't need to worry your pretty little head about it. It's all on me,' he said, his dismissive, patronising tone after our little moment in his office irking me to no end.

'Really? What kind of bullshit was that? You know what? Humour me, slap this dick a little harder on my pretty little head, O' Great Alpha Male, and enlighten this inferior human on what will happen because, for some weird reason, I actually care about... what happens.' I said, wincing at my clumsy attempt to hide my concern, which, at the sound of snorting laughter, had been very amusing to the arsehole vampire.

'Oh, forgive me, Mistress, I forgot. I am but your lowly servant, ever willing to follow your commands. I shall endeavour to ensure my body is intact and able to perform in whichever way you desire.'

'You know, if Leszek doesn't kill you, I will,' I said with a huff before the spark of mischief inside me made me add. 'As for your performance, I haven't seen much of it yet. I approve of the equipment, but maybe I should sample more before I decide to buy the complete package. After all, what if it malfunctions?'

The reaction to my jibe had me screaming as Adam stopped watching the road, and we ploughed into a deep puddle, the car swerving from side to side.

Adam cursed up a blue storm, getting us back under control. In the end, both the tension and near-death experience were too much, and I burst out laughing like a maniac.

'Are you trying to kill us both?' I asked, gasping for breath, tears streaming down my face, but the laughter didn't want to die down.

'Well, one of us maybe, vampire here, remember? Of course, that might not be such a bad idea, especially if I drained you first. Then I could revive you and turn you into a good little vampiric doll. You'd look exquisite in some gothic Lolita dress, and I could show you how well my *equipment* works.' Adam's eyes shone with unholy joy at the kinky little scene he'd described, his grin widening at my punch to his shoulder.

'No fucking way that'll happen, you cut-price Lazurus. No one can force me to wear such a monstrosity.' I said, and he made this clucky, disapproving noise with his tongue that made me roll my eyes.

'Cut-price? Do you think Lazarus could afford the latest Armani suit? The cheek. I should mention that fledgling vampires are unable to disobey the will of their Sire. They crave to please the one who gave them a second life. You would have to do exactly what I say, and I would use your body in so many exciting ways...' Adam paused, looking at me with those hooded, dark blue eyes in a way that made heat flush across my cheeks. The desire in his eyes was searing, and I instinctively tilted my head, presenting him with the long expanse of my neck.

Adam's mouth parted, and in my peripheral vision, I saw the tip of his tongue trailing over the vicious fangs that had lengthened with his need for my blood, and my breath hitched. The burning intensity of his gaze dimmed, turning into pure delight when he finished his thoughts.

'Yes, using you in so many exciting ways... washing my underwear, cleaning the bathroom... Seeing you on your knees scrubbing the floor. That would be better than drinking my fill of blood. Princess, I so want to turn you right now.'

'You already have one woman chained and collared to your needs, you idiot,' I said, laughing even harder, partially with relief, because we both know only his restraint allowed us to joke about the situation.

It was the most carefree experience I'd had in days, and I found myself enjoying Adam's company without worrying about threats and uncertainty. I had never laughed like this with my ex. It was either fiery passion or cold distance, but never carefree laughter that felt much more intimate than any erotic encounter I'd previously shared.

'You are impossible,' I said, looking at the man who never failed to surprise me. Adam slowly nodded, a playful smile ghosting on his lips, and I wanted to kiss him. So fucking much.

'I strive to live up to your expectations,' he answered, parking the car before hesitantly reaching for my hand and lifting it to his lips, kissing my knuckles. 'Thank you, Nina. Thank you for bringing light to my darkness,' he murmured, and I tensed in the chair. Adam must have noticed because he released my hand and pointed toward the door.

'Go, have a chat with Sara. There's no need to worry about me.'

We entered the house together before we parted ways. I headed toward Sara's study while Adam went to Leszek's office. Before he even closed the door, I heard the Lord of the Forest's booming voice.

'Adam, what the fuck were you thinking?'

'Come here, Nina. The boys will need to beat their chests for a while yet. Hopefully, they won't break anything too precious this time.' Sara sounded strangely relaxed when there was such a tense atmosphere emanating from Leszek's office, but after one last look over my shoulder at the firmly shut door, I shrugged and joined my friend in her study.

The sofa Sara waved me toward was arranged into a cosy nest that I knew she loved almost as much as the scarred cat curled up on the cushions. The area around the plush seat was a disorganised mess of half-opened books, most of which seemed to be written in ancient runes, with a few penned in Sara's neat handwriting.

'Studying much?' I asked when Sara cleared the space next to her, and my friend smiled.

'Always. You know I love to learn new things, and I feel I have to catch up for my misspent youth. There are so many things I have to learn after wasting so many years not knowing who I was and what was possible with my gift,' she said before taking my hand. 'What happened? Nadolny called this morning, and it was bad, Nina. Adam left behind a scene of absolute carnage in his wake, not to mention the drained body. Leszek is furious because he didn't even bother erasing the camera footage. Adam can be violent, but he was never careless, so we are worried, especially Leszek. Whatever those two might pretend, they are as close as we are,' Sara bit her lip, and I saw her struggle with her next words. 'I shouldn't ask, but... the two of you... I know it's complicated,

I get it, but did something happen? Were his actions triggered by anything unusual?'

I knew she was trying to be gentle and not upset me with her questions, so I smiled to reassure her before reaching for her hand.

'Yes, he mentioned struggling with the hunger and that he was afraid he would hurt me. That's part of the reason I'm here. I need to talk to you because I think I'm going crazy,' I said, and Sara instantly went on full alert.

'What happened? Did he hurt you? He didn't bite you, did he? I will fry that motherfucker's arse!'

'No, he didn't, but... I think I wouldn't mind if maybe he did? Sara, it is so messed up. He's changed so much, and I like it. I don't know if I should, or maybe it's just stress, but I like him, and he makes me feel all hot and bothered, which ends up with me saying crazy things. That's why I'm losing my mind,' I answered, frantically trying to gather my courage.

'You know I wanted nothing to do with men after my husband. I just... it is so hard to trust, and without it, I didn't see the point. I was happy with a vibrator and the occasional hook-up when needed, and that was it.' I took a deep breath as the next part was even more difficult. Without even looking at Sara, I blurted out the next part as fast as possible.

'Adam wants something I don't think I can give him, but it doesn't stop me from wanting it. Tell me why, when I met the perfect man, did he have to be an immortal vampire? I always wanted a man I could grow old with, but this one? Adam doesn't even have a single wrinkle, and I don't know what I want any more.'

'He wants forever with you, doesn't he?' My friend was, as always, blunt and to the point. When I nodded, unable to find the words, she asked. 'And you don't know what this forever means for you. What do you know of the vampire Seethe structure?'

'Not much. I know that there is an Alpha Baddie and his minions, and as Adam mentioned to me earlier, the minions would do anything to please their maker,' I replied, and Sara chuckled.

'It's more complicated than that. The Seethe, as they call it, is built like a hive, with the monarch, soldiers, and workers. Most of them are created by one sire or swear allegiance to him or her. They are a family with such strong ties that, as the vampire matures, they inherit the supernatural traits of their maker.' She said, and again, I nodded, absorbing the information.

'Adam didn't have a proper sire. He was abandoned, and the only semblance of family he had was Leszek. Adam has built a small Seethe over the years, but none of the vampires there are his spawn because Adam never killed while he was feeding. Until last night.' She sighed, and I felt more deflated than ever. Guilt tore at me so hard that I felt tears building in my eyes.

'He didn't tell me the situation was that desperate. He was great one moment, and then he wasn't. He stormed off, explaining nothing. I would have done it. I shouldn't have told him I wouldn't give him my blood, but after you unlocked the memories of my assault, it's not something I wanted to do. Still, I would have dealt with it because it's Adam, and it was my fault he ended like this in the first place.' I closed my eyes, rubbing my temples with the knuckles to give myself a moment to gather my thoughts.

'He scares me, not as a vampire, but as a man. When I'm with him, I start believing there's a future for us. Then I remember what happened the last time I gave all my heart and trust to someone. He turned out to be an unfeeling bastard who thought visiting a brothel wasn't cheating but a form of executive stress relief,' I said, shaking my head before I bit my lips. 'And, of course, there is the issue of time. I'm sure my immortal vampire would take great pleasure in fucking and feeding from a dried-up prune of a grandma.'

Sara moved closer, embracing me and stroking my back. We held each other for a moment before she pulled away.

'Would it help if I told you his feelings for you are genuine? You are not the only one who keeps their guard up. Adam never let himself care for anyone, except maybe Leszek. That's why we get along *so well*, but he cares for you. I can see it even without my Seer senses.' She said, rolling her eyes before she sighed. 'If you really can't deal with all this, I can ask Leszek to move Adam out of Tricity, or I can help you relocate somewhere else, maybe in the East?'

'Why such extreme measures?'

'Because I believe he loves you, and he won't give up. Adam never pursued a woman, even if he fed on them or used them to warm his bed, but this changed since he met you. He hasn't touched another female since you kicked him out, not even to feed. He's been living off bagged blood. Now, with this incident? This behaviour will only escalate if you don't come to some sort of agreement,' she said, playing with a loose thread of her jumper. 'Leszek asked me to see if you'd reconsider, but I won't. You are my priority, Nina. I won't let Adam's unrequited feelings destroy you.'

'They aren't unrequited,' I heard myself mumbling.

Sara raised her head, looking at me as if seeing me for the first time.

'Are you sure? Don't let anyone guilt trip you into this. Not Adam, not the situation with Pawel, and definitely not me.' She said, and I felt like laughing.

'Just because my emotions are a mess doesn't mean I can be manipulated, and I know that sexy-arsed vampire is just as clueless about my feelings as I am, but he's good to me. Ok, maybe not good. He is caring and considerate, and he makes me laugh. Even when we drove here, we bantered like there was no tomorrow, and I loved it, Sara. I fucking loved it. Each time I have a wobble, he steps away, respecting that just because I didn't say no, it doesn't mean I said yes.' The more I talked, the more I realised I wanted to give Adam a chance, a real chance and that maybe my foolish kiss was a good place to start.

'I know you understand me. How lonely it is to be constantly on guard. When Adam stumbled into my life during your troubles, it was too much, and he was so cocky and annoying and so convinced that with a few fancy gestures, I would fall at his feet in awe of his awesomeness. So, I started setting challenges and obstacles for him to overcome. I needed him to prove he wouldn't hurt me and that I could trust his promises. I wish I knew how to stop it because he started calling me his Obsidian Princess. It serves me right for all those trials and tests I subjected him to,' I said, thinking about earlier when I fed him a drop of my blood.

'Obsidian Princess?' my friend asked, and I saw amusement twinkling in her eyes.

'Yeah, weird, but what can you expect from an ancient vampire?'

'An obsidian blade can kill a vampire even better than an aspen wood stake, and a wound caused by obsidian will never heal on its own. I never suspected Adam had such a dark sense of humour,' she said, and I rolled my eyes.

'He called me his death? What a jerk.' As we burst out laughing, Sara took my hand.

'What are you going to do?' She asked.

'Be honest and see where it takes me, but first, I need to find Pawel, then deal with the bastard that bit me. Adam is my best bet unless Leszek can intervene,' I said, looking hopefully at Sara, but she shook her head.

'He can't. When he regained his power, the wonderful council of Gedania, our oh-so-wise rulers from the Nether, decided he couldn't use his power to solve a mundane crisis, but he released Adam from any duties and ordered him to help you,' she said.

'Did he? Well, that means he will be home a lot right now, right when I agreed to live with him for the time being. I don't know, maybe it could be a good test run for us,' I suggested, hoping for Sara's opinion.

'Try before you buy?' Sara chuckled, and I nodded solemnly.

'Oh yeah, and he'll get a helluva run for his money before I forgive him for this Obsidian Princess bollocks,' I said, noticing wariness on Sara's face and waving it off. 'I promise I won't throw a tantrum or run away like some skittish doctor did. I will let you know if I decide to leave so you can restrain the unruly vampire.' I said, feeling much lighter now that my mind was set on the task.

CHAPTER 13

Leszek went on the offensive before I'd even closed the door to his office. I could see how angry he was, but I couldn't bring myself to regret what happened.

'We both know the scum deserved to die. They murdered those guards for the thrill, not for any valid reason. Nadolny tells his men to back off if things get nasty, then hit the panic button and let the video surveillance cover the rest. Fuck, everyone knows this, that's why no one touches his businesses. That and his policy on revenge, so I didn't overstep. Besides, I know you, if you saw what they did, you'd have ripped them limb from limb.' I finished my argument with a truth neither of us could deny, but I felt the sweat sliding down my spine until Leszek's angrily glowing eyes faded back to their usual verdant green.

'That's not the point, and you know it. You know the rules. No draining a victim to death. Damn it, that rule was your idea, a way to help keep the vampires hidden. How do you expect to enforce a rule you broke yourself? What got into you, Adam?'

'We both know it is not a what but who, and spare me your pitiful compassion. I miscalculated my feeding, and blood loss from the fight caused me to lose control of the hunger. I should have shifted to the void to heal the wound, but I didn't want to leave Nina alone, so don't start preaching. You were just the same over Sara, and we're still dealing with the aftermath of that mess. Should I remind you of Grabowa Mountain, when you were happy to let my Seethe bleed humans dry because your precious Firefly was hurt?' I lashed out, angry because Leszek should understand. He'd been there, falling for a woman who resisted his every attempt, yet here he was, chastising me.

'It doesn't mean you have to repeat my mistakes,' he grumbled, calming down and pointing to the chair. 'Sit down and tell me how I can help. If I can't stop you, I may as well help you survive this madness. I can't let my friend and security chief run around draining humans because he doesn't want to leave his precious woman alone.' I sat down, and he poured us both a good measure of mead before sitting opposite me.

I appreciated the gesture, but there was nothing he could do.

'There's no need to worry. I think I found the way to change Nina's heart,' I said with a smile, and he raised the tumbler to his lips, gesturing for me to continue.

'Tell me your miracle solution and where you hid your will and all the passwords,' he said, and I bent forward, placing my tumbler on the table.

'I submit to her,' I said, enjoying the moment Leszek choked on his alcohol, his face reddening as he gasped for breath.

'You what? You... I mean, Adam, you can't follow my fucking orders, even when you agree with them. What makes you think you can submit to Nina?' The sheer disbelief in his voice was worth the teasing.

'Because each time I let go, she steps closer. Each time I react differently to her expectations, Nina tries to rip a reaction out of me. Today, she purposefully nicked her tongue on my fang and let me taste her blood.'

Leszek leaned forward on the edge of his seat. 'And what did you do?' He asked while I sat there, grinning like the Cheshire Cat.

'Sucked the droplet down, panting like a dog eyeing a bone without touching her. I was a cursed god of patience, but it was worth the effort. The next thing I knew, she proposed a "no strings," fuck and feed. As long as no feelings are involved, she said she would welcome it.'

Leszek looked so sceptical it was almost comical, but I was figuring out why Nina reacted the way she did, and talking it out with a friend who understood actually helped me decide what to do. At least now he knew my motivation for any future decisions.

'When I met her, I thought Nina wanted a human, but my woman craves a monster that will never turn on her. Yesterday was a mistake. I pushed myself to the breaking point, but I don't regret it because today... she thought I was injured, and she freaked out so much it gave me hope,' I said, playing with the glass, recalling the moment I saw her fear vanish and the mask slip, revealing the Nina who cared for me, frantically searching my body for any signs of damage. Even through her worry and my drugged-induced haze-I could smell her arousal, and I almost reacted to it.

'I know what she's been through, I understand. Even if it kills me, if she wants to take it slow, we will. If she needs control, I will give it to her. The more she feels safe, the more she opens up to me, and the more she enjoys the thrill of being with a vampire. So, I can be the monster she tames. For her, I can be whatever she needs. I will bow to Nina's will until she feels so empowered that she realises I can be so much more than the fuck buddy she thinks she wants.'

Leszek's gaze softened when he poured another measure of alcohol and pushed the tumbler in my direction.

'That's the most grown-up thing I've heard from you in years. I will drink to your success and to your luck because you will need it. Just... in your crusade for Nina's love, try to remember she is a heart-sister to Sara, and if you upset my wife, one drained burglar will be the least of your worries,' he said, and I smirked.

There was no sense in arguing with Leszek when it came to his wife. He'd overseen the human realm and the Gates to the Nether longer than anyone who'd ever lived and never shirked his duties, but he would drop it all in a second for his Firefly. I hadn't understood it before, but I did now. For Nina, I would drown this world in endless night if I lost her.

I would abide by Nina's new rules for now, joining her in the pleasure she craved, and when I found and protected her brother, she would see just how much I could be trusted. In the meantime, I would give my Obsidian an insight into the life of a monster who loved only her and would never betray his heart.

'Adam, you're doing it again.' Leszek's voice brought me back to reality, and I realised my body had slipped into the shadows, unconsciously seeking Nina.

'Sorry, I was a little distracted. Do you have the data I asked for, and did you contact the client who wanted to hire me to find his heirloom?'

'Yes, he wants to meet in person on Friday. He asked for the appointment to be at the Anchor, but I don't want Nadolny involved and certainly don't want to have two Vampire Masters in a club full of sweaty humans. You can have my downtown office, or I will have the eastern warehouse cleared for your use.' Leszek said, and I frowned. Friday was almost a week away, and the delay seemed excessive for someone who was initially in such a rush to recover his property.

'If he wants to wait, fine. I have other things to do. I found digital traces of Nina's brother, but I'll need a couple of wolves to track him physically. There's no way Tomasz will help after my last prank at his expense. However, a word from you will....' I left the sentence unfinished, hoping Leszek would help without making it a formal request.

With that, I constructed a plan of action. I needed to do a more thorough background check on Pawel. Rather than concentrating on his whereabouts, I would need to look into his phone records and full financial history, including all his associates and former employment. I couldn't stop the twitch in my neck when I considered my newest client and the coincidence of his arrival and business. My gut feeling told me the man looking for the heirloom and Master Vampire who freely hunted on my Seethe's territory were one and the same person.

'You two are worse than children, what did you... No, forget I asked. Why do you need the wolves when your Seethe has more than enough manpower to chase down one human?'

'Because the digital trace puts him in, or very close to, the Kashubian Forest. I might punk their Alpha for a little stress relief, but I respect the pack's hunting ground. Pawel went off-grid, so rather than someone getting hurt over a misunderstanding, I thought it better to speak to you.'

I had a vague idea where Pawel might be, but after slipping Tomasz a potion that turned his fur pink, I knew he wouldn't cooperate.

'I'll see what I can do. Does Nina know you're so close to finding him?'

'She knows I'm looking for him but not that I started before we had an agreement and how close I am to getting him. I didn't want to give her false hope. There's no need to tell her until I'm sure it's him and that the threat to his life is dealt with. Knowing Nina, she'd insist on joining the search and the fight. She'd try to be in charge of everything, endangering not just her idiot brother but also herself. I know keeping her in the dark will most likely bite me in the arse, but I cannot allow her to be hurt,' I said, and Leszek nodded.

'Fine, I'll talk to Tomasz, and I won't say a word to Sara... but if I've learned anything about those two women, I can tell you she will make you regret keeping it a secret, and with Sara's talent, she'll know sooner rather than later.'

'I know, but I can deal with that when it happens. Nina has been attacked already. I can't believe that motherfucker bit her in a public place, but that only shows he is not above using dirty tricks. I don't want her to be used as bait or get hurt because she wants to help her brother.'

The laughter from outside was so loud that it interrupted our conversation. Leszek stopped looking at the door of his office and involuntarily smiled.

'I could die happy hearing her laughing like that. I have not once regretted sharing my spirit with Sara,' he said, and I nodded, standing up.

'Let's join them before they concoct some devious plans to make our lives more difficult.'

We found Sara and Nina standing next to the coffee machine. I watched in amazement as Sara furiously whipped cream with the speed of Stribog's tempest while Nina stood next to the cup, with a syringe in her hand, measuring out a transparent liquid with scientific precision. The bottle next to her had no labels, yet my woman held it like it contained liquid gold.

'Please tell me you didn't steal Michal's moonshine?' Leszek's heavy sigh from beside me held the weight of the world, but when Sara turned to him with a mischievous grin, his mouth widened as he returned the smile.

'With his permission. He understands we need a calming remedy after hearing your roaring. We were beginning to wonder if we would have to scrub Adam off the wall before he had a chance to show us how to slap a dick on a woman's head.'

Leszek looked at his wife, confused at Sara's reference to my argument with Nina.

This woman will be a death of me. They both will, I thought, when he next glanced at me, and it was clear he required an explanation. Ignoring his curiosity, I turned to Nina. At least I now knew why she was being so precise. Michal made a mean plum moonshine. The liquid was transparent like water, almost tasteless, with only a hint of plum blossom scent, and it kicked like a horse. The shifter's special, tailored to their metabolism, was made from ninety-five percent pure alcohol, and it could poison an average human if taken in large amounts. And our women were mixing it in their drinks.

'What are you making?' I asked, and Nina turned to look at me with a mischievous glint in her dark eyes.

'Homemade Irish Coffee, it will be so yummy.'

Her lips parted, and I saw Nina's tongue darting along the upper lip, and all I could think of was how perfect it would taste with a droplet of two of her blood.

'I hope you're willing to share with a thirsty vampire,' I suggested, surprising myself with the low growling purr in my voice. The memory of her taste in my mouth left me thirsting for more of her delicious nectar.

Nina tilted her head before slowly sucking her lower lip. There was a dare in her gaze, and I had to slip behind the counter to conceal my bulging erection. If it weren't for the fact that Leszek and Sara were right there, I would take advantage of her fucking and feeding contract that very second, no questions asked, and perform the task as if my life depended upon it.

I cleared my throat. 'We will need to go home soon. I have several leads on your brother's whereabouts to chase down,' I said, but Sara waved me off.

'You go, I'm keeping your Obsidian Princess here for the night. We need to catch up, and there's nothing better than a girlie sleepover from time to time,' she said, and I saw Leszek's eyes flash gold. Sara must have noticed it, too, because she waved him off, laughing.

'Oh, please, you're a grown man. You can sleep alone once in a millennium,' she scoffed, and I had to school my face to not burst out laughing. Being amused at Leszek's expense was a hazardous state to be in as an annoyed Leszek turned in my direction, cursing through clenched teeth.

'This is your fault, vampire. You owe me big time,' he said.

Sara walked up behind him, slipping her arms around his body and stroking his chest. Instantly, his anger subsided, replaced by affection as he covered her hands with his own, showing a tenderness that was still surprising from such a dangerous being.

'I need this, Wolfie. If I could ask a favour, would you mind bringing the patchwork quilt from the attic? You know, the colourful fluffy one Nina likes so much,' she asked, and I realised how monochrome my apartment was, nothing like the bright explosion of colour in Nina's home.

Leszek turned his head, kissing Sara's cheek, so I took that as my cue to leave, standing up and heading for the door.

'I'll be on my way then. Please let me know when I can come and pick up Nina,' I said, hearing the lady in question grumbling in the background as she drank her fully loaded coffee.

'I'm not some package to pick up and drop off as you wish,' she grumbled, but I heard the amusement in her voice, so, taking a chance, I approached her.

With slow, deliberate movements, I reached over, cupping Nina's cheek, and leaned down till my lips hovered millimetres above hers. She exhaled slowly, and a shy smile ghosted her lips. I counted the seconds, and on the count of five, hearing no protest or denial, I closed the distance and kissed her with tender care. Nina tasted divine, and I wanted to prolong the moment forever, but I was walking on thin ice and feared to break this delicate truce between us. I stepped back and gave her a cheeky smile while bowing slightly with a medieval courtier's gallantry.

'You are no package, my lady. You are a treasure, and I intend to cherish you till you shine for all to see. Call me when you are ready, my princess.'

'Aww, such grand words from my knight in shining armour,' she teased, shaking her head with a soft chuckle. 'You are impossible, cute, but absolutely impossible.' However, her lips parted, inviting me back into her embrace, but I was already turning toward Leszek.

'I will be working throughout the night, so call me if you need anything,' I said, wishing I could wipe the smug look from my boss's face. He knew exactly what I was doing and took great pleasure in observing my efforts.

'Of course,' he replied, but before I left, I saw Nina pouring an unhealthy amount of Michal's moonshine into her cup.

'I need more of this, so much more, if I'm going to stay sane,' she muttered.

The walk to the car was filled with visions of my kiss with Nina, ones I never wanted to forget, the taste of her lips still lingering on my tongue. By the time I was sitting at the wheel, my determination to prove myself to her had me dialling the clinic's security team, resolving to do whatever was needed to find Pawel and keep him safe.

'Adam Lisowczyk here. Verification code three-zero-alpha-kilo-eight. Send all the footage from the last week to my address via the encrypted VPN,' I commanded as soon as they answered my phone, disconnecting as soon as I heard confirmation.

My next stops were the Syndicate warehouse and Nina's apartment. I needed to secure her home, and while I knew there was no way to stop a determined thief, especially one that walked in the shadows as I did, I could make damn sure they didn't escape undetected.

The warehouse manager didn't question me, only raising his eyebrows when I asked for enough equipment to safeguard the national reserve. I picked up several large motion-sensing military-grade cameras, twice as many covert cameras with infrared capability. I added enough arcane detection devices as backup, including those capable of identifying the passive magical fields of the Elder Races.

After wiring up the outside of Nina's apartment, I hesitated. I knew I should ask permission before going inside, but with Nina now living with me, I didn't think it would infringe too much on her privacy. Just to be sure, though, I sent her a brief text.

I need to enter your home to install some sensors.

After a few minutes, I received a reply.

Sure thing, Sparkles, just don't steal my knickers.

I snorted at the exchange and the nickname she gave me. With a woman like this, I would never be bored. I slipped into the shadows, being careful to search for magical traps as I entered the apartment. I remembered this place so well that I had no issue finding my way around, but after Sara's seemingly casual comment earlier, I was seeing her home with fresh eyes. When I was staying with Nina, I was so focused on her that I'd never paid attention to the furnishings, but now, something that seemed so insignificant in the past meant the world to me. I wanted to know more about the woman I planned to spend my eternity with.

Nina's apartment was filled with colour and gaudy clutter, mostly handcrafted items that looked like they'd come from a flea market's bins. I couldn't deny the items seemed to have some charm, and it was clear the artists had a passion for their work, but the pieces in Nina's home were flawed in ways that made me wonder why she would buy them. One thing was obvious, though: Nina clearly loved them, imperfect as they might be, as each was clear of dust and placed with care in prominent positions.

I focused on the soft furnishings, taking in their loud, bright and often clashing colours, their plush, deep cushioning and the surprising amount of almost neon fur. How I'd missed seeing these things, I don't know, but I did remember the soft, welcoming feel of relaxing in their soft embrace with Nina in my arms.

Two things that didn't match the rest of the decor were a punching bag and a knife. The knife especially caught my attention, giving me an idea for later.

When I finished installing all the security equipment, I closed my eyes, memorising my surroundings before returning home.

It wasn't easy to find local craftsmen who would deliver colourful quilted blankets and cashmere throws after being disturbed in the middle of the night, but after offering outrageous amounts of money and continued patronage, their attitudes changed, and deliveries were arranged for the next day.

There was one thing no amount of wealth could provide. Something that I needed for Nina because the only way to earn her trust was to show her how much I believed in her. For that, I needed to swallow my pride and ask for help.

'Veronica? Good evening, Coven Mistress,' I said politely when she picked up the phone.

'What now?' she answered curtly. I closed my eyes, counting slowly, holding back the vicious retort I wanted to use.

'I'm calling to formally ask a favour. I need an obsidian knife.' I could almost hear the gears turning in her mind, wondering what I was planning, but Veronica surprised me by simply asking.

'You need an Athame? Why would you need a blade of earth and fire if you can't perform spells? Wait... you're not planning on ending your life, are you? I want no trouble with the Leshy if he learns I gave you the knife plunged into your rotten heart.'

'It's not for me. Nina was attacked, and I need something she can use to defend herself, so no, I don't need an Athame. A plain obsidian knife will do, but if you are willing to bespell it, I would be more than grateful.'

'Adam, I can't give an Athame to a human. Not even your human.' She said.

'Sara wanted Nina to have it.' I lied flawlessly, knowing it would work.

Even with Leszek's tumultuous relationship with the witches, Sara's status within the Coven had gradually grown. It started from a kind of hero worship after she survived Czernobog's assault, but now she was seen almost on a par with Dola herself, and there was nothing Leszek or the old gods of the Nether could do about it. More importantly, with the fragment of Leszek's spirit embedded within her soul, Sara's power was growing, fuelled by this worship. I asked once why he hadn't told her about it, and in his own inimitable fashion, he replied that he wanted to give her as close to a human life as possible.

I didn't question his reasons; Sara still didn't fully grasp the changes to her life, but I felt he was making a mistake.

Of course, I knew, and because I was an unscrupulous vampire, I was more than willing to use it to protect Nina.

'Fine, I'll have something ready for you in a few days, but Adam, don't make me regret it. I don't want to explain why some human with a grudge is going around killing vampires with a weapon I made. Oh, and this stays between the two of us. It's bad enough that people think I don't hate you. If they knew I'd actually helped you....'

'Thank you, Veronica,' I said, refraining from making any comments as I ended the call.

She was being overdramatic, but I understood. My thoughts slipped back to the kiss with Nina, and I felt my heart beating faster. Just as I was savouring the memory, my computer chimed, announcing the arrival of the clinic's security footage.

'Lorelai, I've ordered several packages for Nina. When they arrive, please ensure they are taken to her room. I must not be disturbed. Order some normal food to be delivered as well and… some coffee liqueur,' I requested.

'Yes, Master. Will Nina be living with us then?' My assistant asked, tilting her head and the beak made her look like a preening bird. I reached out, patting her affectionately on the head.

'What's your opinion?' I asked, curious after seeing their interactions.

'I don't know. She is kind and likes you. I want her to stay, but there is a sadness in her that festers like a wound. May I decorate her room? I will make it pretty. Maybe that will help?' She offered, and I nodded. Lorelai wanted this, even knowing such a physical task would use a lot of her magic, meaning she might not be able to manifest again for several days afterwards.

The kikimora was wise and helpful. She could see deep into a person's soul, but even so, she was still naïve and prone to exaggerated emotions, occasionally acting almost like a child.

'I'm sure Nina would love that. Just be careful to not deplete your magic.' I said, turning back to my computer. It was time to show why I had a reputation as the best cyber security analyst in Northern Poland, while Lorelai would ensure Nina felt so cosy that she never wanted to leave.

Chapter 14

I should have realised that a sleepover with Sara was a bad idea, with my emotions still in turmoil. Somehow, we emptied Michal's moonshine, inventing new and exciting cocktails whilst setting the world to rights and trying to decipher the mysteries of love.

Every now and then, our discussions were interrupted by Leszek as he came to check up on us under the guise of grabbing drinks and snacks for himself. Each visit, we sat in silence, looking at each other, trying not to giggle as the increasingly worried Forest Lord stared longingly at his spouse. Leszek was fooling no one as he made a mess, creating unappetising sandwiches and overfilled drinks.

As the alcohol continued to disappear with increasing speed, I found myself getting frustrated with Leszek's visits, till in one booze-fuelled moment of clarity, I realised I was jealous and that telling Sara was the right thing to do.

'I want that!' I stated, slamming my cup onto the table. The tacky monstrosity with a painting of clashing bucks chipped on impact but largely survived my enthusiastic handling.

'What? That thing?' Sara looked at me, then spent several moments trying to focus on the cup in my hand as I waved it around.

'No, this!' I pointed to Leszek, who had once again appeared like a bad penny, now with a panicked look in his eyes.

'What?! Hell no, missy! I love you, but that hunk is mine. I'm not sharing, but if you want a date, Gedania is full of horny gods. I can ask Leszek if he'd take you there. We could do it like that programme, with the roses where they have to woo you to get picked.' Sara swayed as she talked, and her "woo you" sounded like a bad impression of an ambulance. She also waggled her eyebrows and moved her hands closer, then further apart, to indicate... Well, even drunk, I understood what that meant.

'Ooh,' she continued. 'Antlers, you must get one with antlers, or horns; they'll do. Damn things are sooo useful. You grab the tips, and then you rock up like that,' Sara began demonstrating but misjudged her balance, screeching with laughter as she fell backwards. The two thumbs up had me joining her in giggling, and it took several minutes for us to calm down.

'You're drunk, doc, and a nut job.' I said, throwing myself next to her and placing my head on Sara's lap. 'I don't want antlers, but feathers would be nice. Nice, cuddly feathers and a man that looks at me like Bambi looks at you. Adam has feathers, you know, and those wings. I mean, he chopped another vampire's head off with them, but I bet they are still cuddly,' I felt my mood shift, and I got dangerously close to flipping from happy drunk to mushy mess.

'Then give Adam a fucking chance, oh, and stop calling Leszek Bambi.' Sara rolled her eyes before pinching my nose. 'That vampire's chasing after you like some lost, bloody puppy, so grab those wings, hop on his dick, and see what happens.' She lectured, pressing a hand to her mouth when the hiccups started.

'What if things go wrong? What if he wants me only because he can't have me? I like him. He's changed, but what if I spoil everything? What if he sticks his dick in me and …poof, he's back to being a toad, I mean, an arsehole?' I couldn't help but play out my worries in my head.

'Oh, for fuck's sake, what if you die tomorrow? Between us both, shit hitting the fan is a daily occurrence. We see enough of that crap at work not to say "fuck it" then carry on. You like him, and he likes you, so why not give yourself a chance? You deserve to be happy. I know most men are shit, but some of them are trainable. I promise if Adam acts like an arsehole, I'll get His Furriness to send him to Siberia to cool off.'

With a few unsteady movements, Sara sat up straighter, then, as she slid back down, pointed her thumbs at her own chest. 'Then this mighty Seer right here will help you forget the bastard ever existed.' My friend looked so pleased at her solution that I couldn't burst her bubble.

Thankfully, Leszek, or as Sara dubbed him, His Furriness, stepped in at that point.

'No one is sending anyone to Siberia at five in the morning, and this mighty Seer is going to bed. Nina, Michal made up the bed in the guest room for you. Walk if you can, or I'll come back after tucking in Twinkle Toes here.' Sara giggled, kicking her feet up into the air, and I raised my head just in time for him to scoop her up, leaving me alone in the nests of cushions.

Sara hung over Leszek's arm like a sack of potatoes, but before they left, she pointed her finger at me. 'You do it, missy. Everything will be all right, trust the Seer,' she said before turning to her husband, tugging his ear. 'You are mean. I'm not sleepy. Stop behaving like you're my daddy.'

'Say that again, and I'll show you who your daddy is. You need rest, and so does Nina. You'll be suffering enough already after drinking Michal's brandy. Now let me heal you and get some water.' The rest of Leszek's words faded to white noise as he walked further into the house.

I sat alone, looking out the window and listening to the incoherent buzz of voices while Leszek tried to force my rebellious friend into bed. Somehow, it helped me to decide. Sara was right, deep inside, I knew it already, but I needed this push. It was now or never, and I needed to see Adam.

I staggered to Michal's room, knocking lightly. After a rather long pause, I heard a lot of shuffling until the tired shifter opened the door.

'I'm so sorry to wake you up, but could you take me to Adam's, please?' I asked, putting my entire focus on clearly enunciating my words. His assessing stare didn't make it easy, leaving me feeling like an entitled brat, my embarrassment growing as the seconds passed.

'Give me a minute,' he said, closing the door in my face.

I visited the bathroom, and my reflection told me I was a mess, so I washed my face and raked a hand through my hair, then returned to the living room.

'Still want to go, pet?' Michal asked, standing in the hallway, car keys in hand. I nodded, rushing outside before the drunken courage evaporated from my body.

I must have slept during the journey because the next thing I knew, Michal was parking the car in the underground garage. Luckily, he had access to the lift, otherwise, my grand plan of seducing Adam would have ended with me sleeping in the car park.

I thanked him profusely before stepping into Adam's penthouse.

'Lorelai, where is your Master?' I asked the guardian spirit, and her answer came from the speaker above my head.

'In his bedroom, sleeping. Do you want me to wake him up?' She asked, and a moment later, the quiet sound of *Smooth Operator* filled the air.

'No, I want to surprise him. Just light the way a little, and what's with you and Sade? You keep playing it each time I enter the house.'

'It can help prepare humans for moments of passion,' she said before ghostly fingers wrapped around my wrist, pulling me deeper into the house. *Great, a household spirit is pimping me out*, I thought, but tonight I didn't mind and let Sade and the kikimora lead me through the apartment until we stopped in front of a heavy oak door.

'They are locked, but I can sense my master is dreaming of you. I like those dreams. They are so full of life and feed me well.'

She disappeared, and I wondered whether Lorelai desired to see me in Adam's bed purely for the energy such an encounter could produce.

A moment later, the quiet thud told me whatever locks protected Adam's sleep were now open. I walked inside. The heavy curtains were drawn shut, and the only source of light came from halfway behind me, revealing Adam sprawled on the bed.

He looked so peaceful laying on his abdomen, arms holding the pillow in what I could only describe as a lover's embrace. Dark hair shone with a blue iridescent sheen when the light caught it. Adam was beautiful in an ethereal, alien way, and my doubts melted when my gaze slid lower to where the blanket barely covered his pert backside.

The view sent a wave of heat and dizziness through me that ended when I grasped the door frame, whispering to the housekeeper.

'Lorelai, is there a way you can brighten the room? Maybe a candle or something?'

As soon as I'd asked, the ceiling glowed with soft, warm light projecting the moon and night sky. It looked so realistic I gasped, moving inside, barely aware that the door closed silently behind me. There was just enough light to walk toward the bed without breaking a leg or hitting something on the way, but I was grateful it wasn't bright enough to illuminate my features. I didn't want Adam to see how scared I was or how vulnerable I felt, stepping out from behind the walls I'd so carefully built around me.

I undressed, discarding my clothes on the floor, but I couldn't bring myself to remove my underwear. Not yet. If Adam said no, that would be my only protection as I retreated, preserving the shreds of my dignity. Taking a deep breath, I sat on the edge of the bed and looked at the vampire. Adam could give me all I ever dreamed of, the complete opposite of the man I'd foolishly married who'd shattered those naïve dreams into pieces.

This is too good to be true, I thought. My resolve was fading, the memory of my past mistakes souring the moment, and I knew I had to make a move now.

'Please don't break me,' I whispered, placing a hand on his back before I lost my nerve and changed my mind.

Adam's skin was cool and so soft I shivered in delight. I remembered the pleasure his bite gave me, but this was different. This feeling was pure, not fuelled by the magic of a vampire's venom, and I revelled in the sensation.

Before I knew it, I was sliding my fingertips along his spine, and he arched under my caress like a giant cat. My touch caused that, and his reaction sent a wave of desire through my body. My movements became more decisive, and I scratched his skin, my short nails barely scraping the surface, but this was enough to make him moan, and his low guttural sound raised the goosebumps on my skin. My nipples hardened, and painful pleasure radiated through my body each time they rubbed on the lacy fabric of my bra. For so long, Adam had been my forbidden fruit. Now, when I made my choice, I was trembling like a teenager before her first time.

Adam's eyelid fluttered, and I knew it wouldn't be long until he awoke from his dream. It was now or never. I brushed the hair off his neck and kissed the place behind his ear, inhaling the sandalwood scent of his aftershave.

'I want you,' I murmured when his eyes fluttered once more.

'Nina,' he muttered, turning onto his back and reaching for me. 'I love to dream of you, baby. Come to me. I will do whatever you want. I need you so much. My beautiful, unyielding treasure, let me cherish you,' he murmured, wrapping his arms around me and pulling me all the way onto the bed.

I could feel his sizable erection pressing on my hip, but before I could comprehend what was happening, Adam's kiss erased all rational thoughts from my mind. Gods, he knew how to kiss. Slow, sensual, and enticing, his lips brushed over mine, teasing my senses. Adam didn't rush, didn't push me to open my mouth. He savoured my taste, his tongue barely touching me, and when I opened my mouth, he sucked at my lower lip. Pleasure bloomed inside me. It felt like paradise, and I wanted it to last forever.

'Please, I want to be yours... I want to feel you inside me,' I moaned, my tongue darting out to meet his, but as soon as I spoke, Adam stopped, licking his lips before pulling away. I saw the moment his eyes opened fully as he realised this was no dream. *Why did he stop?* My thoughts rushed in panic. I didn't want to hurt him, not again. I just assumed he wanted this, but I should have asked....

'What...? How...? Is this not a dream? I'm sorry, Nina, it's all right, sweetheart, please stay,' he said, his arms tightening around me when I tried to get away, his confusion sending me into a panicky explanation.

'I'm not playing games. I just wanted to be with you tonight. Fuck, I'm sorry, this was a stupid idea, we haven't even talked about it.' I said, pushing at Adam's shoulders to escape.

'No, sweetheart, it's alright. It's the perfect idea, but not tonight.' He said, pulling me to his chest.

'Why not? No, don't answer that. Adam, it's fine. If you don't want me, just let me go. I'm embarrassed enough. I'm sorry I woke you up with my clumsy advances. I thought you wanted me, and Sara said... I just... You know what, forget it.' I kept talking, wishing the earth would open up and swallow me whole.

How could I ever think slipping into a man's bed after barely even kissing him the other day was a good idea, and why was Adam behaving like a reasonable adult? It had taken all of my courage and copious amounts of moonshine to come to him, and his refusal stung more than I cared to admit.

'Oh, baby. I want you so much that it hurts. I want to touch you, taste you, make you cry my name when I make love to you,' he groaned out before his lips found mine, and I yielded, melting in his arms as his hips ground against mine. Adam's pupils widened, the crimson hue visible even in the dim light before he whispered.

'There are so many things I want to do with you. All the sweet, perverted things I've dreamed of for the last two years. I will do them all. I will own your delicious body and make you beg for more, but not tonight.'

He was panting. The passion that roughened his voice both calmed and excited me. Everything will be all right, and gods, I wanted him, just like this, raw, true, and so devoted to me. I was wet and ready to mount him when his arms tightened around me and his pressed forehead to mine.

Adam was fighting his desire for me, and it felt so good that I wanted to push him over the edge.

'Can't we... do some now, the nonperverted things?' I asked, scraping my nails over his chest.

'Fuck, Princess, you will make me a martyr, but no, we cannot. You are drunk, sweetheart, and you might end up calling me an arsehole, but I won't do anything you might regret later. We've come so far. I won't destroy it in a moment of passion, not even if you ask me to. Tonight, we sleep, and tomorrow, if you still want me, just say the word, and I will do all those dark and dirty deeds with you. I promise,' he murmured, pulling a blanket over us.

'You are showing an inhuman amount of restraint for a man-whore,' I snapped, annoyed that Adam kept resisting, and he chuckled.

'I stopped being a man-whore the day I met you. Since then, I've only ever belonged to you,' he said tenderly, kissing my forehead. 'Sleep, Nina. You need it.' Wrapping his arm around me, the frustrating vampire started slowly stroking my back.

My drunk brain objected. I came here for a lust-filled night, to do the deed I finally felt ready for, not for cuddles, but the way

Adam touched me made me forget I'd snuck into his room and molested him like a horny teenager. Adam was mine, and I knew it. My body knew it, as I felt safe with this dangerous killer. His slow, gentle stroking, the fingertips pressing in just the right places, made me so relaxed that I yawned and snuggled closer to his chest.

Not having slept with anyone in a very long time, I was surprised by how perfect it felt to lay my head on Adam's chest. I'd made a fool of myself, but it was so worth it that I decided I might as well enjoy this cosy, warm sensation Adam awakened in me for as long as it lasted. Still, there was a lingering part of me that struggled to understand why he rejected my advances.

'Why did you have to be so fucking noble?' I muttered, angry and relieved at the same time because Adam's erection was still pressing against my hip. Yet he'd proved to be a much better person than I'd given him credit for.

I assumed the frustrating male hadn't heard me as I lay there falling asleep, but as my breathing relaxed and my heart slowed, I felt the feather-like touch of his lips on my forehead, followed by a single sentence.

'Because I love you.'

Nothing else was said by either of us, and I wondered if he knew I wasn't asleep. *Does it matter?* I thought as the meaning of his words wrapped around me like a warm blanket.

When did this happen? When did we fall in love?

I knew I wasn't in love with him two years ago, there'd been something between us, attraction, maybe? But it never blossomed. The last few weeks had been a rollercoaster. I felt I'd discovered the real Adam. He was the same, but so much different from the man I'd hosted under my roof. He was honest. Adam had dropped the mask. I couldn't trust the polished façade of a cyber-tech mobster, but I could trust this monster who did nothing but care for and protect me, who let me decide what I wanted to do.

I came to him tonight because I was tired of playing the tough. His quiet admission was his last move in our game of chess. Now, it was my turn.

Unless I allowed him to turn me, eventually, my heart would be broken, but at least I knew that by trusting him, I was choosing the risk of being hurt instead of letting fear destroy my spirit. Whatever years we would have, I could live them happily, knowing that loving Adam was my choice. I promised myself, placing my hand over his heart.

The path in front of me never felt so simple. I could let fear dictate my choices, living my life, missing out on joy and warmth that Adam awoke inside me, envious of my friends' affection. Or I could grasp it with both hands, even if I burned to ashes.

Adam shifted slightly, his arms wrapping tighter around me as if sensing my dilemma, his lips pressed to the top of my head as he inhaled deeply. I snuggled closer to my noble bloodsucker, unbothered by the lack of a heartbeat. He could have had it all tonight: sex, my blood, possibly even my submission. I was ready to surrender, but instead, Adam chose us, proving to me how wrong I was about him.

Now, I only had to show him I loved him, too.

CHAPTER 15

'Wake up, wake up. You must see the Master before he leaves. Wake up.' The bed shook violently under me while I tried to remember where I was and what the hell was going on.

'Lorelai, please stop it,' I moaned, and the cheerful female voice changed into the hoarse and commanding tone of an old crone.

'Wake up,'

'Fine, just... give me a moment. Fuck, I would kill for a glass of water,' I complained, and almost instantly, a healthy measure splashed into my face. 'I got the message, Lorelai. Gods, why couldn't I have died peacefully in my sleep?'

Okay, I was being dramatic, but at that moment, it felt like a reasonable request. My eyes didn't want to open, and my stomach somersaulted each time I valiantly tried to rise from the dead, but the worst was my heart, which hammered in my chest like I'd run a marathon backwards and not just tried to sit up straight in bed.

A pitiful moan escaped my lips as the attempt to sit up made me fall back onto the cold, damp pillows. This was a hangover from hell, and the Veles spawn next to the bed kept snapping her beak, condemning my lack of effort.

I hope Sara feels this bad, too. I loved my friend, but I hoped she felt the brunt of last night's indulgence, as she was the one who'd procured the moonshine from Michal's secret stash. My mind ran through the sequence of yesterday's events until the point of coming to Adam's bedroom and trying to make him have sex with me.

'Oh fuck,' I muttered, grimacing when the reality of the situation hit me with the force of a runaway train. After all, I'd just barged in and thrown myself at him. I wasn't ashamed of wanting him. Women who didn't initiate things from time to time missed out on many good things in life, and it wasn't the first time I'd been straightforward in my approach. The shame lay elsewhere. I'd rebuffed Adam so many times, only to say yes when I was drunk and horny.

'Oh, Nina, you are such a mature, responsible person,' I said out loud, ignoring the pacing kikimora.

I forced my eyes open and turned my head toward the other side of the bed. Adam's impression was still there on the pillow, but I had to check one more thing. I raised the blanket and sighed with relief. I was still wearing my underwear, which meant Adam behaved like a gentleman, while I...

Suddenly, another memory surfaced, and I gasped, recalling his embrace and those few words of affection he'd whispered before I fell asleep. That jolted me out of bed, and fighting with nausea, I rushed to pick up my clothes and sneak back to my room. It felt too much like a dream or a hallucination brought on by my drunk mind, but I wanted it to be real. Consequently, there was a sliver of doubt that left me not knowing what to do or how to behave. My courage from last night evaporated with the first rays of the morning sun, but I wanted to make things work between us.

In vino veritas, the old Latin proverb rang in my mind: *In wine, there is truth.* My truth came with a dreadful headache and upset stomach, but the clarity was there. I just didn't know how to act on it, and I had to find a way to not spoil it because I wanted to hear Adam repeating those few words to my face while I was sober. I wanted to hear those words whilst looking into his eyes, knowing I didn't imagine them.

I quickly showered and put on the comfy loungewear Lorelai placed by the bed. Only now did I notice my room had gone through a transformation while I was with Sara, each corner now filled with vibrant fabric and handcrafted decor. It resembled my old apartment so much it couldn't be a coincidence.

'Lorelai,' I called quietly, and the kikimora emerged from the shadows. 'Did Adam order all these things for my room?'

'Yes, do you like it?' She asked, coming closer.

'Yes. I didn't think he cared... Never mind. Would you mind if I call you Lori? Why do you keep insisting on me seeing Adam?'

The kikimora looked at me, tilting her head to the side, repeating the nickname I gave her before she nodded vigorously.

'Lori, I like it. You can call me Lori. He is mine. The house is mine. I look after him. That's my purpose. That's who I am. You make him happy. Will you stay? He needs you. You strengthen him, make him better, and make his dreams happy. Will you sleep in his bed tonight? I can move your blanket there,' she said, and I snorted in laughter, but the kikimora's eyes were serious, and she waited for me to answer her question.

'I don't know. Last night was kind of an accident and... I wasn't entirely myself. This thing... arrangement between us, to say the least, is complicated,' I answered, and the creature frowned. Lori's shape wavered, becoming less human and more primaeval, and I felt her stare bore into my mind.

'You will sleep in his bed, Nina. You are his tether to the light. You must stay,' she stated, but it sounded more like an order or a threat. However, I wasn't in the mood to be bossed around by a household spirit who thought she owned the house, Adam and now me.

'That is for Adam and me to decide, Lori. That reminds me. I need to talk to him. Where is he?'

'In the kitchen,' Lorelai answered with a disapproving snap of her beak before disappearing into the shadows.

I looked in the mirror and frowned at the dark circles under my eyes; their depths enhanced my pale complexion. The combination of so many sleepless nights and my hangover made me look so ghastly I could have been possessed by a Lichoradka[15] . Not the best look, not after last night's antics, but staying hidden wasn't the solution. The longer I sat in my room, the more my anxiety spiked.

I walked to the kitchen, stopping at the threshold to stare at the usually be-suited vampire dressed in black combat gear and toasting bagels. He looked like death incarnate, with two long blades attached to his belt whilst spreading orange marmalade on a hot piece of toast. That had to be the sexiest but most fucked up image I'd ever seen, and now it was firmly etched in my memory.

'Hi,' I said, trying to balance the impossible duality of this situation.

'Nina, ah, you're awake. I asked Lorelai to let you sleep. She can be a little noisy sometimes. Let me guess, she woke you up?' He said, looking me over with visible pleasure.

---

15. *Lichoradka – In Slavic folklore, the demon of fever.*

'Yes, but don't blame her. My hangover needs to be subdued, anyway. I may have overdone it last night,' I admitted, feeling a blush crawl up my neck.

A small smile curved Adam's lips upwards, but he didn't say a word, and an awkward tension grew between us. I saw uncertainty in his gaze as if he didn't know what to do either, but there was also a flicker of hope. *What a bitch I must have been to him that a bit of civility makes him light up like the sun*, I thought.

I realised Adam was letting me set the tone of our conversation, whether to greet him as a friend, lover, or hated partner, and with that, I felt the tension ease from my shoulders.

Somehow, that made me braver. Whether or not it was true, I could still hear the words he'd whispered when he thought I was sleeping. *Because I love you*. I thought about the decision I'd made. It was all on me now. It was time to put on my big girl pants and admit I cared for him. I wasn't ready to say *L*-word out loud, but it didn't mean I couldn't take our relationship a little further.

I walked across the kitchen, stopped next to Adam, stood on my tiptoes and gave him a light peck on the cheek.

'So handsome, will you forgive me for last night and tell me who you're hunting down today?' I asked, nodding toward his combat gear whilst reaching for a bagel.

I never got to touch it as I was swept off my feet in a blur of shadow and heat to find myself staring up into the crimson eyes of an impassioned vampire,

'Please tell me you don't regret last night. You can't regret it, I... I've waited so long to hold you as you slept. Please tell me it wasn't just one night, my sweet Obsidian.'

'No, I... I only regret that I put you in such a difficult position. I enjoyed being in your arms... erm, maybe we can do it again sometime? Lorelai would certainly approve,' I joked, at a loss for words and stunned by the intensity of Adam's voice. I was deflecting, but I had to dispel the tension.

'Fuck Lorelai. Only you matter.' Adam's lip descended on mine like a starving man. His kiss was a black fire, an all-consuming darkness as he devoured me, and I lost myself in the pleasure of his touch.

Suddenly, the sound of the toast being ejected made me jump, and Adam cursed loudly, looking at the appliance as if it were his mortal enemy. His exaggerated reaction made me laugh, and I reached out, placing a hand on his cheek.

'Hey, we have plenty of time for this. Let's take it slow, so give the poor toaster a break; otherwise, your stare will melt the metal,' I said, and Adam cuddled to my hand before releasing me, pushing the toasted bagels in my direction.

'I wish I could stay. I would show you how slow I could take... you.' His voice was practically a purr, the hesitation purposeful and sexy as hell, as if my acceptance had released a caged animal, and all he wanted was me. I had to admit it thrilled me to be desired like this. Pressure built in my belly, and I stepped closer, my body yearning for his touch, but Adam moved away, shaking his head.

'I have to go, Nina. I just didn't want to leave before I saw you and made sure there was something for your breakfast. I wouldn't want you to think I ran away. If I'd caused any more misunderstandings between us, I would lose my mind. Unfortunately, I have to go now, sweetheart. Eat something, and help yourself to the painkillers in the drawer,' he instructed, pointing to the cupboard.

Adam still hadn't explained the combat gear, and I wasn't happy with him avoiding the subject.

'All right, but I want to know where you're going and who's going to die.' My tone was questioning, but the look I gave my evasive vampire was one of command, demanding an answer.

With a sigh, Adam sat beside me, reaching for my hand.

'We should have talked earlier, but I was waiting for a better time to tell you. Now is as good a time as any, I guess. Nina, your brother, he's in bigger trouble than I expected. I'm trying to find out more about the vampire who attacked you and why he is so obsessed with his family heirloom. I need leverage because he is not just a man with significant power. He is of old noble blood with a commanding presence, not only within the Elder Races but also in the human world. We may need to strike a bargain for Pawel's life, and I need to know what this item is worth.'

I put my half-eaten bagel back on the plate, suddenly losing my interest in food or any physical activity other than listening to Adam's explanation.

'You're going after him? But we have nothing to bargain with. Do you know where Pawel is hiding or if he still has the necklace?'

'Not yet, but I'm working on it. This morning, I got a message from a small Seethe in the south of Poland. They have information about the artefact your brother took, but they insist on meeting in person. I will be back tomorrow,' he said, but I didn't like it. Something inside me protested the idea, and I always trusted my gut instincts.

'Don't go. What if it's the same people who tried to take me? Maybe they're trying to lure you away. What if they want revenge? Take Leszek with you, or we can ask Sara for a prediction,' I said, but Adam shook his head.

'Leszek is still tied to this land despite his growing power, but don't worry, everything will be fine, sweetheart. I'm not a defence-less kitten. This is what I do. I hunt people down and enforce Leszek's orders. Before I drag Pawel into the light, I want to make sure the threat that hangs above his head is dealt with or that we at least have a plan,' he said, giving me a reassuring smile.

I don't know what got into me, but in a panic, I pulled my oversized jumper down, exposing my neck.

'Fine, but don't take any chances. When did you last feed? Do it before you go. You need your strength, and I... please feed on me.

I need to do something to help,' I insisted, shivering slightly when Adam's eyes were drowned in a crimson wave.

He bent to my neck, and the memory of the other vampire forcing himself on me and feeding on my blood overwhelmed my senses, but I fought it, pushing the terror and helplessness away to hold my position.

I closed my eyes when his lips touched my neck, fangs grazing lightly over the sensitive skin, but Adam didn't bite. Instead, he kissed me just above my artery, sucking it gently.

'Our relationship is changing, Nina. I want more than this. I want you. Not just your blood or your body. You. The entire package. I won't take your blood as payment. I won't taste you until your brother is safe and you are free to refuse me, but I want a promise. Promise that you will wait for me here, safe and protected. The penthouse is warded, and nobody can come in without an invitation. As long as I know you are safe, it is enough for me... for now.'

I opened my eyes to look at him. My offer triggered his transformation, and the person I saw now was no longer a dangerous man, ready to fight. Adam was now a lethal, avenging spirit, deadly to anyone he encountered.

'Promise me, Nina, because if something happens to you, it will be the end of me. The beast you saw when I lost control of the hunger will be nothing compared to what I will become if I lose you. Anyone who has ever caused you pain, their families, their friends... they will die, and even that won't satisfy my fury.'

There was a certainty in his voice that reminded me he wasn't a man; he was a vampire that thrived on blood and violence, and now he acted as if my existence was the sole source of light in his life. It was alluring and terrifying at the same time. Looking at the crimson death swirling in his eyes, I could say only one thing.

'I promise.'

Chapter 16

ADAM

Nothing was making sense this morning. After Nina's drunken escapade last night, I was expecting an embarrassed, defensive attitude, but seeing her happy and confident had me reeling, unsure how to react. When Nina kissed me tenderly, I'd been unable to control myself, transforming as I swept her up into my arms and only stopping myself from burying my teeth into her flesh by the thinnest thread of self-restraint.

Whatever caused Nina's change of heart, I wanted more of it, but my analytic mind refused to stop wondering why the cold, reserved woman suddenly opened herself to the possibility of my love.

I studied the situation, my brain hard-wired to replay every detail, afraid to spoil this delicate truce between us. I was going to take this chance, hold it tight because if last night proved anything, it was the fact she was perfect for me and holding her in her sleep made me feel at peace. Even my thirst for blood eased in her company as if her mere presence was enough to sustain my life.

If not for the trouble of rescheduling this meeting and my need for answers, I wouldn't leave at all. Nina's scent was all over me, my body reacting in the most primal way. I had to keep it together because we were at a delicate stage in this complicated dance, and rushing into sex was the quickest way to reinforce her poor opinion of me.

As the elevator took me to the garage, I chuckled, replaying the disappointment in her eyes when I so valiantly refused her blood offer. If she only knew how much it cost me to keep my cock in my pants and fangs away from her svelte neck, she wouldn't question my commitment.

'Well, she already gave me wings. Now she has me learning fucking morals,' I huffed, jumping into my sports car, but deep down, I knew I'd made the right call. Our first encounter happened during a time of danger, with Nina being forced to accept the existence of a whole new reality, which resulted in distrust and anger. I had to ensure she wouldn't run away this time. That Nina came to me so confidently this morning was a good sign.

'You will be mine, my sweet Obsidian, and I will make you happy because if I fuck it up this time, I may as well turn to ash.' I said, starting the car.

The engine roared as I burst from the underground garage onto the busy street. It would take several hours to drive to my destination, but I didn't have a choice. I couldn't Shadow-Walk to a place I hadn't seen before, and I sometimes wondered why my kind was given such an interesting but dangerous ability. It could be so handy to relocate in the blink of an eye if not for the fact I could end up in a brick wall or someone's closet. Instead, like most of my kind, I only tended to use this ability to return to my resting place or, in a state of emergency, somewhere fresh in my mind.

The downside to human transportation was that I had too much time to think. My worry for Nina was a distraction during the journey, but I had no choice. I had to sort this out, as the threat to her brother weighed heavily on her mind. My promise to find Pawel and keep him safe was looking more difficult as I unearthed more and more information. Sapieha was not only old but also well-connected, and I was desperate for anything that would give me the upper hand in the upcoming struggle. I briefly considered engaging Leszek, but it would paint me as a weakling and attract all sorts of unwanted guests to my territory. Even if I could fight them all, it would cost me my men and my reputation.

Pawel gave me so much trouble that if not for Nina, I would have taken his life myself and turned him. Whilst not ideal, it would undoubtedly make protecting him easier with the added bonus of being able to force the little shit to act more responsibly in the future.

Spawning a fledgling vampire was a tremendous responsibility, one I'd avoided this far in my long life. Many vampires felt the need to expand their nests, building generations of soldiers with unquestionable loyalty devoted to keeping their master safe. Maybe because of my own spawning, I didn't feel the need to be surrounded by my own kind.

That abandonment had bothered me for years, but after witnessing the inner workings of other seethes, I was grateful my life wasn't tethered to my maker. Forced obedience didn't sit well with me. All vampires sworn to me were free to leave whenever they chose. They were loyal, following my commands, but because their obedience wasn't blind, they could offer ideas and contradict me without fear of agonising pain.

I might be a demanding master, but my nest worked like a well-oiled machine. I prided myself on being fair, giving my Seethe something they couldn't get anywhere else. Freedom of choice.

That's why I couldn't let the recent encroachment slide. I couldn't let visiting vampires run around my territory unchecked, especially when they threatened my woman. Such an event could lead to more, and before I knew it, my city would be overrun by rogue vampires, thinking they had a licence to kill here. Still, I didn't want to start a war, especially not with Sapieha.

The best way to deal with a more powerful enemy was to learn their weaknesses. What I told Nina was just the tip of the iceberg. After crossmatching hospital footage with the patient's name and that of my client, which Leszek so helpfully supplied, I knew he was Leon Sapieha. "*The*" Leon Sapieha, Prince of the Vampires.

To say learning who my opponent was sent a shiver down my spine was an understatement. Sapieha wasn't just a Vampire Prince; he was an actual prince from medieval Poland, a man renowned for brutality and the oppression of his subjects. He'd been driven from his homeland during the Napoleonic wars whilst masquerading as his own great-grandson.

I needed to find out what was so special about the necklace Pawel had stolen and why it had enraged the ancient vampire so much that he returned to Poland in order to retrieve it.

I'd called in several favours and broken even more written and unwritten laws to track down Sapieha's descendants. They all seemed to be mundane humans, but the difficulty tracing Polish nobles was exacerbated by the purges of the Second World War and the Communist era, neither regime wanting anyone alive that could lead a successful resistance. When I finally found someone, they'd tried disappearing, but I'd kept track of their digital signature, and this morning, I'd received a message requesting a meeting.

I'd submitted the standard visitation request to the Master of the local Seethe, and my access was instantly granted; the Elders didn't even bother to question my petition. That was the reason I wore combat gear this morning and placed a tracking device in my hair.

I didn't trust the vampire's welcoming attitude. We were territorial; I was encroaching on the territory of another Seethe, and no one seemed to care. I checked the tracker's signal, making sure the GPS coordinates were on my phone and backing up to the cloud. It was a simple tool connected to my personal network. One tap would send my location, but if I held it down, an alarm would be sent to my apartment and also immediately alert Leszek to my plight.

All because Nina asked me to not take any chances. I was going soft.

Several hours later, I arrived at the picturesque village of Koden, where Sapieha's original settlement once stood. Its ruins were almost entirely eroded by time. I don't know why this was listed as the residence of the family's remnants; the largest building in the area was the local church, and the houses, whilst quaint, would be no home to any noble I knew. In fact, the only interesting part of this area was the local legend.

Every vampire in Poland knew the story, or at least part of it. Leon Sapieha, having been injured in one of his various battles, was dying from an infection and following his wife's advice, they went on a pilgrimage to the Holyland. She returned first to manage their household and carry their child to term while he stayed behind in order to recover under the care of an Italian medic.

During these turbulent times, a neighbouring nobleman took advantage of the Prince's absence, laying siege to Kodan. In the ensuing battle, Sapieha's wife was killed, whilst his newborn son somehow survived his home's destruction. The Prince returned home to find nothing but ruins, and it was said his revenge was so complete that no record of the neighbouring towns or the noble families ruling them survived.

I'd done my homework on the Prince and his family, delving into the facts behind the myth, only to find the story mostly true, the survival of the Prince's son the only lie. It appeared Sapieha himself took on that role in later years to hide his newly acquired immortality.

None of this helped me discover why the vampire was so fixated on Pawel; my only clue was a line in a manuscript next to a description of Sapieha's wife, mentioning Sapieha never parted with a golden locket similar to the one Nina told me her brother had tried to sell her.

It was almost dark when I exited the car, and the meeting place was deserted except for one man, who I assumed was my contact. As I moved closer, I studied the relaxed male as he leaned against a crumbling cross, seemingly without a care in the world. His face was in shadow until I was about ten metres away, and he moved, allowing me to recognise the man from my file.

I paused as he straightened, looking around and listening for any interlopers to our meeting, but seeing and hearing nothing but the natural sounds of the countryside, I stepped closer.

'Good evening, I hope you weren't waiting long. I set out as soon as I received your message,' I said, and he gestured me toward the ruins that housed a small chapel.

'Welcome to Sapieha's ancestral grounds. Please let me show you the reason you needed to attend in person,' he said, and I followed him at a safe distance. Something didn't feel right. The human in front of me was acting strangely, his movement awkward and uncoordinated, making me warier the further we walked.

I reevaluated the situation, weighing up whether it was worth pushing onwards, but I'd made a promise to Nina and continued, following the quiet figure into the chapel as he opened the door.

Heavy darkness surrounded me as I entered, a strange feeling I had to admit, the sensation that the absence of light could weigh you down, but that's exactly how it felt. The only feature of the interior was a stone sarcophagus placed precisely in the centre, a painted sculpture of a woman holding a book and a handful of lilac flowers.

'So the reason you dragged me here was to visit someone's grave?' I asked, turning to leave, the confined space feeling more like a trap than a tomb, but I couldn't move fast enough to prevent the door from being slammed shut, the sound of a heavy bar falling into place to lock it.

'Fuck,' I cursed with a snarl, grabbing my knives.

My wings snapped open, the sharp edges of my feathers tearing through my clothing, catching the flickering light of the candles that flared into life. Movement from the left was met with violence. I swung my knives across my body, barely slicing the flesh of the figure that leapt away, its movements a blur. I grimaced, recognising a fellow vampire tasting its blood in the air.

A disturbance behind me had me whipping my wings in a lethal arc to engage with the vampire that stepped from the shadow realm, smiling with satisfaction at the cry of pain.

My laughter, when it escaped my lips, was cut short as someone swung a candelabra so fast its heavy weight smashed into my head and sent me staggering, my vision unfocused and blurry. Before I had time to recover, I felt myself picked up and thrown backwards, a curse barely leaving my lips before I crashed into the door, unsure if the crack was the wood or my bones breaking.

It hurt more than it should, especially my wings and head, and when I tried to move, to banish my wings, agony ripped through my body, and I screamed.

'Sit still. You'll only injure yourself more if you struggle. Also, I would appreciate it if you refrain from using such language in my wife's tomb.'

The soft, masculine voice came from the figure emerging out of the shadows. The man was well built, with a neat, old-fashioned three-piece suit that complimented his tawny hair, giving him a distinguished, refined look that didn't match the dispassionate ice in his eyes.

'It took too much effort luring you here for me to allow you to bleed out, so stop squirming,' he ordered, pulling a thin sword from a cane I'd failed to notice before and pointing it at my heart.

I couldn't believe I'd allowed myself to be so easily captured, fooled by a human into falling into this simple trap. I'd counted on Sapieha's descendant being unaware of the Elder Races, but clearly, Tricity wasn't the only place that shared such knowledge, and now I faced a Master Vampire without backup.

'Ah, Leon Sapieha, I presume? We were supposed to meet on Friday. I didn't realise you were so impatient to see me. Was this ploy the reason for delaying our formal meeting?' I asked, biting back a curse when two more vampires walked out of the shadows.

'Of course. I wanted to talk to you with no one disturbing us. Your current employer can be rather bothersome. Tell me, Adam, how much did she pay you for protection? You killed two of my men and injured a third, and all because of a contract with a woman?' He came closer, and I felt a wave of dizziness that muddied my senses.

I could feel myself wanting to kneel for this man, but something was stopping me from moving, and I flinched at the power emanating from the Master Vampire. Uncertainty washed over me, and I saw the same feeling reflected in Sapieha's eyes before he threw his head backwards, roaring with laughter.

'Well now, isn't that interesting? How does it feel to finally meet your maker?' He asked, still chuckling to himself.

Nothing made sense until I realised why I hadn't bowed. Sapieha had told me to stop moving, and I'd obeyed. *Fuck, this bastard is my Sire? No wonder I didn't bow to his power; his magic was fighting itself.* My thoughts must have been easy to read as he waited until I looked at him in horror, only then gesturing for me to move closer.

'Come here, my child. We have a lot to discuss. Oh, and hide your wings. I don't need a reminder of the savage who took you in,' Sapieha commanded, and I walked toward him.

My wings snapped, vanishing into my body with a groan that was my only concession to the agony as I complied, Sapieha's presence settling deep in my soul. I was his, like a hive worker designed to serve him, but a small part of me resisted. I tried to tap my tracking device to send the warning to Leszek, but Sapieha noticed my actions and shook his head, and my hand dropped, never sending the signal.

I stopped before my newly found Master, and he took my chin in his fingers, turning my face from side to side, assessing me.

'You are strong and handsome. No wonder I bled you dry. How old are you?' He asked, assessing me like a prized bull.

'I was reborn in eighteen-sixteen,' I answered, struggling under his power. The first shock of the encounter was wearing off, and now I wanted nothing more than to escape this cursed crypt, but he held me enthralled.

'Ah, that was a difficult year. I was forced to flee, to abandon my home. I think I remember you, a young merchant's son too pretty for his own good. Your blood sustained me in my hour of need, but I thought I'd disposed of you properly,' he mused, hands never leaving my skin, squeezing muscles, probing, assessing, until finally I was released.

'No wonder you defeated Greg despite his telekinesis. You will be his replacement in my nest and, maybe in time, even in my bed.'

'You sick bastard, you'll get nothing from me willingly,' I answered through clenched teeth, unsure of what angered me more. The fact he abandoned me or that he thought I would want to share his bed.

'You are not my son, Adam. My boy died like his mother to a friend's betrayal. No, you are my spawn, my slave, and unless you have the strength to free yourself, you will remain in my service. You are exceptional, and, with my guidance, none shall be your match, but first, you will learn how to serve,' he said before sinking his fangs into my neck.

There was no blood to drain from me. Instead, Sapieha injected venom into my arteries. Pleasure I didn't desire washed through my body, reminding me of Nina's kisses. I'm sure that wasn't his intention because instead of relaxing in his arms, I felt anger roaring through my being like black fire, and I focused on thoughts of Nina, using my feelings for her as a shield to protect me from his overwhelming possession.

I saw him frowning and had to hide my smirk. *There you go, you arsehole, learn your lesson. There is only one person who can bend me to her will,* I thought as he withdrew his fangs, already turning toward the sarcophagus.

'Do you think you've won, Adam? You've given away your greatest weakness. She is not your At'kar. Vampires are not made to love or to be faithful. In the end, we always lose those we wish to protect. Come, let me show you something.'

The depth of sorrow in the Master Vampire's voice surprised me, and I followed him to the stone sarcophagus to stand by his side. Sapieha raised his hand, laying it on my shoulder, his fingers entwined with my hair, absentmindedly playing with strands. The other hand traced features of the female face etched in the pale marble.

'Maria was my weakness. She was beautiful, was she not?' He asked, cupping the statue's cheek in his palm. 'But she was so much more. She loved her books, her garden with its lilac bushes and the sun that warmed her face when she read for me.

'Even before I was turned, I lived for her, to see a hint of her smile and fulfil her wish for a child of our union. I wanted to be a man she could be proud of, a warrior, protector and husband. I sacrificed everything for her. I gave my soul to the vampire so I could live for her, and yet she died. I should have ignored her pleas to let her live as a human, to carry that baby to term. I should never have waited.' His hands slid off my shoulder, grasping the dainty neck of the statue instead.

'I hate her. I hate loving her so much that I wish I could take her remains and bring her back to life just so that I could punish her for choosing the child in her womb instead of me. I could inflict this pain on her again and again, then hold her close and whisper words of love for eternity. Do you think loving a woman will be your salvation, a way to free yourself from me? She will shackle you to her soul, taking all that you are and burn it to ash as she dies. If you are smart, you'll kill her before it's too late.' The vampire stated bitterly, and I watched as his fingers gripped the marble so tight that hairline cracks appeared on the statue's neck.

A single tear slid down his cheek when he bent forward to kiss the statue's stone-cold lips, whispering an apology. 'I'm sorry, my love, so very sorry.'

Sapieha fell silent, the moment stretching out until his finger slid to a freshly repaired crack in the lid of the sarcophagus.

'Look at what those filthy pigs did. They broke in and opened Maria's tomb, defiling her resting place as they ripped away her jewellery and scattered her bones. My wife, the mother of my child, was treated like a pile of bones. I can't let it go. You will find the last one for me, Adam.'

His voice echoed with pain and anger, but the worst part was feeling his emotions radiating through our bond. I understood his actions. Now, the gruesome deaths of the grave robbers made sense, but the man he wanted next wasn't some nameless idiot. He might be scum, but I'd promised to protect him.

'I don't know where he is,' I said, happy I'd dragged my heels in my search for Pawel.

'Not yet, but I know you started searching. Use his sister if you must, but you have to find him. I don't care if you bring him to me dead or alive, but you must find the locket he stole from the coffin.' Sapieha said, and my fingers curled into fists, sharp claws piercing the skin of my palm.

The pain helped a little, and I tried to call back my wings, but my injured body refused to cooperate. It was time to reevaluate my situation. Sapieha had control over me, but he was volatile and stuck in the past. If I could manipulate him into thinking I was going to cooperate, he might even let me go, and I would be able to get a message to Leszek.

'You know I won't let you hurt Nina. It's too late for me, but if you promise to stay away from her, I will help with the rest. Why the locket? Does it have any real value, or is it simply a sentimental attachment? Do you really need Pawel after killing the other members of the Lost Ark?' I asked, and he turned around. I felt the Master Vampire take my measure as he stared before his lips tightened into a thin line.

'Pawel will die. He dared to touch my wife, so I refuse to let him live. If you behave, I will let you quench your thirst first. I know the Leshy holds you all on a tight leash. As for the locket, it is priceless.'

'So you agree? You will give me your word that if I cooperate, Nina will be safe?' I asked, and Sapieha laughed.

'I don't have to give you anything, Adam. You will do as you are told because you are mine. Let's go. I want to rest in my own home before we return to Tricity. After all, what's yours is mine now. Old Gdansk sounds like a perfect place to settle, and you will make sure the Leshy welcomes us with open arms.'

He was delusional if he thought Leszek would let him take over Gdansk, but Sapieha didn't need to know that. He also didn't need to know I was stronger than most of his Seethe. I was his accidental creation, not born of his blood but by the magic of Old Gdansk, free to think for myself for a very long time. He'd caught me by surprise, but I could feel the blood enthrallment already starting to wear off.

CHAPTER 17

That damned vampire promised he'd be home after one day, but here I was, prowling around Adam's apartment like a caged animal at breaking point. I'd been annoyed when he was late coming back, so it was no surprise I was ready to strangle the unreliable idiot after an entire week.

So many potential scenarios ran through my head. I had pictured him broken and bloody in some dark alley or trapped somewhere. I bit my lip, trying to banish the image. I wanted him safe. I would have preferred it if he were hip-deep in some woman's thighs, happy and carefree. It would break my heart, but at least he would be all right. Still, after the earlier breakthrough in our relationship, I just couldn't imagine that being true.

I'd tried calling him so many times I half expected to be told I was being a crazed stalker and blocked, but the calls kept ringing through to his answering service.

I was keeping my promise, knowing the last thing he needed was a woman with a target on her back wandering around town, but it was increasingly difficult to stay put. I didn't want to drag Sara into this again, but my resolve broke on the third day, and I called my friend, asking her to use her talent to see the future. Sara promised to try, but minutes later, she called back, saying she couldn't see anything.

I knew Leszek was trying to find Adam, deploying teams of shifters to the town where he was last seen, but my vampire had disappeared completely. However, they promised to keep investigating, asking me to stay safe in Adam's apartment, or, as Leszek bluntly told me, *"It'd be easier to find Adam if his female would behave and stop bothering me."* There'd been the sound of breaking crockery in the background at that statement, but I'd taken the hint and hung up.

Unfortunately, I was now going stir-crazy, jumping every time Lorelai tried to start cleaning the apartment.

There were so many things I wanted to say to Adam, to ask him about, but no, the damned bloodsucker had to choose this moment to disappear just when I'd opened up to the possibility that there could be an *"Us."* Now, I missed him so much that I slept in his bed, cuddling the pillow that held his scent.

On the fourth day, I recruited the kikimora and broke into Adam's office, not caring whether it was wrong or that it might land me in trouble with Leszek and his Syndicate.

I'd had a brief look inside before, but the amount of tech had been dizzying, and I'd zoned out, not paying attention. Now, without the vampire to distract me, I entered Adam's inner sanctum. The space looked terrifyingly futuristic, with machines that would look at home on the set of some sci-fi movie and screens everywhere looking at me like dark, reproachful eyes.

It took several deep breaths to gather my courage, but I knew I had to search for clues, for anything that might help me find Adam.

I sat on the chair and started the main computer. A quiet hum filled the air, and the lights on several servers blinked and started pulsing, awakened by my touch, but the screen remained black. I frowned, wondering what to do next, tapping on the keyboard when something stabbed my finger, making me hiss.

I jerked my hand off the desk and sucked my finger, licking the blood that appeared on my skin.

What the heck was that? Should I be worried? I wondered, gasping, when the main screen came to life, displaying a security message and asking for a password.

'Lori... Lori... for fuck's sake, Lorelai, come here.' I shouted into thin air, and just as I was about to call again, the kikimora appeared next to the chair, startling me with her presence.

'I have work to do,' she answered petulantly, her cheerful atti-tude strangely absent. We had been clashing continuously for the last few days. It was clear she was worried about Adam in her own way, as she hadn't stopped cleaning even for a moment, driving me mad with a never-ending whirlwind of activity.

'I'm sure it's not as important as finding your Master,' I said, unable to keep myself from snapping back. 'What's Adam's pass-word?'

The kikimora looked at me for a long moment, her eyebrows rising when she noticed me sucking my finger. I thought she was going to object before she flashed me a half-smile.

'Your blood was the password. Now, you only have to type Master's favourite word, and you will have access to everything.'

After a moment of thinking, I quickly typed in "*Obsidian*", my jaw dropping as the system unlocked.

'You have got to be kidding me. Why that? What kind of pass-word is Obsidian? Shouldn't it be something complex or impor-tant? Wait... my blood is the password? Did he somehow code the computer to my blood?' I asked, shocked by the skill, audacity, and trust of such a feat. I was amazed at Adam's confidence that I wouldn't betray him.

'I guess you're very important to him,' she replied, the blunt answer making me want to cry.

'Who else has access to Adam's computer?' I asked, because there must be more people. I couldn't be the only one. I knew how important his computers were to him. Adam took his job as Head of Syndicate Security seriously. It was his pride and joy to be responsible for something so vital. The paranoid vampire had turned this penthouse into a fortress, guarded equally by tech and magic, and now I was sitting in the heart of it, learning that despite my terrible treatment of him, Adam still trusted me.

'Did your Master talk about me often during the last two years?'

'No, but he knows I watch his dreams, and he dreams about you a lot.' She said, looking at me with ancient, all-knowing eyes. 'You are his heart, and he didn't have a single peaceful night until you came to his bed.'

Talk about hammering the final nail into the proverbial coffin, but I couldn't think about that now. I leaned forward and started opening Adam's recent folders, hoping I wouldn't see anything that would get me concrete boots and a one-way trip to the bottom of the Motlawa River.

'You've been watching too many mafia movies,' I muttered to myself before jumping headfirst down the rabbit hole.

The next few days were a blur. There was so much information I felt overwhelmed just looking at how many folders there were. Once I began opening them, I immediately wanted to stop, wishing I could unsee what was before me.

I knew the Syndicate had its own moral code, and Adam never claimed he was a law-abiding person, but some of the things they'd caught people doing? I stumbled over the footage showing a local politician in a dubious situation, along with Adam's demands for keeping the information off the internet. What surprised me wasn't the blackmail itself but the demands. Leszek's second in command never once asked for money. There were nature preservation orders, conservatorship over important architectural and archaeological sites, and protection for the Elder Races that guaranteed certain activities were overlooked by the police. Even if the methods to achieve it were dubious, I could not fault the intent behind it.

I didn't feel pity toward Adam's victims. Especially after I saw the pictures from some of their activities. On several occasions, I had to look over some files twice just to make sure I didn't miss something critical. Not that wearing a gimp suit and muzzle or having a threesome with a couple was a bad thing. Still, those people made their careers by preaching fidelity and honesty, with a hefty dose of patriarchal and family values. So the idea of their electorate seeing Mr Oh-So-Righteous with a purple tail sticking out of his rear end being ridden by a sex worker made me snort with laughter.

Adam, you mischievous little vampire, maybe I should accompany you on a visit to the brothel for your special recording sessions.

I thought, enjoying a slight, humorous respite during this dire situation. I needed it because I was at my wit's end.

Today, my already sour mood worsened. I'd been working nonstop for the last couple of days, digging into the reams of electronic evidence from the Syndicate's business. Most documents were operational procedures or financial reports and trade spreadsheets. I was about to lose my patience when I stumbled on a folder called *Eternal*. The name matched nothing I'd read, and as soon as I opened it, I knew I'd hit the jackpot, as a picture of me was the first file.

It was a security camera at the clinic, the room instantly recognisable as the triage cubicle. Immediately, I felt myself break out in a cold sweat because, despite the weird angle, I could see my face as clear as day, along with the looming figure of the man who introduced himself as Leon Sapieha.

My breath hitched, and my fingers trembled as the memory of his fangs sinking into my neck and the foul pleasure he forced onto me made the bile rise in my throat. That sick bastard had dug into my mind, sifting through my memories, until he came to the moment Pawel showed me the locket. When he couldn't find anything else, he compelled me to serve him, to deliver my brother to him on a silver platter.

I didn't hate many people, but I would enjoy watching this vampire suffer for what he'd done to me.

I was staring at Sapieha, hoping Adam had found him and sliced his throat open with his beautiful, deadly wings, when out of the blue, the room was flooded with crimson light, and an alarm blared from the speakers. The monitor screen flickered, showing me a topographic map of Tricity with a red pulsing dot on the border between Gdansk and Sopot.

I sat up, tension thrumming through my body, as I frantically looked around, unsure if I'd pressed something or somehow triggered an alarm. My heart pounded like I'd run a marathon, and I yelped as a shadow appeared in the room.

'Go to the safe room, Nina.' Lorelai's appearance in her elder form didn't ease the tension, and my hands shook so violently that I had to curl them into fists.

'What's going on?' I asked through clenched teeth.

'Master activated his emergency beacon. He is sending us a warning. You must hide.' She said, reaching for my hand, but I pulled away.

'That red dot on the map, is it Adam?' I asked, but deep down, I already knew the answer. 'Lorelai, is this dot tracking your Master?' I grasped her shoulders in fear she would disappear.

When the kikimora nodded, I enlarged the map. Why in the middle of the forest? What on earth was out there? I kept asking myself as I memorised the location.

It was off the beaten track, in the forest that divided the two cities, or I should say, it connected them, as the citizens loved the pathways and old Second World War bunkers. They didn't know, however, about the ancient ruins from the times before the Nether was created, when magic filled the forest with strange and fantastical creatures.

That magic still lingered, making the forest much bigger than the official maps showed, and if you strayed from the beaten path, you could wander for days. Time and space would twist as the magical amber that was buried deep underground warped the very fabric of reality. The Syndicate protected, but could not fully control this space. No one could. Instead, Leszek made it into a natural reserve with clear paths and dense overgrowth to deter the unwary traveller from wandering into danger.

I couldn't get there by car, and I didn't think anyone would give me a hand with any magical means of transport, but Adam was in danger, and I needed to help. I cursed up a storm, slamming my fist into the desk before I remembered something. Adam was a collector. I'd seen several fancy cars under his name in the files, so maybe he had a motorcycle as well.

'Lori, does Adam own a motorbike? Is there anything in the basement I could use? Any type will do. Fuck, I'll take a horse if I have to,' I exclaimed, jumping off the chair as soon as she nodded. 'Get the keys for me.'

I was halfway through zipping up my riding leathers when my phone rang.

'Nina, Adam is in trouble. He used his emergency signal. Leszek is heading to the location and asked me to tell you to stay away so he can handle it.' Sara's words hit me like a punch to the chest as I listened.

'Really? Since when does he get to tell me what to do? I'm sorry, Sara, you might listen to Leszek, but not me. I'm going after Adam. I'm not sure what I'll do, but I'm going to get my man back.'

'Your man? Nina, whatever's happened, it must be bad for Adam to activate his beacon, and definitely supernatural in origin. You saw Adam fight; if he's in trouble, how do you expect to help?' The worry in my friend's voice was unmistakable, but I had already decided. I didn't know if my brother was still alive, but right now, I knew Adam needed me. I would not sit on my arse when I knew he was in danger.

'I have to help him, Sara. He's doing this for me, I... What if he needs my blood? I can't leave him if he needs me. I just can't.' I was crying on the phone. There's nothing like a few days of solitude and worry to focus a person's feelings.

'I'll call you back when I return. I'm sorry, Sara. We both know you wouldn't sit back and wait if Leszek's life were at stake,' I said, pulling myself back together, and I heard my friend sigh on the other side of the line.

'I knew you would say that, but... I had to try. I'll be there shortly,' she said. Sara's steadfast friendship and willingness to assist me warmed my heart.

'No, I'm taking Adam's bike; the trail's too narrow for a car. Besides, Leszek will be there, and no one will touch me if your husband has my back. Love you, Bestie, now wish me luck.'

I disconnected the call after Sara's tearful farewell and grabbed the keys before heading toward the lift with Lorelai on my heels. When I turned to say goodbye, ancient eyes looked at me from the housekeeper's face, the knowledge of aeons shining out.

'I'm going to bring him back,' I said.

'I know. Remember, you are his heart, and Adam would never willingly hurt you.'

I wasn't sure what she meant by this, so I nodded, bending and kissing the kikimora's cheek, breathing in the cosy scent of a warm fireplace and drying herbs. Lorelai looked startled by my gesture. Her beak clacked, and she backed off slightly. Somehow, it helped to calm my nerves to know I had just surprised an ancient spirit.

There you go, Nina, fake it till you make it. I thought, bracing myself for the upcoming challenge.

CHAPTER 18

NINA

The trees and undergrowth blurred into one while I mar-
velled at the nimble Japanese machine as I swept through
the twists and turns of the bumpy road. Despite riding toward
unknown danger, I was enjoying the speed. I knew once everything
was calmer, I'd be asking Adam to let me use his bike again because
it handled like a dream.

When Lorelai told me Adam had a motorcycle, for some reason,
I expected an old, custom Harley he'd use to pose on to pick up
women, not the ultra-fast, high-tech machine that stuck to the
road like glue. It felt like I was riding a cloud as it glided over the
uneven road, the speed and the wind making it more exhilarating
than anything I'd ever ridden. It was a shame when I had to slow
down as the destination drew closer, making sure to keep my eyes

open for anything out of place. The satellite picture had shown nothing but a small clearing and a single small cabin that would struggle to be more than a storage room for hunters.

There was only one reason for Adam to be out here: Pawel. *Had my quick-witted vampire found Pawel's hideout and gotten hurt when he saw him?*

I came as close to the location as possible, cutting the engine and coasting to a thicket near the clearing's entrance, sneaking the rest of the way until I could peer from behind the overgrowth. There were people in the distance. Their voices, fuelled by anger, were loud and discordant. There were also muffled screams of pain, and I felt fear firmly gripping my chest, but I had to see, so I shuffled forward for a better view.

The scene unfolding before my eyes when my head cleared the bushes had me biting back curses and desperately trying to convince myself not to run out there screaming bloody murder. There were five people in total, two standing guard, staring outward, looking for suspicious activity, whilst another leaned in, whispering to a sentry before slipping into the cabin. The last pair were why I was frantically trying not to scream out in anguish.

I recognised Adam instantly. He was kneeling on the ground, his forehead pressed to the earth, and his wings stretched out on either side of his body. The reason I was struggling to stifle my screams was the other figure. That man casually strolled back and forth, each step placed with languid precision onto Adam's wings, and the sound of creaking bones tore something in my chest each time I heard it.

Adam didn't even flinch. The heavy boots caused appalling damage, but my vampire didn't even lift his head. I could hardly imagine the state Adam must have been in to not react, but as I looked closer, I noticed the deep wounds on his back, both old and new, turning the skin of his back into so much ground meat.

He was untied, and yet Adam didn't resist when his tormentor took a bloody knife and nonchalantly trailed the sharp edge over the bloody wounds. I couldn't believe I was looking at the same man who effortlessly took out three vampires as Adam stayed precisely where he was, just like a statue you'd expect to find in an old temple.

Is he too injured to escape? Or is there something else that's keeping him in place? A spell, maybe? I thought, noticing movement in the cabin doorway. The whisperer from earlier emerged, joining Adam's tormentor and kicking dirt at the kneeling vampire. Still no reaction. The situation was so bizarre, and suddenly, I realised what I was seeing. Adam looked like a catatonic patient that I'd cared for a few years ago. Locked in his mind and unable to do anything, stuck in whatever pose someone placed them in.

'Stand up, Adam. C'mon, why doesn't the self-styled Master of Tricity get up and show me what he can do? ' Mr Whisperer said, but again, there was no response. Instead, the doors to the lodge opened, and the vampire who haunted my nightmares walked out.

'Stop messing around; I don't want him too damaged. Adam won't move until I allow him. I'm impressed that he managed to pretend acceptance of his place, only to alert his Seethe. At least the boy has courage, unlike the rest of my pathetic spawn,' Sapieha sneered before inclining his head toward the other man. 'You can play with him a little longer until he learns his place, but make sure to clean him up afterwards. I want him ready for my bed tonight.'

The one with the knife threw his head back and laughed, showing long, sharp fangs. 'Of course, Master. Thank you for the opportunity to teach your little bird.'

I'd had enough. Leszek still wasn't here, and looking at the cruel face of the knife-wielding vampire, I knew it wouldn't be long till he started slicing up Adam. I retreated to the bike and started its engine.

It was a ride-or-die moment, and I hoped I could buy my man enough time for the horned cavalry to arrive and save the day. I only hoped Sapieha still needed me alive because I sure as hell wouldn't win this match. This entire idea was a risky bet, but as I couldn't do anything for Pawel, I'd be damned if I didn't do something to save Adam. *No one will die today.* I promised myself, spinning the tyres on the gravel road.

I gunned the throttle, the bike leaping from the forest and right between the two sentinels. With a grunt, I leaned over, nearly dropping the motorcycle as I planted my foot and spun in a circle, spraying dirt and stones into their faces. I didn't wait for their reaction. Straightening up and lifting my foot, I rolled the throttle and shot forward, the front wheel threatening to lift off the ground.

Just as I neared the vampire with the knife, I grabbed the front brake, the handlebars hitting my chest as the bike dipped. I leaned over, feeling the rear wheel lift and swing around, crashing into my target's body and knocking him over. I struggled with control as the wheel hit the ground, but once I had the bike upright again, I reached out my hand, looking down at my vampire.

'Get on the bike,' I commanded, my hopes rising as Adam looked up. I saw the desperation in his eyes when his muscles tensed, attempting to move, but he remained frozen in place. The only change was the tension that caused blackened blood to gush from a wound in his neck.

The two sentinel vampires launched themselves at me, but Sapieha's voice rang out as he raised a hand, stopping them in their tracks.

'Nina, how very nice to see you again, my sweet morsel. Adam won't get up. He is mine, and I'm afraid that even you can't make him disobey my order, but I'm not cruel. Please join us. You can stay with him as long as you want. He thought his feelings for you would protect his mind, but, as you can see, they didn't. It is time for him to learn love is a mirage for fools,' he smirked, and I saw Adam tense, his eyes crimson with rage.

Sapieha stood there, still smiling, and I wanted to wipe the expression off his smug face, preferably with my fist. Instead, I got off the bike and turned to face him.

'Well, thank you for your offer. I need to ask why you're doing all this, though. I know my brother crossed you, and I can only apologise for his actions; he never was the smartest boy. However, Adam and I are your best chance of finding what my brother stole from you, and this is hardly the way to motivate your workers.' I said, amazed at how calm my voice sounded.

I gave myself an imaginary pat on the shoulder for digging into Adam's computer files and reading all his thoughts on this case. I even managed to keep my flinch to a single step backwards, hardly revealing the terror I felt as Sapieha approached.

'What a brave little mouse, defending the big bad vampire. What will you give me for his freedom? Your life? Your brother's life? Aren't you afraid I'll just take it all, just like I did in the clinic?' He said, licking his lips.

'You can keep me as your guarantee. You can... you can feed on me. Just let Adam go.'

'Are you tempting me with your body, Nina? I have to admit your blood tasted exquisite, especially laced with your pleasure. Maybe this time, we can let Adam watch? His mind is full of pictures of you and the things he wanted to do...' he said, practically purring.

He was the second vampire that had mentioned the taste of my blood, and Sara used it to attempt scrying. What was so special about it? Could it break Adam's thrall? I had to think about something fast because time was ticking, and the one-god rescue team was nowhere in sight. To make matters worse, Adam's body shook with tension as he growled wordlessly in rage.

'Do you think I'm afraid of you? Just because you tricked me once, it doesn't mean I won't rip out your fangs if you attack me again. However, here I am, offering myself freely if you let Adam go. Or, if you prefer, we can make a wager. You said Adam thought his feelings for me could save him. Well, then, I bet it's true. If I'm right, you will let us go; otherwise….' I shrugged when I finished.

At Sapieha's amused nod, I lifted my hand up and bit into the webbed skin between my thumb and index finger.

Motherfucker! I cursed in my head.

The pain was worse than I'd ever imagined. Of all the ways to draw blood, I had to choose the worst, but I didn't have time to remove my leathers. Still, I achieved my goal. My teeth pierced the skin deeply, and it bled a lot. I looked at the crimson liquid streaming down my wrist and rammed my hand straight into Adam's parted lips before Sapieha could stop me.

For a moment, nothing happened. Adam talked so much about biting me that I thought my blood, the taste of it, could make a difference, and I would be able to break his enthralment. Something like blood magic works in Coven spells. No such luck. The initial shock on Sapieha's face turned to glee at the tears pooling in my eyes. I was a fool who'd acted rashly, placing a bet that would cost me more than I was willing to pay. I rolled the dice and lost because I had nothing else to offer.

'I told you, Nina. He belongs to me. You will be such a sweet addition to my menagerie, but if you find your brother and bring back my locket, I will allow Adam certain freedoms. After all, I will need a capable man by my side once I take over the Tricity Seethe.'

'And why do you think I would allow that?' Leszek said, emerging from the forest's edge. He was calm, but I could hear the raw menace in his voice. Sapieha's eyes narrowed, but the imposing aura of the Forest God made him take a step back.

'Adam is my spawn. Everything he owns is mine, you know our laws. Look at him. He will do what I say, and when I say it, even the woman he thinks he loves can't free him. You are a reasonable man, Forest Lord, and should know better than to interfere in local politics,' Sapieha answered smugly.

'You want me to believe after all these years, Adam found his maker? Or that he fell for the Blood Bond so easily?' Leszek moved to stand next to Adam and look down at us. I saw the frown on his face, and my heart skipped a beat when he turned toward the older vampire.

'You are barely able to control his actions, let alone his thoughts. Otherwise, he wouldn't have sent the distress signal, but as you said, I'm a reasonable man. What do you want for his life?'

'He is strong, but I would expect nothing else from a vampire I created. Unfortunately, he learned to think for himself. I suppose I have you to thank for that, judging by those... things.' Sapieha said, grimacing when he gestured toward Adam's beautiful wings before continuing.

'I admit he needed the blood ties reinforcing after the last incident, but he still belongs to me. Now more than ever, and even you can't take him away from me by force. I ensured his mind would shatter, turning him into a feral beast. If you care for my spawn, Leshy, you will help me search for the thief who plundered my wife's tomb and say nothing when I take Adam's place in Tricity.'

Leszek muttered a curse in a language I'd never heard before and moved toward the older vampire.

'Or maybe I should just kill you. How dare you threaten my kin? Release Adam this instant, or I will turn you into a pile of ash,' he said, and the ground shook as the surrounding vegetation responded to the forest god's magic, growing at such a rate that saplings exploded from the earth. The fresh growth impaled Sapieha's sentries and tore them apart before they could take a single step. The remaining vampires died soon after. Unfortunately, Sapieha was faster than his minions and stepped aside, gesturing toward Adam with a casual wave of his hand. Adam made a strangling noise that stopped Leszek's advance, showing how much the vampire meant to him.

'Adam belongs to me. I won't leave this land before I get what is rightfully mine, and if you try using your magic again, I will make Adam tear his lover's throat out with his bare hands. I may become a pile of ash, but my laughter will echo down eternity knowing you had to kill your friend.'

It was a stalemate. Silence descended while the two men measured each other's resolve. I bent down to Adam, placing my other hand on his cheek. I didn't care about the politics or who ruled the Tricity vampires. I only wanted him to return to me because the thought of losing him was unbearable. The last few days had made me realise how much I cared, and despite Sapieha's claim, I knew Adam was still there. I just had to reach him.

'For fuck's sake, you damn bloodsucker, shake it off. Adam, please. I need you.' I whispered, pushing my wounded hand back into Adam's mouth while Leszek and Sapieha decided whose dick was bigger.

Something dark shifted in Adam's eyes as his mouth clamped onto my injury, sucking hard. The next thing I felt were fangs piercing my flesh, and I whimpered at the pain until euphoria rushed through my body, making me whimper for a different reason. Even through the mind-numbing pleasure, I felt the pain of his fangs scraping against the bone, but I would endure so much more for him, and looking into Adam's eyes, I tried to silently convey those feelings. If Sapieha held his mind in some sort of spell, I wanted Adam to know just what he was fighting for if he resisted.

I blinked away the tears, clearing my vision. Adam's eyes were a sea of crimson, the frightening sight strangely reassuring as we connected, an intense sense of belonging, of love, binding us together. Whatever horror Sapieha had done to control Adam's mind, I felt it fracturing. My vampire was a ruthless killer, a domineering arsehole, but he was my killer, my asshole, and my protector. I couldn't let him suffer under Sapieha's power.

He was my beloved monster, and there was one last thing I could give him. Something that hurt more than the fangs in my hand and scared me more than the leech behind my back.

I pulled my hand from his mouth and placed a kiss on his bloodstained lips.

'I love you. You are mine, only mine. Come back to me so we can be together.'

The Vampire Master howled in pain behind me. The next thing I knew, pain exploded in my head when Sapieha hit me, sending me flying. My vision blurred, but even through the haze, I saw Adam rise to his feet, launching himself toward his former Master. His lips drew back, showing sharp fangs, and his damaged wings snapped open, ready to rip his enemies to shreds, but Adam was still severely injured, and when the boulder behind Sapieha shuddered and broke free of the earth, I knew it wouldn't be an equal fight.

The rock hurtled toward Adam, almost flattening him, and the forest behind us erupted with wild, untamed magic.

'Enough!' Leszek's voice cut into the whirlwind of aggression.

'I will never acknowledge my spawn as the Master of the Tricity Seethe. Do you think this is the end? You saw what those bastards did to my wife. You really think I would leave without finishing what I started?' Sapieha said through clenched teeth, his contour melting into the shadows behind him.

I watched as Adam shifted, following the retreating vampire, his body an explosion of leashed violence about to erupt at any moment. *Fuck, he's going to chase after the bastard.* I thought as soon as his contours shimmered.

I bit my lip, hating myself a little as I spoke.

'Adam, I need you,' I said.

I didn't raise my voice, yet his head snapped round to look at me, and his body returned to its solid form.

In a blur of movement, he was by my side, lifting me from the dirt and cradling me to his chest like his life depended on it. 'I'm sorry, sweetheart. Please tell me what you need,' he said. His voice was so rough, it was like he'd screamed till he was raw.

'Let's go home. I need to patch you up. You're still bleeding.' I said, and he nodded, turning toward the bike, but as we moved, my gaze caught the older vampire's regard.

Sapieha looked me dead in the eyes. I saw the promise of pain and suffering in his gaze, but also something else. Envy, greed and hesitation, as though he saw me with Adam and wanted that feeling more than life itself. The vampire had almost disappeared, but the smile he gave me was cruel and filled with rage.

'Enjoy this time, Nina. I will give you some to return my locket. If you fail, I will hunt you to the end of time to show my unruly child how it feels to lose a piece of your heart.' His voice was barely a whisper, but it shook me to the core, and I was left breathless despite his shape completely melting in the shadows behind him.

We were alone. The vampire bodies Leszek had impaled turned into dust, but the Forest God ignored them as he walked toward the cabin entrance, likely to inspect it, but I suspected he was also giving us some space. As soon as Sapieha disappeared, Adam dropped to his knees, panting heavily, still holding me in his arms.

I placed my hand on his cheek in a soothing gesture, trying to slide from his embrace.

'It's alright, you can let me go now,' I said with a reassuring smile.

'Never. I will never let you go. Fuck, Nina, I thought I'd lost you. The things he said he'd do to you, the things he would make me do...,' Adam growled into my neck. 'No, I need to take you away from here. Why did you leave our home?' I saw the wildness creeping into his eyes, scarlet swirls taking over their infinite depths.

'It's alright, I'm safe,' I tried to say, but before I knew it, Adam wrapped his wings around us, the world darkened, shifting into a void, and I fainted.

Chapter 19

Darkness surrounded me, and I blinked to test if my eyes were open, scoffing at my actions when I felt the softness that covered me, warming my shivering body. I could barely move as every twitch or deep breath pressed against the un-yielding walls of my comforting cocoon. I didn't know where I was or what exactly had happened, my last memory was being enveloped by Adam's broken wings.

I drew a breath to curse the damn vampire's stupidity for hurting himself that way when a rasping voice stopped me.

'Nina, my heart, come back. Please don't leave me.' The curse died on my lips. Why did he sound so terrified? Instead, I stretched out, trying to reach Adam's face. This time, I did curse as my cocoon refused to budge, tightening to keep me in place, and I realised what, or rather, who was holding me.

'Adam?'

'Nina, oh sweetheart, you were so cold. When your heart stopped...gods... I thought I'd lost you to the shadows. I'm so sorry, I wasn't thinking...' the broken answer came from the darkness.

It was Adam's voice, but I'd never heard him so scared. I lifted my hand to where his voice came from, accidentally touching the torn flesh on his neck.

'Are we dead?' That explained the overwhelming darkness, the ice that flowed in my veins, chilling me to the bone and his injury. A raspy laugh answered my question.

'I thought you were. I thought I'd killed you. The Shadows of the Nether are deadly for humans. Gods, I'm an idiot. I could only think about getting you home,' he said, and I sighed.

'Well, let's never do that again. I feel like a half-frozen corpse. Are you sure this isn't the afterlife?'

'I long to spend eternity with you, but no, you are very much alive, and I will ensure it stays that way by any means necessary,' Adam asserted, taking my hand and placing it on his cheek. I felt his lips graze my wrist, and my pulse quickened. *I have a pulse, and I can feel him*, I thought, but with this came another question.

'Can this Shadow Walking make you blind? I can't see anything. Where are we?' Adam chuckled, pulling me closer, and I felt his chin resting on my head.

'In our home, and you are not blind. It is simply very dark in here. I keep my walk-in closet pitch black and empty in case I'm forced to use this mode of transportation,' he explained, and I exhaled, fighting with a sudden wave of relief.

'So why the hell are we still in the closet?' I asked, shaking my head and attempting to brush away the feathers from my face.

'Because I thought I lost your soul in the shadows, there is no coming back from that, and... in the darkness, I could pretend you were just asleep, safe in my arms.' I felt a shudder run through his body, and his grip around me tightened again. It appeared our little escapade had traumatised my vampire much more than myself.

'I'm alright, I promise. My face hurts where Sapieha backhanded me, but I think the cold eased the swelling. I can barely feel it. We need to go to the hospital. What those bastards did to you... oh Adam, your beautiful wings...' I said when reality snapped back into place, and I recalled the torture he experienced, but he didn't let me finish.

I felt his lips on mine. Adam nipped my bottom lip only to let the tip of his tongue soothe it soon after, and any words I wanted to say were quickly forgotten.

'No. No hospitals, not for the moment, at least. I only need you, Nina. I will heal, my love. Shifting through shadows helps my wounds knit together as we move, but I can't leave your side. To hear your breath, feel your touch and hold you in my arms as if nothing else exists; that's what I need. Did you mean it? That you love me?' He asked, placing soft, loving kisses all over my face.

'Of course I do. It comes with the obligatory "I'm looking after your injuries" package. So, let's get you fixed,' I insisted, suddenly shy of my previous declaration.

'Please... don't. Let me hear it again.' There was a yearning in Adam's voice, not fitting his usual blaze attitude, making my heart soften.

'I mean it. I love you. It's still not easy for me, but... I said it, okay? So let's focus on what I know and patch you up.'

'Yes, ma'am,' he replied.

I felt a smirk so sinful when he kissed my temple that I nearly purred. I did, however, close my eyes as his fingers slid through my short hair till they were stroking the back of my neck.

'You're such a bad boy, locking your girlfriend in a dark, windowless room for no apparent reason. Take me to the light, Master Vampire. I need to see you because after you chose to bleed on Leszek's carpet instead of getting help, I have trust issues each time you say you will heal.'

'Oh no, you will not stitch me up again. After last time, I have a scar on this perfect body of mine,' Adam complained, and if I'd known where his shoulder was, he'd have a bruise to go with it.

'Alright, but let's take a shower. I can still taste the dirt on my tongue from my little flying lesson. I want to know what happened. Do you have any idea how worried I was when you disappeared? I thought I'd lost you. No one could contact you until everything started flashing red, and Sara phoned. What happened? If you could send a signal, why did you wait so long?' I was frantic. Days of worry spilling over as I vented. I knew I was being unfair, but Adam didn't seem to mind.

The weight of his wings disappeared when he lifted me from the floor, his foot kicking out and smashing the door open, making me squint as the room flooded with light.

'I can walk, you know,' I said, blinking to clear my blurred vision while feeling my body shake from Adam's laughter.

'Oh, I know, but I'm your bad boy vampire, and I couldn't possibly give up my prize now that I have her,' he replied with such smug arrogance that I couldn't help but laugh.

'See, that's why I shouldn't have said those words. You got cocky all over again,' I said, meaning it as a light-hearted joke, but Adam paused, looking down at me.

'I cannot change who I am. You've seen what I'm capable of, and I'm not ashamed of that. I can kill with ease, and I like to make my enemies suffer... a lot. I will never be one of the good guys doing what's right, no matter the cost their loved ones have to pay..., but with you? I will always be someone you can trust. I waited so long to hear that you loved me, so please, never hide your feelings from me.'

'Adam, I love you, just as you are, but I'm still in my leathers, sweaty, dirty and with more questions than I know what to do with. You are covered in blood and... whatever this crust is on your body. So I promise, if you take me to the shower, I will shout my love from the roof of the building, bouncing a tambourine off my naked arse....'

He roared with laughter before silencing me with a kiss.

'You are impossible, woman. I never stood a chance, did I? So, my Obsidian Princess, what does my lady want to know? What information is worthy of the privilege of peeling these leathers off you?' Adam teased, walking us into the bathroom.

'Just tell me what happened and why you didn't send a message earlier. I was going crazy here,' I replied when Adam finally put my feet on the floor.

'I couldn't. Initially, I was so stunned to discover Sapieha was my Sire that he'd taken control over me before I could fight back. We are supposed to obey our Makers to prevent newly raised vampires from running rampant. It didn't help that he's a powerful psychic, so when I did finally fight back, he imposed his will using magic.'

Adam wouldn't look me in the eye once he'd finished, but before I could do anything, his hands slid through my hair, and he leant down to kiss his way along the column of my neck. When his hands withdrew, only to capture my zipper and begin slowly drawing it downwards, I dragged in a deep, ragged breath before stopping him.

'So how... damn it, Adam. Stop distracting me!' I snapped, pushing him away when he nibbled at my earlobe.

'Distract? I want to do so much more than just distract you, but I will stop if you want me to,' he whispered, sliding the jacket off my shoulders. 'Do you want me to stop?'

'Yes... No... Just tell me what happened,' I groaned, almost forgetting what we were talking about when he hooked his fingers under the hem of my tank top.

'I gave up, well, I pretended to at least. I did what I was told and agreed with every idea the bastard had. Finally, he eased his relentless focus, and I was free to act. I sent the distress signal, but as I was readying to leave, one of Sapieha's goons saw me. When the bastard tore into my mind, he found out what I did, and the next thing I knew, I wasn't in control of my body. That's why you found me helpless in the dirt.' Adam's voice sounded distant as he drew my top over my head, pausing as my lips were exposed, the kiss that followed so gentle that I almost didn't feel it, and I pushed forward to increase the pressure, only for Adam to withdraw, chuckling.

It was a strange mood as Adam, with slow, deliberate movements, stripped away my clothing whilst sharing his traumatic experience. It was incredibly erotic that he felt so safe around me he could show his vulnerable side, my powerful leader of men and the supernatural, admitting to being helpless in the hands, or rather, the power of another vampire. He did all this whilst taking control of my body. I knew I should stop him, my medic's brain shouting it was just trauma-related hypersexuality, but I didn't care. Adam wasn't bleeding anymore, and most of his cuts were healing, so

I told myself to shut up and enjoy the fact we had survived the encounter in more or less one piece.

Adam's growl, full of desire, had me throwing away my top, and the look in my vampire's eyes sent me shivering and grabbing his shoulders. I'd forgotten I was wearing a thin scrap of a lace bra. I may have a boyish figure, but I was proud of how I looked, and my one feminine indulgence was now being scrutinised by a beast that wanted to rip it away with his teeth.

'Nina, how do you feel? Can we...? I need you, sweetheart, so fucking so much, but we can wait.' How he held back, I didn't know, but he stopped undressing me, waiting for my answer.

I moved closer, my eyes hooded, taking him in. With his clenched jaw and hands tightened into fists, Adam was like a loaded spring, and only I had the key to release him. Slowly, sensually, I placed a hand over his heart.

'Wait? No, I don't want to wait any longer, but... I haven't finished asking my questions, and I still have my trousers on.' I said, scraping my nails over his skin. Adam immediately dropped to his knees, reaching for the buttons of my leather trousers.

'So... what was this arsehole's end game?' I asked. I was enjoying our little roleplay but knew I wouldn't be able to keep it up much longer as he slowly opened my trousers one button at a time, and I had to grab the sink to steady myself.

'His goal is to retrieve the locket. Pawel's death is the only way he can enjoy the moment of revenge and is his way of sending a message, so not as... fuck Nina, I can't think straight.' Adam's breathing was ragged as he carefully peeled my leathers down my legs, his eyes glued to my matching lace panties while I played with his hair.

'Undress, I want to see you, all of you.' I commanded when he pressed his forehead to my stomach, inhaling deeply.

I was definitely on a power trip and so turned on I could barely stand, watching as Adam reached out and turned on the shower, his fingers shaking. When he tore away the ripped shirt from his torso, I gasped, pressing my thighs together to restrain my own reaction. Adam's trousers soon followed, and I wondered how long he could keep his feral nature on a leash.

'Stand still, I want to touch you,' I murmured, half hoping he would lose control.

Adam was so hard. His cock stood straight out, jerking slightly when I traced my hand down over his chest, following the narrow band of hair. I pressed a small kiss to Adam's heart before wrapping my fingers around his shaft, smiling as my vampire's eyes turned crimson, his control fraying, but he didn't move, just as I asked.

'Will you let me lead?' It wasn't a question. I unhooked my bra with one hand, still holding his cock with the other, slowly moving along his length until the silken skin was drawn back, exposing the head and bead of liquid at the tip. I needed this. To take control and reclaim my desire after Sapieha stole it from me, but this wasn't just about me. I wanted Adam more than anything else. When he nodded, his eyes staring at my breasts, I licked my lips, making him moan softly while I played with him.

'I want to hear you say it, Adam,' I said, stroking him firmly. He pulled me closer, and his mouth invaded mine in a harsh, unyielding kiss before I drew away, filling the room with throaty laughter. 'Tell me, Adam.'

'Yes, fuck yes, do whatever you want, just don't let go of my cock. Your touch... please, Nina, you are driving me mad,' he said through clenched teeth. He reached between my thighs, and I felt his fingers hook the lacy fabric of my panties before he yanked them away.

I gasped as the lace tore, tightening my grip on Adam before leaning forward and biting his ear, tutting with mock disapproval.

'You are such a brute, but you are mine, and you will do what I ask, yes? Take me to the shower,' I ordered, and when he did, struggling not to throw me against the wall, I issued another command. 'Hands on the wall, Adam.'

It thrilled me that he obeyed. A man who could easily overpower me, pick me up and fuck me till my brain turned to mush was doing as I demanded. I was going to ensure he didn't regret it, but before I allowed him to unleash himself, I had a confession to make because our conversation about the past was long overdue.

I took the sponge and lathered it with soap before I moved toward his back and started rubbing it in slow, sensual circles.

'I'm sorry I was such a bitch to you two years ago,' I said, gently wiping away the dry blood from Adam's back. He drew a breath to speak, but I continued before he could interrupt. 'Shh, just listen. I'm trying to apologise.' I waited until he nodded, then renewed my efforts, smiling as his body tensed.

'You are not at fault for how things turned out last time. It was the wrong time for us, and with my past, it wasn't easy to trust a man who was pushed into my life without my consent. Initially, I was angry that my choice was stripped away, but that time with you… it felt good. I was afraid of how you made me feel, so I blamed you because I felt vulnerable.' I kissed his shoulder before my hand slid down to his tight buttocks.

'It is not an excuse for how I treated you, just an explanation. It was wrong of me to try changing you and then tell you we couldn't be together because of who we were. You are perfect, and you are mine, my beloved monster. I love you, I'm still afraid, but we will work through it together, yes?' I asked, and Adam moaned when my hand slid between his legs.

'Nina, I don't know if I can hold…' he groaned out through clenched teeth, his body shaking with barely restrained desire.

I turned him around, pressing his back to the wall, fascinated by the rivulets of water turning pink as they ran down his blood-splattered chest.

'You can, and you will, because I have so much more to say,' I said, brushing the dark, wet hair from his face.

'I love how you fight. I love how brilliant your mind is. I love the possessive streak that prevented you from giving up on me when I pushed you away. I love your loyalty and your sense of justice, and I'm pretty sure I will love sex with you because you turn me on so much I can barely stand.'

I kept talking while cleaning him, letting the water wash off the last remnants of Sapieha's cruelty from Adam's body and the foul touch from my mind. Everywhere I cleansed, I kissed, gradually moving down his torso.

Adam stood as still as a statue, but his muscles were trem bling with strain, hands balled into fists, a silent witness to how he held himself back. I wasn't trying to test him, but the way he followed my wishes soothed the wound deep inside me. Adam would put my needs first, even when it cost him dearly, using actions instead of flowery words to prove how deeply he cared for me.

It wasn't long before I was on my knees, hands sliding along the length of his cock when I kissed the head, teasing him a little, then taking him deep into my mouth. Adam groaned, his knees buckled, and I knew I was ready.

I looked up to see my lover's expression filled with pleasure and need, fangs bared as he panted, gazing at me with desperate entreaty in his eyes as I stroked him with my tongue, working around his length, cheeks hollowing when I sucked on his cock.

'Fuck, sweetheart, please...'

His moan was almost painful, and I tasted the saltiness of his pre-cum before I released him from my mouth.

'I love you, and I want you to make love to me. No holding back, just you being you. I trust you.'

I'd barely finished when he roared, lifting me off the floor and pressing my back to the wall. He kissed me like a man possessed, tongue sliding in my mouth and playing with mine while his hands grasped my butt, holding me effortlessly in the air.

I wrapped my legs around him, feeling his shaft rubbing against my throbbing clit. It felt so good I pressed myself harder to increase the friction.

'You will be the true death of me, Princess, and I will die happy,' Adam said, rocking his hips, but despite the head of his cock teasing my entrance, he stopped and looked at me with eyes as crimson as Veles' pit.

'Tell me you are mine, Nina. There will be no one else for me. I belong to you, my Obsidian, but make no mistake, there will be no one else for you, either. I will never share you, and I'm done pretending I would let you be with another. I will be your safe harbour, but if anyone dares to touch you, I will tear them apart in front of you. So please... tell me... you are mine, my At'kar.'

It was pure madness, but I believed every word he said. If he thought he would scare me with this vampiric version till death do us part, he was sorely mistaken. I needed this. That's why the failure of my marriage hurt so much. Deep inside, I was an old-fashioned woman who believed in everlasting love, and my winged vampire had just promised himself to me.

'Adam... I'm yours. There will be no one else, ever, but please...please fuck me.' I begged, tilting my hips.

His throaty laughter, full of dark promise, gave me goosebumps. The bastard held himself back, teasing me.

'It appears you like to dispense sensual torment but not receive it. Is that how it is, my Obsidian? Maybe I also have something to say. A long confession while my hand and tongue drive you mad.' Adam pulled away slightly, and I moaned, aroused and frustrated by his teasing.

'Adam, don't you dare...'

Now I was impatient, wrapping my legs around his hips, holding him in a death grip, trying to pull him closer. My need, my scent, did something to him. His nostrils flared before he pressed his face into the crook of my neck.

'You are mine, Nina.' He snarled, thrusting into me.

I gasped when he entered me, then paused, his breath uneven. He was stretching me, even with my arousal easing his passage, but my body adjusted.

Adam moved; it wasn't fast or brutal, but there was a finality in it. There was no space left to fill, no feelings left unanswered. I knew my future was with him, and I felt bound to him beyond any physical connection, strange emotions overwhelming me. Love, joy, freedom… hope. I raised my face to the water cascading over us to hide the tears brought to my eyes by the maelstrom inside me.

Adam rocked his hips with slow, deliberate thrusts as if he was savouring the moment, showering my neck with tiny nips and kisses. The pleasure built up each time he moved, and I moaned forlornly, begging him to take me harder.

Our breath mingled when he kissed me. His body trembled, and his moves became more insistent while I circled my hips to take him deeper, imposing a faster pace as I drew close to the edge.

'Nina,' Adam's husky voice gave a warning when I moved my hips back, only to impale myself on him a moment later.

'Bite me, my love, I want it, then fuck me hard and make me scream,' I cried, desperate for him to ravage me as I yielded to him.

My plea unleashed the beast, my back hitting the tiled wall when he rammed into me with wild abandon.

'Fuck Nina, I can't. I will hurt you… You're not thinking…' he moaned, slamming into me, but I saw his eyes burning with hunger as I rapidly approached my climax. I raised my hand, grabbed the hair on the back of his head, and pulled his mouth to my neck.

'Please…' I gasped, moaning when Adam's fangs penetrated my skin, and my climax hit me with the power of a hurricane. My body contracted around him while his venom filled my veins. He was still moving inside me while my orgasm milked his shaft, but lost in my rapture, I could only whimper when he shuddered, ramming into me as he drank my blood and came.

It was beyond perfect, my happiness so complete that I couldn't contain it, but as I sobbed, Adam instantly withdrew his fangs, his wings reappearing, filling the shower as they wrapped around me.

'Did I hurt you? If I made a mistake, I'm sorry. Tell me where it hurts. I shouldn't have lost control, not after what that bastard did to you...please, don't cry. I love you so much. I will live off bagged blood and never bite you again. I'm so sorry, my love.' There was an edge of panic in Adam's voice as if he were afraid he'd misread my intentions.

'Men,' I sniffled, hiccupping as the tears slowed. 'These are happy tears, and you will bite me again because I liked it. This... I'm not saying I'm over what happened, but I refuse to let that arsehole ruin our love. It matters what you do and how much you care. I wanted this, and I told you to do it. Even if I had any regrets, I wouldn't face them alone, but I regret nothing.' I took his face in my hands and pulled him in for a kiss.

'The pleasure your bite brings when we make love is, let's just say, I almost fainted because it was so good. I know your experience tells you I'm not the most emotionally stable person, but I'm getting there. Sometimes, it just takes a little longer to realise the happiness you seek has awfully sharp fangs. Still, we have to talk about your wings. If they keep sprouting during sex, you're going to need a bigger shower. It is crowded enough with you and me in here, and those enormous beauties have enough personality to make things awkward,' I said, and Adam flashed me the most dazzling smile before pulling an adorable pout.

'Oh, well, a bigger shower it is then. Better get used to this because wrapping you up in my wings when we make love, knowing you are entirely mine to do with as I want? I cannot think of anything more alluring. In the spirit of our mutual honesty and respect, I have to tell you, if ordering me around is all it takes to hear you moan my name so beautifully, I find myself strangely susceptible to following every word of a certain bossy woman.'

That was the Adam I knew, the arrogant arsehole who could light up a room with his smile, and he was entirely mine.

'I'm sure you'll learn just how bossy I can be, but right now, maybe you could feed me. We both know I have to call Sara before she goes full Soul Shepherd on my arse. We also need to discuss how we get my brother back and what the hell is going on with Sapieha's locket. I may be getting paranoid, but I don't like the way he looked at us... like he wanted us, and not just to soothe his anger,' I said, stepping out of the shower as soon as Adam retracted his wings.

'Here is your towel, Nina,' Lorelai appeared from nowhere, and I screamed, not knowing whether to cover my body or Adam's. As a last resort, I jerked the towel from her outstretched hand, throwing it at my vampire while I grabbed another one from the railing, wrapping it tightly around me.

'Lori, could you please not appear when we are in the bathroom or bedroom... ehh... anywhere where we're naked?'

'Why?' the spirit asked in complete innocence before her eyes flashed with understanding. 'Oh, that's why,' she said, and Sade's *Smooth Operator* blasted from the speakers.

'Oh, gods, someone kill me,' I begged, watching Adam double over, laughing.

Chapter 20

Adam

Nina was growing restless, and I couldn't blame her. After the shock of discovering the magical world two years ago, my incredible woman had taken it in her stride, settling into her new reality with confidence and a silver knuckleduster, but now? The danger posed by Sapieha left Nina trapped in my apartment with only the occasional trip to escape her growing frustration.

It had been a week since I'd broken free of the Master Vampire's control, thanks in no small part to the woman sitting next to me with a surprisingly delicate smile on her lips. It had taken that long to gather my resources to retrieve Nina's brother. I had to admit I quietly admired the little rat's skills in finding a way to hide in the Kashubian forest without being eaten or driven mad by the creatures that called that eerie domain their home. Thankfully, I didn't need to sell my soul to find Pawel. When you had a working relationship with the Alpha of the local werewolves and called their god by his first name, the price was significantly discounted. I'd been more than happy to give Tomasz a controlling interest in the largest meat supply company in order to use his pack.

So, now I had a location and several wolves hidden in the houses surrounding the one place Nina's brother frequented, a little family-owned shop that looked more like a ramshackle hut than a thriving business. All it took then was patience, and after learning his schedule, we knew he was due to visit the shop again tomorrow. Pawel would be getting a little surprise with his supplies this time, and so would Nina. As I watched her munching on the egg royale sandwiches I'd made for her, I knew just how happy she would be when I brought her brother home safely.

It's strange how much you learn about yourself when you are held captive with your life hanging by a thread. I wish I could forget the feeling of Sapieha rifling through my memories, thoughts and desires, making me suffer through countless nightmares as he searched for anything he could use. How he mocked my longing for family, my dedication to the Syndicate, and all it represents and protects. I could still feel his fangs sinking into my throat over and over as he tried to break my loyalty to the Leshy. He did it so many times that, despite my enhanced healing, it would leave a scar.

And Nina? I still couldn't believe she came for me. Out of all the supernaturals in Tricity, all the people who owed me their lives, it was her, a regular human, powerless but full of courage, who stood up to Sapieha and his thugs before Leszek arrived. The spirit, the steadfast loyalty I'd seen when we first met as she fought for Sara's life, was still there, but this time, my Obsidian fought for me.

I didn't deserve it, but I promised myself she would never regret choosing me.

My hand tightened on the cup of herbal tea I'd been sipping, and the delicate ceramic shattered, splashing liquid all over the counter.

'Adam, is everything alright?' Nina jumped off her seat, taking my hand in hers, but I'd already directed my body to heal the superficial cuts.

'It is really freaky watching you heal like that,' she commented, watching as the skin closed, completely fascinated, while I cleaned up the mess. The frown Nina gave me when I remained silent should have warned me, but I didn't elaborate.

'Don't make me guess. What triggered this? Is something wrong with the search for Pawel, or is there a problem with the Syndicate?'

'Nothing's wrong, the operation is on track, and I promise you'll see your brother tomorrow. It was just a bad memory. Nothing your tender, loving ministrations couldn't fix, Matron,' I said, giving Nina a playful smile, which just made her roll her eyes.

'Just be serious for a moment. We've been humping like a pair of randy rabbits, but I can see something's bothering you, so come on, Adam, spill.'

I held myself back, but I knew I couldn't avoid the conversation for much longer. I'd been joking when I used Nina's job title, yet whenever she used her no-nonsense Matronly tone, I knew better than to argue. I walked to the sofa and pulled Nina onto my lap, wrapping one of her colourful, fluffy blankets around us.

'I'm worried about Sapieha. He ripped open my mind with such ease, pulling out everything I wanted to hide and dissecting it. That itself gives me nightmares, but there's more. He thought he had me enthralled. That made him careless and allowed me to peek into his thoughts whenever he was distracted. He is obsessed. There is a thing vampires don't like to talk about. A sickness, or more accurately, an addiction we call the Blood Fever,' I said, pausing for a moment, savouring the feeling of Nina's fingers stroking my chest.

'There were moments I thought I was afflicted. After we split up, I could do nothing without thinking of you,' I recounted, kissing the top of her head. Nina looked up, and I saw the amusement in her dark eyes.

'Well, I'll take it as a compliment that I'm not your vampire version of herpes, but go on,' she said, and I chuckled at her joke.

'I'm still obsessed with you, my Obsidian, and I crave you with every fibre of my being, but you're free to live your life with or without me. That's the difference. However, since you insisted you're mine, I'll never let you go,' I teased, playfully tapping my finger on the tip of her nose. Nina rolled her eyes, and I heard her muttering *Yeah, right* before she snuggled closer.

'Sapieha had Blood Fever, no, he *has* Blood Fever. Even though his wife has been dead for centuries, the Prince still craves the taste of her more than he cares for the world around him. I don't know how he's survived the madness for so long without going on a rampage or being put down for the excesses the sickness usually causes.'

I shuddered at the memory of my ordeal and what I'd seen.

'When Sapieha feeds, he always picks women that remind him of his wife and... it's brutal. It's as if he's punishing his victims for not being her. He should be put down like a rabid dog, but I don't have the manpower or resources to do it. That's why I'm worried.'

'Is his search for the locket what's important, or is Sapieha so desperate for revenge that we'll have a bigger problem if we don't kill him?'

Nina's insight was spot on, and I wasn't sure I had a straightforward answer, but as she slid from my embrace to pace, it appeared she wasn't finished.

'What are we going to do about it? Is there a way to talk to him, to pay him off?' Nina looked at me, and I saw the moment she came to the same conclusion I had. 'We have to kill him. It's the only way to ensure Pawel survives,' she finished, and I nodded.

'Yes, however, therein lies the problem. Sapieha is much older than I am, and that makes him ridiculously powerful. Add in his psychic abilities, and to say we don't stand a chance is more than an understatement. What good is a pair of wings against that?'

'You could ask Leszek for help,' Nina offered, but I shook my head.

'You heard those arseholes that attacked us in the playground. I'm not recognised as the Master of Tricity Seethe. The only way to prevent a never-ending stream of challengers for the position is to sort this issue out for myself. Besides, I can't ask Leszek. His status as the Guardian is at stake. The council of gods wasn't thrilled when he gave Sara a piece of his soul, unwittingly making her a minor deity. He can't interfere in a vampiric power struggle without being accused of abusing his position.'

Nina smiled as she retorted. 'But I can ask him. I'd kneel and pray for divine intervention if it would help. They can't blame mortals for asking a god for help.' I chuckled at the image but shook my head.

'Even if you were one of his tree-hugging zhrests[16] , it would still put Leszek and me in a difficult position. I will do what I do best. We have a potential weakness, so I will find out what's so special about the silver locket and blackmail him to leave us alone. I don't want to fight him, not now, Nina. I'm not strong enough to face

---

16. *Zhrests - priests in the Slavic religion whose name literally means "one who makes sacrifices."*

him, but I'm smart enough to buy us some time, and once I build up my Seethe's power and hone my skills, I promise to take him out,' I insisted, frowning when the Lorelai appeared, announcing that we had a visitor.

I looked at my watch, accessing the lift security camera, and noticed the Coven Mistress, Veronica Sandoval, heading toward us with a sour expression on her face. I stood up, letting Nina slide to the side before I moved in front, moments before the lift door opened.

'I'm assuming you have a good explanation for demanding an obsidian athame, then forgetting to pick it up and not returning my calls?' She snapped without even saying hello. If anything, this let me know how royally pissed off she was because Veronica was so uptight she never missed an opportunity to use social pleasantries to make a person feel small.

'Hello to you too, Veronica. It appears you're losing your touch. Or are you ignoring the reappearance of an ancient Polish Prince and his obsession with kidnapping other vampires? If you're here to deliver the athame, then you have my gratitude. I will double the payment to reflect the inconvenience you've suffered,' I offered, unsuccessfully trying to keep the hostility from my voice.

'Veronica, so nice to see you. Would you care for a drink?' Nina smiled as she slipped past me to greet the Coven Mistress warmly. 'Please ignore His Grumpiness. Adam is a little twitchy since he had his arse handed to him by his sire, but it doesn't mean he can be rude to our guests,' she said before turning toward me with daggers in her eyes. 'So, my love, be a darling and make us some tea, preferably without poison.'

I saw the corner of Veronica's mouth twitching in barely re-strained amusement when she moved her gaze from me to Nina before she shook her head and burst out laughing.

'That was so worth my time. Seeing you being put in your place by a human was worth every moment of driving in city traffic,' she said, still chuckling to herself before turning to Nina. 'Good to see you again. I am, as Adam stated, here to deliver the athame he purchased for you, but if you don't mind me asking. What are you doing here? You seem too comfortable for this to be a brief visit.' Veronica was too observant for her own good, and I grimaced, trying to hide my pride as Nina answered, directing the witch to the lounge with another smile.

'I'm living here for now as Sapieha is targeting me in order to get hold of my brother,' Nina said, and I winced at how temporary her statement sounded.

'Adam moved you into his home? Interesting.' Veronica glanced at me before changing the subject. 'Your vampire mentioned you were having a little trouble when he commissioned the athame, but I assumed you needed it to keep him from being too forward.' With an amused snort, the witch placed an engraved wooden box on the table. 'Be careful with the blade. It is sinfully sharp but quite brittle. As it's not meant to keep Adam honest, you should make sure to keep it away from any part of him you find precious. Vampires cannot heal wounds made by obsidian.'

Nina looked entranced when she opened the box, gazing upon the black blade with its contrasting aspen handle. The wood almost glowed next to the reflective surface of the obsidian, and she couldn't resist tracing her finger along the blade, hissing slightly when the sharp edge cut her finger. A single droplet of blood beaded on her skin, and I closed my eyes, inhaling deeply. Her scent was so tempting, but Nina didn't invite me to taste it. Since I struggled to restrain myself when it came to her blood, I concentrated instead on the kettle, willing the appliance to boil. It wouldn't be appreciated by either woman if I lost control over something so insignificant.

'Sharp little bugger,' Nina said with a chuckle, sticking a finger in her mouth and sucking it, testing my already tenuous control as I pictured her lips on my wrist as she drank my blood, choosing to stay with me forever.

'Oh, get a grip,' I muttered through clenched teeth. I knew Nina didn't want to become a vampire, but I couldn't help fantasising about it.

'Adam?' Nina looked at me with concern as if she sensed my struggle, and I flashed her a smile.

'The tea is coming, ladies,' I said, pouring the hot water and heading over, giving Veronica the evil eye as she chuckled.

'This day will go down in history; the day Adam Lisowczyk became domesticated by a woman. Even serving tea like the perfect househusband.' The witch's tone was biting, but as used to it as I was, I had a retort ready, an insult on the tip of my tongue. However, before I could speak, Nina jumped in with a comment of her own.

'I know, right? He's amazing. One day, he kills three dangerous vampires; the next, he breaks the psychic bond of his maker. Then, to top all of that, he serves tea and makes the most heavenly pancakes. Adam is a man of many talents, and I'm lucky to have him. He can even convince the Mistress of The Coven to run a delivery service and bring me such a precious gift.' She said without even batting an eye. It was all I could do to not snatch her up from that damn sofa and cover her with kisses, telling her how much I loved her.

'Touche, my dear. He is an exceptional man, and I see he's finally met his match,' Veronica said, leaving me speechless because not once had I heard praise coming from her.

'Thank you,' I said, settling next to Nina and pulling her to my side, only for Veronica to surprise me again.

'Do you need the Coven's help?'

'No, if it comes to a confrontation, I will need to face him alone, but I appreciate the offer,' I replied, and something akin to mutual understanding passed between us.

Conversation from that point was strangely mundane and pleasant, with Nina nestled in my arms, asking questions about the athame and magic in general until Veronica bade us goodbye. As soon as the Coven Mistress left the apartment, Nina turned toward me.

'Why did you have a knife made for me that could kill you, Adam?'

'It was before you trusted me, and I needed to give you a weapon that would help you feel safe. After we found out Sapieha attacked you, it... well, if you'd never wanted to see another vampire, I'd have understood, even if it would have meant you were defenceless,' I answered and saw tears suddenly appear in Nina's eyes.

'What's wrong, love?' I asked before she pushed me down on the sofa and sat on my hips, straddling me.

'You! You happened. You are the most reckless, most romantic man I've ever met, and to give me a knife that could actually kill you? What is wrong with you?' She questioned, emphasising each word with a firm punch in the chest.

'I just wanted you to feel safe. I wanted to look after you, hoping that one day you would accept me for who I am and maybe love me enough to stay with me. If an obsidian blade could help you feel more secure, I was ready to place one under every pillow. There is nothing I wouldn't do for you. If one day you decide to take my life with this knife, it would mean I deserved it,' I said, biting my lower lip. My words came so naturally, but they still resembled an ancient vampiric oath, one I wanted to share.

'There is also a custom that a vampire will offer an obsidian dagger to his At'kar as a symbol of his absolute trust. In essence, he offers her his life to take.'

'At'kar? You called me that in the shower,' she queried, and I took her hand, placing a kiss on her fingertips.

'It felt right at the time, but I will understand if you don't like it. It means "beloved." It is an old vampiric term of endearment used only between mated couples.'

'Mates, hmm...' Nina took the knife from the box and balanced it on one finger.

I tensed when she moved it over my chest. It would only take a little pressure to pierce my heart, turning me to dust. I had never been closer to dying a true death than now, but somehow, it didn't scare me.

'My At'kar, I trust you completely,' I said, closing my eyes.

A shiver ran down my spine when the blade touched my body. I was at Nina's mercy, but instead of pain, one by one, the buttons of my shirt fell to the floor, silken thread giving way under the pressure of the blade. I opened my eyes to see my lover's expression, and Nina tilted her head, her mischievous smile widening when she pointed to my trousers with the tip of the knife.

'You're going to take those off and fuck me, or should I help myself using this knife,' she said, and I laughed, taking the obsidian blade and putting it safely back in the box.

'You're not waving that thing around my junk, young lady. Being dead, I can deal with, but being out of commission when I have such beauty in my bed is a hard pass,' I said, and as soon as the knife was secure, I flipped Nina onto her back.

'I have a meeting with Tomasz in half an hour. We need to run through the plan for your brother's retrieval, and you don't want me to miss that,' I said, kissing behind her ear.

'I won't need that long,' Nina answered, taking my hand and sliding it down into her lounge trousers. Nina was already wet and arched her back as my fingers slid through her folds, her moans so sexy that I surrendered to her desire.

'Fuck it. The damn wolf can wait,' I growled, tearing her trousers to shreds.

'Fast or slow, Princess?' I asked through clenched teeth, ripping away my own trousers, pleased when Nina's eyes widened at the sight of my cock. I knew what I wanted, but it was her call.

'Fast,' she managed, her voice breathy with need. 'Fast... and hard. I want you to fuck me like you mean it, like the man who killed three vampires with his bare hands.'

'Gods, you are perfect,' I groaned, gasping her hips and thrusting hard. She was more than ready. My shaft slid in as if we'd been fucking for hours, and I bit my lip, trying to control the overwhelming pleasure.

Nina arched her back, tilting her hips to take me deeper. I'd learned how rough she liked it, and I was more than happy to give her everything she wanted. I withdrew till my head teased her entrance, then thrust till our hips crashed together, holding still as my lover's open snapped open.

'That's it, sweetheart, I want to see your beautiful eyes,' I said, looking into her wild, desperate gaze. 'Is that how you like it? Fucked by a monster, helpless with desire and unable to escape the pleasure?' I withdrew slowly as I questioned her, then plunged deep inside, demanding my answer.

'Yes,' she answered hungrily, and I wished I could sink my fangs into her neck, tasting the metallic sweetness of her blood, but I'd fed deeply already, and Nina needed time to recover.

Instead, I manifested my wings.

Nina's moan as she saw my wings appear was filled with longing, her eyes fascinated by the light playing over the iridescent feathers, green and purple flashes shivering over their length. Even though I was almost blinded by pleasure, I noticed the wonder in Nina's eyes. She reached to touch them, but I moved them out of reach, grabbing her wrists to hold her defenceless beneath me.

'You are my everything,' I ground out, feeling my control fraying as I fucked my delicious woman.

'I know. Fuck. You are gorgeous,' she moaned, leaning forward and scraping her teeth over my chest, leaving red marks on my skin.

I wouldn't last long and struggled to control my body when Nina lost herself in desire, but I knew what this vixen wanted and bent down to lick the hard nipple she pushed toward my mouth. As soon as I sucked it into my mouth, Nina's legs wrapped around my hips, holding me tight as her ankles locked behind me and my lover impaled herself on my cock.

'You drive me wild,' I groaned, releasing her hands as Nina moved her hips. My no longer helpless lover circled her hips, taking her pleasure as I ravaged her body.

'Oh, you want it that hard,' I said, pushing her down. 'Buckle up, sweetheart, because this monster is going to fuck you until you're hoarse from screaming my name,' I said, a cruel smile on my lips. Nina whimpered when I grabbed her legs, withdrawing completely before flipping her onto her stomach.

Her heart-shaped arse looked delicious from this angle, and I slapped it hard, leaving the imprint of my hand on her milky white skin before ploughing into her. The impact pushed Nina's face into the pillow, but I heard a muffled cry, and for a moment, I thought I'd been too forceful before I heard a quiet plea.

'Please... harder.'

'Fuck, you own me, Nina. I cannot refuse you. You own my fucking soul.' I groaned, pistoning into her like a madman. I felt her clenching, speeding my own release. Suddenly Nina was sobbing, her body shaking, gripping my cock, squeezing it harder than a fist, and I plunged into her one last time, shooting inside with blinding, overwhelming pleasure before falling forward and wrapping my wings around this remarkable woman.

'I have never felt more alive than when I'm with you. You are my salvation. I will lay the world at your feet and bring you the heads of your enemies. Whatever you wish will be yours, my Obsidian. Just like my heart belongs to you,' I whispered in her ear, unwilling to move, savouring our connection.

'I only want you.' Nina answered, her breathing slowing, and I wanted to stay like this forever.

'Don't go back to your apartment. I noticed you said you were only staying here for now when Veronica asked. Nina, I want you to stay, to consider this your home. We can redecorate as you please, make everything fluffy and colourful if that's your wish. Just... please stay.'

'And if I don't?' she asked.

I couldn't restrain my sigh before giving her my answer.

'Then it will be very cramped when I move into your place, but I can live with it as long as I live with you,' I answered, and she raised an eyebrow, her expression challenging me.

'Who said I'd invite you?' There was a teasing tone in her voice that made me relax and return her challenge with a wicked smile.

'Who said I won't make you beg for me to move in? Once you accept a gorgeous vampire into your life, there's no escaping the pleasure he'll give you. You know how good it feels to fall asleep embraced by such soft, warm feathers.' I moved one wing slightly, brushing it against Nina's cheek and grinning as she pressed against it.

'Well, your feathers are nice, but who would clean up when you moult all over the place?' She asked, and for a moment, we looked at each other seriously before we burst out laughing.

'I... I'll stay, I just... you are...' Nina said, trying to catch her breath between bouts of laughter before sliding from the couch. 'Get your perky arse to the meeting. I'll take a shower, and when you get back, you can help me find a scabbard for this beauty.' She said, tapping the wooden box. I pretended to pout, but I was already late, and the Tricity Alpha was not known for his patience.

'I will prepare the bath for you, Nina.' Lorelai's voice came from the speakers, and I saw Nina's shoulder sagging slightly.

'Have you been eavesdropping again?' she asked.

'Yes, and I was looking, too. A very entertaining technique but I advise buying a bigger sofa. This one could barely accommodate...'

'What's next? Notes on my performance?' Nina muttered quietly

'Nine out of ten points. Master's knee was slipping off the edge.' Lorelai deadpanned, and Nina elbowed me in the side when I snorted, trying to contain my merriment. I had no shame, but Nina's face was burning red. Wrapping herself in the blanket, she marched to the bathroom.

'I'll either choke this bloody Spirit or put her box in a nunnery.' I heard her saying before going into my own bedroom to get dressed.

Chapter 21

I looked at the map, analysing the topography of the forest. I had to admit Pawel chose his hiding place well. It looked uninhabitable, a place no human would be expected to survive. I knew he was using this area of the primaeval forest since he'd been caught on camera heading in this direction at the train station, but at the place Tomasz indicated, there was nothing. Just before the war, it was a forest lake. Now, it was just swampland in the middle of nowhere, with nothing there even close to being a building.

'Are you sure this is the place? Did he dig a hole in the peat or something?' I asked Tomasz, who gave me a smug, superior smile.

'You may be better with computers, but I know how to track and have an entire pack almost as good. If they tell me your man is there, then he's there. I also sent a few friendly faces to question the locals. They told my wolves all about the local legend. According to the villagers, sometime in the past, before the swamp took over the lake, there was an island there with a small hut. Eventually, the hut fell to ruin, but the stone basement remained, and that's where you'll find your prey.'

'Perfect, keep your sentinels in position. We will take him from his hideout instead of the village store. It will make things easier, though I still expect some trouble. Pawel has an artefact that belongs to a powerful vampire, and the owner may try to retrieve it by any means necessary. Make sure your wolves are ready for a fight.'

I wasn't taking any chances this time, as this would be the only thing I had to bargain with.

'Make sure you have the money ready for my people, and don't worry about my fighters. They'll be ready. The forest is their home.' Tomasz said, irritation clear in his voice, and I nodded. I didn't care about the money. Years of working for the Syndicate and doing various side jobs allowed me to accumulate wealth that almost rivalled Leszek's hoard.

'I've transferred enough money to the pack's account to cover this job three times over, but make sure your team knows Pawel must be handled with kid gloves. No bites, scratches or bruises, please,' I instructed, and Tomasz laughed, getting ready to leave.

'Spoilsport. You're getting soft in your old age, but fine, we won't nibble on. You will still be in your nurse's good graces once we drag the rat from his hole.'

As soon as I was left alone, I travelled to Syndicate's downtown office. I needed to check for any reports of unusual activity in Tricity. I wasn't so naïve to believe Sapieha would peacefully leave my territory just because Leszek told him to. After what I saw whilst held captive, I knew the Master Vampire was obsessive and beyond caring.

From the moment I'd watched Sapieha stroking the marble sculpture of his dead lover, the way he'd spoken of her with a mixture of love and hatred, I'd known exactly why he was so dangerous. The man was affected by the Blood Fever and would stop at nothing to find the necklace stolen from his wife's body, then punish all those who lay their hands on her crumbling bones. *Am I any better?* I wondered. There was no way I'd let the bastard get away with his assault on Nina. Sapieha would die, maybe not tomorrow, or even in a month, but die, he would.

I'd never cared for power or vampire politics, but a week in his company was enough to convince me I needed both if I wanted to avoid being powerless and on my knees. I would build up my Seethe, and when I was sure we could win, I would attack.

Nina might recover from his assault, and she had, thankfully, already taken those essential first steps, but I wouldn't. What he did to her was unforgivable, and there was no doubt I would separate his head from his shoulders, not only for sinking his fangs into my woman's neck but also for treating my city as his own personal playground.

I shook my head, trying to clear my thoughts and push away the burning anger. *Focus, Adam. Get the locket from Pawel and leave him to Nina's tender care.* She was angry enough with her brother that he'd regret his latest fuck up. The problem was, would using the locket to force Sapieha to leave actually work?

Once I had it in my hands, I'd at least be able to examine the damn thing. *Maybe Sara can help, use her magic to see if the Master Vampire will honour his word,* I thought, but instantly dismissed it. Leszek clearly stated he didn't want Sara to be put at risk, and the only thing that could genuinely enrage the Forest Lord was someone placing his Firefly in danger.

I closed another window on the computer. None of the recent reports mentioned anything unusual. No new arrivals, strange emergency calls or bodies floating in the Motlawa River. Even the Gates to the Nether realm were uncommonly quiet. I briefly spoke with Nadolny, Leszek's human counterpart, but he had nothing to report either, and that worried me. Gdansk was never peaceful. Since Leszek's powers had been restored and Sara's became stronger, Tricity had become the hub for the magical community in Eastern Europe, attracting many supernatural beings. This quiet felt too much like the calm before the storm.

I signed off on the few projects awaiting my approval, noticing that in my absence, Leszek had been more lenient than usual in his rulings. I was grateful for his help, but his attitude was bound to cause problems in the future. When I was done, I phoned my

Seethe's compound, confirming the details with Brygid, my second-in-command for the operation the next day.

My Seethe was based in Oliwa, a convenient location I'd actually chosen on a whim in the first year of my new life. The small villa was surrounded by churches and places of worship, and I'd half hoped some avenging priest would put an end to my miserable existence. Instead, I'd ended up protecting the area after a chance meeting with a rabbi. The old man was being beaten up, and I'd stepped in using the opportunity to feed. I'd expected condemnation from the rabbi; instead, he'd offered me a blessing. Somehow, we became friends, and I stayed in the area till my friend died of old age.

My reputation had drawn several weary vampires to join me, each grateful to escape the absolute obedience demanded in other Seethes. When I left to travel as an amber merchant, I gave them the villa, simply asking them to support the other Elder Races and agree to abide by Leszek's rule to never kill whilst feeding.

The last task for today was one I wished I could put off. My mind went blank whenever I wondered how to convince Nina to stay home during tomorrow's operation. I knew that for her safety, I would most likely have to hurt her feelings, but knowing it was the right thing to do didn't make it any easier.

Nina was stubborn and protective, and she would argue she needed to be there to ensure Pawel's safety and compliance. She was right, but the memory of her attacking four vampires on my motorcycle was burned into my mind, and I couldn't have a repeat of that. I was too afraid she would die if Sapieha once again incapacitated me with his magic.

I returned home to the sound of Nina screaming curses at my computer as she mashed the keys on the expensive keyboard. The image on the screen was one of bloody carnage as an animated and surprisingly busty version of my lover ripped apart a werewolf with a whip and a sickle. With a whoop, she punched the air, turning around at my polite cough, her grin wide as she pointed toward the screen.

'Now that's what I'm talking about. You don't mess with Nina, the Destroyer, and not pay the price.' With a casual click of the mouse, Nina closed the game down and stood to give me a slow, lingering kiss. 'So how did it go? Are we still a go for tomorrow?' she asked.

'Tomasz located your brother, and we are ready to retrieve him. It's in an almost inaccessible part of the forest, so we're heading in early to take advantage of the daylight,' I said, sliding my hands up Nina's spine and enjoying her shiver as we kissed again. 'Care to help me in the kitchen? I bought something nice for dinner.'

It wasn't my best idea to change the subject, but it was all I could come up with. Part of me hoped that if I satiated Nina's hunger, this conversation would be easier.

'Sure. Do you have any combat gear that would fit me, or should I use my bike gear? Oh, and I'd better take the dagger you gave me. Just in case Sapieha shows up,' she said, smiling while I braced myself to break the news.

Nina kept talking whilst taking out the fresh produce I'd brought home. She must have sensed there was a problem from my silence because she grabbed my hand and looked at me with a question in her piercing eyes.

'You can't go with me. I'm sorry, but you would be a liability,' I said, watching Nina's eyes widen. I promptly raised my hands in a gesture of surrender. 'I know Pawel's your brother, but we are going deep into the forest. If Sapieha attacks us there, I have to be able to focus on fighting him, not defending you.'

Nina carefully put a box of eggs on the counter, but judging by her tense shoulders, she wasn't happy with my explanation.

'What about Tomasz's pack, the members of your Seethe? What about my brother? How are they, not liabilities? It's not like any of them can resist if that arsehole decides to mind-fuck them. What is it, Adam? Are you sidelining me because I'm human, because I'm your girlfriend, or maybe because he fucked me up once already, and you're afraid I liked it?'

I felt like an arsehole when her voice trembled at the end, but I couldn't give in. Nina was human, brave, resourceful, and loyal to her very last bone, but still a human with no magic and no combat skills. She was a liability, but I had to soften the blow. I came closer and put a finger under her chin, tilting her head up to look at me.

Nina initially struggled but finally surrendered, and I saw she was trying to blink away tears.

'None of those. I am at fault. The wolves and vampires can fight for themselves, your brother.... I don't really care what happens to him, but if I see you in danger, I will let every single one of them die before I allow you to be harmed. You are strong and capable. You stay calm and level-headed in difficult situations. You even saved my arse when I was forced into submission by Sapieha's psychic abilities, but you are my weakness. Don't belittle yourself because I am a weak man,' I said, stroking her beautiful face.

'What? I don't understand....'

'I can't think clearly when you're around. Everything I've built, everything I own, and the people who depend on me are important, but on the scales of my life, none of that matters because you are everything to me. The mere thought of you being hurt brings out the worst of me. I will kill for you, I will die for you, but I cannot lose you. Please, for your brother's sake and mine, stay in the apartment.' I kissed her, hoping that telling her the truth would change her mind, but Nina stiffened in my embrace.

'I wish I had a hint of magic in my veins. I could help you instead of being a burden,' Nina said before straightening her back. 'I'm sorry for my outburst. Please understand. It's my messed up family that caused all this, and I don't like that instead of doing something about it, I'm being forced to stay behind like some pathetic damsel in distress. I've fought for my place all my life. Now I feel like everybody else is moving on, and I'm stuck looking on from the sidelines,' she said, and I saw tears glistening in her eyes.

'You are not pathetic, far from it. Nina, please... don't cry, my love.'

I was at a loss. Why couldn't I keep Nina safe and happy at the same time? Why did it have to be a choice? My thoughts were racing, trying to find the best way to console her. I hadn't realised she felt that way and how much this temporary isolation in my penthouse affected her. I stilled when she pushed at my arms to free herself from my embrace, then reluctantly let her go. I hadn't seen her so tense since I'd invited her to the restaurant to discuss our contract.

'I will stay here because it's the reasonable thing to do, but as soon as we find Pawel and get Sapieha off of his back, we need to talk. I want to be with you, but not like this. I don't want to be your porcelain doll, observing the world as it passes me by. If you can't deal with that, then we can't....' Nina faltered at the last, and I instantly pulled her back, silencing the rest of her words with a kiss.

Nina was right, and I intended to give her as much freedom as I could, but as long as she remained human, there would be a part of my life she couldn't share. Sapieha's obsession opened my eyes to what Nina had always said was the biggest hindrance to our relationship.

Nina was human, and I was a vampire. She would wither and die while I remained ever youthful... unless she allowed me to turn her. I wouldn't force this change on her, but there was one secret I would never reveal. If my love died, her soul travelling beyond the Veil, she would not journey alone. I would not suffer the loneliness and madness of Sapieha's existence.

'We will talk, I promise. We will make it work, and I may even allow you to scratch me a few times if you promise to kiss them better afterwards,' I said, trying to ease the tense atmosphere, but when Nina looked up, daggers in her eyes, I backed up.

'Good, and stop calling me Princess,' she said with the cutest pout.

'Of course, my Queen, whatever the lady commands.' I said, ducking when Nina lunged forward to stake me with a crooked carrot.

The next day came much too soon for my liking. I could feel the unmistakable warmth of the rising sun even through the tightly drawn curtains. Nina was still asleep, and I turned my head, looking at the woman cuddling to my chest. She was perfect. She was my life, and leaning over, I placed a gentle kiss on her forehead before sliding off the bed.

'Come back to me in one piece, bloodsucker,' she murmured, reaching for my hand, and I couldn't help smiling.

'Always, my love,' I replied, lingering a little longer, unwilling to leave her.

Once I'd dragged myself away, I dressed quickly in combat gear and went to the kitchen, noticing the house spirit had already started the coffeemaker.

'Lorelai, ensure the house is secure after I leave. Monitor all movement in the basement. No one except the Forest Lord can enter this house until I come back,' I commanded, and sudden tension in the air told me the kikimora understood the gravity of the situation.

I went to the Syndicate office to meet Tomasz, who turned up with a Żmija, an old army reconnaissance vehicle that his mate called his big-boy toy, driving us to the Kashubian Forest with the proudest smile on his face. It wasn't the best day to stroll in the swamp. The sun barely showed itself from behind the clouds crowding in from the sea, making the air feel heavy with moisture, but the Żmija got us a fair distance before we needed to rely on stealth.

We met the rest of the Alpha's team and a few fighters from my Seethe in a small clearing deep in the forest, the mud making everyone annoyed and surly.

As we headed further into the swamp, I heard the muttered curses of annoyed shifters each time condensation fell from the tree branches, sliding beneath their collars.

'It's starting to smell like wet dog and snot,' said one of my vampires, and I sent him a thunderous look.

'It'll soon start smelling like vampire blood and ripped entrails if you don't shut up,' I growled, watching him visibly pale.

'How far do we have to go?' I asked after grabbing Tomasz's attention, and the Alpha nodded toward where the gaps between the trees widened.

'We're almost there. I've sent a group to secure the other side of the swamp. How do you want to do this? Should I send my team to drag the rat out kicking and screaming, or are we going to walk in and politely ask him to join us?'

'Neither. I'll walk in and ask Pawel politely to visit his sister. He won't refuse. I don't think we've been followed, but just in case, keep your men out of sight and ready to fight,' I said, considering whether to manifest my wings, but in the end, I decided against it. I could unfurl them in moments, and I suspected Pawel would be calmer if he saw a human, not a winged demon.

Tomasz nodded, and I trudged toward the centre of the swamp. I could see broken wooden posts with hints of dressed stone hidden beneath the tall reed grass.

I cursed as I stumbled, slipping from the broken path into rancid, muddy water.

'Fuck,' I muttered as my wings tore through my clothing, my sigh of frustration loud enough to make the werewolves snigger. Still, there was no point worrying, and I used them to lift myself from the grip of the mud, grimacing at the squelching as my leg was released.

'Stay where you are or I will shoot you, I swear, I'll fucking shoot you!' The voice, muffled as if spoken from the depths of the grave, was panicked, so I held my hands up to show I had no weapons as I settled on the path.

'Hello Pawel, we both know shooting me won't make a difference,' I said, slowly moving forward, making sure my wings were clearly visible. 'If anything, Nina would be upset that you'd injured her favourite vampire.'

A hidden door burst open, revealing the emaciated figure of a young man who looked around with terrified, blood-shot eyes.

'Nina? If you've hurt her, you motherfucker, I'll fucking kill you,' He rasped, raising his weapon in one shaky hand.

'Your sister is safe in my apartment, and if you want to see her, you...' The gunshot reverberated throughout the forest, and my flank exploded in agony.

It was a weapon designed to kill humans, but having something tear into your body at the speed of sound still hurt, and I was airborne before I realised. I had Pawel's throat in my clawed fist as I lifted him off the ground. The damn fool whimpered, and I dropped him, landing next to his prone body, giving a quick kick as he attempted to crawl away.

I closed my eyes against the pain, shifting partially into the Shadow Realm, allowing my body a moment to expel the small projectile and begin healing. I tried to ignore the begging from my erstwhile attacker, but it was difficult.

'Please...please don't kill me, I'm sorry, I didn't mean it. Ask Nina, she knows me. I'm so sorry.' Pawel repeated mechanically, his gaze fixed on my bleeding side.

'I'm not your enemy, but the longer you're here, the more likely your last victim will appear to collect his property and payment in blood. Get up because I promised I would deliver you to your sister, but nobody said anything about you being in one piece.'

My words hit Pawel as hard as the bullet had struck me, and Nina's brother fell back, looking around like a cornered animal. Not that I felt any pity for him, only a twinge of uneasiness when his pale blue eyes caught mine.

'Is Nina... God, what have I done? How did she... did you take her blood?' He asked, and I couldn't help feeling guilty about Nina's original offer.

'She's fine,' I answered, annoyed that this thief was making me feel bad when he caused this whole mess. I leaned down and grabbed him by the collar, lifting him effortlessly. 'Do you still have the necklace?' I asked, feeling uneasy.

I didn't like it here. It was too quiet, too peaceful. It all was too simple, with no trap, no attack. The ease of this retrieval was making me worry. I'd come here with a small army, expecting to face Sapieha's forces, and all that happened was a trembling fool accidentally shooting a gun and rolling in the mud.

'Yes, it's here,' Pawel answered, pulling a dirty silver chain from his pocket.

I grabbed it, hissing when its protective magic hit me, almost freezing my hand to the bone. Nina told me that Sara couldn't find Pawel through scrying. Now I knew why and how Pawel had managed to hide so well. The magic in this artefact was so strong that if not for modern technology and a shifter's nose, I would never have been able to find him.

I wanted to see what was hidden inside, but as soon as I touched the lock, a wave of nausea brought me to my knees, almost making me pass out. This little thing had more wards than my apartment, and I'd need Coven witches or even Leszek himself to help me deal with it.

That also meant Sapieha wouldn't find us here. Instead, he'd likely wait until I retrieved both the necklace and the thief, delivering them into whatever trap he'd laid in Gdansk.

I needed a safe house and a diversion until I knew what I was dealing with.

I grabbed Pawel by his shoulder in one hand while the other held onto the necklace and walked toward Tomasz.

'Take your men and return to Tricity in three teams. Make it loud and visible. I need to take this one and his little trinket to the Coven,' I said, Tomasz nodding at my order.

'Fine, just don't die, bloodsucker. I don't want to explain to Leszek why you died on my watch,' he replied, and I rolled my eyes.

'Too late for that, so leave me a car and bugger off. It really does smell like wet dog here.'

Chapter 22

NINA

Adam had left, and I was stuck here, a virtual prisoner, which did nothing for my feelings of helplessness and failure. I hated having others fight my battles, but while I couldn't fault his reasons, I still wanted to punch the damn vampire for pointing them out. I didn't have Sara's foresight or time manipulation abilities and no special skills or magic like the Elder Races. Except for a few boxing moves and self-defence classes I'd taken after Kosovo, I didn't even know how to fight.

I was a boring, ordinary human who had fallen in love with a vampire that, for whatever reason, returned those feelings. Talk about feeling inadequate. Adam treated me like a strong, independent woman right up to the moment my safety was involved, then it was off to my ivory tower like a fairytale princess. It made it very difficult to be angry at him, but I was managing.

My phone chimed with a message just as my pillow took another punch to its smug vampire face, and I instantly grabbed it.

Has Adam found my brother already?

The message came from the hospital service, and I frowned while reading it. I'd told the team I was off to deal with a family crisis, and that was the one time the staff would never disturb you. Yet, the message was definitely from the clinic.

'Hi Nina, sorry for asking, but we have a problem. Please call ASAP.'

It was a simple, brief text, but I was calling without hesitation. If the clinic staff were disturbing me, then the shit must have really hit the fan. Of course, it didn't hurt that this was the perfect opportunity to take my mind off my own situation.

The call was answered in record time, and I nearly jumped at the greeting.

'Hi, it's Nina. Please tell me no one's eaten a patient.'

'Nina? Thank the gods. I mean, really, thank you for calling back. I'm so sorry to bother you, but we have a problem.' I heard the edge of panic in the manager's voice and instantly sat up straighter.

'What kind of problem?'

'I don't know how, but a water pipe burst in the basement. Before we knew it, storage and the archives were flooded. We lost everything. I had to report us as closed, but no one informed the ambulance service, and they keep turning up with patients and... fuck Nina, it's such a mess.' I slowly exhaled at the explanation, as garbled as it was.

'Set up a fast triage area and send away anyone able to walk under their own steam. I'm on my way.'

I ended the call, a shiver of foreboding running down my spine, but it didn't matter; this was too important. If this were some ploy to get me out of the apartment, then they'd get Matron Nina Zalewska, and Lord help them if they tried to stop me.

I quickly changed and went to the living room.

'Lori, when Adam returns, please tell him I went to the hospital,' I said to the Spirit, pulling my heavy boots on. My gaze fell on the carved box containing the dagger capable of killing a vampire. I smiled at my thoughts. Adam gave it to me to help me feel safe in his company and for his surprisingly sexy *vampiric mating* ritual, but I didn't need protection from him. My personal bloodsucker may be brutal to his enemies and may have a talent for being an arsehole, but for me, he was always gentle.

I picked up the knife and the leather scabbard I noticed beneath the fabric padding. It looked very mystical, covered with swirls and runes. Witches preferred to wear their athames like necklaces with the blade resting over their hearts rather than as knives at the belt, and I copied their style.

'Nina, you must stay! Master won't like it. I can't let you go.' Lorelai appeared in front of me, looking at me with a deep frown on her ageless face.

'Did he tell you to keep me imprisoned?' I asked, trying to find out the truth before I jumped to conclusions and killed him with the very knife he gave me.

'No,'

'Then what exactly were his instructions?'

'To guard the penthouse and prevent anyone other than him and the Forest Lord from entering,' she answered, and I felt I could breathe again. Adam would protect me with his life, but he hadn't imprisoned me, and I wholeheartedly welcomed such possessiveness.

'See? You're doing nothing wrong. Follow his orders, but please pass on my message and let him know I took the dagger just in case,' I said, throwing a leather jacket on my back. 'Oh, and that I took the bike again.'

The feeling of freedom as I rode Adam's bike was cathartic but far too brief. If not for the fact that there was an emergency, I would have simply let the road carry me wherever it chose; the rush of the wind and salty tang of the Baltic always took me on the greatest of adventures.

I parked the bike in front of the hospital and promised myself that as soon as my life had some semblance of order, I'd take Adam to the cliffs and have a picnic there, looking out at the stormy sea.

In the meantime, I had to tackle the problem at hand. The hospital entrance was heaving, people rushing back and forth with building materials or water-logged supplies, storing them in old army tents that must have been borrowed from the surplus store around the corner. All of this was being watched over by hulking men and women openly carrying highly illegal automatic weapons who scowled at anyone they didn't recognise.

'Right!' I said, diving right in, nodding to the relieved personnel as they greeted me.

It took us the whole day to organise the chaos, and although I worked hard, it was a blessing in disguise. I didn't think about Adam or my brother once, trusting my vampire to do what he promised while I did my job.

Tackling the chaos gave me a boost of confidence. This was something I was good at, and after days in lockdown, I finally felt useful again. The pipe was repaired, although the plumbers were very cryptic about what caused the problem in the first place. Supplies were sorted into salvageable and non-salvageable piles. As we had all the paper files backed up in our computer system with servers located outside of the hospital, all thanks to Adam's intervention earlier during his unique pursuit of me, we didn't lose any data. So, I blissfully ordered a small bonfire to be lit for the damaged records.

The last of the sun's golden light was disappearing over the horizon when I sat down in my office, stretching out and enjoying the view from the bay window. Spring was in glorious bloom in our little haven, the first bright green leaves sprouting on the trees with snowcaps and daffodils breaching the clinic's lawn.

The sun, low over the horizon, gave the waters of Gdansk Bay a golden red hue. I didn't turn on the light just yet, wanting to enjoy the soft shadows in my office together with the tranquil surroundings. I loved this place. The shelved walls, full of medical journals and administrative folders, and a large desk with a crinkly leather chair were all mine. My safe space, and I didn't realise how much I'd missed it.

The clinic would stay closed until tomorrow, with giant heaters in the basement drying the walls, and as the last people left the building, only two members of security and I remained. I wasn't in a rush to leave, despite knowing it was time to go home and meet my brother. The anxiety that vanished during hard labour returned with a vengeance, and I pulled out my phone.

'Hello Nina, so nice to see you again,' the voice, with its distinctive French accent, whispered in my ear. The phone fell from my shaking hand. I bit my lip to stop myself from screaming while my mind went blank for a moment.

No,

Please, no, how did he get here?

The voice that haunted my nightmares, its owner standing behind me, so close his breath whispered over my ear while his hand slid around my waist, pulling back against the creaking chair. His fangs lightly scraped over my throat, so close to my carotid artery that I trembled like a helpless rabbit, frozen in terror. I heard Sapieha chuckle as he enjoyed my fear, but all I could do was whimper, realising I was alone with an absolute monster and no cavalry would arrive to save the day this time.

The arm around my waist slid over my shuddering body to my shoulder as Sapieha moved to stand in front of me.

'That's my girl. Now, you will do exactly what I tell you. Pick up your phone and call my rebellious spawn. He has something that belongs to me, and it would be impolite not to tell him I have something of his.' The vampire spoke with such calm composure that I struggled to realise what he was saying, horror making me slow.

The memory of Sapieha's threat in the forest flickered before my eyes. I knew I was going to die, and all I could do for those I loved was die alone.

'No, I won't lure him into your trap,' I retorted, bravado steadying my voice as I defied him.

'I can make you, Nina. I can even make you like it. Do you want to feel me in your mind that much?' He asked.

I felt something strange, a darkness pressing against my thoughts, and bile rose in my throat to burn the back of my tongue. I swallowed it back, refusing to surrender. I gathered my courage, and I looked into the Master Vampire's eyes.

It was a mistake. I knew it as soon as our eyes met. His soulless gaze was even more frightening with its lack of emotion, only a mild curiosity giving them a false sense of life as I pushed his hand away in defiance.

'Why are you doing this? You know Adam will destroy you for this, and Leszek... he told you to leave his land. Do you think he will forgive your disobedience? He's a god, for fuck's sake. For you, I'm nobody, but I'm loved by a strong vampire and am friends with the most powerful beings in the country. There's no way you'll survive this. Why are you risking death for revenge?' I asked, and he tilted his head before extending his hand to touch my cheek. I managed to brace myself to avoid flinching but couldn't stop the shiver down my spine.

'Foolish child, a nobody like you has the power to break even the strongest of men. Maria, my wife, was my everything. She knew it, but she wanted a child more than she wanted me. She promised to join me once she delivered our son, but ultimately, she chose death over me. She broke her promise, and I refuse to allow her any peace until I find mine.' My jaw dropped at Sapieha's rant, completely at a loss for how to deal with him.

'I'm not your wife,' I said warily, regretting it when his fingers stopped stroking and started squeezing my jaw.

'No, you are not, but just like her, you refused Adam. I gave you time. When you freed him from my power... it made me curious. I wanted to see if he succeeded where I failed, but no. You are still entirely human, toying with his emotions. If you loved Adam, you would join him in eternity, but no, you are happy to see the light die in his eyes at your passing.'

He pulled me so close our lips almost touched, reminding me of the unwanted pleasure he'd forced on me. My breath hitched, and despite trying to control my muscles, I was shaking like a leaf, unable to say a word.

'I will turn you for him, Nina. He will follow you because the fool loves you. I will have you both in my Seethe and in my bed. You, my sweet, beautiful Nina, will show me how to love again. Maybe then I will be strong enough to get rid of her.'

Sapieha grabbed the hand I was still using to push him away and forced it beneath the collar of his shirt, pushing it down till my fingers rested on a cold, round pendant.

I turned away, refusing to be a part of whatever sick game he was playing, but his free hand grabbed my hair and forced my gaze downward.

I glanced to where my hand lay, noticing the golden locket, almost the twin of the one Pawel tried to give me, except for Pawel's being silver and less worn. I could tell the vampire never removed this piece, as its decoration was almost rubbed away entirely.

'Her lies condemned me to this empty existence, but I punished Maria for her crimes. I carry her heart with me, a small piece entombed in amber and necromancy spells. Maria cannot cross the Veil until my death, our souls entwined forever. I came here to punish your brother and retrieve the piece of my heart entombed with my love, but thanks to you and your foolish lover, I have found a new reason to live.'

I hadn't realised the Master Vampire was still connected to my mind until his unguarded memories flooded my head.

I held a woman in my arms, no, not my arms, Sapieha's. He held the woman tenderly as the pallor of death stole over her features. The moment seemed to last forever until, with a wordless cry, the vampire reared back and stabbed the dead woman in the heart with a stiletto knife. The words Sapieha said next made no sense, their meaning lost even to the vampire, but as he spoke, he twisted the knife and tore it from her body. A small piece of tissue remained on the blade, and he took it to an altar, laying it carefully on a delicate-looking obsidian plate.

The following image shook me to the core. Sapieha plunged the same bloody knife into his own chest, repeating the procedure. It was clearly the ritual he'd spoken about, so twisted and dark that I gasped, shifting backwards, but Sapieha's hands tightened their grip.

'Now you know, I let you see because I wanted you to know why your brother must die, why I need the locket back. I am a monster, my pet. Your mistake was to show me how lonely I was. Pick up the phone, Nina. My Adam has your brother, and it is time for us to finally meet,' he said, and the mental cage around my mind tightened.

I saw my hand reaching out and dialling Adam's number, helpless to stop it.

'Nina? Hey love, I'll be home soon. Pawel is safe, so please don't worry. This locket is strange, and I need to check on a few things before I bring it home. Do you need anything?' he said, pausing and waiting for me to answer.

'Nina? Is everything all right?' I could hear the growing concern in his voice.

I was quiet. My body trembled as I fought the mental command to lure Adam here, resisting the best I could, tears streaming from my eyes.

'Sapieha's here... don't come.' I croaked, forcing the words through clenched teeth. With a disappointed shake of his head, the vampire calmly took the phone from my hand, bringing it to his ear.

'Nina is a very naughty girl. If you don't want her to learn how I punish disobedient children, you will come to her hospital. No tricks, Adam. Only you and the thief. Don't forget my locket,' he said, and I heard Adam release a stream of curses.

'If you hurt her, I will hunt you down. The entire Syndicate will fucking hunt you down. I don't care who you are and if this causes a war. I will burn your nest to the ground. I will fucking destroy you until not even the wind that blows your ashes away will remember your name. Do you hear me? Touch her, and you die.'

'Then you had better hurry. Nina is alive and unharmed. We are just getting to know one another for now, but you know I am not a patient man. Oh, and don't even think of bringing that savage of a god with you if you want to see your woman alive.'

As soon as the conversation ended, Sapieha turned in my direction.

'How strange that I see myself in him. He is a powerful man, willing to destroy the world for his woman. A fine vampire and yet a foolish one. You will make an excellent leash for him because if he strays, you will suffer,' he said, and I felt chills running down my spine. The only thing good about it was that his mental hold on me relaxed, and I was finally able to speak freely.

'You're insane. Adam will never serve you, not even for me. You can't control him, just as you couldn't control your wife,' I said, and he sent me an indulgent smile.

'My poor Nina, you will learn. A man will fight to the last breath if you threaten his life, but threaten those he loves?' Sapieha's chuckle was chilling, and I fell back, horrified. 'Sit down, child. We should relax as we wait for your brother and Adam. Later will be the time for pain and woe, but I want to enjoy a moment of peace with you now, listening to the sweet beating of your heart.'

Peace, pain, and woe in the same breath. This man is as mad as a hatter. I thought, studying him but still obeying for the moment. I fell back into my chair, pushing it away for a little breathing space.

'What are you going to do?' I asked quietly, looking at the man who could lock my mind in a steel vice at any moment.

'I'm going to kill your brother, then I will drain you, letting my spawn wallow in despair while I take every drop of your blood. That would be a suitable punishment for his disobedience, but don't worry; I will allow you to be reborn. I will even ensure Adam knows he can still have you... if he follows me. I will make the experience pleasant for you, just like I did last time. When you resurrect... we will enjoy you together,' the vampire said with a dreamy smile on his face, and I couldn't help but shudder. Sapieha had a perverted idea of love, but the worst was that he genuinely seemed to believe what he was saying.

'Do you have a death wish? Adam will never agree to this and certainly won't share anything with you.'

'No child, no vampire wants their second death. Nothing waits for us on the other side of the Veil. No peace, no afterlife, no rebirth. We simply cease to exist. We only have one existence, and once I take my revenge and secure the locket, I will spend the rest of eternity with you and Adam, and I will ensure you learn to like it,' he said before his power swept over me.

'Be still and be quiet. It won't take long now until your lover arrives.'

CHAPTER 23

The phone call from Nina left me stunned. I'd been in the Coven manor, sitting impatiently in a comfortable leather chair, one eye on Pawel and his twitching knee. I hadn't expected it to take so long, but Veronica's witches had been trying to crack open the locket for several hours now, and it hadn't helped to calm my nerves.

The spell was ancient, the engravings worn away by time and challenging to decipher. Worst of all, it was warded by a type of vampire magic I didn't recognise, which left the women working on it cursing in several languages. If I weren't so desperate to learn its secrets, it would have been amusing, but I felt the growing need to go home.

Amidst all this, the last thing I expected was Nina warning me she was held hostage by my enemy.

When the conversation ended, I stared at the phone, its protective case cracked by my anger as I fought the urge to smash the damned thing against the wall. I still needed it, though, and with a sigh, I scrolled to Leszek's emergency contact. A few moments later, I was directed to an automatic response. I tried Sara's, to no avail, before I dialled their landline.

'What do you want, Adam?' It was Michal, Leszek's assistant.

'Where's the boss? It's urgent.'

'Good question. I'm guessing he's still in Gedania, as he and Sara got summoned for a Council meeting. What do you need?' He asked.

I cursed, unable to stop myself. Gedania, the mirror city of Gdansk, existed behind the Gates of the Nether, and no modern technology could reach it. I could travel there if I had to, but not to Temple Hill, and I couldn't walk into a Divine Council session and demand the Forest Lord come to my aid.

'Nothing you can help with, but when they return, tell Leszek Sapieha has Nina at the clinic, and I'm going after her.' I ended the conversation, turning toward Pawel, who'd eavesdropped on my exchange with wide eyes.

'Get up! If something happens to Nina, I'll kill you myself, so go to the car and don't try escaping. I can't promise to keep you alive, but for Nina, I will try. Give me any trouble, and I'll let Sapieha rip you apart.'

He paled but nodded, moving toward my parked vehicle while I went to retrieve the locket. The Coven Mistress protested, but I didn't give her a choice. Open or closed, I needed it with me. If I was lucky, I could persuade Sapieha to exchange the locket and Pawel for Nina. She might hate me for it, but if it kept her alive, I was more than happy to trade her brother's life for hers.

It was a quick journey. I drove like a maniac. Tomasz's off-road car was unwieldy on the streets of the city, but people were too scared to argue when I pushed out into traffic or cut off their precious little babies. Pawel kept his mouth shut the entire journey, and after his third fearful squeak, I was grateful for small mercies. It was only as we entered the docklands that he tried talking.

'Will you look after her? I heard what you said on the phone. You love Nina, don't you? When I'm gone, she'll have no one. Promise me you'll look after her,' he babbled.

I turned to look at Pawel, measuring the dirty and starved human in front of me.

'A little late for brotherly love, don't you think? Besides, Nina has a family, and they're better than the people who share her blood,' I retorted, and he shrugged.

'Better late than never. Still, she needs a man in her life, someone who can protect her. We both know this arsehole won't let me live, and you know what? Fuck it. I'm tired. I've never made a good choice in my life, and living like this? I'm just tired. If my death can buy Nina's life, then at least I'll have done something worthwhile. So promise me because I know your word means something, not like that useless wanker of an ex-husband.'

I should have told him that Nina didn't need anyone to protect her. That she was the one who protected others, a strong, battle-scarred, but triumphant warrior. I could have rubbed it in, pointing out she'd shielded him his whole life and that he was no better than her ex, scrounging money for drugs and gambling. In the end, I said nothing because even this small amount of love he had for Nina could help her if he lived or be a consolation after he was gone.

'I promise. Now shift your arse, because the longer she's in his company, the more likely she is to get hurt.' I said, stopping the car in front of the hospital. Even in a deepening dusk, I noticed the welcoming committee.

The entrance to the hospital stood open. Aluminium framed tinted glass marked with traces of blood. I could smell its metallic scent even at this distance, and the vampires in front of me looked like they'd recently fed, their skin flushed with a soft pink hue.

As I suspected, our shifter security hadn't stood a chance against a psychic vampire and his enforcers. I hoped the two men hadn't been aware when their throats were ripped out. Their healing ability would have made their suffering endless, but I had no delusion about Sapieha's views on mercy. The former Prince was from a time where might meant right, and he'd always been right.

The locket felt heavier in my hand, the silver so cold that it burned me as I wrapped the chain tighter around my fingers. Would it be enough?

'Follow me and remember to stay quiet,' I said, exhaling slowly before opening the car door.

The smell of damp and burned paper, with the sight of a pile of wet supplies, confused me as I stepped out of the car. The quiet hum of fans coming from the basement helped me figure out what had happened. They'd used a problem with the clinic to draw Nina out, and she rushed here without a care for her own safety.

My wonderful, selfless woman, and she was surprised I was so protective of her.

Whatever they'd done, the clinic was now as quiet as a tomb. Here, with night falling, the sun was out of sight but still painting the sky with the bright shade of blood, a dark omen for those who believed in such.

It felt as if the magic of the Nether had seeped through into the human realm, eddies of dust stirred by the breeze from the Baltic, giving the emptiness a life of its own.

However, the feeling of emptiness was an illusion broken by the five vampires standing guard at the building entrance.

'Remember to stay out of the way,' I told Pawel, who wrapped his arms around himself, his breathing fast and shallow. I hoped he'd stay calm, as he had to live long enough to be useful. I had enough on my plate without defending him if he did something stupid.

'Did you bring us a snack, Lisowczyk? Such a good boy, especially as the Master refused to share the delicious morsel he has inside.'

The group's spokesperson knew my surname, but I didn't know his, except for the knowledge that he was an Elder Vampire who'd stayed bound to Sapieha despite his own strength. That made him second only to the Prince in the Seethe's hierarchy.

Still, nothing and no one would keep me from Nina. I tensed my shoulders, and in a show of strength and control, I slowly manifested my wings. My features remained expressionless as the razor-sharp feathers tore through my flesh, growing and expanding until they stood out at full stretch, shining with my blood.

'I have no time for your games, old man. Get out of my way or die. I don't care which.' I said, without a hint of emotion.

I was alone, and there were five of them. I'd bet my wings Sapieha hadn't used newly turned novices. At least two of them had the presence and bearing of Elder Vampires, likely with their own powers. As if to confirm my suspicions, I felt a mental touch skimming over the surface of my consciousness while the eyes of Sapieha's second changed to the cloudiness of death.

'You are outnumbered and outmatched, Adam Lisowczyk. My Master ordered me to keep you alive, but not necessarily the human you are hiding. So please, go ahead and entertain me with your pointless resistance,' he taunted, stepping toward me before mockingly gesturing to the doors as if daring me to enter.

I briefly considered the possibilities. I could let the vampire lead me inside, but leaving four enemies at my back was not an option. I smirked while looking into the leader's eyes.

'Are you willing to die for your Prince?' I asked, and he laughed, not that I was surprised by this.

He was still laughing when I leapt into the air, twisting my body to give myself forward momentum and thrusting the leading edge of one wing toward his neck, the faint whistle of its razor-sharp feathers slicing through the air with the precision of an obsidian knife. Only my opponent wasn't there. His body was a blur as it disappeared into the shadows, only to emerge closer to the hospital doors.

Instead, my attack ripped through the torso of his companion, opening his chest with ease. I saw the vampire's diseased heart before my claws sank into his chest, crushing the vital organ and tearing out its remains. I used the force of my attack to intercept the two vampires rushing toward me, my feet kicking out to force them back and give myself some space.

One down, four to go, I thought, wincing as someone attacked using his psychic powers.

The psychic grip of an Elder Vampire intensified in my mind, agonising spikes piercing my brain and forcing me to stumble back. I recognised this power. Sapieha had used a similar technique to immobilise me, but this bastard wasn't my maker, and my will was stronger than his. Still, I nearly fell as I fought him off, hearing Pawel's muffled shout when I regained control.

'Behind you!'

I turned, sweeping my wings out as half shield, half bludgeon, and felt them collide with the vampire who'd been sneaking up from behind. I pulled back my wings and snapped my head forward, fangs sinking into the flesh of the flailing attacker. This time, I had no thought of strategy, inflicting as much damage as I could before he regained his footing. When my victim seemed unable to recover, I pressed my attack, grasping his jaw while my other hand pressed down on his collarbone, and with a scream of triumph, I ripped his head from his body.

Three more left. Or maybe two, the youngster keeps hesitating. My thoughts were crystal clear as I assessed my attackers, but it was an illusion as the image of one flickered, closely followed by excruciating pain smashing into my back. The vampire had fooled me by using his magic as a distraction, intending to disable my wings before killing me. When the damn fool tried to bite me, I nearly laughed. Despite the mess my wings did to my clothes, I was still wearing the remnants of my combat gear, the collar still protecting my vulnerable neck.

'Wrong move,' I hissed through clenched teeth. As my attacker's teeth caught in the kevlar, my fist struck out, crushing the idiot's skull in an explosion of bone and brains.

There were only two vampires left, but my luck was running out. I was injured and struggling to catch my breath. The mental band around my mind tightened with each passing second, slowing me down, so I needed to end this before the last of my energy bled out onto the tarmac. I should have brought my own Seethe to aid me, but I didn't have the time, nor did I want to lose any friends to this bastard. My cockiness and soft heart would be my downfall this time, and it meant that Nina was now vulnerable.

The vampire with the psychic powers withdrew to the hospital doors. His eyes, moving rapidly under their white veil, told me he was probably talking with his Master. The other vampire, however, was looking at me with a mix of fear and respect in his eyes.

I let my hands fall to my sides, relaxing my wings as I faced the young vampire.

'You don't need to die. Not for that piece of shit Prince who hides while you fight, uncaring of your fate. He is using you to slow me down, to weaken me. If you leave now, I'm willing to offer you a place in my Seethe,' I whispered.

His eyes widened, and he glanced nervously at the corpses littering the ground and his Elder, who seemed to be oblivious to our conversation. He briefly nodded, withdrawing before he disappeared into the shadows.

I smiled as I stepped forward. It had been a brutal fight, but I was enjoying myself, and there was only one more obstacle to overcome before I could face Sapieha and take Nina away to safety.

I sprinted toward the doors. The longer the psychic vampire was oblivious as he communicated with his Master, the better chance I had to end his miserable life.

When I was only a few steps away, the door crashed open, and Sapieha emerged from the shadows, holding Nina by her neck.

She looked like a marionette whose stings had been cruelly cut away. Her limp frame hung bonelessly in Sapieha's grasp. Only her eyes held any hint of life, begging me for something I couldn't fathom.

'Let her go, it's me you want. I stole the locket.' Pawel pushed in front of me, his voice tremulous with fear. He kept his gaze on Sapieha, and I made the mistake of disregarding him until I felt Pawel ripping the necklace from the pocket I'd placed it in during the fight.

Nina's brother rushed forward, hands outstretched, and I cursed as Sapieha smirked at me, tightening his grip on my lover's throat to keep me still.

Blinding rage clouded my mind, but all I could do was watch as Nina looked at me with fear and anger in her beautiful eyes.

She seemed so calm, but her pupils widened when the other vampire intercepted Pawel. He held the struggling man by the scruff of his neck like an unruly puppy while ripping the locket from his fingers and passing it to Sapieha.

My gaze shifted to the Master Vampire. The hatred in his gaze as he stared at Pawel told me the thief's death would be long and agonising, but I ignored it, hoping I could still negotiate a way out for Nina.

'I delivered your thief, and you have the locket in your possession. You can keep both, but release my woman,' I said, taking a step closer.

Nina's eyes widened, filling with tears. I saw her jaw clench as she attempted to speak. I knew this helplessness all too well after being subjected to the power of Sapieha's mind magic.

I knew if I let Pawel die, Nina would never forgive me, but I would suffer her hatred as long as she survived.

'Yes... so you did. I see you are learning, Adam. Still, Nina is mine now. If you continue to cooperate, I will... ensure she comes back to you. As for our dirty little rat here, he will get what he deserves. His death is barely enough to pay for desecrating my wife's grave, but it will have to do,' He said, turning toward the Elder Vampire. 'Do it slowly. I want to savour his suffering.'

I saw the other vampire tighten his grip on Pawel's neck while Nina's lips parted in a silent scream.

'I don't care about the thief's fate, but I will offer myself freely if you release Nina. I will serve you and surrender my Seethe,' I said, watching Pawel's face turning an interesting shade of purple from the corner of my eye.

'Oh, you will, will you? Should we hear what your woman thinks about that?'

The moment Sapieha's mental grip on Nina lessened, she jerked in his grasp, hitting his chest while attempting to turn toward Pawel.

'Tell him to stop! Tell your thug to stop! You're killing him. For fuck's sake, you're killing my brother!' she shouted before turning toward me. 'Adam, he's going to kill me, anyway. He told me I'd be your leash. Please, do something! You promised me you would protect him!'

Sapieha laughed, his voice hollow in the darkness, so inhuman that even Nina stopped thrashing.

'Oh, my little pet, did my spawn promise you that? Let's give him the first lesson of his new training. Should we let him know how it feels when a woman who is his entire world detests him?' He said, gesturing toward his minion. The other vampire instantly relaxed his grasp, letting Pawel take a lungful of air.

'You can have her, but you have to kill this rat. I want you to stand in front of your lover, look into her eyes, then take his life. Show me you can listen to your Master. Do it for Nina.'

If I had a heartbeat, it would have faltered at the cruelty of Sapieha's offer. I couldn't save Pawel. If I attacked the vampire holding him, Nina would die, the same if I attacked Sapieha. All I had was one slight chance. I just had to play it well.

That meant killing Nina's brother in front of her without letting her know, so the bastard digging into her mind didn't see.

'I will do it, but I want your word that you'll free Nina,' I said, closing my eyes briefly when Nina screamed.

Rage, guilt, and betrayal filled the sound that pierced my chest like a dagger. My Obsidian fought with all she had to free herself, to hurt her captor, but nothing worked. After a brief struggle that broke my heart, the love of my life stood there powerless, clutching her hands to her chest, looking at me in disbelief. What shattered me was the hope, the tiny sliver of trust that made her believe it was all just a hoax.

'It's alright, sis, everybody dies.' Pawel said, his voice hoarse from his injured throat. 'Hey, at least your man won't make it too painful, I hope.'

Pawel was trembling. A pale, dirty scruff of a human who, in his last moments, acted with dignity and courage whilst somehow still trying to comfort Nina. The older vampire released his hold on Pawel's body, and he walked toward me, his head high, even if he was tense and visibly shaking.

'No, just fucking no! Adam, you can't, please,' she begged before turning toward Sapieha.

'You win. You can turn me. I'll do anything: blood, sex, everything. You can even kill me, but let Pawel live, let Adam go, and I will never fight you again.' Nina was crying, but he only gripped her neck tighter, digging his nails into her throat.

'Watch!' he commanded as she grasped his hand, fighting to free herself.

'Do it quick, please,' Pawel asked, tilting his head to the side, exposing a rapidly pulsing carotid artery. I moved to pull him closer, and this slight gesture sent shooting pain and a fresh stream of blood down my arm. I tensed my muscles again to increase the flow.

The thought of it made me smile. I pulled Pawel closer, pretending to play with the overgrown strands of his hair.

'You don't get to set the terms. We will do it slowly... very slowly. This is your fault, the heartache you've caused your sister, the families of the dead shifters; everything is your fault. I will enjoy feeling you die,' I said, laying his head on my shoulder and brushing his hair to the side to obstruct the view.

'If you want to live, drink as much of my blood as you can. It's not a guarantee, but it's the best chance you have. The wound is on my shoulder; now brace yourself, this will hurt,' I whispered, slowly pressing my teeth into his skin. Pawel's breath stuttered. I could only hope he understood what I offered because, seeing Sapieha's fingers tightening on Nina's neck, I knew I wouldn't hesitate to end his life to save hers.

I sank my fangs into his artery and started drinking. I purposefully withheld my venom. I needed him to be conscious and able to follow my instructions, not writhing in my grasp, overwhelmed by a mind-altering substance.

His screams and sobs echoed around the car park, but I felt Pawel's tongue lapping at the blood seeping from my wound.

Good, let's hope this works. He would be my first. I'd never spawned a vampire, but my body reacted instinctively. The world drowned in a red hue as I siphoned his blood, this time without reservation.

Nina closed her eyes, and I saw tears escaping from her tightly pressed eyelids, but our enemy didn't allow her even this slight respite. Sapieha took her chin, his fingers turning her head toward her dying brother, a whispered command forcing her eyes open.

Pawel's body stiffened before convulsing in my grip, his oxygen-deprived brain firing impulses uncontrollably as it shut down. As soon as his heart stuttered to a halt, I felt it, the newly forming link to the man who was dying in my arms. Vampire blood magic was potent, and it had already started transforming his body.

Pawel would survive, maybe not unchanged, but he would rise with the dawn. I hadn't broken my promise. Now, I had to save my woman.

'I trusted you, and you....' Nina's voice was broken and numb. She looked me in the eye as I let Pawel's body drop to the ground. 'Why don't you kill me too, Adam? Just like this arsehole planned. You know he's going to turn me anyway, so the three of us can be one happy family? That's all you bought with Pawel's death. The privilege of seeing me fucking your Master.'

The vitriol in her voice and the pain in her eyes told me the woman who loved me was gone.

It was my fault. I'd created a situation where she could be taken. I should have kept her with me when I went for Pawel or ensured she was adequately protected, but I expected Sapieha to come for me, not Nina. My oversight was to blame, and I could only pray to all the gods that she let me explain and that she'd forgive me for what I'd done to her brother.

Still, if I'd learned anything about Nina, it wouldn't be easy to explain my actions.

CHAPTER 24

A dam had done it. He'd killed Pawel, all whilst looking me in the eye. I could barely breathe. Sapieha's fingers tightened on my throat each time I tried to fight, cutting off my oxygen. I wished he'd killed me instead because watching my brother being bled dry by the vampire I loved was the most excruciating pain I'd ever experienced.

I stood there frozen in horror, clutching my hand to my chest, unable and unwilling to continue breathing. All my senses felt like they were shutting down, refusing to deal with what had just happened.

I thought I'd been through heartbreak before. The hopelessness after the betrayal of my ex-husband, seeing the truth after all the lies. All that had been nothing compared to this.

I'd trusted Adam to keep us safe. I believed he would make the right choice, knowing me well enough to understand I would never let him trade his or Pawel's life for mine. *Better die with honour than live in shame.* I don't know who said it, but those words rang true in my mind. Adam's actions condemned me to live my life in shame. A plaything for a mind-fucking vampire, a leash for the man I loved, a pathetic life paid for by Pawel's blood and Adam's submission. A life where I would never be free. I wanted to hate Adam, but I couldn't. Instead, I hated myself for still loving him.

'I trusted you,' I heard myself say as the numbness spread through my body.

'I know,' he answered.

Adam looked at me, and I saw the pain that filled those beautiful eyes. He was battered and bloodied, and I wished I could wake up from this nightmare. I loved him, and I hated myself for loving him. It hurt so much that I wished I could tear my own heart out to stop this feeling.

My heart. I looked at Sapieha's locket, feeling the heaviness of the obsidian dagger resting against my chest. Adam thought he bought my freedom with Pawel's death, but I wasn't interested in living any more. All I wanted was revenge and to take Sapieha with me. I would happily rot in Veles' cauldron if I could wipe that smug smile from that bastard's face.

Hysterical laughter burst from my lips. Could my life get any more fucked up? Each time I allowed myself to love, my heart was burned and branded, the scars left behind for all the world to see. I thought this time would be different. I'd thought Adam was different. I could survive anything else, justify any other outcome, but not the corpse of my brother abandoned on the ground, staring sightlessly into the vast, indifferent universe. The voice of reason whispered that Adam was, in fact, different, that he'd had no choice, but reason had no place here, and I ignored its whispered platitudes.

I felt the tears stream from my eyes, but my laughter didn't stop. From this point, everything was a fucking joke. Good riddance, poor naïve Nina and the happy ever after she'd thought she'd won with her Vampire Prince.

'I wish I'd never met you. I hate myself for loving you. I hate that I can't stop. Gods, I wish I'd never been born….' I choked on my words, and Adam paled, shaking his head as if I'd slapped him.

'Nina, please…' He begged, his eyes pleading for mercy, but I had nothing left.

'Please, what? Please trust me? Please live with me? Please give me your heart because I will never hurt you? You had it all. You fucking had it all! I trusted you, I lived with you, I… I love you. And what did you do? You killed my brother because your Master commanded it. You could have saved him and yourself, and I would die happy knowing you both would live. I told you this bastard was going to kill me, anyway. Do you think I want to live as his slave? Do you think I want it when the price is Pawel's life and seeing you in chains?'

Adam's pained expression told me my words hit the mark. I tilted my head to look at Sapieha. He observed me with a cruel, smug grin, almost as if he were a butterfly collector who wondered how many pins it would take for his newest specimen to die.

'You think you've won, don't you?' I asked, shaking my head, realising he'd released my mind. The bastard wanted to see my grief, to hear me weep, but I had a nasty surprise for him. All it needed was the right moment.

'You think this, controlling and destroying people's love, means you've proved your point? Maria would look at you now, at the monster you've become, and spit in your face. She would curse your name and crush the locket beneath her heel, destroying that rotten heart in disgust. How happy she must be to be free from you and your twisted love.'

'Nina, stop!'

Adam's warning made me scoff in defiance, fuelling the flames of my rage. I needed Sapieha to release me so I could reach my dagger, and there was no way I was stopping now.

'I bet she truly hated you, only using you for your position and a child she could actually love. Why else would she refuse to stay at your side? You, the coward who failed her to avoid death. How she must have hated you, you sad, pathetic old leech!'

Sapieha pushed me away, and the other vampire rushed to grab me at the same time Adam shot forward.

'Stop!' Sapieha's raised voice stopped them in their tracks. I felt a wave of psychic power washing over me, but I wasn't the target. Only the two vampires stood frozen by their creator's magic.

The former Prince stepped in front of me, still smug, still entirely in control.

'Be quiet, you foolish child. As if you could understand the love we shared. I admire your courage, Nina, but it is time for you to learn your place. I will work on your temper when you are reborn. However, I cannot let your insults pass, so you will feel the pain of death as I drain you. I look forward to making you yearn for such pain when you join me in bed, my fierce human.' Bile rose in my throat at Sapieha's threat, but I didn't back down. I needed him as close as possible to execute my plan. Instead, I pressed one hand to my throat, masking my other hand with the sleeve of my shirt while I grasped the handle of the obsidian dagger.

Something akin to respect flashed in his eyes when I stood tall and proud with a sneer on my lips.

'Oh, will you? How arrogant of you to think I would take pleasure from anything you do. Oh yes, your "*Special Powers*". Pathetic! How does it feel? Knowing that unless you inject your venom into them, no woman will get off on your charm? Maybe you should take lessons from Adam; I long to see you calling him

Master as he teaches you how to use your shrivelled cock,' I scoffed as I slipped my fingertips into my open collar.

'We shall see how easily you succumb to ecstasy at my touch, woman. I will let Adam hold you, unable to stop me when I take your body and mind, when I make you moan my name in pure ecstasy. You have a fire in you, Nina, and I will enjoy breaking you almost as much as I will enjoy breaking him. Look at his face and see his devastation. He knows he's lost you. The child of my blood was willing to give you up if it saved your life. The poor, trusting fool can see it now, can't he? Adam knows everything he did was all for nothing. Look at him. He can't do anything about it, and it's killing him.' Sapieha said, pointing toward Adam's struggling form.

Adam's snarling, thrashing struggle to free himself matched the pulsing vein on Sapieha's temple, and I felt a strange pleasure knowing that the Master Vampire struggled to maintain control over his former spawn. I watched as Sapieha ground his teeth, his fangs elongating, scraping his lower lip until little droplets of blood dribbled down his chin.

Laughter bubbled up again as I couldn't help but be reminded of a nineteen-fifties B-movie. *Oh fuck, I've really lost my mind this time.*

I glanced over Sapieha's shoulder, causing the former Prince to follow my gaze, turning his head to look at the scene behind him. With him focused on the snarling Adam, I made my move.

With one hand still covering my chest, I slipped the other underneath my blouse and grabbed the dagger, pulling it from the scabbard. The blade skittered across my other hand as I withdrew it, the keen edge easily slicing through the skin, and the blood that poured from the wound covered the handle, making it slippery and difficult to hold. It was easy to see why so many people believed obsidian to have the sharpest edge on the planet.

I couldn't tell if Adam saw what I'd done, but I heard his shout of triumph as he broke free and rushed toward Sapieha.

With clawed hands raised, Adam launched himself forward. Just as I thrust with my dagger, the Master Vampire twisted to avoid his fist and grabbed me by the throat. The icy fingers of the Void ripped through me as we disappeared into the Shadows, freezing the blood in my veins. The place we'd stood moments ago was filled by the magnificent avenging angel, bloody and screaming his frustration.

'Get back here, you coward. I challenge you!' Adam's voice was more like a roar as he stood there, but then Sapieha's abandoned minion attacked him. Claws tore into Adam's chest, and for a moment, I forgot about the lifeless body under their feet that used to be my brother, my heart leaping to the man whose blood spattered the steps to the clinic.

Sapieha emerged from the shadows, far away from the fight, but I could still see Adam locked with the other vampire. Contradicting emotions ripped through me. I wanted to sink the knife into

Sapieha's heart, but I was too shocked from travelling through the Shadow Realm, my hand barely holding onto the dagger. I suspected the only reason my heart didn't stop this time was because it was only a short distance. Still, I could only stand there watching the battle, held tight against Sapieha's body.

With a pained roar, Adam fell back, twisting to the side to avoid another slicing attack, and I saw the deep gash caused by the vicious claws of his opponent. I gasped as Adam's wings flared out crookedly, still managing to slice forward and force Sapieha's second to scramble away backwards to avoid decapitation.

In a blur of movement, Adam struck. His wings swept back, and his clawed hand shot forward, smashing into the vampire's chest with vicious finality. With a last contemptuous kick, my fury incarnate ripped out his opponent's heart.

There were no shooting flames or anything so dramatic. The vampire simply fell to the floor, folding like a puppet with cut strings.

The sound of cursing came from my captor as he grabbed my hair to wrench my head to the side.

I sucked my breath as Sapieha dragged me onto my toes. I knew I was on the verge of passing out, but I couldn't give in. Not until I killed the bastard who held me captive.

Raising his voice, Sapieha taunted Adam as his hand twisted painfully in my hair.

'You keep killing my spawn, so I think it's past time to replace them.' His laughter as he smacked his lips together chilled me to the bone, and I screamed as a pair of sharp fangs pierced my neck.

'No! Fuck, no!' Adam bellowed desperately as he launched himself into the air.

I couldn't see what was happening as Sapieha savaged my neck. It was all I could do to hold on to the slippery dagger, but I fought against the agony. I knew I had to grip it tighter as I choked on my own blood, air bubbling from the gaping hole he was creating in his frenzy. *I hope life is better on the other side*, I thought, jerking my body to the side, and with the last of my disappearing strength, I stabbed my dagger between his ribs.

The obsidian blade sank into the vampire's flesh like a hot knife in butter. So sharp it was probably painless. The vampire, busy gorging on my blood, didn't react at first, and as my body was shutting down, I knew this was it. I pushed harder, forcing the thicker part of the knife under the vampire's ribs, and Sapieha ripped his fangs from my throat. I watched the beautiful arc of my blood as it sprayed across the car park, smiling.

The bastard must have realised what I've done, I thought, my satisfaction tinged with exhaustion.

'You...' he snarled, reaching for my hand, but I didn't let him finish. I gathered what was left of my strength and pushed so hard that my hand and the knife disappeared into his chest.

The screech of a mortally wounded animal echoed in the air long after the vampire collapsed at my feet. The volcanic glass had fulfilled its purpose. I had channelled all my hate, my fear and my pain into the knife Adam had given me, killing the scum that turned my life into a nightmare.

Holding my hand to my throat to slow down the stream of blood, I collapsed to my knees. Everything was so very dark. My gaze slid over the shape of my brother's body and the corpses of the vampires littering the parking lot. Finally, my gaze caught on Adam as he landed and caught me up in his arms.

'Nina, my love, hold on. Please, please hold on.'

I looked away from those pain-filled eyes to stare out toward the Baltic Sea. If this was the last thing I saw, I didn't want it to be filled with remorse or guilt. I was going to die, but I wasn't afraid. In the clarity of death, I accepted Adam for all he was, and I truly believed he loved me.

'Nina!' His cry filled the air.

Strong hands lifted me from the cold ground, and the world disappeared behind a curtain of feathers.

'Nina, please hold on. Your brother will live. I let him drink my blood, please, my love, don't give up. I'm sorry. I'm so sorry. I will spend my life repenting for the pain I've caused you but don't leave me. You have to fight.'

Pawel will live? As a vampire? My thoughts were sluggish. My fluttering, frantic heart stuttered with the lack of blood. Deep regret rose in my core. Adam hadn't betrayed me, and my last words to him were full of hatred. I wouldn't be able to say goodbye or apologise. I couldn't tell him he showed me what real love is.

I felt the warm liquid falling on my lips, but I didn't drink it. I saw firsthand the blind obedience between a Master Vampire and his spawn, and I didn't want that, not between me and Adam, not even at the price of my life.

With one last effort, I raised my hand and touched Adam's cheek. My vampire was crying, bloody tears staining his cheeks. I smiled, and a loud crash of thunder broke the silence of the night, followed by a single thought.

I didn't know vampires could cry.

CHAPTER 25

ADAM

The only light in my dark was dying in my arms, and I couldn't do anything to stop it. Nina refused the gift of my blood, and there was nothing else I could do.

'No, fuck no. Sweetheart, please... without you, nothing else matters,' I cried, my voice hoarse from begging, but despite my pleas and the frantic efforts to stem the blood, Nina closed her eyes, and her head sagged against my chest while the ominous sound of thunder boomed overhead.

I prayed to Perun[17] for a bolt of lightning to incinerate me. I didn't want to live without her, so I might as well be a pile of ash.

---

17. *Perun - one of the most revered Slavic gods. He is considered a thunderer, the god of warriors, and a rival of Veles.*

I barely registered the change in air pressure while I rocked back and forth, unable to believe in a world without Nina in it. When a wave of magic crashed over me, I was shaken to the core. A force so strong it felt like the Gates of the Nether had been torn asunder. The night sky exploded into a kaleidoscope of colour, and when it hit the ground, flowers and grass erupted from the ground, blooming with otherworldly speed. I stared open-mouthed at the miracle before me, then screamed as my wounds began knitting together, disappearing so quickly it left me panting.

That wasn't good, and with my strength returning, I knew it could mean only one thing. Someone had released the Nether's magic into the human realm, but why?

My wings had instinctively swept over Nina and me as if I could still protect her from anything that might happen, but they were now obstructing my view. With Nina's heart beating its last slow, erratic pulses, I couldn't gather the courage to look past them; then, something changed when I heard a strong, commanding voice coming from the seafront.

'Adam!'

My wings snapped open, revealing an uncanny picture. A portal had opened over the sea, and a majestic stag galloped over the waves. On the top of the divine animal was Sara, her body glowing with the same magic that surrounded me. I couldn't tear my eyes from the sight as the Soul Shepherd leapt from Leszek's back and rushed toward us.

She opened a fucking portal!

I'd heard that before the Gates had been created, those with potent magic could conjure portals to the other worlds, but no one had made one since the Gates were built. Somehow, I knew Sara had done it, and the magnitude of the power coming through it took my breath away. Time slowed down for everything not touched by the riotous power. I'd known Sara could use a god's divine energy, but this was both wondrous and terrifying at the same time.

'Adam, what the fuck did you do?' Sara shouted before dropping to her knees and slamming her hand onto Nina's chest. The woman in my arms convulsed, her eyes opening suddenly. I couldn't contain the sob that burst from my lips as her heart stuttered once more and stopped, but Nina's soul didn't escape. I could still feel her. My woman was still there. Despite the pale cheeks and unmoving chest, there was still a soul.

Sara Wilska, Soul Shepherd and force of nature, held her friend's soul tethered to her body while looking at me with a rage that burned so hot I felt it would consume me.

'Turn her!' She commanded, but I shook my head.

'She refused. Don't you think I haven't tried?' I cried, my throat tight with grief.

'I'm not asking, Adam. Turn her. Now! I won't lose her. They can lock me behind those fucking Gates, but I won't lose Nina to this madness.'

If I thought Sapieha's psychic torture or torn wings were the pinnacle of agony, it faded into insignificance when compared to the all-consuming compulsion in Sara's voice. Blinding bolts of power erupted from her body, flaring and shimmering behind her like giant wings.

I couldn't avert my eyes, and I couldn't deny her. The power that pulsed from Sara crashed into me in unrelenting waves, and I watched myself open a vein on my wrist and press it to Nina's lips.

'Stop, my love, don't force this. Everything will be okay.' Leszek's sharp voice broke through, interrupting Sara's command, and I pulled my wrist back.

I looked toward the stairs where, in his primal form, the Leshy walked toward us. His eyes locked on Sara's as her fury scorched the air.

'I won't let her go. Even you can't make me. I don't fucking care about the politics involved. If Gedania has a problem with it, then tough shit, let them do their worst.'

The sheer defiance in Sara's voice gave me a sliver of hope. If anyone could keep Nina in this world, it was her unyielding, steadfast friend.

'No one is going to take her, my love. I told you it would be okay, and I wasn't lying. Vampiric magic is already changing Nina's body. Aren't you surprised she lasted so long with her throat ripped open?' He asked gently, and I saw Sara hesitate, uncertain and scared.

'Adam?' she asked, but I shook my head.

'I tried, but she wouldn't accept my blood. There's only one other possibility.' I pointed to the rapidly decomposing body next to us.

'And... you let him?' she asked, and this time, it was my anger that echoed through the car park.

'I didn't fucking let him! I was retrieving Nina's brother when that bastard targeted the one place she would never abandon. I came as fast as I could, and I killed every vampire he commanded. He was my sire, for fuck's sake, an ancient vampire able to squash me like a bug, but I did everything I could!' I shouted, feeling the desperate need for someone to believe I hadn't failed Nina.

'You can't hold on to her spirit, my Firefly. Vampires cannot awaken with their spirits intact. Let her go, and Nina will return to you in no time. Look, her body is already healing.'

Leszek's gentle words and his hand on Sara's shoulder told me he was determined to stop whatever his wife was doing, so I turned away, focusing on Nina. Knowing I hadn't lost my love forever allowed me to concentrate on the changes happening to her body, but everything about this whole situation felt wrong.

'I turned Pawel, but he won't awaken till tomorrow. Why is Nina reacting differently? Is it something you're doing, Sara, or is this because Sapieha was so old?'

I looked at Sara, but she shook her head. Her features went slack for several moments. She was using Seer magic, and I remained silent, afraid to even breathe. Finally, she shook her head, looking at me in disbelief.

'You gave her an Athame?! The Obsidian Athame? Oh, Adam, you wonderful idiot,' she exclaimed, tears streaming down her face as she laughed.

'I wanted her to feel safe,' I retorted defensively, and then I felt it, a single, miraculous thump of Nina's heart, then, moments later, another.

Sara's power withdrew, the otherworldly glow diminishing as the portal over the sea slowly closed. She bent toward Nina, cradling her face in her hands.

'C'mon, Biker Bitch, don't make me wait,' she whispered, kissing Nina's forehead.

I didn't know what was going on, but as long as Nina was alive, I couldn't care less. I would forever serve the annoying Soul Shepherd for bringing her back to me. My wings wrapped protectively around my woman, nudging Sara aside.

'Let her rest,' I insisted, indulging my possessive instincts before Nina could wake up as I turned to Sara. 'Please, can you tell me what you saw and what this means for her future?'

'The athame you gave Nina was made of obsidian and aspen and blessed by the Coven. It appears Veronica has taken a liking to her and wanted to protect her from a certain winged lothario. Of course, I don't think the Coven Mistress was expecting Nina to get her blood on it first. She effectively made an offering of human blood and vampire immortality with a blade blessed by fire, air, water and earth. Do you get it yet?'

Sara looked at my confused expression and rolled her eyes.

'Don't they teach you anything at Vampire High?' As she laughed at her own joke, I tried to answer, angry at her flippancy, but she waved her hand, dismissing me.

'Nina sacrificed Sapieha to the gods. When my girl goes big, she goes really big. I don't know what that'll mean for the future, maybe nothing, maybe she'll get Sapieha's powers. Who knows?'

A grumbling growl from Leszek made me turn in his direction.

'But you just had to hold on to her spirit, didn't you? And don't get me started on the whole portal mess. Now we have a vampire with a soul and, if we're lucky, only half a city that witnessed magic exploding over Gdansk Bay. Gedania's council won't be happy. I barely kept you out of their dungeon last time. You can't keep breaking the rules, my love.'

Leszek was back to acting surly, which he only did when he was feeling protective, so I tried to ignore their discussion and looked instead at the miracle in my arms.

'I'll be fine. I will simply explain the situation calmly and have you stand there glowering behind me. C'mon, Nina is my friend. If I can't help her and the people I love, then why am I even here?' Sara's frustration was obvious, and Leszek sighed in defeat, taking her hand to kiss her delicate fingertips gently.

'I know my Firefly. All I'm asking is for you to be careful,' Leszek answered as he looked into his wife's eyes.

Despite trying to ignore the lovebirds, I'd been so engrossed in their exchange that I nearly missed Nina's eyes opening, but the smile that stretched my lips wide was the most joyous I'd ever felt.

'Welcome back, my love,' I said, pushing an unruly strand of hair from her eyes.

I was entranced. Nina's eyes were swirling crimson with no iris or pupils, just two hypnotic glowing whirlpools.

She looked back at me and smiled, reaching out for my face.

I exhaled, hopeful that this reaction meant I was forgiven, but my relief was premature as Nina's hand paused and her features twisted into furious outrage. With unexpected strength, Nina tried to push me away. When that didn't work, pain exploded in my cheek as she slapped me with all her might.

'I thought you killed him. You let me believe you killed him! Then I told you all those hateful words, and I fucking died. Do you even know how it feels to die after that?' She snarled, clawing at the tarmac to get away from me, and I tightened my arms, hugging her to my chest and burying my face in her hair.

'I know, I'm sorry. I didn't have a choice,' I whispered, kissing her desperately, ignoring her fists as they beat against my back. 'Pawel will return tomorrow, I promise. Please say you'll give me a chance to explain.'

Nina's pummelling of my back seemed to slow, and I hoped that meant she was just angry and not succumbing to a feeding frenzy. I relaxed my hold and cursed as Nina sank her teeth into my shoulder. My blood flowed into her mouth, and her struggles ceased as she began stroking my back until her hands were caressing my wings.

'Why do you taste so good? Gods, I'm so hungry,' she mumbled before looking up at me. 'What did you do to me?'

'Nothing. I swear. When you killed Sapieha, something happened. Sara said it was a ritual sacrifice, and that did something unusual. Nina... you're a vampire.'

She looked at me with shock and reached up to touch her new fangs. I breathed a sigh of relief as the crimson in her eyes slowly bled away, but my heart nearly broke when Nina started shaking, and a sob broke free from her lips.

'I need to take her home,' I said, looking at Leszek, and he nodded, pulling his phone out from... somewhere.

'I'll arrange the clean up. Where do you want us to put Pawel's body?'

'Deliver him to the Seethe's compound. Tell them to lock him in the basement and feed him when he wakes up. I'll come talk to him as soon as I'm able.'

Leszek nodded and looked around the hospital car park and the various bloodied corpses.

'And... which one is Pawel?'

I couldn't help it; I laughed. The confusion in Leszek's voice was amusing, and I pointed at a small heap at the bottom of the stairs.

'The only one with no missing parts? The others, I'm afraid, you'll have to collect with a shovel.'

Sara approached me, shaking her head, before she looked at Nina.

'Adam...' I heard the warning in her voice and bowed my head in response.

'I know you think the worst of me, but I love Nina. I will look after her. I promise she'll feel better soon, but right now, there is no better person to look after a vampire with no Master than me.' As if to confirm my words, Nina lifted her head.

'I feel strange. I need... something. Gods, that's confusing.'

I kissed the top of her head.

'I know what you need, my Obsidian and I will provide it as soon as we're home.'

I carried Nina to the car while Leszek phoned our associates to clean up what had essentially been a vampire gang war. As I settled her in the passenger seat, the vampire I'd allowed to live stepped out of the shadows.

'Sir, what about your oath?' I frowned before I remembered I'd promised him a place in my Seethe for withdrawing from the fight.

'Help in cleaning up, and you may bring the rest of your brethren if they would like a new home,' I replied, and he bowed deeply.

'Yes, sir, and thank you.'

CHAPTER 26

We travelled in silence, the rumble of the engine making it easy to avoid conversation as Nina sat, lost in thought, and I tried desperately to think of a way to reassure her. When we arrived in the underground garage, I parked Tomasz's vehicle in front of the elevator and leapt out to open Nina's door. With her head lowered, she slipped out and silently waited for me to enter the passcode.

I held my tongue, waiting till Nina was ready, proud that she was dealing with it, taking her time to process this traumatic change without losing control of her hunger. Once we entered the apartment, I coaxed Nina into the kitchen, pulling out a chair with a slight flourish. The hint of a smile was all I received as she sat down, but it felt like I'd been handed the Nobel Peace Prize. I went to my cooler to retrieve two units of blood, warming them in readiness.

'I can't...' Nina paled as she looked at the bags, and I frowned.

'You have to feed my love. I can call for a donor if you prefer, but you need to feed. What you feel, the hunger that is gnawing at your insides, it will only get worse. Remember what happened to me when the hunger got too much?' I said, crouching next to her chair.

'Are you sure Pawel will be all right,' she asked, avoiding the subject.

'He will. He will wake up confused and hungry, just like you did, but we have the supplies at the compound to deal with that. Nina, it may be for the best. What happened with your brother... I'm his sire, so he will have to listen to me, and I can make sure he stays out of trouble.'

'What about me?' she asked, biting her lip, 'Will you command me as well?' Nina was so serious, as if the rest of our lives rested on my answer, so I paused, thinking of the best response.

'You, my little miracle, are not my spawn, and I, for one, am truly grateful for that. I'm not responsible for your transformation; you are. No blood ties are holding you back, and you never have to worry about being forced to do anything against your will. I have no power over you other than being Master of the Tricity Seethe, but that won't mean any changes to your life. Your choices will always be your own, but I hope you will choose to live with me,' I said, caressing her cheek and tilting her head back, stunned by the immense relief I could see there.

'Good. It would make things too complicated,' Nina said, sitting still and tense but with that hint of a smile again.

'Oh, my beautiful warrior, who could ever command such fierce beauty?' I attempted to break the tension and cheer her up a bit, but Nina's reaction shook me to the core. The upturned lips fell, and a soul-wrenching sob tore through her body.

'I'm so scared, Adam. What am I supposed to do now? How can I live like this? Will I have to kill people? Fuck, I feel like I'm losing my mind.'

'It will be all right, my love, I promise. Please look at me, Nina. You are not alone. I will be with you every step of the way, and Sara will be here whenever you need a break from me. I can't promise life won't be different and even a little weirder than usual, but I'll do everything in my power to make this work for us.' I stroked her hair, rocking her like a child.

It took Nina several moments to relax into my embrace, and I sent a silent prayer of thanks to whoever was listening when she buried her head in my shoulder, her sobs easing and turning into quiet sniffles.

'I thought you'd killed him.' Nina's muffled words made me tense, but I stayed silent, waiting. 'I was so angry and felt utterly betrayed. It was like every fear I'd ever had about us came true, but more than that, I hated myself because even then, I loved you. I wanted to die, Adam, because I couldn't live with myself for loving my brother's murderer. I wouldn't have been so reckless if I knew you didn't... then I was dying, and you told me he would live, and I couldn't even tell you I loved you or apologise for what I said. I was so scared you wouldn't forgive yourself when all you'd done was try to save us,' she sobbed, still hidden against my chest. 'You should have told me that was the plan. Somehow, you should have let me know.'

'I know, and if you need to hate me for what happened, I understand. Everything I did was... I didn't have a plan. When I heard Sapieha took you, I lost it, and nothing mattered except getting to you. I should have been sensible, should have called in every favour and turned up with an army. I'm sorry, Nina. I failed you, and saving Pawel was pure luck. If it hadn't worked, I would have gladly sacrificed his life for yours. The simple truth is that I would sacrifice anything and anyone for you. I would die for you, and even if you hate me for saying this, know that I am, and always will be, in love with you.'

Something flashed in her eyes, a hint of amusement or outrage; I couldn't be sure until that small, sly smile teased her lips once more.

'Adam, you are an idiot,' she said, and happiness exploded in my chest.

'I am, it's true, but I'm your idiot, Princess.' That earned me another twitch of her lips.

In a moment of inspiration, with an elegant, manly flourish, I knelt in front of Nina, pressing her hand to my forehead. 'I promise to be your knight in shining armour, a dark and sinister lover, or a pale and sparkly vampire. As long as you allow me to provide you with the sustenance that you crave so deeply.'

'Get up, you idiot. This is a serious matter. Gods, why do I have to spend eternity in the company of such a ridiculous vampire?' Nina's eye roll was one for the record books, and I grinned, knowing I had eased her pain. There might be rainy days ahead, but seeing Nina smile again was more than enough for now.

I took the blood from the warmer and grabbed a couple of crystal wine glasses as Nina silently watched on. I don't know if she realised, but the cutest set of fangs were peeking from behind her lips. I had to turn away for a moment to calm myself. She was mine, and we had all the time in the world to get to know each other better.

Contentment had always felt like the death of fun to me, but today, I felt as if I'd almost explode with the feeling. However, telling Nina how happy I was after what we'd just been through would probably be a bad idea.

'Can we try something else?' She asked, and I turned back, wondering what Nina had in mind. 'I don't know if I can do it... I mean, I should, you know, drink it to feel better... but... Well, maybe I could try some raw steak instead? At least for now, to get used to the idea.'

It only took one look into those eyes, and I caved like a house of cards, even though I knew animal blood would never quench the thirst that must feel so overwhelming right now.

One indulgent smile later, and I was dragging two Wagyu Tomahawk steaks from the fridge. I always kept something in, just in case I had a shifter client. Now, it was a blessing in disguise, and I sent Lorelai a silent word of thanks for stocking the kitchen. I could give it to Nina completely raw, but somehow, I had a feeling my newborn vampire needed the reassurance of normality more than the blood, and if the thirst became too much, I knew how to assist her.

After heating a little butter, I gave the slab a few seconds to fry. Just enough to brown it slightly and lock all the goodness inside.

As soon as the smell of seared meat permeated the kitchen, Nina jumped off her chair and yanked the fork from my hand, stabbing the beef with a vengeance before lifting the whole chunk to her mouth.

'Shit... shit, it's hot. Gods, it's delicious. I love you so much,' she muttered, stuffing her mouth with the bleeding meat while I observed her, trying my best not to laugh at the comical sight.

Nina looked ridiculous, but for the first time today, she was relaxed enough to be unguarded and silly, blowing on the sizzling meat and trying to lick her lips as its juices squirted everywhere. It was so adorable that I couldn't help but tease her.

'Me or the meat?' I asked, and her confused frown nearly broke me.

'What?'

'You said I love you, but I'm not sure if you meant me... or the steak you're salivating over right now. Frankly, I'm jealous. You never looked at me like you're looking at that prime piece of beef right now.'

Nina pushed the last piece into her mouth before she came closer.

'Hmm, tough choice. I mean, you do taste delicious, but a good steak can really get a girl going.'

Nina's answer broke my self-control, and I laughed until she moved so close that our breath mingled, and she looked at me from beneath the curtain of her eyelashes. I couldn't look away as my temptress pursed her lips, her tongue peeking out to tempt and bewitch.

'Adam?' she said, practically purring, 'May I ask you something?'

'Anything, my love,' I managed, swallowing hard. Her body, the way she moved, and her low, raspy voice sent shivers down my spine. Whether or not she was conscious of the fact, Nina drove me wild.

'Good, so can you tell me why I've felt so horny since we arrived? Is this normal? Or will I always feel like I want to rip your clothes off and ride you till you're begging for mercy? What is wrong with me? I've just been through the worst night of my life. I killed someone, for fuck's sake. How can I be thinking of pushing you back on the table and licking you from top to tail?' She asked, looking at me with lust-filled eyes whilst wearing a worried frown.

The sweet torture Nina was struggling with wasn't helping my own difficulties as I gripped the marble beneath my hands whilst hiding my almost painful erection behind its surface.

The soft tones of *Smooth Operator* and Sade's sensual voice filled the room, adding to my torment.

'Lorelai, you are not helping!' I bellowed while Nina laughed.

'Are you all right? Maybe I should take a look at what's causing you so much pain.' Nina smiled, and I nearly whimpered.

'Nina, all newly turned vampires have heightened senses, and it can be overwhelming until they can adjust; eyesight, taste, smell, and even touch can be difficult. You will be so sensitive that the sun will make going outside during the day impossible until you've adapted.' My explanation was meant to discourage Nina from doing anything she might regret until after she could think a little clearer, but I was a vampire who preyed on lust, and this woman before me was everything I'd ever dreamt of.

Adrenaline was still coursing through Nina's veins. I knew just how that felt. I'd been so close to losing her that the need to reaffirm our survival was difficult to deny. For a newly turned vampire, it would feel more urgent.

At any other time, I would be happy to oblige, but I didn't want to take advantage even if my own body protested this refusal.

'You're saying this will fade?' She asked, without realising she was stalking me in a predatory manner. Nina's transformation was progressing faster than I'd realised. I twisted around, keeping my posture relaxed even as she leaned forward, placing her hands on my chest.

'It won't fade, but it will get easier to deal with. You'll adjust, adapt, and learn to enjoy your new abilities. For now, you're driven by your body's needs, and it's clouding your judgement,' I said, gasping when Nina's hand stroked downwards till it rested on my crotch.

She began running her nails lightly over the bulging fabric. My wings nearly burst from my body as shivers ran down my spine, and I heard marble cracking as my grip on the table tightened.

'I don't want to adjust. I want to enjoy these feelings with you,' she insisted, pressing up against me.

'This isn't a good idea, my love. I want you; there's no denying that with my hard-on beneath your hand...' I tried to talk, but Nina kept rubbing my manhood, making my thoughts an incoherent mess. 'Sweetheart, I'm no saint, so could you please not....'

I fell silent as Nina slid her hand into my trousers. That was it; I'd reached my breaking point, and this vixen had gleefully pushed me well beyond it with a smile on her lips. I didn't care about anything now except showing Nina exactly why you don't tease a Master Vampire when you are his sole desire.

I grabbed my prey with a swiftness that made Nina gasp, lifting her up and throwing her onto the tabletop. My gaze dropped to the clothes that concealed my woman's beautiful body, and moments later, their tattered remains fell to the floor. Now, it was my lips that held the predatory smile, and as I leaned close to breathe in her delectable scent, my hands lightly traced over her thighs, enjoying the way she trembled under my touch.

'Adam, don't you dare tease me right now,' she commanded as I paused to run my fangs over her collarbone.

I looked at her heavy-lidded eyes and pressed a nail to her inner thigh, smirking as she opened her legs to invite me closer.

'I shall take you as I desire, sweetheart. If you insist on destroying my self-control, then I insist on you enjoying the consequences.' Nina's throaty chuckle when I stepped back was music to my ears, and I slowly drew down my trouser's zip, allowing my hard cock to spring free.

The growl that Nina made as she looked down made me even harder, but when she reached forward, I pinned her arms back and revelled in the sight of her skin blushing pink. Nina arched her back as my tongue teased her pebbled nipples, her breath hitching.

'Tell me, beloved, tell me how much you need me inside you,' I teased, sliding the head of my manhood between her folds and stroking it over her clit. Nina was already wet, and the sensation was deliciously sinful. I held back as much as I could, wondering which of us would break first, knowing I would crack if she didn't answer soon.

'Oh gods, Adam, you want me to beg? I want you, I want your cock. Fuck me till I no longer can scream your name,' she answered, moaning when I teased her nipples with my fangs. 'I am going to get you back for this, so fuck me till the table breaks and then keep doing it till I beg you to stop.'

I couldn't take it anymore. Changing the angle, I slid inside her. Her muscles gripped me tight, increasing the friction, and I felt myself descend into savage, passionate madness.

'Finally! Gods, I love your cock,' Nina moaned, wrapping her legs around me and pulling our bodies hard against each other. So beautiful, so precious, so... insatiable. With her body on display, dark hair contrasting starkly with the white marble, I was stripped of my sanity. I'd almost lost her today, and as I thrust deep inside her body over and over, I gave in to the desperate primal need to make her mine forever.

There was no subtlety to our lovemaking. It was pure lust, the need to claim, the need to own every dark corner of Nina's soul. I would allow nothing to keep her from my side ever again.

The fast and brutal pace drove us both to the edge too fast, with my lover urging me to ravage her body with each thrust. We lost all awareness of the world as our bodies collided with bruising force, but that just drove our crazed desire onwards, Nina's nails tearing deep furrows in my flesh.

When her climax hit, Nina screamed, her tight walls contracting and milking me until I couldn't take it anymore. As I reached my peak, sinking my fangs into her throat, I unleashed my passion.

Delicious, powerful blood filled my mouth, surprising me with its potency. I'd never bitten another vampire before, but here I was, drunk on her life, while I couldn't stop releasing my seed deep inside her.

Nina tasted almost human, reacting to my venom with the same euphoria as usual, but the energy, the magic contained within, was incredible, increasing my pleasure till I nearly passed out.

As my awareness of the world returned, I withdrew my fangs and my cock, cradling Nina in my arms as I moved her to the more comfortable couch.

'That was... extraordinary doesn't even come close. I... please tell me I didn't hurt you, my love,' I asked, and to my relief, Nina shook her head, smiling as she cuddled to my chest and smiled.

'No, but do you have some more steak? I feel so hungry again, and I'll need all my strength for round two.' She finished with a mischievous glint in her eye.

CHAPTER 27

*A*dam is sleeping like the dead - pun intended, I thought as I chuckled at my own joke. Unfortunately, our vigorous activities hadn't pushed me past the point where my mind stopped working, and now I lay here cuddling to his chest, pondering over everything that had happened.

I'd died, my brother had died, Sapieha and the Elders of his Seethe died. Everybody fucking died except Adam, and he came too close for comfort; it was one big, bloody slaughterhouse. I didn't think I'd ever be able to erase the image of my brother's body as it crumpled to the ground, and here I was, cuddling with his killer. No, not a killer. Adam's actions had actually saved Pawel, but the image simply refused to go away.

I tightened my hold on my lover's body, pressing my face into his chest, trying to block out my thoughts. Adam had promised Pawel would awaken soon, and I trusted his word, but the spectre of relationships past kept trying to sneak in, whispering, '*All men lie.*' The insidious words still affected me despite all the evidence to the contrary.

I didn't care if my brother was a vampire; I mean, pot, meet kettle. Maybe it was, as Adam said, a good thing that he would be under such strict control from now on, and this new life would be the second chance that actually worked.

My thoughts circled back to that memory again and the worry with it. What if Adam did everything he could, but something went wrong, and we weren't there to fix it because we were fucking each other's brains out? As much as I loved this incredible man, if I had to bury my brother because of our neglect, I didn't know if I could live with myself... or him.

I looked at Adam lying peacefully next to me, and I felt so anxious I could barely breathe. It took me a moment to slowly untangle myself from his embrace and go to the kitchen. I didn't bother to fry the steak this time. No one was watching, so I simply put the bloody slab in my mouth, chewing slowly as the juices flowed down my throat.

The sudden appearance of Lorelai startled me, and it took a moment to realise she was holding my vibrating phone out to me.

As I grabbed it with a shaking hand and a shakier smile, I saw Sara's name and answered immediately.

'Hey, you do know it is four in the morning, don't you?' I said, but my friend simply laughed in reply.

'Yeah, of course, but you know me, I had a feeling you needed a chat, so I called,' Sara answered, and I couldn't help but roll my eyes.

'I'm sure there was mention of how much I dislike you using your Seer abilities on me.'

'I didn't. I'm just worried. Yesterday was a lot. I know you're a tough cookie, but this... well, we both know I'd be halfway across Poland by now and eating enough garlic to keep anyone away, not just vampires. I just wanted to check in with my best friend and see how she was doing. Just... you know, if things get too much, then you can always crash here, and we can steal Michal's brandy again,' she said, making the tears well up in my eyes.

'Yeah, yesterday was crazy. I'm still processing the whole dead-not-dead bloodbath, but I think seeing Pawel will help. Guess what? I'm chewing on raw meat. It feels like I'm constantly hungry now. Oh, and worried and horny and then hungry again,' I said, and Sara chuckled.

'Well, I can provide you with meat, and if Adam isn't up to the job, one of the new nurses mentioned a website with all sorts of interesting monster... parts.' I snorted at Sara's lewd suggestion, and as the smile settled on my lips, I realised how relaxed I felt, the tension washed away by her eccentric support.

'Adam is more than enough, thank you very much,' I replied, as prim and proper as any aristocratic lady. 'Go to sleep, woman, and stop talking about my vampire's performance.' I paused a moment before continuing. 'I'd really appreciate seeing you later. I think I need it and... you know, things may not go that well.' I said, unwilling to disclose my concerns, but Sara seemed to know without my saying a word.

'Whenever you're ready, hun, the hooch will be in your hand as soon as you walk through the door; no invitation needed or questions asked. You are always welcome here,' she said, and I heard a grumpy male voice in the background.

'Sara? Is everything okay? Why did you sneak out in the middle of the night?'

Leszek sounded wary, and I heard Sara's deep sigh.

'I'm sorry, Nina. I need to go. Leszek... is worried. We had a little trouble in Gedania, but we'll catch up later,' she said. I bid her goodbye before curling up on the sofa and gazing through the massive window at Gdansk's old town.

That's how Adam found me several hours later.

I woke up to the soft caresses of his lips on my cheek and a voice filled with tenderness.

'Hey, sleepyhead. Ready to see your brother?'

I sat upright abruptly, blinking away my exhaustion. A fluffy, colourful blanket that must have been wrapped around my body slid to the floor as I looked at Adam.

'It's still dark. How long did I sleep?'

He smiled mischievously and pointed to the clock.

'About fourteen hours, according to Lorelai. Anyway, your supper is ready, and as soon as you've finished eating, we can go to the Seethe's compound. Your brother woke up a short while ago.'

'What? Why didn't you wake me up earlier? We can go right away.' I said, rising from the sofa, but Adam's hand on my shoulder stopped me.

'First, you were tired and needed to rest. Second, although your transformation was quicker than expected, Pawel's wasn't, so there was no point leaving earlier. I made your supper and woke you as soon as I got the call. You were recently turned, and I'm not risking a hungry vampire on the streets of the city.' I instantly bristled at his lecturing tone.

'Since when are you in charge... *daddy*?' I asked, trying to annoy Adam enough to avoid eating. I didn't expect his lips to twitch as he turned away, attempting to hold back laughter before he composed himself and looked back.

'Be a good girl, Nina, or *daddy* will spank your bottom.'

'What? No... you're supposed to be angry, not teasing me.' I said with righteous indignation, but he leaned over to kiss my forehead.

'I like this new kink of yours. I can be your daddy anytime you want, baby girl,' he whispered into my ear, and I swore as I pushed him away to make space to stand up.

'I just said it to piss you off, you idiot. Stop it now. Where's the food?' I desperately tried to distract myself from the sudden flood of arousal. *Calm your titties, Nina. First, your brother, then Sara, and if all goes well, you can play with the winged Adonis afterwards,* I thought, trying to talk myself out of the images that appeared in my mind.

Adam smirked as if he could read my thoughts, busying himself with his phone as I went to the table. He made a few calls while I was eating, and as soon as I finished, he gestured to the hallway.

'The car is ready. I have to warn you. Your brother is going through the normal stages of vampiric transformation, and right now, he is... a little feral. I don't want you to worry. It will pass, but this first meeting won't be pleasant.'

'Adam, as long as he is alive, I don't care. I know you will help him through his transition,' I affirmed, noticing his relieved sigh.

We drove for half an hour. I had never been to the Seethe's compound and wasn't sure what to expect. Maybe some gothic manor, but certainly not Fin de siècle[18] architecture. The house was beautiful, the colourfully decorated front and fantastic carvings

---

18. *Fin de siècle, (French: "end of the century") – relating to, characteristic of, or resembling the late 19th-century literary and artistic climate of sophistication, escapism, extreme aestheticism, world-weariness, and fashionable despair.*

harmonising perfectly with its stained-glass windows. Set inside a generous walled garden, I half expected Victorian couples to be strolling around outside with parasols and fluttering fans held aloft.

'Whoa, that looks amazing. Why are you living in that concrete penthouse when you have something like this here?' I asked.

'Because I like my solitude. This pretty building is a communication hub for the Tricity vampires and a guest house for visitors. Or maybe I should call it a beehive? I like old Gdansk, and I prefer my modern conveniences over the beauty of this place,' he insisted, and I rolled my eyes.

'Solitude, my arse. If you wanted solitude, why would you allow a kikimora to stay there, or me?' I teased.

'Because she is useful. You get to stay because I love you.' Adam replied with such a matter-of-fact tone it left me unsure what to say, but something pushed me to test the waters.

'You know I have a home, too. I should move back there now that everything is settled,' I said, watching as his body stilled.

'No! I mean, please, you don't need to do that. I know you may not like my style, but I hope you'll stay, and we can make it a home for us both.'

I didn't answer as Adam parked the car and came around to the passenger door, opening it for me with a shy smile. I liked his cute, old-fashioned gestures, which contrasted with his usual no-nonsense professional brusqueness.

As we entered the building, the vampires that greeted us nodded their heads respectfully but avoided looking directly at Adam or me.

I leaned closer to whisper into Adam's ear. 'What's wrong with them?'

'They've heard about Sapieha's demise and are trying to avoid challenging you, or me for that matter, but I'm well known here, so....' The look of shocked disbelief on my face made Adam smile, but I could see the pride in his expression.

'You're saying they're afraid of me? This is a joke, right?'

'I wouldn't say they are scared, my love, but you achieved something that most here couldn't accomplish without a significant increase in power. Love, you are friends with the Soul Shepherd, the Forest Lord and the Coven Mistress. All of that would make anyone wary of you, but you, a human, enchanted me, their Master, then killed the most powerful psychic vampire in Poland and became a vampire during a magical explosion that half of the Tricity area witnessed. Like it or not, you are a force to be reckoned with.' Adam replied calmly. He looked me straight in the eye with pride burning in his gaze, then turned and walked away, leaving me speechless in the middle of the beautiful hallway.

It took me a moment to shake off my surprise at Adam's speech, but as I rushed after my lover, I couldn't help but wonder if the pride I'd seen in his eyes meant more than I realised.

We entered the basement together, and I couldn't help the little moue of disappointment at the sight before me. My expectations of damp, dark cells filled with moaning, starving captives couldn't have been further from the truth. Instead, I was confronted by a long, well-lit corridor with well-spaced doors along its length, most of which were open with comfortably appointed suites. At the end of the corridor was a large communal area filled with plush sofas and chairs, as well as a large flat-screen television, a stylish coffee maker and a large fridge.

When I turned to Adam, he couldn't hold back his smirk as he directed me to one of the closed doors and knocked on the door.

A young-looking, petite woman opened the door and nodded to Adam, then to me, before stepping out and walking away. I looked inside and nearly bit my lip at the sight before me. A bedraggled, shivering male lay on a bed, surrounded by several empty blood bags.

'Pawel?' I asked quietly, and he turned to me.

His eyes were wild, but after several seconds, he seemed to focus, and recognition brightened their depths. After a few moments, he sat up and tried to straighten his unkempt hair.

'Sis? Am I in jail?' He asked, his voice hoarse as if he'd been screaming all night.

'Kind of. Adam thinks it's the best for the moment. Pawel, I'm so sorry, but you're a vampire now.' I said, and he nodded before his head hung low.

'I thought so, the bags, and... I'm so hungry. I shouldn't have raided that tomb, but they said it was safe, that the whole family was long dead. Then that man, that vampire, came after us. I saw him rip my friends apart. He didn't even use a knife...' Pawel's voice trailed off before changing into an inhuman growl.

'It's all right, Pawel. Sapieha's gone . You're safe now, I promise.'

Pawel looked at me before his gaze moved toward Adam.

'You killed me,' he said. I could almost see the memories surface before his face transformed into a rictus of fury, and he leapt forward, clawed hands reaching for Adam's throat, 'You fucking killed me! Then I woke up here, surrounded by bags full of blood. I called, and no one, not a single soul, came. I didn't know where I was, what time it was, and what was happening to me....'

'Calm down.' Adam didn't raise his voice, but the command was unmistakable, and Pawel reacted instantly, his body relaxing, hands dropping to his sides.

'Yes, I killed you. You asked me to, remember? You wanted to save Nina, sacrificing your life for hers, and for that, I let you live. I could have simply ended your existence, but I love your sister too much to see her suffer grief at your death,' he said with a menacing undertone that affected me in ways I didn't fully understand.

'Yes, you were left alone. A newly raised vampire is a danger to everyone around them. Only their sire is able to control their feeding frenzy. You should be grateful that Brygid was willing to risk herself to replenish your supply and make sure you didn't hurt yourself. Let me make one thing very clear to you, boy. This new life that you've been given? It belongs to me, and there will be some significant changes. You will stay in this cell until you learn to control your hunger. Then, we will find you a job, and you will apply yourself with due diligence. After you've proved yourself trustworthy, you will gain your freedom. However, if you do anything to cause Nina pain, I will make your life a living hell.'

I looked at Adam as if it were the first time I'd ever seen him. The Master of the Tricity Seethe had somehow replaced the carefree, annoying vampire, and this new, menacing, and commanding presence was incredibly alluring. Unfortunately, the overprotective threats ruined the moment.

'Oh, right, Mr High and Mighty Vampire Lord, maybe you should try remembering I defended myself last time a vampire threatened me, so... May I talk to my brother now that you've finished measuring your manhoods? Preferably alone?' I arched an eyebrow as I looked at Adam, half expecting him to object. To my surprise, the unyielding look on his face softened when he glanced at me and bent to kiss my forehead.

'Don't provoke his baser instincts if you can help it. At the first sign of trouble, run. That will keep both of you safe. Brygid will be outside; she has experience in these situations. Come out when you are done, I'll be in my office.' I touched his cheek, noticing the roughness of the stubble he must have forgotten to shave. Adam looked tired. He must have been working non-stop whilst I slept on the sofa.

'I need to go to Sara's later. Just go home and have a rest. I will take a taxi,' I suggested, but he looked at me as though I'd grown horns.

'We will go together. I wouldn't mind a little of Leszek's expensive whisky. I'm sure he won't mind sharing while you two have a chat,' he said before walking out, leaving me alone with my brother.

Two hours later, I emerged, my eyes puffy from the tears I'd shed, but my heart felt much lighter after I'd aired all the family's dirty laundry. I asked the nearest vampire for the way to Adam's office, and he pointed me to a room on the second floor.

I climbed the beautiful oak stairs with its ornamental copper balustrade and stumbled to a halt, noticing a significant queue of petitioners in front of the *vampire boss's lair*. I squeezed through the annoyed crowd until I reached his door and knocked.

'Adam, may I come in?' I asked, intending to tell him I was going to Sara's and he could join me when he finished. The door swung open, and I yelped in surprise when a strong masculine arm wrapped around my waist.

'We are done here. Send the important requests to me via email. The rest can wait till tomorrow. Office hours will resume over the next few days, so expect some disruption. Just remember, I'm not your babysitter, and if you send me any more petty complaints, you'll be paying for them in blood,' Adam snapped, holding me tight to his side.

I noticed a few murmured remarks and sharp stares aimed in my direction. Adam must have sensed them, too, but his following statement baffled me completely.

'Nina is a new vampire, and she is my At'kar. If any of you think of using her in your petty power plays, forget it. Any trouble you cause her, I will take personally. Very, very, personally, and you will beg for death when I catch you.' Adam seemed to grow as he made his point, the threat clearing a wide space around us, especially when his wings tore through his shirt and he turned their vicious edges toward the crowd.

'Well, that escalated quickly,' I muttered before stepping forward and turning to the gathered vampires. 'First, I'm not here to cause trouble. I'm not interested in taking anyone's position, and I prefer to keep my life as it is. Second, if you have an issue with me, please talk to me directly because apparently, your boss skipped his conflict resolution training,' I said, and a few covert giggles followed my statement.

I reached behind me and grabbed the tip of Adam's wing, the feathers instantly softening under my touch.

'Let's call it a day for now. I'll take him for a drink or two, and he will come back in a much better mood tomorrow. It's a big ask, but could someone keep Pawel company? I will treat it as a personal favour,' I offered, pulling Adam down the corridor, and he followed me with a bewildered expression.

Strangely, the mood had shifted, as if my berating the Seethe's Master somehow created a balance the place needed. When we were passing people, I noticed a few friendly smiles and one or two nodes of appreciation. It almost felt like I was in my element, directing a crowd of people to do what was best for them.

'Well done, Matron. You will have them all under your thumb in no time.' Adam said as we drove to Sara's. Something in the way he spoke gave me pause.

'Did you just... Please don't tell me you were an arsehole on purpose. And why? What did you gain from it?'

'Nina, by being with me, you will become the Mistress of the Seethe. You are not a blood donor or a side chick. You are my equal, my partner in everything, and if my nest want to have their Seethe Master to deal with all their bullshit, they will have their Mistress too,' he insisted, and I felt warmth spreading inside, but I had to ask.

'What if I don't want to?'

'The choice is yours, my love. Not theirs. You can be as involved as much or as little as you want to be. I won't press you to do anything, but if you decide to stay by my side and help me run the Seethe, they will accept you. That, or they can find some other place to live.'

The intensity of his voice made me smile. I reached out and placed my hand on his thigh.

'Thank you for not giving up on me,' I said. Adam turned his face toward me, and I saw the love shining in his eyes.

'Never, my love. After all, one of us had to be the responsible adult,' he teased, and when I tried to smack him playfully, he raised my hand to his lips, kissing my knuckles.

Raised voices and the sound of an argument assaulted our ears as soon as we entered Leszek's home. This was so unusual in this tranquil dwelling that Adam's wings instantly snapped open, and he positioned himself in front of me.

Suddenly, the Coven Mistress, Veronica Sandoval, stormed from Leszek's office, her stilettos grinding to a halt when she saw Adam in all his winged glory.

'Oh, cut it out, budgie boy,' she snapped, her mouth thinning in disapproval before her gaze met mine. 'Hi, Nina. I hope it was fucking worth it.'

She rushed to the door, angry tears in her eyes, leaving us in utter confusion. Adam raced to Leszek's office, snapping the door open.

I saw a handsome man in his forties with a salt-and-pepper-short beard gesturing toward Leszek before he noticed our arrival.

He looked me in the eye, and I felt all the secrets I'd ever hidden reveal themselves to him. Next to him was Sara, and I instantly recognised her 'stubborn doctor' glare. Something was wrong, and my friend was in the middle of it.

'I will be going. Nina, it is a pleasure to meet you,' he said, and I blinked rapidly, taken aback that he knew my name.

Before I could answer, he vanished.

'I regret nothing, and if those arseholes have a problem with it, they can fuck the hell off,' Sara said, glaring at Leszek. Her husband sighed before looking at Adam.

'I need a drink. Care to join me?' The Forest Lord was already walking towards the small bar before Adam hurried to catch up.

'What happened?' I asked, confused by this entire situation.

'Sara wasn't supposed to be able to create a portal or a vampire with a soul. It's caused a problem with the flow of magic, destabilising the Nether. Clearly, impossible magic doesn't resonate well with the old spells, and portals are difficult to close completely,' Leszek said, rubbing his temple.

'How could I know it would open a rift? Besides, nothing much happened, and it is not like we are draining the Nether of its magic,' she snapped back with a determined expression.

'What rift? What magic? Was that the reason Veronica was here?' I asked, feeling even more confused. 'Can someone please explain to me what exactly happened?'

Leszek took pity on me, and while passing his wife a glass of sweet Tokaj wine, he answered.

'Maybe you should ask your house spirit? We were getting peacefully berated by the Council of Gods because Jurata was being a bitch again, accusing Sara of exploiting the Coven when your kikimora turned up, shouting that Nina was in danger.'

'Lori?' I gasped, unwilling to believe our *Smooth Operator*-loving spirit could do something like that.

'Yes, next thing I know, Sara had bolted, and I followed. While we were riding to the Gates, there was a huge influx of magic, and this insane woman decided it was taking too long, so she invented a portal spell. Next thing I know, we're bursting out of the Nether and landing in a flower-covered bloodbath,' he explained, while Adam looked at Sara like she was his hero.

'I thought I closed it, but magic is still seeping through; then Veronica came complaining that Coven spells had become overcharged and unpredictable,' Sara said.

'After that, Stribog came here to warn us that after this latest incident, the council is divided on whether they should keep Sara in Gedania or allow her to live with me. They are afraid she could cause irreparable damage to the barrier.'

'I'm going nowhere,' Sara growled, and Leszek stroked her hair.

'No, you aren't. I won't be separated from you, my Firefly, but that creates a problem. Your intervention created a small hole in the over-inflated balloon that contains the Nether's magic, and now this power is trickling into Tricity,' Leszek said, and I bit my lip. Sara was always there for me. Maybe it was the time I paid back my debt to her.

'So... what now?' I asked, wondering what could be a better solution.

'Now we wait and see. The rift is small, and the good citizens of Tricity shouldn't notice any changes to their daily lives, but I expect we'll receive more visitors from the Nether. The fact Stribog could hold his physical form for so long speaks for itself.'

'Stribog? God of air and change, that Stribog?' I asked as I finally connected the man with the name. 'But I thought the gods couldn't enter this world in their physical form.'

'Well... they couldn't, except me,' Leszek said, and I looked at Sara, my eyes wide from shock.

'Oh, fuck!' I swore, and she sighed.

'Yup, oh fuck indeed.'

CHAPTER 28

Six months later

'Have I told you I'm too old for night shifts?' I grumbled, packing another bloody sheet into the bag. Sara smirked, rolling her eyes at my complaint.

'Yeah, you did. It's such a shame your old, decrepit body will have to endure it for eternity,' she answered. I snorted and stuck my tongue out at her.

Today, we were repaying a favour to the staff that had covered our shifts during Yuletide, and that meant getting our hands dirty working at the major trauma unit. It had been a long time coming, but at least they weren't waiting till the approaching Yule.

As usual, there was plenty to do. I could feel the sun rising even in this windowless room. It was one of the little treats my

441

transformation had gifted me. Adam reassured me that the feeling was entirely normal, and I trusted this, even if it came from a man who sucked blood to survive.

When I caught Sara giving me the side eye for the third time, I straightened up and looked at her till she met my gaze.

'Okay, I know I'm cranky, but you don't need to hover over my shoulder all shift,' I huffed.

'C'mon Sister, you keep repeating it every time we clean up after a trauma, but look on the bright side. You haven't licked your fingers clean once today, and you didn't even lick your lips at that gusher earlier,' Sara's grin was mischievous enough that I felt like smacking her across the head with a dressing pack.

'Stop calling me Sister, you wicked woman, and you can definitely stop making fun of my problem. It happened once, Sara, once, but of course, you keep bringing it up,' I complained, pretending I was deeply offended, but Sara saw through my act right away. I was embarrassed that she still remembered my return to work and the first patient we had.

'But you're like a sister to me, Nina. Are you trying to break my heart? Besides, seeing you licking up the blood with that dreamy expression was an unforgettable experience. Oh, how I wish I'd had my phone on me.'

It had been unforgettable for me, too. I'd just come from my leave of absence, and minutes after my shift started, Sara's boys brought in a man from a factory accident. Before I was able to put a compression dressing on the bleeding stump, arterial blood sprayed over my face, and I instinctively licked my lips, then stuck a finger in my mouth, moaning quietly at the rich metallic taste.

'Yeah, unforgettable is the perfect word, especially after we made everyone else forget it.'

'Well, that's part of my job now. To protect the delicate balance between the Nether and the human world. Admit it, you enjoyed using your mojo on Karina. It was so funny afterwards, seeing the looks of confusion on everyone's faces every time I licked my lips,' Sara said, wiping the blood from the metal tray.

I was grateful for her help. I'd struggled to use vampire compulsion in those first few weeks, and covering up the mistakes I made because of my cravings had been hard work.

My new life was still a voyage of discovery; hence, the Wicked Seer of the West constantly looking over my shoulder. I was still regularly surprised by the hand I'd been dealt.

I didn't need human blood to survive, although I still craved it. I could live well on the hefty supply of the best beef steaks that Adam kept stocked in his fridge. The biggest surprise came when Adam and I found out he didn't need to feed elsewhere.

At first, we hadn't realised, but we were in the honeymoon period, and sex had been... well, let's just say we enjoyed each other's company. Adam liked to bite me when passions were high, and our first discovery was that vampire venom still worked on me. Our second revelation was that my blood heightened Adam's pleasure. We had explored that little quirk thoroughly.

After several days of bedroom gymnastics, we'd emerged to enjoy a nice meal. However, instead of opening a unit of blood, Adam only had a glass of whisky. When I expressed my concern, my winged lover simply shrugged, saying he wasn't hungry. After two weeks, I'd been ready to tie him to the chair and pour a unit or two straight down his helpless throat, but Adam insisted he felt the best he'd ever been. Once I made him talk to another vampire, and they analysed his blood, we found out that not only was my blood nourishing his body, but it was much more potent than anything a human could provide.

I also discovered I wasn't as affected by the sun as fledgling vampires. That discovery came after I lost my temper when Adam told me to wait before returning to work. After I'd stormed out and stolen his bike to blow off some steam, I realised, two miles down the road, that it was midday and my skin wasn't a blistered mess. Both Adam and I were relieved when I returned unharmed. I had taken my telling off for that one very contritely.

'I hope you haven't forgotten about tonight?' I blinked, my musing interrupted by Sara's question.

'What?'

'Tonight? Autumn Equinox? The Harvest Festival? Please don't tell me you forgot about Leszek's birthday and the party on the island?' She asked with a gentle frown, and I slapped my forehead.

'Shit, yes. We have a gift and everything,' I said, suddenly remembering Sara had picked this ancient pagan holiday to celebrate Leszek's birthday when we found out deities didn't have them.

It was meant to be a surprise for him, and I hoped he wasn't so surprised that he unleashed the power of the forest upon us in what was supposed to be the celebration of his magic.

'Perfect, let's do the handover so we have time for a beauty sleep,' she said, stretching once we'd finished organising the room.

That's what I loved about Sara. She might be at the top of the pecking order, but it never stopped her from doing the menial jobs if it meant she could help someone.

An hour later, we left the hospital to see the soft glow of the Autumn sun. Adam and Leszek were already outside, waiting for us to finish our shift. Sara's husband was, as always, impeccably dressed with the obligatory caramel latte. I didn't need small gifts. Seeing Adam's roguish smile was enough to improve my day.

'See you later, Matron. Don't forget to bring your wellies,' Sara called, taking Leszek's arm. They were going for a walk so she could vent all her work frustrations while he quietly listened. Somehow, it had become their ritual to stroll along the banks of the Motlawa River, and I noticed more and more supernatural citizens joining them. It was both a fashion statement and an opportunity to exchange a word or two with the power couple.

'Shall we head home or to the Seethe to see your brother?' Adam asked, bending over to tenderly kiss my lips.

'Home,' I said, 'We can see Pawel tomorrow. I need some sleep before the party... I mean ritual.' I chuckled slightly, but we both knew there wouldn't be a sober soul left after Leszek finished with the harvest spellbinding.

'As you wish, sweetheart. If you don't object, I think it's time for Pawel to rejoin the world outside the of the Seethe. He's made significant progress, and we have a vacant porter position at the clinic. It will be the perfect new start, not to mention you can keep an eye on him,' Adam said, leading me to the car.

I gasped slightly, but it was welcome news. The first few weeks were hard for Pawel. His vampire thirst, mixed with his forced sobriety and subsequent detox, had caused him to experience excruciating pain and inflicted him with a foul temper. I'd spent almost all that time nursing him until he was healthy enough to unlock his room.

I'd taken on Pawel's care in part to remove the burden from the vampires that lived in the compound, and it gave me the opportunity to become closer to them and learn more about being a vampire. I became an unofficial messenger and the buffer between the Seethe and Adam's explosive temper.

After the short drive, Adam parked the car in the underground garage, and I took his hand when we talked toward the elevator.

'You make me happy,' I said when the elevator pinged and started moving.

'What's up? Is everything okay?' He asked, taking my chin and lifting my face to look me in the eye.

'Everything's fine. I was just thinking about life and how my worst fears turned into my greatest strength. I'm not afraid anymore. With you and Sara around, there is nothing I can't face. You are the best, my Cyber Prince Charming.' I said, slowly stroking his chest. Adam smirked, leaning into my touch before pushing me until my back pressed against the elevator wall.

The next thing I knew, I was caged between my lover's arms as he placed his lips next to my ear, my skin caressed by his breath, giving me goosebumps when he spoke.

'Prince Charming? I prefer Dark Prince because I want you trembling beneath me. I want to impale you on my cock while I feast on your blood and you scream my name,' he whispered.

I could feel the hunger in his voice. The bloodlust and desire that drove us both to new heights. I moved the hand that was resting on his chest, sliding it down until I cupped his erection.

'Oh, do you? Maybe I will even allow it. I believe the marks on my neck need refreshing,' I murmured, giving him a few firm strokes through the fabric.

'Shit, can't this thing move faster?' Adam hit the wall, visibly frustrated by the elevator's speed, and I took way too much pleasure in teasing him.

'Tut tut, is Loverboy in a rush? Didn't your female friends ever tell you never to rush a lady's seduction?'

'Lorelai! *Smooth Operator*, now!' Adam shouted, lifting me into his arms. As soon as the doors opened, he rushed to the bedroom while I laughed like a crazed jockey.

After a few incidents where his housekeeping spirit accidentally, or maybe not so accidentally, appeared in our bedroom while we were doing the deed, Adam came up with the code phrase. *Smooth Operator* put the apartment on lockdown and forbade Lorelai from coming anywhere near us unless the world was ending.

Music filled the house when Adam threw me on the bed so hard that I bounced. He hadn't tasted my blood for some time. We couldn't do it too often, and after deliberation, he agreed that once a month would be safe. Since I gave him my permission in the elevator, Adam was like a possessed man and eager to make his threat come true.

The ripping sound surprised me. Adam didn't waste time undressing. He simply grabbed the front of his shirt and tore it apart, revealing his chest and the tattoo of a winged obsidian dagger over his heart. I liked to look at it, especially after he explained its symbolism: the two of us forever bound together, protecting our love.

'On no, you are not ripping off my clothes. I like this outfit,' I squealed, crawling away from him, laughing.

'Oh yes, I will,' Adam said with a low predatory growl in his voice that made me shiver with anticipation.

'Adam!' I screamed when he ripped away my clothes.

'I'm going to worship you, Nina. I'll worship my At'kar until she whimpers my name,' he said before descending between my thighs.

His tongue caressed the most sensitive part of me, bringing me to my peak with an expertise that did, in fact, make me whimper, but Adam was merciless as he rose up and pulled me closer. When his shaft pressed against my entrance, my whimpers turned to growls, and my legs wrapped around his body, trying to drag him forward.

'You are perfect. If there is an afterlife for vampires, my paradise is in your arms,' he said, thrusting forward.

I moaned when Adam breached my entrance, arching my hips to take him further. He rocked back and forth at a slow, measured pace, driving me mad with need. The fullness was overwhelming, and even more so was the love that shone in Adam's eyes. I saw how much his control cost him, the strain of holding back fangs so sharp and elongated while his gaze slid to my neck. He waited for me to be ready, to add the venom to the bliss of our bodies moving together.

I was close, so close.

I turned my face to the side, exposing my neck. Adam growled, his teeth gliding closer. I felt his stubble sliding along my skin while he thrust harder.

'Adam, please,' I moaned, on the verge of climax.

His shaft pulsed, shooting its load as I shattered around him.

Sharp pain urged me on as ecstasy rolled through me, the hot bliss of vampire venom filling my veins. My body shivered with euphoria, squeezing Adam's cock as he came, the blood he fed on extending his rapture.

Adam didn't rush, savouring the moment and prolonging my pleasure. I could easily understand why vampires didn't have to hunt anymore. If I'd known before that such bliss could exist, I would have frequented every disreputable club in Tricity.

'You are my miracle, Nina,' Adam murmured, withdrawing his fangs and turning, placing my head on his chest. I yawned, embracing him, feeling tired but completely sated.

'You mellowed me, you wicked man. How can we go to a party if I feel like this?' I complained, half asleep.

'You will rest, my love, then I will feed you a nice, juicy steak, then we will dance the whole night away,' he promised.

'What? We?' I asked

'Yes, we. You are mine, Nina. For better or worse, especially given that death will never do us part.'

GLOSSARY

Amber/Jantar –a magical gem created from the resin of Leshy's trees and Jurata's magic (otherwise named Jurata's tears after she cried at the failure of her magic). It can store, alter and release magic, affecting time and space. Its purpose was to allow the gods to exist in the human realm without losing their power to the Nether; however, it is also used to create various magical artefacts.

At'kar – "Beloved" both the term of endearment as the official honorific name for a vampire's spouse.

Adam Lisowczyk – a 150-year-old vampire. Master of Tricity Seethe, a ward and a friend of the Forest Lord Leshy. The Syndicate cyber-security and tracking expert and second in command.

Czernobog – an Eastern Slavic deity of darkness, misfortune and calamity. The antithesis of life and light.

Damian Rus – One of 'The Boys', a paramedic and Sara's friend.

Dola – a Slavic goddess of fate similar to the Greek Moirae. She holds power over the fate of every living being and the universe itself and the ability to end even god's life with her silver scissors.

Gdansk – Part of the Tricity; an old Hanseatic city, the centre of maritime commerce of Northern Poland, and an ancient gateway to the sea with ports, shipyards, and waterways (an actual city).

Gdynia – Part of the Tricity, a community and military port founded after the Second World War (an actual city).

Hel – fishermen's town on Hel's Peninsula (actual place).

Jurata – Goddess of the Baltic Sea who created amber. Also, the Leshy's ex-lover. She wasn't willing to sacrifice her powers to stay with him in the human world.

Kamil Walicki – an undercover policeman, Sara's ex, human liaison officer to the Syndicate.

Kikimora – (pronounced Kih-kee-mora) a female house spirit from Slavic lore who can be helpful or malevolent depending on the behaviour of the homeowner. In differing versions of her stories, there are two kinds of spirit, one generally helpful and the other hurtful, both depicted as a woman sometimes with a bird's beak and legs.

Kris Borecki – chief firefighter, leader of Tricity's search and rescue team, Sara's friend.

Leszek Borowy/Leshy/Forest Lord – the human name of the Leshy, The God of the Forest and wilderness, who sacrificed the majority of his power to create and sustain the Gates to the Nether. Posing as a human, he is a philanthropist, environmentalist and leader of the Amber Trade Syndicate, the clandestine leader of Tricity's Elder Races.

Makosz – Slavic goddess of the earth and fertility similar to the Greek Demeter.

The Nether – A sphere of reality in between the physical world and Nawia(the afterlife). Hidden from non-magical humans. It was created after the expanding humanity, fighting for space with the Elder Races, threatened the extinction of magical beings and the ancient gods. As an act of defence, the gods withdrew magic from the physical world, leaving only a trace of it for their descendants and created the Nether. Currently, the sphere of the Nether is housing several cities all over the world inhabited by those who, for their existence, require a large quantity of magic. Entrances to the world of the Nether are called Gates, and each Gate is tied to a Guardian, usually an ancient god or spirit who sacrificed their power to erect the Gates and sustain the Nether barrier. This sacrifice allows the Guardians to remain permanently in the human world when other deities can only visit for a brief time.

Nina Zalewska – Sara's best friend. She is a human nurse with no special powers who works with Sara in the Emergency Department and runs the Elder Race hospital in the Dockyard area of Tricity.

Ryszard(Rysiek) Izbicki – One of 'The Boys', paramedic and Sara's friend.

Sara Wilska – a human with magical powers that were latent until her thirties. Emergency Doctor by trade, Soul Shepherd by birth. She has the ability to bind the spirit to living flesh, manipulate time and space and cross not only into the Nether, but to Navia as well. She married the Leshy, the Forest deity after they defeated Czernobog.

Sopot – part of the Tricity. Initially built as a spa resort for wealthy tourists (an actual city).

Soul Shephard - a rare type of spirit magic that allows its user to bind a spirit into living flesh or hold it into dying flesh. It also allows its user to speak to the spirits who are close to death or didn't cross to the afterlife. Lesser-known abilities are time and space manipulation by interacting with both the physical world and the Nether and Navia spheres.

Stribog – a Slavic god of wind, air and destruction, who offers wealth to worthy people.

Svarog – a Slavic god of fire and blacksmiths, but also an instigator of quarrels. Known to have a fiery temper.

The Anchor – a popular nightclub and trade base for the human mafia of Tricity and their leader, Zbigniew Nadolny.

Tomasz Szary – wolf Shifter and Alpha of Tricity pack.

Veles - a major Slavic god of earth, water, livestock, and the underworld. His mythology and powers are similar, though not identical, to those of (among other deities) Odin, Loki and Hermes.

Veronica Sandoval – Air Witch. Leader of the Tricity Coven.

Zbigniew Nadolny – half-human, half-unknown Elder Race. A human presenting mafia boss and owner of the Anchor.

About Author

Olena Nikitin is the pen name of a writing power couple who share a love of fantasy, paranormal romance, rich, vivid worlds and exciting storylines. In their books and out, they love down-to-earth humour, a visceral approach to life, striving to write realistic romances filled with the passion and steam people always dream of experiencing. Meet the two halves of this Truro UK-based dynamic duo!

Olga, a Polish woman, has a wicked sense of humour with a dash of Slavic pessimism. She's been writing since she was a small child, but life led her to work as an emergency physician. While this work means she always has stories to share, it often means she's too busy to actually write. She's proud to be a crazy cat lady, and together with Mark, they have five cats.

Mark, a typical English gentleman, radiates charm, sophistication, and an undeniable sex appeal. At least, he's reasonably certain that's what convinced Olga to fly across the sea into his arms.

He's an incredibly intelligent man with a knack for fixing things, including Polish syntax in English writing. If you give him good whiskey, he might even regale you with his Gulf War story of how he got shot.

Olena Nikitin loves hearing from their fans and critics alike and welcomes communication via any platform!

For more, check all in one social link: HERE

For updates and Newsletter, sign in: HERE

ALSO BY

Season's War: Epic Romantic Fantasy (4 books in the series) — series compleated https://geni.us/SeasonsWar

In the land where the Old Gods still walk on earth, the antihero, the harbinger of Chaos, and the daughter of the Autumn, lady Inanuan of Thorn have to face her magic and choose between power and the life she always wanted.

For many, known as Striga for her explosive temper or Royal Witch for her role, she is just Ina, a woman of many colours, craving to live her life free and without too many expectations.

With a rare Chaos magic, she becomes the centre of a power struggle between those who desire to rule the world with her hands. And when her life gets tangled with Marcach of Liath and Sa'Ren Gerel, her heart has to choose between them even if her magic has already claimed them both.

The same magic that long ago changed the shape of the known world.

Meet the land of Cornovii, a merchant kingdom and the bubbling cauldron of human and non-human races living together and follow the adventures of incorrigible Ina, her men, her friends, and Leshy, the Old God of the Forest, who chose her to be his herald.

(The series contains mature themes and language, violent scenes and steamy content that some readers may find distressing)

Milton Keynes UK
Ingram Content Group UK Ltd.
UKHW010654080324
439098UK00001B/45